"One of the leading novelists of the younger realistic school in Germany." – *The Bookman*

PRAISE FOR THE DIARY OF A LOST GIRL

"The saddest of modern books." – *Nelson Evening Mail*

"There are many readers . . . who find it very shocking." – *New York Times*

"A terribly impressive book, full of accusations against society." – Preussische Yearbook

The "poignant story of a great-hearted girl who kept her soul alive amidst all the mire that surrounded her poor body." – Hall Caine

"This moving confession . . . is an important social document." – *Bibliothèque universelle*

"A complete inventory of the sexual trade." – Walter Benjamin

"The fact that one German critic asserted the impossibility of a woman herself immune from vice having written such a book, is proof that besides truth of matter there was compelling art in Margarete Böhme's book." – Percival Pollard

"The moral justification of such a publication is to be found in the fact that it shrivels up sentimentality; the weak thing cannot stand and look at such stark degradation." – *Manchester Guardian*

THE DIARY OF A LOST GIRL

(The Diary of a Lost One)

Louise Brooks, during the making of **Diary of a Lost Girl**.

THE DIARY
OF A LOST GIRL

BY

MARGARETE BÖHME

≡ LOUISE BROOKS EDITION ≡

edited, and with
an introduction, by Thomas Gladysz

The Diary of a Lost Girl, by Margarete Böhme.

Originally published in Germany in 1905 as Tagebuch einer Verlorenen. Von einer Toten.

Published in English translation in 1907 as The Diary of a Lost One. English translation by Ethel Colburn Mayne.

Special contents this edition copyright © 2010 by Thomas Gladysz.

Introduction copyright © 2010 by Thomas Gladysz.

Front cover: Louise Brooks, in Diary of a Lost Girl
Back cover: German film poster, 1929

Cover design by site bilder.

Book design by site bilder & Thomas Gladysz.

Unless otherwise noted, all images are from the collection of Thomas Gladysz / Louise Brooks Society. Images from early 20th century copies of Tagebuch einer Verlorenen, and vintage material related to the book and subsequent films, are considered in the public domain.

Published by PandorasBox, with the cooperation of the Louise Brooks Society. (A limited edition of this book has been privately printed.)

Printed in the United States of America by Lulu.com

ISBN 978-0557508488

First Edition
10 9 8 7 6 5 4 3 2 1

CONTENTS

Introduction, by Thomas Gladysz ix

Author's Preface xxx

Publisher's Note xxxii

Foreword xxxii

A Note xxxiv

The Diary of a Lost Girl

Chapter I 2
Chapter II 12
Chapter III 22
Chapter IV 34
Chapter V 45
Chapter VI 58
Chapter VII 67
Chapter VIII 79
Chapter IX 96
Chapter X 110
Chapter XI 124
Chapter XII 139
Chapter XIII 153
Chapter XIV 164
Chapter XV 179
Chapter XVI 183
Chapter XVII 195
Chapter XVIII 206
Chapter XIX 216
Chapter XX 228

Chapter XXI 245
Chapter XXII 228
Chapter XXIII 271
Epilogue 279

This Austrian card, series III, number 237, was distributed along with Samum cigarettes. It depicts Louise Brooks dressed as Thymian, and dates from the early 1930s. The sentiment, "Die Schonheit im Wandel der Zeiten," notes her beauty through the ages.

Introduction

In the first decades of the last century, **The Diary of a Lost Girl** was nothing less than a literary phenomenon. Today, it is little known.

The book purportedly tells the true-life story of Thymian, a young woman forced by circumstance into a life of prostitution. Due in part to its sensational subject matter, the book was a tremendous bestseller in its native Germany, where it's now considered among the bestselling books of the time.[1] One contemporary scholar has called it "Perhaps the most notorious and certainly the commercially most successful autobiographical narrative of the early twentieth century." [2]

First published in 1905 as **Tagebuch einer Verlorenen. Von einer Toten**, this *succès de scandal* has proved an especially enduring and engendering work. It brought about not only a popular sequel, a controversial stage play, a parody, and two silent films – but a score of imitators as well.[3] Lawsuits arose around its publication, and the book had a small influence on social reform. There was a movie made from the book's sequel, and in France, a novelization of the 1929 film was issued. All this kept Thymian's tragic story before the public. By the end of the Twenties, more than a million copies had been published.

---

[1] According to Donald Ray Richards' **The German Bestseller in the 20th Century: A Complete Bibliography and Analysis 1915-1940** (Herbert Lang, 1968), **Tagebuch einer Verlorenen** was among the bestselling books of the period. Richards ranks it eleventh. By comparison, the third bestselling book was Erich Remarque's phenomenal bestseller, **All Quiet on the Western Front**, which sold nearly twice as many copies.

[2] **Truth to Tell: German Women's Autobiographies and Turn-of-the-Century Culture** by Katharina Gerstenberger (University of Michigan Press, 2000).

[3] Ibid. After the publication of **Tagebuch einer Verlorenen**, there was a wave of similarly themed female autobiographies – many were a confession, and each told the tale of its heroine in what was considered frank and sometimes indecent detail.

This five act play was one of a handful of works inspired by Böhme's book. It was written by Wolf von Metzlch-Schilbach, and published by Theaterverlag Eduard Bloch. Performances of the play were banned in some German cities.

Today, however, few are familiar with this once controversial and contested work. In Germany, the book has been reissued in recent years – but is given scant attention in literary and cultural histories. In the English-speaking world, the book is even less remembered. Long out-of-print, it is known only to collectors and readers of antiquarian literature, and to a few scholars in academia. The memory of it is largely preserved by fans of the American actress Louise Brooks, who appears in the second film based on the book. That silent film is available on home video, and is still shown in theaters around the world.

. . . .

The Diary of a Lost Girl was penned by Margarete Böhme, arguably one of the more widely read German writers of the early 20th century. Böhme authored 40 novels – as well as short stories, autobiographical sketches, and articles. **The Diary of a Lost Girl** is her best known book.

Böhme was born Wilhelmina Margarete Susanna Feddersen in 1867. The future writer grew up in a modest house in Husum, a small town in Northern Germany. It was dubbed "the grey town by the grey sea" by its best known resident, the novelist and poet Theodor Storm. According to family lore, there was something of a storytelling tradition in the Feddersen household. Her mother's aunt was Lena Wies, a longtime friend of Storm who furnished the well-known novelist with legends and tales for his later work. As a child, Böhme too was said to have made-up elaborate stories for neighborhood children.[4]

Böhme began writing early. At age 17, she published her first story, "The Secret of the Rose Passage," in a Hamburg newspaper. She then went on to place pieces in weekly

---

[4] The factual record of the author's life is established in **Margarete Böhme Die Erfolgsschriftstellerin aus Husum** by Arno Bammé (Profil, 1994). This introduction relies on that groundbreaking sourcebook.

magazines, both under her own name and under a pseudonym. Later, while living in Hamburg and then Vienna, Böhme worked as a correspondent for North German and Austrian newspapers.

In 1894, at age 27, the then still struggling author married Friedrich Theodor Böhme, a newspaper publisher 20 years her senior. After six years, the marriage ended in divorce. Böhme moved with her daughter to Berlin, where she attempted to make her living as an author.

This 1902 portrait of the author appeared in *The Bookman* in 1912, at the time **The Department Store** was published in the United States.

Böhme was not only a working writer, but a single parent – both somewhat unusual for a woman in Wilhelmina-era Germany. Portraits from the time depict her as attractive, with up-swept hair, and fashionable clothes. She was considered tall, and is remembered to have sometimes worn an embroidered velvet ribbon around her neck.[5] She was also independent minded. When Böhme married for the second time in 1911, she insisted on a marriage contract which reserved her earnings as a writer for herself.

---

[5] **Das Tagebuch einer Verlorenen: aus dem Nachlass einer Toten: der Welterfolg eines Buches und die Folgen** by Heide Soltau (Klagenfurt Institute für Interdisziplinäre Forschung und Fortbildung, 1993). This is the transcript to a German radio broadcast about Böhme which included the writer's granddaughter.

Throughout her life, Böhme complained about the small sums she was paid for her work. As a consequence, she was a writer who out of financial necessity wrote prolifically. She wrote articles and essays as well as short stories for the newspapers and magazines of the time. Some of her early novels were also serialized. At first, Böhme wrote what would today be termed popular fiction – but as her work matured, she turned to more serious themes.

Böhme's novels were issued in book form by Germany's leading publishers. Some would go into a second printing, and some were translated into other languages. Most would be concerned with the social conditions and everyday lives of women.

Beginning in 1903, Böhme produced within the span of two years some six novels. Few of them, however, met with much success. With the publication of **The Diary of a Lost Girl** in 1905, the author's fortunes changed. The book was an overnight bestseller, and Böhme's reputation was secured. Her succeeding books were met with serious consideration. They were reviewed in literary periodicals across Europe, and her work was favorably compared to that of the French writer Émile Zola.

Dida Ibsens Geschichte (The History of Dida Ibsen), from 1907, is a kind of sequel to **The Diary of a Lost Girl**. The title character, a friend of Thymian, suffers a similar fate and also falls into a life of prostitution. As Böhme states in the forward, the book was written in response to a flood of letters she received regarding her earlier book. People from all walks of life had written to the author. Some wrote to say they had cried over the book. Others, wanting to pay their respects, enquired as to where Thymian was buried.

Critics consider **W.A.G.M.U.S.**, the story of a department store, to be Bohme's best work. This 1911 novel chronicles the growth of a colossal business which crushes its smaller competitors by systematically underselling them. The book touches on emerging modern business methods, the treatment of employees, and issues around commerce and consumerism. Shoplifters, then a new phenomenon, also come into the story. **W.A.G.M.U.S.** surveys the social milieu of Berlin at the time; the novel is also a sweeping family saga. It was published in the United States, where one leading literary review called it "a distinctly remarkable book."[6]

Much of Böhme's later fiction has a strong social message. **Christine Immersen,** from 1913, concerns the unpleasant working conditions faced by women telephone operators (then just coming onto the scene). **Sarah von Lindholm,** from 1914, puts forth progressive ideas on the role of the worker, while outlining a model workers city. **Kriegsbriefe der familie Wimmel (War Letters of the Wimmel Family)**, written in 1915 during the early days of the First World War, reflects the harsh realities of that conflict. Other notable works include **Im Irrlichtschein** from 1903, **Fetisch** from 1904, **Apostel**

IM GLEICHEN VERLAGE ERSCHIENEN:

MARGARETE BÖHME

IM IRRLICHTSCHEIN
Roman

WENN DER Roman FRÜHLING KOMMT

FETISCH Roman

DIE GRÜNEN DREI
Roman

RHEINZAUBER Roman

ABSEITS VOM WEGE
Roman

Pro Band geheftet M. 3.—, gebunden M. 4.—

TAGEBUCH EINER VERLORENEN VON EINER TOTEN
Herausg. u. überarbeitet von MARGARETE BÖHME
Illustr. Ausgabe. Geheftet M. 4.—, gebunden M. 5.—

DIDA IBSENS GESCHICHTE Ein Finale zum Tagebuch einer Verlorenen
Geh. 4.—, gebd. 5.-

APOSTEL DODEN-SCHEIT BRIEFE AN EINE DAME
Geh. M. 3.—, gebd. M. 4.—

DES GESETZES ERFÜLLUNG Roman
Geheftet M. 5.—, gebunden M. 6.50

---

[6] *The Bookman*, June, 1912.

Dodenscheit from 1908, **Anna Nissens Traum** from 1913, **Millionenrausch** from 1919, and **Roswitha** from 1923.

Rheinzauber, from 1909, focuses on a family feud which ends after three generations when a child brings its hostile branches together. It gained Böhme one of her few American notices when it was reviewed in *The Nation* in a round-up of German-language books.

Despite her European reputation, only two of Böhme's books would find their way into English; they are **Tagebuch einer Verlorenen** as **The Diary of a Lost One** in 1907, and **W.A.G.M.U.S.** as **The Department Store** in 1912. Each was first issued in Great Britain and then the United States; the latter was also published in Canada. The British editions were, in all likelihood, also distributed throughout the Commonwealth. In 1909, a newspaper in New Zealand, the *Nelson Evening Mail*, referred to **The Diary of a Lost One** as "The saddest of modern books." [7] It was that, and more.

.   .   .   .

Today, **The Diary of a Lost Girl** is accepted as a work of fiction. But when it was first published, it was believed to be the genuine diary of a young girl. Böhme claimed only to be its editor. As Böhme states in her forward, she was given the manuscript and intended to rework it into a novel. But, on the advice of her publisher, she instead presented it as an authentic diary.

The book's publication and success led to all manner of speculation as to its authorship. Readers, critics, and the press were divided. The author, and her publisher, maintained their account of the origins of the diary. Some early editions of **Tagebuch einer Verlorenen** even depict pages which were said to be in Thymian's hand.

---

[7] *Nelson Evening Mail*, April 14, 1909.

According to the forward in the 1988 German reissue,[8] as late as 1935 Böhme decided to forgo any claims as author in order to maintain the illusion the book was a genuine diary. Belief in its authenticity continued in some quarters for decades, even into the 1970's.[9]

Why Böhme presented the work as genuine isn't recorded. Some have suggested that the author, facing the double standards of the day, either lacked the courage to publish a novel about the demimonde or realized the consequences she would suffer as a result of having done so. Others have speculated that its claim to be an actual diary was a literary ploy to put over its provocative subject matter. To the attentive reader however – the force of its

---

[8] The 1988 reissue, a facsimile of the deluxe 1907 edition, was published In Germany by Kronacher Verlag Moordeich. It includes a new forward by Jürgen Dietrich.

[9] See **Sperrbezirke: Tugendhaftigkeit und Prostitution in der bürgerlichen Welt**, by Regine Schulte (Syndikat, 1979).

narrative, its detailed realism, its references to other literature of prostitution, and its acute psychological observations all betray a literary sophistication beyond that of a teenage girl.

Whatever Böhme's motivation, she succeeded. Due in part to its sensational subject matter, as well as its contested nature, the book proved extremely popular and was widely written about. More than 30,000 copies were sold within the first four months of publication. After one year, 90,000 copies were in print. A short time later, its publisher, F. Fontane & Co., issued a "Luxus Ausgabe," or deluxe edition, marking more than 100,000 copies in circulation. The book continued to sell and sell, and was reissued in many different editions over the next two decades. By 1929, more than 1,200,000 copies were in print.

The book was a European phenomenon. It was translated into 14 languages, and was widely reviewed and written about. It was published in Dutch as **Eene verloren ziel**, in Danish as **Fortabt**, in Swedish as **Förtappad**, and in Finnish as **Yhteiskunnan Hylkäämä**.

It was also published in Polish as **Pamiętnik Kobiety Upadłej**, in Czech as **Dennik padlého děvčete**, in Croatian as **Dnevnik Jedne Izgubljene**, in Hungarian as **Egy Tévedt Nö Naplója**, and in Russian as **ДНеВНИКЪ ПаВШей**. There was an edition issued in France as **Journal d'une fille perdue**. In Italy, the book was titled **Diario di una donna perduta da una morta**.

Interest was so great there were even pirated versions in The Netherlands (where it was published as **Thymian**[10]), as well as in Poland, where an authorized translation competed for sales with an unauthorized edition published as **Pamiętnik Uwiedzionej**.

---

[10] This unauthorized translation was issued by Albert de Lange, a reputable publisher. The translation was by the poet Hillegonda van Uildriks, alias Gonne Loman-van Uildriks (1863-1921). Now remembered as a translator, she was the first to translate Jane Austen into Dutch. She also translated Robert Louis Stevenson and H.G. Wells.

Tagebuch einer Verlorenen was published in Dutch as Thymian, with the subtitle From the life of a fallen woman. The cover is unusual for its visual representation of Böhme's heroine. When the 1918 film of the book was shown in The Netherlands, it too was titled *Thymian*. (Image courtesy of Digitale Bibliotheek voor de Nederlandse Letteren.)

In England, the book was issued as **The Diary of a Lost One** by Sisley's Ltd. of London. It was first advertised as **The Diary of a Lost Soul**, the title given by its previously unknown translator, the Anglo-Irish author Ethel Colburn Mayne. Because of its subject matter, Mayne elected not to have her name appear in the book.[11]

THE BOOK THAT HAS STIRRED THE HEARTS OF THE GERMAN PEOPLE—125,000 COPIES SOLD.

THE DIARY OF A LOST ONE

Messrs. SISLEY are pleased to announce that they have secured the British rights in "Das Tagebuch einer Verlorenen," the remarkable work which has created so great a sensation in Germany. This book they are issuing under the title of "The Diary of a Lost One." It is outspoken to a degree, but the great moral lesson it conveys is the publishers' apology for venturing to reproduce this human document.

AT ALL LIBRARIES, 6/-

SISLEYS, LD., Makers of Beautiful Books, CHARING CROSS, LONDON.

A British newspaper advertisement proclaimed it "The Book that Has Stirred the Hearts of the German People – 125,000 copies sold." The advertisement stated "Messrs. Sisley are pleased to announce that they have secured the British rights in **Das Tagebuch einer Verlorenen**, the remarkable work which has created so great a sensation in Germany. This book they are issuing under the title **The Diary of a Lost One**. It is outspoken to a degree, but the great moral lesson it conveys is the publishers' apology for venturing to reproduce this human document."

In England, the book proved popular. It received positive notices and went through at least three printings. The *Manchester Guardian* noted "It professes to be an authentic document, the actual diary of the woman it describes, unaltered save for the excision of some passages and the suppression of real names. There can be no doubt this is not the case. It is a careful narrative, directed toward a distinctly moral purpose. The psychology of it

---

[11] Mayne (1865-1941) was an Irish-born novelist, critic and translator of Emil Ludwig, Dostoevsky, and others. With the success of **Diary** in England, Mayne suggested herself as translator for the book's sequel, **Dida Ibsens Geschichte**; it never came to be. Mayne also translated Böhme's **The Department Store**, and is so credited. Thanks to scholar Susan Waterman for this information.

is arresting and unmistakably founded upon experience. It has made, we are told, a great stir in Germany. It may do so in England." The *Guardian* concluded its sympathetic review by stating, "The moral justification of such a publication is to be found in the fact that it shrivels up sentimentality; the weak thing cannot stand and look at such stark degradation." [12]

Three day later, in a letter to the editor, Rev. J.K. Maconachie of the Manchester Association Against State Regulation of Vice wrote, "The appearance in Germany of this remarkable book, together with the stir it has made there and the fact that its author is a woman, betoken the uprising which has taken place in recent years amongst German women against the evils and injustice which the book reveals. . . . It may be hoped that discriminating circulation of **The Diary of a Lost One** will help many here to realize, in the forceful words of your reviewer, 'the horror of setting aside one section of human beings for the use of another.'"

The book was also praised by writer and man of letters, Hall Caine.[13] English editions carried his endorsement. "It is years since I read anything of the kind that moved me to so much sympathy and admiration. More reality, more truth, more sincerity, I have rarely met with. . . . I know it to be true because I know the life it depicts. . . . It is difficult for me to believe that a grown man or woman with a straight mind and a clean heart can find anything that is not of good influence in this most moving, most convincing, most poignant story of a great-hearted girl who

---

[12] H.M.S., "New Novels," *Manchester Guardian*, December 11, 1907.

[13] Caine (1853-1931) was an immensely popular novelist and playwright during the Victorian and Edwardian eras. At one point, he was among the best-selling writers in England; his 1897 novel, **The Christian**, was the first in Britain to sell over a million copies. Caine was secretary to Dante Gabriel Rossetti, and friendly with Robert Browning, Matthew Arnold, and George Bernard Shaw. Bram Stoker dedicated **Dracula** to his friend under the nickname "Hommy-Beg."

kept her soul alive amidst all the mire that surrounded her poor body."

The *New York Times*, surveying the English literary scene,[14] also took note of the book's reception. "At any rate, however, the book is interesting and widely read in England. Mr. Hall Caine has announced publicly and rather ambiguously that he admires it more than 'anything of its kind' which he has read for years. There are many readers, however, who find it very shocking, and Mr. Bram Stoker, the advocate of book censoring (as a London cable to this *Review* announced recently) would ban it promptly."

The book lingered in the British literary imagination. In 1917, the popular novelist Gilbert Frankau published **The Woman of the Horizon: A Romance of Nineteen-Thirteen**. In it, he referenced Böhme's book and other scandalous fiction of the time. . . . "**Fair Game**, she had called it, this wonderful, impossible book. For it was impossible; thinking of all the published tales that had dealt with the same subject – of **Little Sister** and **Quelle Signore** and **Das Tagebuch einer Verlorenen**. . . ." In 1931, a novel titled **No Bed of Roses: A Pathetically Realistic Story of a Woman of the Underworld** was advertised as "The Diary of a Lost Soul." In not unfamiliar language, the ad stated "These are the actual diaries of a prostitute and dope fiend. They form one of the most important human documents uncovered in our time."

In the United States, the book drew less attention and fewer notices. It was issued by the Hudson Press in 1908, and reprinted by the Stuyvesant Press in 1909. After that, **The Diary of a Lost One** largely faded from view. In America, it was referenced only occasionally in scholarly works on sexuality and criminal behavior. However, it did manage to find at least a few readers. The Anglo-American writer and aesthete Percival Pollard praised

---

[14] anonymous. "Alice is London's Holiday Favorite." *New York Times*, December 7, 1907.

it lavishly on more than one occasion.[15] And the novelist Henry Miller included it on his list of the books which influenced him the most.[16]

. . . .

Two silent films were made in Germany based on Böhme's **Tagebuch einer Verlorenen**.[17] Each reworked its source material – and each remained a powerful retelling of Thymian's tragic tale.

The first was directed by Richard Oswald and was based on his adaption of Böhme's book. This 1918 film starred Erna Morena as Thymian, with Reinhold Schünzel as Osdorff, Werner Krauss as Meinert, and Conrad Veidt as Dr. Julius.[18] As a film, this version of *Tagebuch einer Verlorenen* was well reviewed, but demands of the censor at the time led to cuts and even a change in its title. Once censorship was lifted after the end of WWI, scenes thought too provocative or critical of society were restored and its famous title changed back.

Nineteen eighteen also saw the release of a film based on the sequel to Böhme's book. *Dida Ibsens Geschichte* was also

---

[15] Pollard (1869-1911) was a friend of Ambrose Bierce and H.L. Mencken. See Pollard's **Their Day in Court** (Neale Publishing Co., 1909) and **Masks and Minstrels of New Germany** (Luce and Co., 1911).

[16] Miller's list of essential books was included in Raymond Queneau's **Pour une Bibliothèque Idéale** (Gallimard, 1956).

[17] Some film databases, such as filmportal.de and IMDb, list a 1912 German production titled *Tagebuch einer Verlorenen*. It was directed by Fritz Bernhardt and produced by Alfred Duskes. Little else is known of the film, which is presumably lost. Its relationship to Böhme's book is uncertain.

[18] Oswald directed many films including *Different from the Others* (1919). Together, Krauss and Veidt achieved cinema immortality in *The Cabinet of Dr. Caligari* (1920). Schünzel would write and direct; his best known work is *Viktor und Viktoria* (1933).

directed by Richard Oswald, with the leading roles again played by Krauss and Veidt. The infamous German dancer, actress, and "performance artist" Anita Berber played Dida Ibsen. It, like the first film version of *Tagebuch einer Verlorenen*, is thought lost

In 1929, Böhme's book was made into a film a second time. G.W. Pabst's version of **Tagebuch einer Verlorenen** came on the heels of his now classic ***Pandora's Box***, a film based on the similarly controversial Lulu plays authored by Frank Wedekind. Both of these films starred Louise Brooks. Also appearing in Pabst's ***Diary of a Lost Girl*** is Fritz Rasp as Meinert and the dancer Valeska Gert as the sadistic reform school disciplinarian. The well known character actor Kurt Gerron also has a role in this second adaption.

At the time of its release, the film received negative reviews – but for reasons which sometimes had little to do with the movie. As Brooks' biographer Barry Paris notes, some German film critics instead devoted their columns to savaging Böhme's novel.[19] Siegfried Kracauer was a critic at the time of the film's release. In his famous 1946 book **From Caligari to Hitler: A Psychological History of the German Film**, he comments on the Pabst film and its literary source – "the popularity of which among the philistines of the past generation rested upon the slightly pornographic frankness with which it recounted the private life of some prostitutes from a morally elevated point of view."

An anonymous correspondent for *Variety* who saw the film in Berlin early on similarly wrote, "G.W. Pabst is among the best German directors still working here but has had atrocious luck with scenarios. This one, taken from a best seller of years ago, is no exception." [20]

---

[19] **Louise Brooks**, by Barry Paris (Knopf, 1989).

[20] anonymous. "Diary of a Lost Girl." *Variety*, November 20, 1929.

IN DIESER WOCHE

Uraufführung:

TAGEBUCH EINER VERLORENEN

mit

**Louise Brooks, André Roanne
Fritz Rasp, Edith Meinhard
Valeska Gert, Siegfried Arno
Kurt Gerron**

Regie: G. W. PABST

VERLEIH:

Berlin-Osten:
Favorit-Film G. m. b. H., Berlin

Mitteldeutschland:
Siegel Monopolfilm, Dresden

Norddeutschland:
Nord Film G. m. b. H., Hamburg

Süddeutschland:
Union Film Co. m. b. H., München

Rheinland-Westfalen:
Rhein. Film Ges. m. b. H., Köln

This German trade ad states the film will be opening within the week, and notes it will be playing throughout the country. The ad dates from October, 1929 – before the film would be censored.

xxiv

As with the book, the film's implied critique of society would not go unchallenged. Like Oswald's earlier movie, the Pabst film suffered at the hands of the censor. *Diary of a Lost Girl* opened in Vienna on September 27 and made its German debut in Berlin on October 15, 1929. By December 5, the film had been banned by the German state censor and was temporarily withdrawn from circulation.

Various groups, including those representing the German Evangelical Church, a national organization for young women, a national organization of Protestant girl's boarding schools, a German morality association, and even the governor in Lower Silesia all voiced their objections to aspects of the film. Some of these groups were city based, others regional and national. Some were civic, others religious. Despite their differences, each found the film to be demoralizing. Objections were raised to the negative portrayal of the girl's reformatory, and the positive portrayal of the brothel. In particular, censors objected to the death of the housekeeper at the hands of an abortionist, the scene of Thymian's seduction, the removal of her baby in the coffin, the implied sexual activity at the brothel, etc....

Rudolph Leonhardt, the film's screenwriter, wrote in 1953 that ". . . entire filmed sequences were cut without mercy. . . . In one version, if I remember rightly, they cut 450 meters, and either in this or another version, they made another 54 further cuts. . . . The film comes to an end shortly after the middle of our script, inconclusively and incomprehensively. I once saw it myself at a cinema in Paris and stayed in my seat at the end because I thought the film had broken." [21]

After cuts were made to satisfy the censor, the ban on the film was lifted on January 6, 1930. And in this heavily censored form,

---

[21] Rudolph Leonhardt in a letter to Lotte Eisner, quoted in **The Haunted Screen**, by Lotte H. Eisner (Thames and Hudson, 1969).

it went on to play across Europe and the Soviet Union. One cine-club in Madrid screened it as late as 1933.

Released as it was in a heavily censored form and as a silent film at the beginning of the sound era – and with poor reviews trailing it, Pabst's *Diary of a Lost Girl* failed to make much of an impact. It would take time for audiences to catch-up with Brooks' remarkable performance, as well as with the film's still relevant message. It wasn't shown in the United States until some three decades later.

. . . .

This French newspaper ad dates from 1930. It promotes a screening at the Rialto Theater in Paris. The French title of the Pabst film, *Trois pages d'un journal* is given, as is the book's original French title **Le Journal d'une fille perdue**.

A few years after the death of her second husband in 1927, Böhme moved from Berlin to the town of Othmarschen near Hamburg, where her daughter then lived. There, she led a largely quiet life, despite the growing turmoil in the world around her.

In 1933, **Tagebuch einer Verlorenen** was once again the subject of attack. An attempt was made in the early days of the Nazi-era to ban Böhme's book. It was deemed trash, and its author considered suspect. Though an official decree was never issued, **Tagebuch einer Verlorenen** was successfully driven from print more than a quarter-century after it was first published.

By 1937, Böhme's name no longer appeared in annuals devoted to German literature. With a changing century and the coming World War, Böhme's books fell out of print and faded from view. The author died on May 23, 1939 at the age of 72. Like her famous heroine and the book which tells her tragic tale – Böhme became an author lost to history.

In recent years, there has been a small resurgence of interest in Böhme in her native Germany. In 1988, a facsimile of the deluxe 1907 edition of **Tagebuch einer Verlorenen** was published by Kronacher Verlag Moordeich. It was followed in 1995 by a soft cover edition of the book, issued by Suhrkamp, which features Louise Brooks on the cover. Around the same time, Böhme's near sole contemporary champion, the scholar Arno Bammé, published two groundbreaking books on the author. In 2009, a small soft cover edition of Böhme's selected writings was also issued.

Once condemned by critics and embraced by the reading public, **Tagebuch einer Verlorenen** experienced a popularity and notoriety which have obscured its singular achievement. Though what you hold in your hands may well be a maudlin thing, a potboiler, a tear-jerker, a weeper, a story at times both sentimental and sensational – it is also a work of emotional depth, literary sophistication, and unusual historical significance. This edition brings it back into print in English after more than a century of neglect.

Though first published more than a century ago, **Tagebuch einer Verlorenen** continues to find new readers in Germany. In 1988, a facsimile of the deluxe 1907 edition was published by Kronacher Verlag Moordeich. It was followed in 1995 by a soft cover edition, issued by Suhrkamp, which features Louise Brooks on the cover.

· · · · · · · · · · ·

Besides a few chapters in scholarly works, there is little information in English about Margarete Böhme. The information in this afterword is derived from my biographical and bibliographical research, and from a handful of books published by academic presses in Germany and the United States. It is indebted to the work of the German scholar Arno Bammé.

My heartfelt thanks to Christy Pascoe for her help with all aspects of this book. Thanks also to the staff of the San Francisco Public Library, and to fellow fans of Louise Brooks. Along with the works referenced in the introduction and footnotes, I found the following books and websites helpful. Those interested in reading further should consider them as well:

Der literarische Nachlass der Husumer Erfolgsschriftstellerin Margarete Böhme (1867-1939) by Arno Bammé / Klagenfurt, 1993.

"Of Lost Girls and Fake Diaries: Margarete Böhme's and G.W. Pabst's *Diary of a Lost Girl*" by Maggie McCarthy / 1998.

Commodities of Desire: The Prostitute in Modern German Literature edited by Christiane Schönfeld / Camden House, 2000.

Louise Brooks: Rebellin, Ikone, Legende edited by Gunter Krenn & Karin Moser / Film Archiv Austria, 2006.

Margarete Böhme - Einblicke: Eine Annäherung an ihr Werk / Husum, 2009.

http://www.kronacherverlag.de

http://www.pandorasbox.com

Thomas Gladysz

AUTHOR'S PREFACE
From the German Editions

When this Diary came into my hands it was my intention to work up the material into a novel, after a certain time had passed.

On the advice of my publisher, Herr Fontane, I afterwards changed my mind, and resolved to give it (after the necessary editing) in its original form, to the public. The only alterations are those which had to be made in the names of the various persons mentioned in the book, and in certain passages which were quite unfit for publication.

Nothing is further from my intention than to enrich what is called "the literature of pornography" by the publication of these pages. The slight and entirely unadorned narrative has no claim whatever to literary value; it is nothing, and pretends to be nothing, but an authentic contribution to a burning social question.

More powerfully and more convincingly than the most brilliant descriptions of an experienced writer do these pages speak to us, and illumine with a glaring precision that mournful world of the outcasts and pariahs of society.

If the perusal of them should move a reader here and there to serious thought, and show him that no human being, however strong, however highly placed, can be stronger than his fate, that neither prosperity nor culture, nor a high social position, can bid defiance to death and sorrow, and guard impregnably our own young people from such a destiny as poor Thymian's – if this reflection leads him to the conclusion that one should not pass by in thoughtless indifference or in pitiless contempt these unhappy creatures, but should look and look again, and seek to separate vice from misfortune – then the aim of this publication will have been attained. Then Thymian will not in vain have given us the story, the tragic chronology of her ruined life. And perhaps, too, her life will not have been a wholly "lost" one.

MARGARETE BÖHME

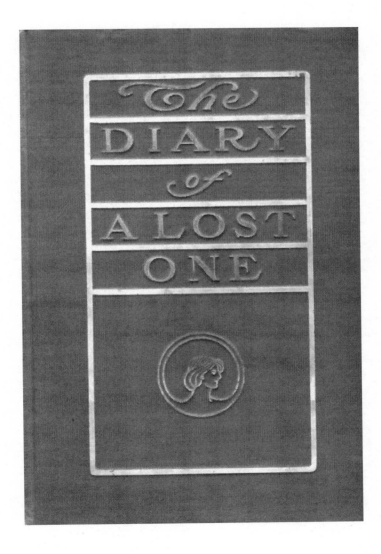

1908 American edition

PUBLISHER'S NOTE
From the 1907 British Edition

OUR chief apology for placing in the hands of the British public this authorized translation of **Die Tagebuch einer Verlorenen** must be the great moral lesson it conveys. The book has been read by thousands in the land where it originally appeared, it has stirred to the depths the hearts of a legion of readers, and has been translated into most modern languages. We sincerely believe it will arouse the deepest and most serious thought among the people of Great Britain and her Colonies, and will compel the grave attention of every humanist who inquires into social conditions. Its appearance in Germany was the signal for an outburst of criticism, and if by some superficial minds it was condemned for its frankness, it was equally praised by the large majority of thoughtful readers who saw in this wonderful human document a work which must exert a vast influence, and one which every grown-up man and woman ought to read.

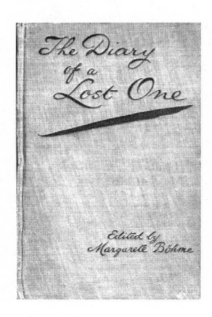

1907 British edition

FOREWORD
From the 1908 American Edition

There can be no doubt that this Diary is a truthful record of the actual life of a woman who had lived in the "half-world." The pages pulsate with a fever of protest; with a longing for unachievable reconciliation with the world of morality. It is a pitiful appeal to the inexorable tribunal of public opinion.

The publication of the Diary in Germany called forth a redundance of criticism. It was condemned, by some superficial minds, for its frankness; but it has been equally praised by the large majority of thoughtful readers who recognize in this wonderful human document a work which must exert a vast influence through the great moral lesson it conveys.

This terrible picture of life has stirred to the depths the hearts of a legion of readers, and it will arouse the deepest and most serious thought among the American people. It will compel the grave attention of every humanist who inquires into social conditions.

Every normal, thinking, grown-up man and woman should read it.

F. F.

A NOTE
About this Edition

The text found in this book is based on the first American edition of **Tagebuch einer Verlorenen**, published as **The Diary of a Lost One** by The Hudson Press in 1908. It, in turn, was based on the first English edition published by Sisley Ltd in 1907. Care has been taken to honor the original efforts of the author and translator. Except for the addition of an introduction and related matter, this edition of Böhme's book is a faithful recreation of the text of the original English language editions. German names, antique spelling (*realise, neighbour, diarizing, etc...*), old-fashioned usage, the author's prolific use of ellipses – and a few dated turns of phrase have been retained. (A few minor typographical errors in the original American edition have been silently corrected.) Footnotes, and editorial notes within the body of the novel, belong to Margarete Böhme.

Vintage illustrations, from a variety of sources including early European editions of the book as well as the G.W. Pabst film, have been added to the text. It is felt they help place this important work within its time, as well as amplify its still relevant message.

T. G.

THE DIARY OF A LOST GIRL

CHAPTER I

AUNT LEHNSMANN brought me a diary yesterday, as a belated Confirmation present. "Such a nice thing for a young girl," she said. "And such a cheap one," thought I. But as it's there I may as well use it, and perhaps I shall discover that I have some literary talent.

Not indeed that much goes on in this God-forsaken hole, and anything that does is scarcely worth putting down; but I'll pretend that I'm a famous person writing my memoirs, and the most unimportant things do well enough for that.

Well, here's my first entry.

I am called Thymian Katharine Gotteball, and I am the daughter of the chemist, Ludwig Erhard Gotteball, of G—, a small, neat town of about 2000 inhabitants, in the North Marshes. The streets are all very, very narrow and extremely clean; no grass grows between the stones, and the cocks and hens are not allowed to run about on the pavements. The houses look as sleek and smooth as men who have just been shaved by the barber.

It's desperately dull in G—. If a carriage drives through the street, everybody rushes to the windows. In the evenings the people sit on benches before their doors, and talk with their neighbours about the other neighbours, and when the other neighbours come up, they go on talking about more neighbours. For everyone is a "neighbour" here; even people who live at opposite ends of the town are "neighbours."

What a mad name my mother picked out for me! It often makes me very angry; the other children say it sounds like medicine, and the boys say something still worse, which I can't write down.

My mother was always delicate as long as I can remember her. I never heard her laugh; and when she smiled, she looked sadder than when she was grave. When I was a child playing in the square with other children, and used to see her at the window, I was almost afraid to look at her. I don't know why. It always gave me a pang when I caught sight of her dear, pale, sad little face up there.

When I was ten years old, mother got so ill that the doctors sent her to Davos. She stayed there a whole year. At first I missed her very much, but afterwards I almost forgot her. It was very gay at home while she was away. Father had lots of visitors. The relations came, too, sometimes, but they are not so amusing. We have a lot of relations. All mother's brothers and sisters live in country places in the North Marshes; only my Uncle Henning and my Aunt Wiebke (she *is* mother's sister) live here. And then there's Aunt Frauke, who is married to Lehnsmann Pohns. She is as miserly as she can be.

Then there's mother's brother, Councillor Thomsen, and another brother, Dirk Thomsen. And a brother-in-law, Hinnerk Larsen, whose wife (also a sister of mother's) died of consumption. Oh! and lots more besides. Father has only one sister, Aunt Freda, unmarried, and hump-backed; she lives here. I like her the least of all. She is always finding fault with me; one day I am too smart, and another day too slovenly. What she would like would be for me to spend every afternoon with her, mewed up in her prim drawing-room. But I think I see myself! Father can't stand her; they are for ever quarrelling. I don't know why father hasn't forbidden her the house long ago, for she is always so disgusting to him. Our dispenser, Mr. Meinert, calls her "Judge Lynch." When he sees her from the shop-window, coming across the square with her big brocade bag over her arm, he calls up into the house – "Here comes Judge Lynch! "Upon which I instantly disappear, and so does father, often.

While mother was in Davos, there was a theatrical company at the German Opera House. I was allowed to go every evening with father, or Meinert. Once they played *Teresa Krones* – that's a wonderful piece, but very sad. Ah! and the actress who played Teresa – simply divine! *Now* I know, of course, that she was painted up, but then I was struck all of a heap by her dazzling beauty. What a baby I was in those days!

The night they played *Teresa Krones* father had invited the actors to supper. I was allowed to come to table. We had supper in the best room, and there was red wine and champagne and I had some of everything. The actresses sang funny songs, and I got merrier and merrier. It was gorgeous fun. At last I jumped upon the table and yelled out – "I am a pudding! I am a pudding! Cut me up and eat me. I am a pudding!"

"Yes, you're a lovely pudding; there'll soon be somebody to cut you up," said Meinert, and all the others laughed. After that we got madder than ever. The chairs were pushed aside, and as there weren't enough then round the table, the ladies sat upon the gentlemen's knees. Teresa Krones sat upon father's.

And then – Just as the fun was at its height, the door was flung open, and there stood Aunt Freda, in her long faded old waterproof, which anybody could see she had pulled on over her night-dress! Goodness knows how she'd found out about it. She was livid with rage, and screamed out in a mad kind of voice, like a hoarse crow's: "This is very nice, very nice indeed! My congratulations! I have absolutely nothing to say to *you*, Ludwig. But to bring your own flesh and blood into such company oh! you – you – "Her rage was choking her; it was as if she was spitting venom at him. "Come, Thymian, you shall spend the rest of the night with me. Fie, child! Aren't you ashamed to stand there in the middle of the table like that!" And she wanted to roll me up in her night-gown there and then and carry me off. But I fled like the wind, over bottles and glasses and dessert-plates, to the sofa, and from there I jumped on to Meinert's shoulders, with my legs round his neck, and he leaped up, and with a loud "Bravo!" and "Hullo!" rushed past Aunt Freda, out of the door and up the stairs. But Aunt Freda was after us. "Give me the child, you brute! You ought to be had up! Thymian, get down at once. For shame, child, for shame! If your poor dear mother saw you. . . !"

So she scolded after us all the way upstairs, and I kept sticking out my tongue at her, and yelling wildly, "Judge Lynch, Judge Lynch! Hateful old Judge Lynch!"

And then she caught me by the foot! But Meinert hurled open the door of his room, and all she kept hold of was my left shoe, and then Meinert slammed the door behind us. And we sat down in the dark on the side of his bed, and laughed. . . . and I was on his knee; and while Judge Lynch was foaming outside, tearing herself to pieces with rage, Meinert kissed me. He is very fond of doing that. When my little friends and I used to ask him for chocolate, we always had to give him a kiss for it.

We sat there for a long time, while Aunt Freda got madder and madder. She kept banging at the door with her umbrella, and I really think they must have heard it in the street. "Open the door, you hound, or I will call the police!"

"Don't be so excited, Fräulein Gotteball," Meinert called out. "It's nothing but a joke. You're only frightening Thymi."

Father came up then, and we could hear him quarrelling with Judge Lynch. But afterwards, he said that Meinert must open the door, and that Aunt Freda might keep me for that night, if she liked. I was very cross, but it was no good. Meinert opened the door, and I had to go off with Aunt Freda. She didn't say a word, but she held my hand tightly, and I could feel how her own was trembling.

She took me into her bedroom, and gave me a good washing, and I had to have a gargle, and then she helped me to undress, and put me in her own bed. She had to sleep on the sofa herself. She was trembling with cold, for she really *had* on nothing but her night-gown and a flannel petticoat under her waterproof!

I shut my eyes at once, and pretended I was very tired, for I was afraid she might still give me a scolding. But it was all right. She just said "Goodnight, Thymian," and then – she is rather religious – she knelt down by the bed, and in a strange passionate voice said this little prayer:–

> "Spread out thy two white wings, O Jesus, King of Kings,
>   And take this little birdie in;
> Then, through the evil day, she'll hear thine angels say
>   'This little child shall do no sin.'"

. . . .

Yes, it was a mad night, and it is still as clear in my memory as if it had been yesterday, although it's four years ago now.

In May, mother came back from Davos. A nursing-sister brought her home, and stayed with her. She was very ill; she moved only from her bed to her sofa, and from her sofa to her bed. And all of a sudden our house got as quiet as a church. I used to sit beside her sometimes on a stool, and then she used to stroke my hair with her little thin hand, and say, "My sweet Thymi, my poor little girl! What will become of you? If only I could have seen you grow up!" I did not know exactly what I ought to say to that; I felt very shy and very sad.

One night they came and awoke me, and when I opened my eyes, the nursing-sister was standing beside my bed.

"Dress yourself, little Thymian, and come with me," she said. "Your dear mother is going to heaven, and wants to say good-bye to you."

I began to cry, but the sister said I mustn't do that, it would make good-bye so much more difficult for my dear mother, and it was a great blessing and joy to her that she was going into God's beautiful Paradise at last, after all her suffering. I choked my sobs back then, for I had a tremendous respect for the sister. Aunt Freda and the clergyman were in mother's bedroom, and on the table beside the bed there were wax candles burning, for mother had had Communion in the night. Father was in the sitting room close by. You could scarcely see mother in the bed, her face was so white and small. I was very frightened; there was such a dreadful rattling going on in her throat. She got very much agitated when she saw me. She stretched out both hands to me, and I had to bend over her, and kiss her on both cheeks, and she held my face close between her damp cold hands, and sighed and sighed, and said something, but I couldn't understand what she said. I think she said that she would dearly love to take me with her. And then she kissed me again, and cried out, and the rattling came back so dreadfully! It was simply terrifying. The clergyman said, "We will ask our good God to watch over your child, dear Frau Gotteball. Let us pray." But mother didn't hear him, she was crying so dreadfully, and so was I. And then I heard the sister saying very low to the clergyman, "The child must go away. It is agony for the poor woman. She will rest easier when Thymian is gone." And then mother kissed me once more, and there came another attack, and Sister Anna took me by the hand and led me away. I couldn't go to sleep for a long time afterwards, but at last I did. And next morning the sister came to me again, and told me that mother had gone to God in the night.

That was on Thursday, and on Sunday mother was buried. Those were terrible days. Mother was in the best bedroom. I was frightened of her, she lay there so stiff and so icy cold, and yet something was always drawing me to her. Sunday was a most beautiful day. Just after twelve o'clock, when I was standing at the door, Fite Raasch and Lide Peters came and asked if I couldn't play marbles with them – "just one round" – and I did. We went under the lime trees in front of our house, and in one game I won twenty marbles from Fite Raasch. When I tried to take them up, he snatched two away from me, and ran off. I ran after him, and so did Lide. And suddenly – I don't know how it was – we were playing "tig" and screaming and laughing, and I'd forgotten all my sorrow, and I never would have remembered it if Aunt Freda hadn't suddenly appeared. She certainly has a talent for arriving just when one least wants her.

"Thymian," she cried angrily, "are you so utterly heartless, child, that you can't even keep quiet on the day of your mother's funeral?"

Then I began to cry bitterly, for I saw that I really had been very naughty. Aunt Freda stroked my cheek and sighed.

"Poor little thing! you're too young to know what they are taking away from you to-day," she said, and her eyes were filled with tears.

At four o'clock we took mother to the churchyard. In the middle of his discourse the clergyman turned to me, and told me I must always be good, and never forget that mother's last thought had been a prayer for me. I didn't hear him very well, for suddenly it all got black before my eyes, and then I knew nothing more until we drove up to our own house. I had fainted in the churchyard, they told me.

.   .   .   .

For some time after mother's funeral it was very dreary. The house seemed to me so frightfully big; it was just as if there was a hole in it. It was quite different from the time that mother was at Davos.

I often stole off by myself to the churchyard and sat on mother's grave. All the withered white wreaths had "Auf Wiedersehen" written on them, and the clergyman is always saying that people see each other again in heaven, but I could never understand how you *could* see anyone again who had once been put so deep into the dark, cold ground. I thought of many things that I'd never thought of until mother died. I thought of how often she used to take me on her lap and hold me close to her, and a great longing for her kisses came over me. I felt so lonely and forsaken all at once.

In the evenings it was lovely at the churchyard. The lime trees were in flower, and the narcissus smelt so sweet. I used to shut my eyes, and dream that mother had floated down to me dressed all in white, and kissed me. Often I saw her so plainly that I stretched out my arms to hold her fast.

Once father came and brought me away from the churchyard at ten o'clock in the evening. He seemed very much upset.

"Thymi, my little angel, I had no idea that you came here all by yourself to the churchyard, and fretted," he said. "Aunt Freda only told me to-day. You mustn't do that, my darling; you must try to get over it now. We must all die some day, but until it comes we ought to enjoy this beautiful life. I will take you with me to Hamburg in August, and we'll go to the Circus, and I'll buy you a doll as big as a baby. Promise me that you won't steal off to the churchyard again."

I promised him, and I never went there again after that. Gradually everything slipped back into the old routine. Aunt Freda came, sticking her nose into everything just as before, and scolding and finding fault and making herself disagreeable. She would have liked father to get a duenna, but father wouldn't. He said mother's long illness had cost him so much, it would be all he could do to get into smooth water again. We could easily get on with two servants; and the cook after all *was* quite an elderly woman, and had been with us for seven years. Our housemaid then was Lena Hannemann, a daughter of Boatman Hannemann, who lived in Wiedemann Alley. Lena was just seventeen, and a very dainty, pretty girl. She knew the most delightful games which we used to play together. But to my great grief, she went away in September, after a great fuss. I didn't know what it was about, and it would not have interested me at all, if it had not been that something happened immediately afterwards, which was a great event for me.

One day Frau Hannemann appeared at our house, making a terrible outcry, and saying that Lena must instantly pack up her things and come away with her. She met father in the back-hall, and stood in front of him, and abused him frightfully, and brandished an iron fish-hook in his face, until I was really afraid that she might hurt him. She talked so fast that I could only understand a very few words, and those were not pretty ones. Father told her to go to the devil, but she stormed on and ran into the kitchen and roared out loud: "He's a damned scoundrel! His poor wife is scarcely cold in her grave, before he is running after his servant-maids. . . ."

It was all terribly mysterious to me, and I thought that Frau Hannemann had gone mad, and was very glad when she disappeared from the house with Lena.

Two days later, when I came home from school, I found at least half the tribe of relations sitting round the table in the sitting-room and drinking coffee – Uncle Henning, and Aunt Wiebke, Lehnsmann Pohns, and Aunt Frauke, and of course the inevitable Aunt Freda. Father was looking very red and indignant. "Oh, there you are! Come here, Thymi," he said; "there's a great family-council going on about you. All the aunts and uncles think you'll have to go to school at T —. What do you think of that? Would you like it?"

"Thymi has nothing to do with *thinking* and *liking;* what she has to do is to listen and obey, and be a good child, and do what her elders think best for her," said Aunt Freda in her sharp, thin voice.

"You old image!" I thought to myself, but of course I said nothing.

"Yes, yes, Thymi must be obedient," babbled Uncle Henning, and the aunts all nodded like mandarins.

I could easily see that father didn't like it, but he is a great deal too good-natured ever to stand out against Aunt Freda's nagging. So it was decided that I was to go to T— on the 1st of October. When the family was gone, father comforted me, and said I should soon be home again, and he would come to see me every month, and always bring me a lovely present.

Father loves me very much.

CHAPTER II

I THOUGHT at first that I should never have anything at all to write in my Diary, but now that I have begun I see that I shall have any amount of things to tell. If I were to write down all my experiences in T—, I could fill half the book with them, so I will keep to the principal ones.

At first I went to live with Pastor Flau. There were two other school-girls in his boarding-house. Our daily life in the pastoral household was exactly like the pastor's name— it was more than flat. Mrs. Pastor had five small children and no servant, but three housekeeping-pupils instead, who each paid her 350 marks. These three girls had each their set work, or "labour," as they called it; one looked after the kitchen, another cleaned the living-rooms, and. The third reigned in the nursery. They exchanged work every week, so that when the year was over, they had each of them learnt cookery, housekeeping, and the care of children. And Mrs. Pastor had all their work for nothing, and more than one thousand marks to the good besides. She herself wrote novels in her leisure-time, and said it was the dearest dream of her life to be able to get out into the garden. We had some cooked-up meat nearly every day for early dinner; on Sunday there was roast meat; on Mondays, fricassee; on Tuesdays, dumplings; on Wednesdays, "mock-hare"; on Thursdays, fried slices of "mock-hare"; on Fridays, huh; on Saturdays. a ragout of soup-meat, or, as a great treat, stuffed celery, or "lost birds" – that is, meat wrapped in cabbage-leaves and fried. Once when the General Superintendent was dining, we had a fricassee as an entree, and the old gentleman praised it beyond measure, and asked for the recipe. *We* had our own opinion about it; the mere sight of it nearly made us sick.

Father came first every Sunday in the month, and brought me a lot of chocolate, and he nearly always gave me a ten-mark piece as pocket-money, so that if I got up hungry from early dinner, I could always eat as many cream cakes as I wanted at the confectioner's. Sometimes Meinert came to see me too. After a year the Flaus got transferred, and then I went to two old ladies who took boarders. We were seven girls there. The others were daughters of Northern country folk, and we were all about the same age, and so, naturally, we all went to Fräulein Lundberg's High School for Girls. The new place was better as regards food; and close by there was a Professor of Gymnastics, who also took boarders — boys, of course, so we got some amusement out of that.

The head of our boarding-house, Fräulein Sass, lived in perpetual warfare with the Professor on account of his fowl. The Professor's fowl were always coming into the Sass garden, and scratching up the asparagus-beds, and breaking down the Hower-borders. Fräulein Sass demanded that the Professor should shut up his fowl, and the Professor maintained that it could not be *his* fowl, for they never did anything like that. But unfortunately there were no others in the neighbourhood. Fräulein Sass and the Professor exchanged dozens of insulting letters about the fowl, and we very seldom talked about anything else at meals.

Although we were strictly forbidden to speak to the Professor's boarders, we got to know them all the same, and chose our opportunity in the afternoon, when the old ladies were asleep, and we were sitting in the summer-house, and the boys were close by in the gymnasium. They used to climb over the planks and come to us, or else sit on the highest bars where they could see us and talk to us. Most of them were Northerners, and some of them I already knew through staying with my relations.

There was also at the Professor's a cousin of my best friend, Annie Meier (she was at the Sass boarding-house), called Boy Detlefs. They were to get married as soon as Boy was a doctor (for he was to study medicine); and then there was a real Count there, too – Casimir Osdorff, with two f's, the "real feudal way of spelling it," he used to say. There exists an Osdorff family with one f, but "they are nobodies and don't count," said Osdorff with the two f's.

Each of us had our special friend, and Osdorff was mine. . . . He is not exactly good-looking. His under lip sticks out a little, his face is rather puffy, and his light-grey eyes seem always asleep. Annie called them cod-fish eyes. He looks exactly the same now as he did then. . . . Boy Detlefs used to declare that Osdorff was as stupid as an owl, and as lazy as a pig. What I liked so much about him in those days – and still like-were his boots and his hands. Never before had I seen such marvellous boots, and such enchanting hands. The boots look as if they grew on his feet, as glossy and as supple as an eelskin; and his hands are white and soft as velvet, with lovely rosy nails, as dainty as a dainty lady's.

Casimir Osdorff is the fifth of six children, and his mother is a widow. They are not very rich. The eldest son will have the property, and as it is heavily mortgaged, there won't be much for the others. When he has done with school he is to study forestry. But he hasn't got his Junior Certificate yet.

Osdorff makes no secret of hating lessons. He says that the social conditions of the present day are absolutely corrupt, and that the State will very soon come to an end if there isn't some tremendous reaction. Instead of so many millions being squandered on wicked folly, and the Government for ever coquetting with the mob, and sanctioning all sorts of tinkering reforms, there ought to be established once for all a Fund for Keeping Up the Position of the Poorer Nobility. This Fund should be managed so that the interest could be divided among all the real feudal families of small means, in such a manner as to provide them with a suitable unearned increment. Then the noblest in the land would not be obliged to compete with the populace in the degrading task of earning their living. This would be a great gain to the State, since the Nobility would thereby grow more powerful. For there are (he says) only three genuine class-divisions-Nobility, Clergy, and Proletariat. The so-called Middle-Class is the canker at the heart of a Feudal Constitution. The Noble is there to command; the Proletarian to labour and to serve; the Clergyman to maintain order. The bourgeoisie is the hot-bed of revolution. . . And what a scandal it was (he would continue) that a young, highly-gifted, well-born man like himself – an Osdorff with two f's-should have to rub shoulders at the same desk with the sons of peasants and shopkeepers, and submit to the fault-finding of low-born school teachers. . . He used to talk to me about his views for hours together. I could not agree with him at all, but I thought him very original and interesting.

The other girls were all to marry their sweethearts, but Osdorff told me from the very first that he could not marry *me*. Years ago, he said, he had fallen in love with the distant relation of a married cousin. As a prudent man, he could not risk too hasty a declaration; so first made a thorough investigation into the lady's family-tree. And thus he discovered that her great-grandmother (on the maternal side) had been the daughter of a Saxon Privy-Councillor called Düppel. He would never have forgiven himself if by an ill-considered promise he had bound himself to bring such disgrace as *that* upon his family. It was his pride and his privilege to keep his escutcheon stainless, and that great-grandmother Düppel would have been an ineradicable blot upon it. I must confess that his nobility touched me very deeply, but nothing else about him took my fancy at all, except his nails and his hands.

So far, I had had a very good time at Fräulein Lundberg's school. I had been in the first class for just six months when the great scandal happened which brought my sojourn in T— to an untimely end. This was how it came about.

There was a fashionable wedding in T— to which Fräulein Sass and the Professor were invited. For weeks the two Sass ladies debated whether they ought not to decline on account of the Professor. The fowl warfare was so fierce that they were more than half inclined to send a refusal, but at last they decided to go, and treat the Professor as if he did not exist.

We had arranged an excursion to "The Green Tree" with the Professor's boys, for the great day. There were to be only Annie Meier, Lena Schlitt, and I; Boy Detlefs, Heite Butenschön, and Osdorff (the other girls were all too proper). "The Green Tree" is a solitary inn, about an hour from T—, and is famous for its excellent rumpunch.

We started about five o'clock, and strolled along slowly, so that it was nearly seven when we got there. Directly we arrived, we ordered six punches, clinked glasses, and drank deep. The fiery stuff burnt one's tongue like flame, and I can't say I enjoyed it excessively, but Boy declared that it was the correct thing to order another go all round and that we must do it, otherwise they'd think we were fools – besides, one couldn't possibly judge by one glass. I thought: "Now for it, then!" . . . held my breath and gulped it down like medicine. . . . But it was funny – either the rum must have been better in the second go, or else there was more sugar in it – for certainly it *did* taste much nicer this time. And it made one feel so warm and happy. We had some more after that, "to show we liked it," said Boy Detlefs; and we got gayer and gayer, and laughed like mad. Then Boy ordered a whole bowl, and said we must drink to his betrothal with Annie, and we all shouted "Hip-hip, hurrah!" and drank again each with the other, all round. At last the hot, strong stuff made me feel ill, and the others couldn't manage any more, either. So about a quarter-past nine we broke up, but it was nearly ten before we really went away. When I stepped from the warm room into the open air, everything seemed to go round and round, and it was a good thing that Boy Detlefs was standing behind me and held me up, otherwise I should have been tumbling all over the place.

"Yes, Thymian, that's right, stay with me, and let a *man* take care of you, instead of that silly fool," said he. "Osdorff has as much as he can do to-night to carry all his f's; he's got four of them now, two in his name and two in his head." And he held my hand tight, and hit Osdorff over the head, and cried, "Hollow! hollow!" Osdorff certainly looked lamentable, but we *had* to laugh. Annie came flying up like an avenging angel, and smacked me on the hand that Boy was holding, and said I must go away, I had nothing to do with her sweetheart. Then she too Boy by his other arm, and we trundled off, reeling all over the road so that nobody could pass us.

The open air was making us worse and worse; Annie was wailing out that she couldn't walk; I could scarcely get along at all, and Lena Schutt was limping like a wounded bird; but the boys – that is, Boy Detlefs and Butenschön – held us up and shouldered us on, and all of a sudden the line broke! Osdorff, who was on the outside, held up by Lena, had come to the ground and dragged Lena with him, and we were all within an ace of tumbling on top of them. But while Boy and Butenschon were picking up the two who were rolling in the mud, Annie and I stumbled sideways towards the side of the road. I sat down on a stone, and Annie threw herself on her face on the wet grass and began to weep bitterly, saying she knew she was going to die, and she wouldn't go a step further, for it didn't matter where .it ended, it was all over with her. Nobody listened to her, for Boy and Butenschön had enough to do with Osdorff and Lena, and although they did succeed in getting Lena on her legs, they couldn't get her to stir a step. So they consulted together as to what they had better do, and at last came to the conclusion that they would run all the way to T— and fetch a carriage, so that we might get home before the doors were shut. Off they went, and. we stayed behind on the road.

Lena and Annie were howling like two mad things; Osdorff was grunting like a pig in the gutter, and finally the two girls began to get very sick. This disgusted me so much that it had very nearly the same effect upon me, and I crawled a little further away from them, but my feet were so heavy that I soon had to sit down again in the ditch. I knew perfectly well that I was just as drunk as the others, but I was conscious of everything. My head ached so dreadfully, though, that I stretched myself full length on the grass, and lay blinking up at the sky. The moon was shining in the puddles, and millions of stars were twinkling; and, looking at them, it seemed to me as if they were clear, human eyes, and as if two of them-two that were very gold and bright belonged to my dear dead mother. And I shut my eyes, for I couldn't bear to look at those two stars; it was my heart that began to ache then, for I was so horribly ashamed. It is not a pretty sight to see little school-girls drunk, and lying on the road like cattle; but how could we know that the abominable stuff was going to have such an effect? . . . That other night-the *Teresa Krones* night – there was something so much nicer about it; and even to this day I will maintain that to get drunk upon champagne is a much daintier thing than to get drunk upon rum – there's just the same difference between them that there is between a well-bred dog and a wretched mongrel cur. . . .

After a while a cart came along, and when the driver heard the whimpering of Annie and Lena he stopped and got down. He was a butcher, who had been into the country with some cattle-dealers; and these were the men who now, with yells of laughter, collected Osdorff and the girls and put them in the cart. I didn't want to stay behind alone, so I climbed up, but I was able to do it all by myself, for I was gradually getting better. Oh I the witticisms and the coarse jokes we had to listen to on the way to T—; about the "High" young ladies and the "Superior" young men! We wanted hides like their own cattle.

It was purgatory. Annie and Lena were still incapable of understanding it, but I expiated then all my sins of that evening, I can most absolutely say.

It was so terrible that I stuffed my fingers into my ears to prevent myself from hearing. When we arrived at T—, the men set us down at the butcher's shop, and Mrs. Butcher came out with a lamp, and so did all the servants and errand-boys, and then there was more laughing and more jocosity. How Osdorff got home I don't know. Fräulein Sass's maid put Lena and Annie to bed, and the doctor had to be fetched for Lena. I tried to prevent that, but Lena was perfectly idiotic, and said she was going to die, just as Annie had said before.

Well, of course, the whole town was talking of our adventure next day. Fräulein Lundberg sent us home from school in the afternoon, for there was to be an investigation into our conduct- the result of which was that we were all three expelled. Fräulein Lundberg said that never in the annals of her school had there been such a case of immoral behaviour, and that our example would be ruinous to our school-fellows. The very existence of her school, she said, depended upon the elimination of all evil elements. Annie and Lena howled like hyenas, and Annie was mean enough to put all the blame upon me – but she gained nothing by that.

As for the boys, Osdorff shared our fate; he was expelled with ignominy, despite his two f's. Boy Detlefs and Butenschon got off with a reprimand, which I thought very unfair, for the only mitigation of their behaviour was that they knew better how to carry their liquor than poor Osdorff did. Some malicious tongues whispered that the Head had not dared to be so strict with Boy, because Frau Detlefs used to bring his wife three pounds of butter and a score of eggs every Saturday as a present, but I don't know whether that was true or not.

The other girls cried all day and all night, for they were afraid of their parents. I wasn't. I knew that father would do nothing to me. But I felt a little nervous at the thought of Aunt Freda's angry eyes.

Father came to fetch me away the next evening. He wasn't a bit cross; he only abused Fräulein Lundberg, and said she was the most petty, narrow-minded old thing he had ever heard of, to punish a childish prank so savagely, and he was very glad I was coming home again, for he had missed me very much. I was glad too.

All the doors were decorated at home, and they had put up a transparency with "Welcome" on it. I cried with joy, I was so delighted.

There were very few changes at home, but the old cook was gone, and there was a housekeeper in her place – quite a nice-looking person, but very stout. Fräulein Reinhard was her name. When supper was over and Reinhard was gone, and Meinert back in the shop, father sat down beside me on the sofa and talked to me just as if I was a grown-up lady. Housekeepers were a nuisance, he told me; this Reinhard was the fourth in two years. He would be very glad when I was old enough to keep house, and we needn't have any of these women hanging about. Then he took my chin in his left hand and looked at me for a long time, and stroked my black hair with his right, and said I had grown pretty, as pretty as a picture, and as soon as I was grown up he was going to travel about with me, so that I might get to know people; it would be a shame to let me moulder away in this hole, and marry one of the infernal Philistines belonging to it.

"Do you know who you're like, Thymi?" he asked.

I shook my head.

"You don't take after your mother. She had a nice little face, but she was no beauty. And you haven't got your good looks from me, either. But you ask Aunt Freda to show you the picture of your great-grandmother, Madame Claire Gotteball, some day – she must have it put away somewhere and – you'll see your own face there. She was a Frenchwoman, and must have been a piquant beauty."

"What is a 'piquante' beauty' " I asked.

Father laughed. "I couldn't explain it to you, Thymi, but a 'piquante' beauty is a beauty whom men admire. Now you know."

Yea, now I knew; but I wasn't much the wiser for it. . . .

Everything went on just as usual after that. The last half-year I went to Fräulein Vieterich's school, and that lasted until the time came for me to be confirmed.

„Das Tagebuch einer Verlorenen"

CHAPTER III

ONE day I had a great surprise. I was going on a message to
Aunt Wiebke Henning's, and at the corner of the Bismarckstrasse
I met – Casimir Osdorff! I could hardly believe my eyes, but it
was he, as large as life. He said he was getting on all right. . . . He
is boarding at Doctor Bauer's, and will soon be going up for his
Junior Examination. Doctor Bauer was once private tutor at the
Count "von" and "zu" Ypsilon's – a great Berlin grandee, who is
Casimir's guardian. Osdorff complains that he is still obliged to
put up with the same kind of "mixed company" as he had in T—.
I condoled with him, and we promised one another to meet as
often as possible. I have no intimate friends now, since I've come
back from school. Annie Meier has gone to Wandsbeck to school,
and Lena Schlitt to Kiel, so that it is very nice to have at least one
chum with whom I can talk sometimes.

Nothing particular happened last year up to the time of my
Confirmation. I get on splendidly with our housekeeper; she is
kind and friendly. If only she wasn't so frightfully greedy! I hate
people who are always eating. It's incredible the amount she
consumes at table; and between meals, she is always nibbling at
something out of her pocket. It's disgusting!

. . . .

I went to the Confirmation class every Wednesday and Saturday.
At first I hated these hours with the old parson, but later on I got
to like them.

I hadn't been at all religious up to that, but the old clergyman has
a wonderful way of reaching one's heart. When the lesson was
over, about six, it was beginning to get dark, and I often went a
roundabout way home so as to think over what I had heard. It

made such a deep impression upon me, to hear about that Love which wipes out all sin, and spread its soft gracious wings over the follies and misdeed of mankind. I never could help thinking, at those times, of our hideous adventure at "The Green Tree," and the terrible home-coming with the cattle-dealers. Even though father, in his great kindness, regarded it merely as a childish prank, I couldn't help feeling that there was something horrible about it, and I never could get rid of the feeling that mother saw me then, and sorrowed over me. At that time I used often to go to mother's grave, and always I felt very good and very serious while I was there. I made up my mind to go to church every Sunday after my Confirmation, and to be a really good girl. The clergyman is a darling old man. There is something so lovable and gentle and natural and human about him, and he's not a bit unctuous, and it always seemed to me as if he regarded me with a quiet special tenderness.

All the relations were there on my Confirmation-day. They came in the morning, so as to go to church with me. I fainted while I was dressing, out of pure excitement, but I soon got all right again. Father wanted to give me a glass of brandy, but I couldn't touch it. Ever since that evening at "The Green Tree," I've had a great horror of spirits.

It was a beautiful ceremony, and the clergyman said such lovely things. I sat there in a dream, and it seemed to me as if the sound of the organ was lifting my soul and carrying it up to another world, where mother was. And when we knelt down and made our profession of faith, and the bells all rang out, I was so overcome that I sobbed aloud. Afterwards we each got our texts. Mine was: Our conversation is in heaven, from whence we await the coming of our Lord and Savior Jesus Christ." The organ played softly while the clergyman blessed us. When the ceremony was over, we took our First Communion.

I was more deeply moved than I had ever been in my whole life, and father had tears in his eyes, too, when he took me in his arms after the Feast was over, and kissed me. Then the whole tribe of relations crowded round and congratulated me, uncles and aunts and cousins of every degree, and I felt very proud to be the centre of all the excitement.

We dined in the big room, which is only used on great occasions, and we had a cook and a waiter in for the day. Uncle Lehnsmann made a speech at dinner and talked about my having entered on a new phase of my existence. But otherwise we were very silent during the meal, and I even thought we seemed a little oppressed, as if it were a funeral Reinhard scarcely showed at all. When we came home from church, she looked just as if she had been crying, from which I concluded that she was moved like all the rest of us, and gave her great credit for it. After dinner the gentlemen went into the sitting-room to smoke, and the ladies drank coffee in the drawing-room, where my present-table was. I had had a lot of lovely presents: from father there was a long golden chain with a little watch on it, and a diamond ring; from Aunt Freda, an old-fashioned gold ornament which is a family heirloom; and I had two bracelets and three gold rings, and three brooches, and a silver filigree ornament, and a lot of books and flowers and other trifles.

While I was standing, apparently quite absorbed, at my table, reading one of my books, I heard Aunt Freda and Aunt Franke whispering to one another, and I managed to catch a few words.

"I do wish that Ludwig could get hold of a nice, sensible wife," said Aunt Freda; "it would be a real blessing for him and Thymi, and all of us."

Aunt Frauke, who looked very hot, sighed and said, "Yes, it's a terrible scandal for the family; my poor sister would turn in her grave if she knew."

That was all I could hear, and I only thought that they were still talking about my adventure in T—, for I couldn't think of any other reason why mother should turn in her grave. I didn't think it at all nice of them to bring it up again on my Confirmation-day, and it was *too* absurd of Aunt Freda to connect father with it. The relations went away about six o'clock, and even Aunt Freda departed.

About half-past six, when they were all gone, Meinert came and called me into the shop.

"There's somebody else there who wants to Congratulate you, Thymi," he said, laughing.

I went in, and found Osdorff. The poor boy had sent me a bouquet, and now he was feeling very forlorn without his little pocket-money. . . . Father brought him in to drink a glass of wine with us upstairs, and afterwards Meinert came up too, and we had great fun.

I'm really sorry for Osdorff. He has failed again in his Junior, and now he'll have to wait until August and stay a year longer with Doctor Bauer. What will become of him after that, he doesn't know.

. . . .

It's five weeks now since my Confirmation; and Aunt Freda has brought me this book to write in. I wonder if I shall have any experiences worth putting down. Aunt Freda insists that I shall go to school, but I don't want to, and father stands by me.

It is a fortnight since I made the last entry in my Diary, and now at length I have something more to tell. It is nothing very important, but in my uneventful life I must use every opportunity, else I shall never get the book filled.

Well, Fräulein Reinhard is gone . . . . I didn't know at all that she was thinking of leaving. One forenoon I went into her room, and found her packing her little all, and crying so that she could hardly speak. I asked her why she was going off in such a hurry. But I couldn't get a rational answer from her; she went on crying and sobbing like a great baby. I'm funny in that way; I hate to see anyone cry. Up comes a big lump in my throat that instant, and before I know, I'm blubbering too. Reinhard wouldn't say anything more, so I ran down to father, who was reading the paper in the sitting-room, and asked him why she was going.

"She is ill. I can't stand her everlasting groaning and moaning," said father.

"Oh!" said I, quite disconcerted. "Why, I never noticed it. What's the matter with her?"

"Leave me alone; don't pester me with your everlasting questions," cried father, roughly. I never knew him like that before. So I went into the shop, for I'm funny in that way too. I always *must* get to the bottom of a thing, and the thought of poor Reinhard was making me very unhappy. Meinert was mixing a powder, so I didn't dare to disturb him, but I sat on the counter and waited till he had finished.

"Do *you* know why Reinhard is going away?" I asked.

"Yes," said he.

"What's the matter with her?"

"She has a pain in her stomach," he replied, and I could see his month twitching under his thin red moustache, as if he was laughing.

"Oh, is *that* all?" I said, relieved to find that it was nothing worse. "No wonder, considering the amount she eats. She nibbles at things out of her pocket all day long."

"Quite right, Thymi! It all comes from nibbling," said Meinert, shouting with laughter. And he laughed and laughed, and held his sides, and couldn't stop himself. "Remember that, Thymi!" he cried. "You should always stop eating just when the thing tastes nicest. If you don't, you'll have the same sort of pain as Ma'msell Reinhard."

I was annoyed by his laughing, and I went away and banged the door behind me. I'm sorry for poor Reinhard, even if it *is* only a pain in her stomach from all the chocolate she eats. Certainly it's nothing to laugh at. That kind of pain can be perfectly awful, for I've often had it when I've eaten too much cucumber-salad at supper.

Reinhard is gone, now, and we have no new housekeeper yet. Father is looking for one at an agency. I hope we shall get a nice one.

. . . .

We have got a very nice one. She is charming and dainty and good-humoured, and quite young only four-and-twenty, and an orphan. She was born at Naumburg on the Taal. Her name is Elizabeth Woyens, and she *is* pretty! I like her golden hair so much. It is so long that she can sit upon it when it's all let down; but she always wears it in two plaits around her head. And she has a darling little waist – slender as anything. I made friends with her directly. It's very pleasant at home now. On fine evenings we go for walks together, sometimes to the churchyard, and sometimes along the avenue into the town. We have drunk to each other's health and sworn eternal friendship in raspberry-vinegar, and she has told me the story of her life. She lost her parents when she wasn't quite seven years old; they died one after the other of typhus fever, and she has no brothers or sisters. Then she was brought up by a clergyman, but he had eight children of his own, so he could only keep her as long as she was paid for, and what money she had lasted till her Confirmation and for just a year afterwards, while she was learning cooking in a polytechnic school. So then she had to look out for a situation; and ever since she has always lived with strangers, and in most families she has had anything but a bed of roses. She has had an unhappy love-affair, too, a very romantic one. He was the son of an old lady whose "help" Elizabeth was, and when they got to know each other he was studying theology, and only came home in the holidays. The instant the old lady discovered what was going on, she turned Elizabeth out of the house; and then she went to a colonial dealer's where she was the only servant and had to do all the work. But she and Johannes (that's the young man's name) still corresponded, and when he came home for the holidays they used to meet, and were quite determined to get married. But years and years passed by, and Johannes passed his examination and was made vicar, and Elizabeth was sure that they would get married *then*. But it all went wrong. His mother died, and it came out then that she had had no money of her own, only her pension and some support from relations. One day after Johannes had been elected as pastor of a little town in Westphalia, he wrote to Elizabeth and said they would not be able to get married, for they were both poor, and nobody could manage decently on eight hundred thalers. Poor Elizabeth cried a lot about it, she told me. It seems strange to me that a clergyman should think so much about money; I always used to imagine that people like that had "their conversation in heaven," but it seems that a parson is a man like other men, and, to judge by this instance, rather worse than the average. For in my opinion it's a very contemptible man who would keep a young girl waiting nearly four years, and then give her the go-by, because she has no money. Thank goodness, Elizabeth has very nearly got over it now; she is quite gay and cheerful.

When we go for a walk in the evening, Osdorff sometimes joins us. Elizabeth never can help making game of him; she says he's *too* funny, with his ridiculous ideas of his own importance. He is certainly rather absurd, as he always was; and I think Boy Detlefs was right enough when he called him a silly fool. But all the same, I'm glad to see him when he comes. Father doesn't object to his visits, and he often spends the evenings with us in the garden. I have never told yet about our lovely big garden, with its fine thick-stemmed old pear-trees, and its flowers –such heaps of them. And big pots of grass, and such a lovely *secret* kind of summer-house, with birds and climbing plants. Casimir Osdorff loves flowers too, and when we are doing the watering in the evening, he often forgets all about aristocratic magnificence and even the two f's, and pumps the water with his own hands and helps me to water, and really delights in the whole thing. Lately he was very proud because he had discovered an old half-dead rose-tree, which he watered well and then loosened the earth all around it, and now it's beginning to look quite healthy again. Osdorff says that he would like very much to be a gardener, but only for himself, not for other people, for that would naturally be impossible in his position; and then he begins to talk about his wonderful social ideals, and father and Elizabeth ask him this, that, and the other, and look at one another and laugh, and Osdorff talks nineteen to the dozen and hasn't the least idea that they are only leading him on.

On fine summer evenings we often sit in the arbour. We have a hanging-lamp there, but it burns badly, so that there's always a sort of delightful half-twilight in the little leafy place. Father and Elizabeth chat together, and I often sit for a long time with my hands clasped round my knees and forget everything, and feel as if I were floating in the dreamy beauty of the deep still night which broods over the garden. And the clouds go drifting over the dark blue sky and over the golden crescent of the moon, and nothing stirs, and the trees stand there so tall and dark and still, and the lilies shine like white tapers through the misty veil of the twilight and pour out their fragrance so that it fills the air and makes you feel faint, like incense – and a strange melancholy comes over you, a twofold feeling of longing and sadness. The thought of mother always comes to me – how she used to sit here once too, and drink in the scent of the lilies and watch the clouds drifting, and how she has lain for three years buried deep in the cold dark ground. How strange it is! We human beings live just like flowers, and wither away and return to the dust like fallen autumn petals. Only the flowers come up again, and the dead never return. In those hours my heart is heavy with longing for something inexpressible, a happiness of which I have only a very vague and indefinite conception. Yet at the same time a dim presentiment creeps like a shadow through my soul, telling me that these dreamy, quiet, perfumed summer evenings in my father's garden will one day lie behind me like a lost Paradise. I don't know at all how it is, but whenever I am enjoying something lovely and calm and tranquil, and my heart is at rest, something sad always comes and overshadows me at the same moment. It was like that yesterday evening. Elizabeth suddenly put her arm around my neck. "What are you dreaming of, Thymi?" she asked. And it wasn't until I looked up that I noticed that we were alone together.

"I am dreaming of happiness," I said. "I should so like some day to be very, very happy. Tell me, Elizabeth, what do you think is the greatest happiness in the world?"

"Ah! that's a difficult question," she replied. "I think our ideas of happiness change with time. When I was a child, my dearest wish was for a doll that could say Papa and Mamma; and when I was in love, of course there was nothing I wanted more than to be able to get married soon. And now – now I should be perfectly contented if the good God would give me a home of my own, a little nest that nobody could drive me away from. . . . Ah! how I should love a tiny tranquil little home like Aunt Freda's—"

"A poky, old-maidish hole like that!" I cried, in astonishment. "Good gracious! I don't believe there could be any real happiness without a. husband."

"Yes, at your age one thinks that," she said, thoughtfully; "but as one grows older, one sees that men don't make one happy either. If a man were to want me now, and I didn't love him, but respected him, and he offered me a home, I wouldn't say no. But I would much rather have it, if, for instance, I were to win a prize in the lottery, and could make a home for myself, without a husband whom I didn't love. Do you understand, Thymi?"

"Perfectly," I said; "and it's just what I think. I won't marry any man either unless I love him, and I'll only love an absolutely ideal one, quite faultless—"

"*Un chevalier sans peur et Sllons reproche,*" laughed Elizabeth. "Perhaps I shall be still here when you're having a look-around for a husband, and I'll help you to find one."

"No, I'll do that for myself, Elizabeth," I said.

. . . .

Aunt Freda goes on finding fault with everything in our household; she considered Elizabeth too young from the first, and she told her so to her face. "A pretty young girl, alone in the world like you, should always look out for a place under a mistress," she said, in her sharp way. "Don't you know that the house of an unmarried man is no place for a defenceless girl? Take care that you aren't led astray."

Elizabeth was quite frightened, but I calmed her down and said she mustn't think anything of it; Aunt Freda was a little cracked. But Aunt Freda seems to have got used to Elizabeth now, for she is very nice to her and often invites her to her house. Everybody who knows Elizabeth loves her, even our relations. We two are always being asked out to coffee. The day before yesterday we were at Aunt Wiebke's – that's Frau Henning – at quite a big party, twenty-two ladies, and Elizabeth helped aunt with the tea, and I heard the older ladies talking about her very nicely.

"Charming person; so quiet," said Frau Jens.

"And so sensible and clever," said Frau Doctor Henning, Aunt Wiebke's sister-in-law. "She speaks French fluently, and plays the piano charmingly, and she can do all kinds of needlework."

"Why, she can even cut out," Aunt Freda told them. "She made the whole of Thymian's blouse and inserted all that lace, every bit, with her own hands—"

"Is it possible?"

"I've often admired her, and thought she must come from Hamburg."

"She's a real treasure."

"Yes, my brother was in luck when he got her."

They did nothing but talk about her, in fact, and then the blouse was examined and admired, and Elizabeth's praises were sung all over again.

The ladies bad all brought a bit of work with them, and whenever there was a pause in the conversation they stitched and hemmed and gathered as if the devil was behind them. There were any amount of cakes – I counted twenty-four different sorts; and after the coffee there was chocolate and éclairs and whipped cream, and I saw one lady having four cups of coffee, and five cups of chocolate, and six éclairs besides any amount of other goodies, and if she *didn't* have a pain in her stomach, she ought to have had!

They didn't gossip at all, for some years ago a horrible thing happened here. They were abusing a lady who was said to be unfaithful to her husband, and they had no idea that one of the women who was there was a friend of hers. She told it all back, and the lady in question summoned all the other ladies who had said these things about her before the magistrate, and there was weeping and gnashing of teeth; and since then, nobody has been slandered at the coffee-parties, they only just talk tittle-tattle. The great piece of news was the story about old Hinze. He was an old cobbler about seventy years of age, who lived down on the Deepwater Quay, and never hurt a fly. The wall of his shop was a little bit out of repair, and as they are just going to build a new post-office behind his garden, and thousands of bricks are lying about, he thought it was no harm to take a couple and mend his wall with them, quite forgetting that these bricks belonged to the corporation. Some fool of a foreman noticed it, and last week the poor old man was sentenced to three days imprisonment for larceny. It would never have come to that really, for the Emperor would certainly have let him off, but he was afraid to trust to that, and hanged himself the same evening in his workshop, and when they found him in the morning he had been dead a long time. It is terrible that such things should happen. I think there ought to be a new law made, distinguishing between "taking" and "stealing" for those bricks were certainly not *stolen*. The people who make the laws can't be very clever, or they would have provided for a case like this, and then poor honest old Cobbler Hinze would be alive to-day.

CHAPTER IV

IF one sits behind the portiere in the drawing-room one can hear what is said in the sitting-room, and if one stands at the window of the sitting-room one can hear what is said in the drawing-room. I found that out a couple of days ago. I wanted to get a book out of the drawing-room, and I heard Aunt Freda and father talking in the next room. Aunt Freda's sweet voice doesn't hold me spellbound as a rule, but I caught a couple of sentences that interested me, and so I listened.

"I don't know what you want," Aunt Freda was saying; "she's a good sensible girl of respectable family and blameless life, and Thymi is very fond of her. Much the best thing you can do is to marry her; everything will be all right then, and Thymi will have somebody to take care of her, and people will stop gossiping."

"Oho!" thought I, "so father's to marry Elizabeth. I wonder if she'll have him – they needn't be so sure!"

But father was saying that he had no idea of marrying at all as yet; he had had enough of matrimony and its bondage through all those years with a sickly wife. Besides, Elizabeth was too young for him. She would probably present him with half a dozen children, and he had to think of me. And if he ever did marry again – later on, when I was settled – it would be an older woman, and very certainly one who had some money of her own. His business was far from prosperous. . . . I heard so far, and after that the conversation ceased to interest me.

I had my own ideas about what I had heard, and was in high feather at knowing so much more than anyone thought I did. Aunt Freda's plan seemed to me not at all a bad one. Elizabeth asks for nothing better than a little house of her own. We can offer her that. And then we shall have her always, whereas now we can never be sure that she won't go away some day. I thought of talking to father and cheering him up, and generally playing the part of a little Providence. If she really did have half a dozen children, I don't see what harm it could do me. I shouldn't have to look after them, though I'm very, very fond of children, for that matter. But on reflection, I think I won't say a word, only watch carefully, like a guardian angel, and keep my own counsel. Yes, that will be delightful. I'll make them both so happy. I love them both very dearly, and I shan't a bit mind if I have to say Mamma to Elizabeth. But only "Mamma," for one can't have any "Mother" but the first. And *my* mother is with the good God.

. . . .

Once or twice I have wanted badly to encourage father and tell him that no one would make him so happy as Elizabeth, and that I shouldn't have a word to say against his marrying again. But I haven't· succeeded in doing it; a sort of shyness has always prevented me. I watch them both silently the whole time, and it seems to me that every day is drawing them closer together. Elizabeth does her hair differently now; she doesn't put her thick golden plaits on the top of her head any more, but wears them in a great twist on her neck. It becomes her tremendously, and makes her look younger. I often notice father looking at her very oddly. His eyes glitter so funnily, and there comes two burning red spots in his cheeks, and Elizabeth always blushes crimson when it happens. I believe it's the way *love* begins. And it's very interesting indeed to look on at, and I want to write it all down, so that I may know how to behave when I'm in love myself some day. It would be strange indeed if father didn't love Elizabeth; she's so charming that I'm quite in love with her myself. She used not to be so dreadfully shy as she is now, and it often seems to me that she is actually a little bit afraid of father. Lately, I've thought that quite often; and it does seem quaint! Why, she's twenty four! I teased her about it once and she got very red and quite angry – that is, angry *for her*. She's much too sweet to get into a real rage. One thing is certain – she avoids being alone with father. That's silly of her! How is he to declare himself? A week ago, I heard a noise at night, and woke up. When I opened my eyes, there was a white figure standing beside my bed. I was on the point of calling out in a fright, when I saw that it was Elizabeth. She was trembling from head to foot, and could hardly speak.

"May I stay with you to-night, Thymi?" she said.

"I should think so!" and I pulled her into my bed with both arms.

"What's the matter with you, Bessie dear?" I asked, for she was still trembling like an aspen-leaf.

"I was frightened upstairs!" she said. "It was so eerie there. I felt just as if there was someone in my room."

I kissed her and hugged her tight, and nestled up to her. It was so delicious to have her with me; and, moreover, I was very proud that my future mamma should come to me for protection.

The next day there came an invitation from Uncle Dirk for father and me, and I was to stay a few days longer" than father. When father read out the letter, Elizabeth looked very miserable all of a sudden.

"Then I can't stay with you," she said. 'I must look out for another place."

I thought it was horrid of her to spring a surprise like that upon us, and I told her so.

"Can't you come with us, if you won't stay here without me?" I said. For I always go and stay with Uncle Dirk for his birthday. Then she dried her eyes and said she would go with us if father would allow her; and so we all came here on Wednesday week. Uncle Dirk fetched us in his carriage.

I always like a week in his place. Our country has no great beauties perhaps – no mountains, no forests; but it has its own peculiar charm, all the same! The estates lie in the green pastures like great islands of trees; and when the evening-mist hangs over the fens in white, thick clouds, they look like real islands in a great, undulating, heaving sea. On such evenings there broods a deep, penetrating stillness over the land. When the setting sun stands and round on the horizon, and the mists rise like specters and envelop everything, and here and there a sleepy cow lows or a horse whinnies, and it's all so big and so silent, I have the same sort of feeling that I have on summer evenings in our own garden.

But on Uncle Dirk's birthday it certainly wasn't quiet! Half the North Country was there. Uncle Dirk was elected to the *Landtag* lately, and so more people than usual came to congratulate him. A great deal of rum-punch was drunk, but I didn't take any, for I have still an extraordinary horror of the sweet, strong stuff. And there were lots of speeches. Then came dancing; and father danced a waltz with Aunt Trina, Dirk Thomsen's wife; and then he had a gallop with Aunt Frauke, and then a waltz with Elizabeth. After that I saw Elizabeth looking for me, but I hid – I don't know why. It was very hot, although it is the beginning of October, and I noticed Elizabeth going outside, and soon afterwards father followed her. Then I ran through the sitting-room and came out just behind them. Elizabeth had gone out by the hall-door into the garden, and father after her, and I crept along behind the gooseberry-bushes that border the path.

"Now it's getting on!" I thought, looking forward to the proposal that I was longing to hear.

Unfortunately I couldn't keep quite close without being seen. They were standing a few paces from me, and father was

Illustration by Ludwig Berwald, from an early edition of **Tagebuch einer Verlorenen**.

speaking so softly to Elizabeth that I couldn't hear anything. I just heard her crying out, "Herr Gotteball!" and it sounded as if she was frightened. And then she said, still more vehemently, "Herr Gotteball!" And then it seemed to me that she tore herself away from him, and rushed up the garden-path like the wind, and into the house, while father followed her slowly. I was very much disappointed and vexed with Elizabeth, who had spoilt everything by being such a goose. And when we were alone in our bedroom later on, I couldn't help telling her my opinion and asking her if she didn't think father was good enough for her, for it seemed to me that we could offer her such a nice little home. She kissed me, and I saw that she was quite pale and very much agitated.

"Ah, child, how should *you* know" she said. "Your father is not dreaming of marrying me."

"But I heard him talking about it to Aunt Freda myself!"

She looked amazed. "Really?"

"Yes, really," said I; and it was only afterwards I remembered that that wasn't quite true. But what does it matter? It will all come right in the end. The great thing is that they love one another.

Father went home next morning, and on the following day he telegraphed to say that Elizabeth must come back, for the servant was ill, and they had nobody to cook their dinner. Elizabeth would have liked me to go back with her, but I wouldn't, for we were to spend the afternoon with the Pohns family, which is always tremendous fun, so Uncle Dirk had to drive her back alone.

The Pohnses are really too funny; they are rolling in money, and they have no children, and are frightfully miserly.

They never sleep together at night like any other married couple – not they! Uncle goes to bed for the first half of the night, and aunt sits in the room where the safe is; and the second half, aunt goes to bed and uncle sits up, for they are terrified of burglars.

In the height of the summer they eat dripping on their bread and sell all their butter. I was there once in the dog-days, and they had bacon-soup, which is a watery, salty kind of broth with very fat bacon in it, and they like it because it's so economical. The great moment of the day was in the evening, when they actually had some stale cheese on the table; and if a neighbour came in, aunt used to hide the cheese under her apron, so that the man shouldn't see how well they lived. They ought to be shot! When Uncle had an operation some years ago at the Flensburg Hospital, and aunt came to visit him, she used to trudge the whole way in streaming rain from the railway-station, because she wouldn't "waste money" on the tramway. Oh! one could write whole books about them. Once when mother was alive, we went unexpectedly to see them in the slaughtering-season. They were up to their necks in fresh butcher's meat, for they had killed two cows and a pig. I but if anyone thinks that we got a good roast joint for dinner in consequence he's very much mistaken – not we! What we had was a piece of tainted salt meat, with black bread as hard as a board and rancid butter by way of a relish. Aunt kept saying: "Other people may eat up all their substance, and then beg from the Government but *we* think a balance at the bank is better. Organised economy, with a nice little pocket of gold behind it, is the best way in the end."

My cousin, Jacob Thomsen, drove me and our cousin, Lude Levsen, out; the Pohnses didn't know we were coming, and aunt was in town with some harness which she had taken to be mended. Uncle Lehnsmann rubbed his hands, and said, "Oh! children, children, you might have written us a little line. I don't know what I can give you to eat now, for aunt has taken the pantry keys with her." I nearly exploded with laughter, but Jacob kept quite grave, and said, "Perhaps another key will fit the pantry door; I happen to have my own bunch in my pocket." "No, no, that "that would never do," said uncle, greatly distressed.

Afterwards uncle and Lude and I went into the orchard. It's not a good apple year, so there wasn't much on the trees, but one biggish pear-tree had some tolerably large pears on it, from which uncle tried very hard to abstract our attention, saying they were frightfully sour. But I didn't believe him, and picked one and bit it – uncle positively shaking with horror – and oh! it was such an exquisite one, juicy, and as sweet as sugar. And when Lude Levsen heard that he pulled down a whole lot of them, and filled his pockets and my own.

"Oh dear, oh dear," wailed uncle, "what will aunt say! The pears were to be sold at the market on Thursday."

"Blood is thicker than water," said Lude, and we stripped the tree, and got a few good apples as well.

In the meantime Jacob had investigated the pantry, and goodness knows *how* he opened it, but he did. And just then somebody came who wanted to speak to Uncle Lehnsmann, and so we all three rushed into the pantry and examined all the pots and crocks. The first thing we got hold of was two jars of quince-jelly; it was too acid for my taste, and Jacob didn't care for it either, and Lude never touches jam of any kind, but out of sheer devilry we ate what we could, so that there was scarcely anything left in either jar.

There was nothing else particularly nice, but at last we discovered a pot of pickled herrings, and that was triumphantly emptied into a dish and carried into the next room. When uncle saw it, he wrung his hands and began to complain bitterly. "Children, children, what will your aunt say? The whole of the pickled herrings that old Peters brought me as a present! Your aunt had put them away so carefully, in case of any illness in the house—"

"They *would* be splendid for that," said we, and fell upon them, tooth and nail. And when uncle saw that we were not inclined to leave any in the dish, he quickly fetched a knife and fork for himself, and tucked in too.

"I think the herring would like to swim, uncle," said Jacob; "haven't you a glass of wine in the cellar?"

"Your aunt has the keys," said uncle.

Then Jacob got up, went out, and sent the servant-man into the village to get two bottles of wine, which were to be put down to Uncle Lehnsmann's account; and when we had finished them, we got off as fast as we could, for if we had been caught by Aunt Frauke there would have been something terrible in the way of a row. It was a fizzing afternoon, and I laughed till I cried.

. . . .

I haven't written anything in for a long time; life is so uneventful here. I'm afraid something's gone wrong about father and Elizabeth getting married, and I'm not going to bother about it any more, for if she won't have him, he must only do without her. I don't believe he really wants her; indeed, it often seems to me that he positively can't bear her.

Elizabeth is often very silent and depressed. I think she is still fretting a little over her faithless clergyman. She is very pale, too, but she won't admit it, and if I ask her if anything is the matter with her she gets red and says "No, no." She is just as wonderful as ever. For Christmas she made me an enchanting dressing-gown of rose-coloured flannel, with a little train; and my brown velvet dress, which was made after a pattern of hers, is tremendously admired at the skating. She has such wonderfully good taste; she skates splendidly, too, and the new young doctor who lives here now always comes up to her, so perhaps she will get hold of him. It would be dreadful for us to lose her, but I should like her to be happy.

Osdorff is always on the ice; and skates a great deal with her too. He seems to me to get stupider and stupider, although he has at last managed with great difficulty to pass his Junior Examination. It was time he did; in April he will be one-and-twenty.

Osdorff loves to do your hair for you, and he does it awfully well I can give him no greater pleasure than to allow him to act as my hairdresser. He combs and brushes and curls and frizzes my long black hair, and makes the most artistic coiffure for me. Sometimes he dresses it low and combs it over my ears and makes a coil in the nape of the neck, and sometimes he dresses it high and makes such beautiful puffs and curls. He tormented Elizabeth for ever so long to let him do hers, and when I joined in and begged her, too, she gave in at last, and he piled up her bright hair like a crown – yes, exactly like a crown, and she looked exactly like a queen.

Osdorff knows lots of people here, and they all run after him, because he is a Count. They know all about this hobby of his, and for the Harmony Club Ball a lot of ladies went to Conrad Lütte's, where Osdorff was staying, and got him to dress their hair for them, and they say that he did it as well as a Parisian hairdresser. The ladies were full of his praises, and said he was a genius. I can't help laughing at that. Poor Osdorff a genius – God help him!

. . . .

Last week Osdorff had to go to the barracks, and was declared unfit for military service. He was simply enchanted, and said he was only sorry he had wasted his time over the confounded examination. He is to stay here one year longer, and then he is to be apprenticed to a land-agency. He *is* a lazy pig! What they ought to do is to apprentice him to a hairdresser; for that is the only thing he has any fancy or talent for. But of course that would never do for a Osdorff with two f's . . . Here at home all is not as it should be; it really seems to me that father can't endure Elizabeth, and probably she's fretting over it, thinking that he will give her notice, but she needn't be afraid of that so long as I'm at home. Father always does what I want. I don't know what he objects to in Elizabeth; at first he used to make such eyes at her.

A few days ago I went into her little room in the morning, and she was lying full length upon her bed and crying, crying. I don't know how it was, but I suddenly felt as if there was an iron band round my heart; and a terrible fear came over me.

"Elizabeth," I said gently, and stroked her hair, and she looked at me with her wet eyes – such an ineffable look! My heart beat quicker and the tears came into my eyes, "What is it, Elizabeth" I said.

"Oh! I'm so afraid."

"What of?"

I don't know," she said, and clasped both hands to her heart. "It's such a dreadful, horrible sort of fear."

I tried to calm her, but I felt frightened myself. I don't think Elizabeth is well; there's something wrong with her. Perhaps it's her nerves. She looks frightfully ill.

CHAPTER V

IT'S nearly three months since I've written up my Diary. I wanted to do it long ago, but I found it impossible to collect my thoughts. Something perfectly terrible has happened to us. I hardly know how I feel; I go about in a sort of dream, and don't know whether I am awake or asleep, and I feel as if I had suddenly grown years and years older. While I am sitting here, writing, my eyes fill with tears again, my cheeks burn, and I feel ashamed and sorry to the bottom of my soul. I can't write it all down, but I'll try to tell the most important part at any rate.

When I made my last entry, I had just begun to notice that Elizabeth always seemed very depressed, and looked terribly ill. I often succeeded in cheering her up, but she would fall back into the old silent mood afterwards.

On the day of mother's death, the 21st of May, she and I were going in the evening to the churchyard with wreaths and flowers. It was a beautiful calm evening. There was the narcissus, smelling as lovely as in the old days, and the sky was so high and blue above us, with little misty clouds floating in it like silver ships. Elizabeth sat down on the little bench behind the cross, and I arranged the flowers, I don't go very often now to the churchyard, but even still, whenever I stand at mother's grave, the same mournful feeling comes over me as on the day of her funeral.

"Isn't it terrible to have to die so young, Elizabeth?" I said. "Mother was only just thirty-one. Oh! it seems dreadful to me to die so soon."

Elizabeth was sitting with her hands folded in her lap, leaning her head against the black marble cross, and looking upwards.

"It isn't dreadful at all," she said; "we should rather envy the dead than pity them. It's so sweet to lie down there in the cool ground; but you've got to get there first. . . . It's the getting there that's so dreadful. . . . but one might be able to force one's self . . . . just clench one's teeth and shut one's eyes —"

"What are you saying, Elizabeth?" I cried, in amazement. And she started as if she had suddenly waked from a dream.

"Nothing," she said, confusedly, and got up.

Exactly a week later, Elizabeth said, at evening coffee, that she was going to take a stroll down to Aunt Freda's. I was just reading a rightfully exciting novel, translated from the English, and didn't feel inclined to go at that moment.

"I'll come along afterwards," I said.

"Good-bye, little Thymian," said she, and gave me her hand, and I noticed that it was icy-cold. Then she kissed me quickly and went out. I watched her going across the square; her black tulle hat with the pink roses in it and her little black cloth bolero suited her so well, and it was delightful to see how graceful she looked in her simple clothes. At the corner of the square she met Dr. Möller, and he bowed low and looked after her. "Ho-ho!" I thought to myself, for I was certain there was something going on there – he had paid her such attention at the skating all this winter.

At half-past seven I made my way down to Aunt Freda's, but there I heard, to my great astonishment, that Elizabeth hadn't been at all. I was completely mystified, for it was not her way to deceive me. I thought it better to stay a while with Aunt Freda and then I strolled on a little. It was an exquisite warm evening, so I lingered in the Gardens and sat down for a few minutes on one of the seats.

As I was sitting there, Police-Sergeant Hahnhaus came hurrying by, saw me, stopped short, and then came up to me. "Ah, Fräulein Gotteball," he said, "a terrible thing has just happened down at the weir. A woman has drowned herself there, and nightwatchman Hinz, who got her out, thinks she is your housekeeper. You'll know, of course, so will you come down there with me? It's only a step or two, and perhaps you will be able to identify her."

I didn't say a word. It was as if my tongue was tied, but as I hurried mechanically after him I didn't seem to feel anything really at all; it seemed like a dream, and nothing was further from my thoughts than that it would really turn out to be Elizabeth. There were five men standing round the lock-gates, and a long, dark object was lying on the ground, and Dr. Möller was kneeling beside it. I ran down quickly. I cannot describe my feelings at that moment for it was Elizabeth. . . . I knew her by her clothes, which clung to her limbs like wet rags. I don't believe I should have known her face, it looked so terrible with green stains on it, and the eyes staring open as if they had been fixed in the death struggle, and all the features distorted and the mouth wide open. Her hair had got loose and hung in long, wet masses over her shoulders. Never in my life shall I forget that sight I couldn't speak; my knees trembled, I shrieked aloud, and then I saw and heard no more.

When I came to my senses again, I heard a familiar voice speaking, but it sounded as if it came from miles away.

"If you ask my opinion, you'll take the body to the morgue. No one could possibly expect Herr Gotteball to keep it in the house till it can be buried."

They dashed water in my face, but I slipped back into unconsciousness again, and when I came to myself I couldn't remember at first what had happened. The body still lay on the same spot, but the police had great trouble in keeping off the crowd which came thronging up, for the news had spread like wildfire. Dr. Möller helped me to stand up.

"By Jove! that was a faint!" he said; and then Meinert took my arm to support me home. It was only then that I really remembered.

"Elizabeth shan't go to the morgue! She belongs to us!" I cried. But they wouldn't listen to me, and Meinert drew me away. . . . The whole town was in an uproar; people were standing at every door, and there were groups at the street corners; and Meinert pressed my arm and said I musn't howl and make a fuss there was enough bother without that.

. . . . I don't think I can write much more about it. The memory agitates me so dreadfully that my hands are trembling while I write. . . . Father was white to the lips.

"Awful – awful!" he said, again and again.

I locked myself into my room and threw myself on the bed and cried. And yet it didn't seem a bit as if it had really happened. It seemed as if Elizabeth must come in shortly and sit down on my bed, and everything be all right again. After a while the door opened, and father came in with his overcoat on, and said he must bid me good-bye at once, for he had had a telegram and was obliged to go to Hamburg for a few days on business. He seemed to be in a great hurry, and I wasn't much inclined for talking. Afterwards I went downstairs again. Supper was all laid in the dining-room, but only Meinert and the apprentice had eaten anything, the other three places were untouched for a place had been laid for Elizabeth.

I didn't know what to do for grief and terror. I ran to the sitting-room window and saw that the square was full of people. Some were standing staring at our house, and one of them said something dreadful – I think it was Hannemann's wife "The

brute! . . . The beast! . . . He ought to be brought to the gallows!"
she kept on screaming. . . .

About eleven o'clock I went up to my own room and lay down,
but I couldn't go to sleep. It was so stiflingly hot, and fear and
horror lay like a weight upon my heart. I couldn't get the terrible
sight of the drowned woman out of my head. My poor sweet
Elizabeth! Now I knew how much I really loved her. . . . It was
very dark, but I was too frightened to light the candle, so I pulled
the bed-clothes over my face and sobbed myself to sleep at last.
But I can only have slept a very short time, for I woke up and
heard one o'clock striking and then again that fearful scene rose
up before my eyes. I trembled in every limb and didn't dare to
move. I felt as if my heart was swelling in my breast and getting
as big and heavy as a millstone. . . . "Why did she do it? "I
wondered over and over again, and a dim suspicion of something
utterly terrible haunted my shuddering soul.

All of a sudden it began to thunder. It sounded like a wild animal
growling in the distance. I cannot describe what I suffered that
night. . . . Then there came a great flash of light, and I leaped up,
and the whole room seemed ablaze with blue fire, and in the
corner stood Elizabeth in her white nightgown, with that fearful
green, distorted face, and the long wet hair and the staring eyes. I
gave one wild piercing shriek and the light was gone, but that
figure still stood there in the corner and stared at me and I
shrieked – shrieked. . . . Oh! I think I should have gone mad if I
had had to spend the rest of the night by myself.

"What on earth is the matter, Thymi? What are you screaming
like that for?" Meinert called through the door, and as I didn't
stop, he opened it and came in and bent over me. I clung tightly
to him with both arms, and was speechless at first, pointing to the
corner where the spectre was standing, and then I tried
stammeringly to tell him what I had seen.

"Why," he said, laughing, "it's a thunderstorm. And we'll soon wring the neck of the spook in the corner! Just look, Thymi!" and he went over and seized the white thing, and then I saw it was the towel which I had caught sight of in the glass; but I didn't feel inclined to laugh somehow, and I implored Meinert not to go away, for I should die of fright if he did. So he sat down beside me on the edge of the bed and put his arm round me, and it did me good and quieted me, to feel a warm living being beside me.

"Why did she do it, Meinert? Why did she do it?" I asked. "Tell me all about it, if you know." He stroked my cheek with his right hand and kissed me, and although I knew it wasn't right I let him do it, for I was so distraught and miserable that I could think of nothing but the one terrible thing.

"Doesn't the little girl really know, then?" he murmured. And his sudden tender tone and way of speaking didn't seem strange to me, although he has never spoken like that since my Confirmation. "Such a big, clever girl, too! Is she so wise and has those great eyes, and yet sees nothing? That flighty young woman had a love-affair with your father and took it into her head that he was going to marry her. And when he showed her he wasn't, and she knew what was coming, she went off like a fool and drowned herself."

"But why wouldn't father marry her? And what did she know was coming?" I asked.

"Goodness, Thymi, you are a little fool!" said Meinert, and sighed. And then he told me that Elizabeth was going to have a baby. But I wasn't to think too hardly of father on that account. A big healthy man like him was bound to have his fling; it was an ordinance of Nature; and father treated these women very decently; he always paid their expenses for them and a thousand marks indemnity, so to speak, and kept the child until its Confirmation. But if father were to marry a woman of that sort, I should suffer for it, for then any children there might be would have to be treated the same as myself, and there wouldn't be any sort of a fortune for me at that rate. Reinhard's brat (Meinert went on) had died almost immediately, so she got the thousand marks for herself and had made a good thing out of it. "We've only got to hold up our finger and *she'd* come back to us," he said, coarsely, "but we don't want her. She's too fat for the likes of us, though she's neat and good-tempered enough. Elizabeth was a different sort of thing altogether. I should never have had the pluck to try at all, and I warned your father. That sort goes in for a proper establishment."

"No, she wasn't a bit like that; Elizabeth was a good girl!" I cried, and pushed away his hand which was still stroking my cheek; for suddenly his touch filled me with disgust and horror.

"Ah! then I'll be off," said he, standing up. I let him get as far as the door, and then the terror came over me, and I began to cry, and he came back and sat down on my bed again and took my head in both hands and bent down, close, close over me, so that even in the dark I could see his blue eyes glittering. I don't know what came over me, and I didn't know then at all what it was that was making me so fearfully afraid. My heart was pounding against my side. I was terrified of Meinert. . . and yet a curious sort of thrill ran through me – the strangest, most mysterious feeling, which I had never felt before. I let him kiss me I let him hold me closer and closer. It was as if I was stupefied. I tried to get out of his embrace, I tried to push him away, but I hadn't the strength. . . .

I fell asleep at dawn and did not wake till quite late next morning. At first I thought I must have dreamt it all, but I soon realised that it had happened, happened really and truly. . . . Then I crushed my face into the pillows and cried, for I was so dreadfully ashamed and frightened at the thought of seeing Meinert and speaking to him. While I was still sobbing to myself, the door opened and Meinert came in. He spoke to me very kindly and gently, and said I was his little sweetheart now, and nobody must know our secret. He said he had loved me ever since I was a child. . . . Perhaps we should get married some day. But the nicest part was before that happened. . . . I said nothing – I couldn't say anything.

Two days later Elizabeth was taken from the morgue and buried. It was done quite early in the morning, so that as few people as possible should know, and there should be no fuss about it. Her grave is with all the poor people's graves. I have planted flowers and ivy on it, and I often go there. Poor, poor Elizabeth! . . .

My heart is so heavy. I am so unhappy. I want to cry all the time. . . . To-morrow – to-morrow – I'll write some more.

.   .   .   .

Oh, goodness! the house *is* desolate since Elizabeth died. We have a widow now as housekeeper – a bland obsequious person, with a smooth white face and black hair. Her name is Frau Lena Peters. She speaks very slowly, and drawls out the end of her sentences, as if she was singing. I can't stand her, though she is very nice to me and quite motherly in her ways. There's something that rings false about her. She is always hanging about father, so if he tries to lead her astray it won't be very surprising – she makes it so easy for him. She won't take to the water; I'm not a bit afraid of that!

Formerly I never thought about such things, but now my eyes are opened to what goes on around me.

Often I am seized with a frightful horror of myself and my surroundings. There is some intangible barrier between me and father. He doesn't feel it, but I do. It is as if I were haunted by the thought of Elizabeth. I know I have no right to condemn father, who loves me so dearly; but in those fearful hours something did die in me for ever, and that was my respect for, and trust in, him.

But, indeed, *I* have no right now to set myself up. My God! how miserable I have been since that night! I wish I could go away. I hate Meinert, and yet I seem to belong to him more and more. I lock myself into my room at night, but it seems as if he had laid a spell on me; I wake out of my sleep at the sound of his gentle knocking, and though I clench my teeth and try to lie quite still and not even stir, some mysterious power, which is stronger than my own will, draws me up and over to the door, which I open. . . .

I am quite changed since that fatal night. Sometimes I think that people might easily notice what has happened to me, for I cannot look them straight in the face any more. I am particularly afraid of Aunt Freda's sharp eyes; she often looks at me so doubtfully that I think she must suspect something, but I know that I myself see people quite differently from the way I did before.

For instance, I've lost all ease in my intercourse with Osdorff. I can't keep my eyes off his hands – those soft, white, beautiful hands that I used to like so much. It gives me such an extraordinary sensation now when I look at them. I sometimes feel a violent desire to be beaten by those beautiful hands. Once the desire was so strong in me that I told him of it.

"Do beat me," I said; "scratch me, or pinch me, Osdorff; I'd like to be hurt by your hands."

He looked at me in astonishment. Our eyes met. There was a curious glitter in his, which are usually so dull the same glitter that I saw for the first time on that secret night, after Elizabeth's death, in Meinert's eyes.

"Ah, nonsense! Why should I hurt you, Thymi? Beautiful girls are meant to be loved and kissed and stroked. I'm not a bully, I assure you." And then he drew his velvety hand very softly and slowly over my cheek. I shut my eyes, so as not to see his face – that stupid, silly face, with the light-grey, fishy eyes. But the hands, the hands! they drive me quite mad. . . . Since then, we call each other "thou," and often meet in solitary places. In spite of his stupidity and his idiotic face, I love him like I don't know exactly – something like the way I used to love, as a child, the doll in the sky-blue silk dress that father once brought me when he came home from a journey. I love him like a thing that I've got accustomed to, like something that one always uses and can't do without. We have promised to keep faithful friends always, whatever Fate may do with us. But his hands always they make me feel crazy. . . . O God! . . .

Another piece of news. Father is going to be married again, and to whom? Frau Lena Peters!

My goodness! she's a clever one. Positively I feel a respect for her 'cuteness, or rather, for her craftiness. It was last Sunday morning that father told me.

He seemed to me to be somewhat depressed. He said that having a housekeeper didn't do; there must be a mistress in a house, and as he didn't feel inclined to go courting again at his age, he was "taking the first person handy," namely, Peters, who was a very nice, sensible, clean, economical woman. Had I anything against it?

"No," I said, turning as pale as death, for my blood seemed to run cold in my veins. I was thinking of Elizabeth, who had had to sacrifice her young life to make room for this false, common woman who is no better than a servant. Certainly Lena Peters is more cunning than poor, guileless Elizabeth was. *She* insists on having everything properly arranged, and a marriage settlement.

"You shan't suffer by it, my darling," said father, who mistook the cause of my sudden pallor. "Your money is settled on you, and you needn't pay any attention to her. She has nothing to do with you. If ever she tries to interfere with you, come to me. Next summer we'll take a little trip, you and I – to Sylt, or Zoppot.

You must learn to know the world, and you must be admired, my own little girl."

I made no reply, and received his kisses like a lamb led to the slaughter.

The banns were called the next day. On Saturday three weeks the betrothal ceremony will take place. For my part I don't care. I wish them luck.

.   .   .   .

And so now Lena is Mrs. Gotteball. I get on quite tolerably with her. Of course I don't call her mother, but for decency's sake I put pressure on myself and call her aunt.

It appears now that the wedding ceremony was urgently necessary – or so Meinert says. I can't understand how she has managed to accomplish what none of her predecessors could. She's as ignorant and stupid as an owl, and has no good looks worth mentioning, only a smooth skin and a plump figure. Meinert says she ought to have married a sea captain. I asked him why, and he made some absurd joke about the "swell" of her bosom, which made me laugh, though I wasn't a bit inclined to.

I don't know why I feel so down-in-the mouth so thoroughly dejected and wretched. I often have palpitations of the heart. Meinert has given me some digitalis drops, but they haven't done me any good. The moral disgust that I have felt for myself for months and months is now turning into a kind of physical sickness.

I haven't said anything to Meinert about it, and of course not to Osdorff either.

One evening, when I saw some pickled cucumbers on the table, I felt such a loathing of them that they seemed to turn into hideous green snakes before my eyes. And the whole night through the abominable green stuff seemed to writhe like worms in front of me. It was perfectly awful. I am so frightened; I don't know what of.

Illustration by Ludwig Berwald, from an early edition of **Tagebuch einer Verlorenen.**

CHAPTER VI

GOD knows I had no notion, when I began to write my Diary, of the sort of things that I was going to live through. I haven't had much that is good and sweet to put down in it, have I? So it would seem that it might just as well never have been begun. But it's really a relief to me to pour out my whole heart into its pages; it feels exactly like talking to a confidential friend.

Things have been going very ill with me, and I have been terrified of some unknown peril that seemed to be threatening. Many a time I locked myself in my bedroom and cried, I knew not why, in utter misery and oppression, and it made me feel better for the time being.

Lena had begun to look at me suspiciously, and once she asked me a lot of searching questions – whether I knew that. . . . no! I can't write them down. I got crimson, and then deathly pale, and Lena turned livid with fury, and suddenly, before I knew, she had given me two great boxes on the ear, so that I lost sight and hearing for a moment, and then I shrieked aloud. Father came rushing in, and when he saw Lena strike me, he caught her by the arm and dragged her away and flung her against the wall and kicked her, and would have hit her, but I threw myself between them; and then Lena screamed and yelled the whole thing out. She had known it for a long time, she said – the disgrace that I was bringing on the house. I was a regular bad lot, a good-for-nothing baggage, and she was only sorry she had married into such a family. Father had better make the best bargain he could for his promising daughter. . . . But he rushed at her again, and I ran away and shut the door behind me, and tore upstairs to my room and locked that door too, and threw myself on the bed and stared up at the ceiling with burning eyes and cheeks.

And I felt so hurt and ill, so I don't know what, and my head ached and throbbed and burned as if there was a fire in it. I couldn't think clearly; my brain was whirling, and every thought seemed to revolve round the one question: What will happen now? Shall I do like Elizabeth and throw myself into the river, or shall I implore Meinert to give me some poison? Or shall I get under the train and be killed? For that I must somehow escape from everybody in the world seemed as sure as if it was written in the Bible.

I stayed upstairs the whole evening and refused to go down; but, later on, father came and begged me to open my door, and his voice sounded so strangely broken, and trembled so much, that I crept across at last and let him in. I saw then with my hot, aching eyes how wretched and stricken he looked and all in a minute, there I was, sobbing in his arms, and he was crying too and kissing me, and we couldn't speak a word at first.

"Child, child! My poor little girlie! Tell me just one thing is that woman right? Was it Meinert?" father managed to say at last. I nodded. Father groaned. "O God! O God!" he said twice. And then: "Promise me you won't do anything foolish, my poor darling. I'll speak to Meinert; we'll see what we can do to set it right." And I had to swear to him then and there that I would do myself no injury. So then I begged to be allowed to stay in my room the next day and have my meals there. Father said I might.

Afterwards Meinert came. He looked very unkindly at me, and was wild with rage. "If you had only told me what had happened, something might have been done," he exclaimed. "We might have managed somehow. Your father is crying like an old woman, and your stepmother's bleating all over the place the whole town will know by tomorrow. Old Freda Gotteball has set up her hunch-back already in the sitting-room, and is getting the whole story out of the old man."

Aunt Freda! That was the last straw for me. I imagined her stern piercing eyes looking at me, and my heart stood still with fear and shame. "Give me poison!" I said.

He laughed curtly. "The usual thing – poison! Oh, of course! No. I shall have to marry you, I suppose. Well, if your father will take me into partnership, I don't mind; otherwise I'm not keen, as they say." He hurried off, and I lay there, shuddering as if with cold. I believed that I should have to marry Meinert and suddenly, mysteriously, I knew one thing, and knew it better than anything else in the world, and would know it for ever and ever I would rather die than do it. I would rather go into the river or under the train than be Meinert's wife, I could not – could not – could not.

It was strange, but it was so. All my feelings had suddenly altered, and in that minute I knew that I hated Meinert. It made me sick to think of him. . . . He is evil. When I think of him, I feel as if a loathsome worm were crawling on my flesh. When I think that for my whole life long I may be tied to that man, that I may be condemned, not only again, but for all time, to belong to him as his property, everything grows dark before my eyes. But no! I will not, will not! . . . More to-morrow.

.   .   .   .

Aunt Freda, of course, couldn't keep the secret to herself, and two days after that frightful discovery, which came even to myself like a thief in the night, she arrived with all the relations, Lehnsmann Pohns and Aunt Frauke, Uncle Dirk Thomsen and Aunt Trina, and they all sat together in the best room, and held a family-council as to what was to be done with me, just as they had, years ago, about my going to T —.

I was upstairs in my room, but as I crouched by my window, I suddenly felt as if I *must* go and hear what was going on. So I crept gently down the stairs to the sitting-room, and listened in the old way to what they were saying. Sometimes I drew the curtain aside very carefully, so as to see, and not one word escaped me.

They were very much excited, and talked vehemently all at once. Aunt Freda hadn't even taken off her things; she sat at the table in her hat and jacket, with a distressed, crimson face. I could hear that all the talk was of my marrying Meinert. Father said that he would take Meinert into partnership, and everything would be all right, and the blessed family needn't get into such a desperate state of mind. The banns could be put up within the next few days. Lena whined, and said that it would injure her children, and there would be nothing left for her, and she might have to go out to service again and send her children to the workhouse, when father was dead. Father told her to hold her row. Uncle Dirk and Lehnsmann Pohns affirmed loudly that it was the only decent way out of the difficulty, and though it was a frightful disgrace for the family, such things had happened before, and would happen again. In the middle of all the haranguing Aunt Freda's voice suddenly broke in, saying coldly and distinctly: "Are you quite certain that Thymi will consent to marry Meinert?"

There was dead silence for two seconds, and then arose a perfect babel of voices, all declaring that that was a matter of course, and I simply would have to. And Lena out-screamed them all: "Upon my word, it would be a pretty thing if she were to set herself up, after all this! She ought to be only too glad to get a husband."

And then, all of a sudden, there was a regular row going on. Aunt Freda was holding her own now: "I'm not at all sure that it's a good plan to rush the child headlong into marriage with a blackguard like Meinert. It's a choice of evils, and to have a stain on her name might easily prove more tolerable than a whole life of misery."

"You must have gone crazy, Freda," cried Aunt Frauke, vehemently; "no one could take you seriously. As she has made her bed, so she must lie on it. Since she has chosen to yield to Meinert, she must marry him."

"That's my opinion, too," said father; "marriage is the best solution."

"Marriage with a fellow like that!" cried Aunt Freda; "a scoundrel who can take advantage of the innocence of a mere child, and bring this misery upon her! Are you a father, and yet cannot see what you would bring upon your child by forcing her to this marriage? You are no true father; you are a scoundrel too, like your precious friend. Yes, you are," she cried, and struck the table with her hand. "Are *you* a man fit to have the bringing up of a child, and especially a girl? Haven't I always said it, and begged you almost on my knees to send her away to school after her Confirmation? It's all your fault; it is you we are to judge to-day, and not the poor misguided child, and you know it. You have been an unnatural father; you should never have kept your daughter in this house."

"*I* ?" cried father. "But I have idolised her, Freda. I am not to blame."

"It's no true love that lets a child do everything it likes, and says 'Yes' and 'Amen' to all its silly whims. No growing girl should be in this house; it has been notorious for ages. Since your poor dear first wife died, the goings-on here have been utterly disreputable. There's no name bad enough for them – no! The only respectable person that's been here in all these years was that poor girl whose death is on your conscience, you black villain."

"The *only* respectable person!" yelled Lena. "Am *I* not a respectable person? Am I supposed to be one of the —"

"It's the best description of you," cried Aunt Freda. Then Lena jumped up from her chair, and rushed at Aunt Freda and seized her by the throat, and screamed, "Is it indeed, you hunch-backed old slut? Take it back, and beg my pardon, or I'll twist your crooked neck for you."

But Aunt Freda was ready for her and nearly scratched her eyes out, and Lena howled, and everybody jumped up, and there was a general uproar: and Uncle Pohns took his stout walking-stick that he had between his knees, and banged on the table between the two women, and hit the hanging-lamp so that all the globes and lustres smashed in a thousand pieces. Then the women were separated, and Aunt Freda smoothed her tousled hair, while Lena ran out of the room, probably to bathe her eyes, on which Aunt Freda had left her mark.

Just then Meinert came in. I didn't know exactly what they wanted with him. The women were still talking excitedly to each other. I think the idea was that he was to be made partner in my father's business, and as Lehnsmann Pohns and Uncle Dirk had large shares in it, their consent was necessary.

It seemed that they had some doubts about it, and Aunt Freda insisted that I must first be consulted as to whether I would marry Meinert.

I pushed the blind of the peep-hole a little to one side, and found myself looking straight at Meinert's pale, sneering face, which had never seemed to me so utterly detestable as at that moment.

"Well, honoured sirs," he said, rubbing his thin, bony hands together, "if that's the way things are, we must speak plainly. It's scarcely to be supposed that *I* am playing the suppliant! On the contrary, I deny nothing. I have had a little fun with Thymian? Good. That's evident from the result? Good again. As she is the daughter of my chief and best friend, I am ready to do my duty and marry her. I'm a gentleman, you see. If I wasn't, and if I wanted to be particular, I might say that I had reasonable grounds for refusing. For Miss Thymian, let me tell you, is tolerably go-ahead; the young lady has a temperament. She has been carrying on with young Count Osdorff, too, so if anyone can demonstrate to me that I am exactly bound in honour —"

I stopped my ears. My limbs were trembling, and everything grew dark before me. I felt as if my brain were an anvil.

So I ran away and fetched my hat and fled from the house, without knowing where I was going. On and on, wherever my feet would carry me, past the meadows, and then down to the weir. I wanted to go the same way that Elizabeth had gone before me; but when I leant over the railings, and saw the dark, restless, whirling waters, a terrible fear gripped me. I clung fast to the iron bar, and tried to lift myself up and swing over it, but my feet were heavy as lead. And there I stood, staring down, and wishing myself under that black flood, and yet so filled with a shuddering horror of the death which awaited me there! "Just clench one's teeth, and shut one's eyes." I seemed again to hear Elizabeth saying it, and I thought of how in these last days I had suffered all that she had suffered the fears, the anguish, the instinctive struggle against an unknown peril that was coming inevitably nearer and nearer.

"Come, do it," said a voice within me; "don't be such a wretched coward." And I drew myself together again for the jump, and again some mysterious power fastened my feet to the ground, and midst all the anguish there was a will-to-live in me which would not be denied, and which streamed like golden sunshine over the spectral will-to-die, and drove it away. Despair possessed me; my reason was staggering, all my limbs were burning with an agonising pain. I wanted nothing – nothing but annihilation.

I don't know how long I stood there. Suddenly I heard my name, and I turned round and looked into Aunt Freda's pale, sad face. Her eyes were wet, and she looked strangely altered not stern any more, nor cross, nor reproving.

"Thymian," she said; "come, my poor child; come home with me."

She drew my hand under her arm, and I followed her as if in a dream. I had never heard her speak like that before. I never knew that her voice could sound so soft and sweet and tender. I had always heard her scolding and finding fault; and now, when I had done so ill and felt so sinful, walking beside her, she had nothing but soft, comforting, tender things to say. And it seemed to me, suddenly, that this wonderful old woman had much to forgive me; that in my childish folly I had been blind for all these years, and had never seen what a faithful, tender heart lived in that distorted body, under all the oddities and absurdities.

It was quite dark in her little sitting-room when we came in. I sat down on the sofa, and laid my arms on the table and covered my face with my hands, and Aunt Freda stroked my hair, and said again gently, "Poor child, poor unhappy child, what have they done to you?"

"I am very wicked, Aunt Freda," I said; "it would be better if I were dead."

"No, Thymian," she said earnestly; "the dead cannot repair their faults, and you must repair yours. You must learn to rule yourself, so that in spite of everything you may still be a good, brave girl."

"But I won't merry Meinert," I cried; "I'd rather drown myself."

She nodded. "I thought so, and I don't blame you. Be calm, dear. I will speak to father. We will get him to come here and see what is to be done."

She talked to me for a long time. I don't remember everything she said, but it was all good and dear and kind; there were no reproaches, no wounding allusions. Finally she told me about the beautiful Frau Claire Gotteball, my great-grandmother, whom Great-grandfather had brought with him from Paris as a poverty-stricken girl. Her name is erased from the Gotteball archives, but a few drops of her gay irresponsible French blood have been instilled into her posterity, and are always corning out like an hereditary curse.

"The sins of the fathers shall be visited unto the third and fourth generation," murmured Aunt Freda, "Yes; that's true, that's true."

. . . .

Later on, father came. He was in terribly bad spirits. His house was a hell, he said. Lena was nagging, and Meinert was sneering and mysterious.

Father and Aunt Freda talked in low voices, and I was so worn-out that I fell asleep on the sofa.

When I woke up they told me what they had arranged. I am to go to Hamburg. Father will take me within the next few days. I am to stay in a home until it is all over, and then I am to go away and live *en pension*.

I feel so dreadfully indifferent to the whole thing! I wrote to Osdorff just now, for I should very much like to talk to him before I go away. But he won't be able to get off for a couple of months. I am so utterly wretched! I am still with Aunt Freda. All my things have been brought here. I shall not go home again before our departure. I am afraid of meeting Meinert.

I hate him so unspeakably!

CHAPTER VII

I HAVE been five weeks in Hamburg now. Frau Rammigen is the name of the nurse with whom I am staying. She lives in a little house which stands all by itself on the Eimsbuttler Road, with a small garden at the back. There's another lady here with me, who expects her confinement as soon as next month. Her name is Frau Liesmann, she says. But I don't think she is married, or else she wouldn't be here. She is from Hanover; a beautiful woman with red-gold hair and a creamy white skin with some pretty freckles on it here and there. We often go for walks together, for we both get frightfully bored sometimes.

What is one to do the whole livelong day?

Frau Liesmann is twenty-four. Goodness! but she has got pretty clothes! I wish I had some lovely things like that. Every finger on her hands is flashing with splendid rings.

There was a gentleman here lately to visit her her husband, she said, but of course he isn't. He left a handkerchief behind him, which I found, and it had the initials "V. von V." on it, and her "husband's" name ought to be Liesmann. They seemed to be very much in love. One evening they took me to the theatre with them, and afterwards we had supper at Ehmke's in the Market Square. It was very nice indeed, but I felt rather in the way, for they didn't in the least mind kissing each other before me, and that sort of thing. And then the man made some remarks and allusions which I thought very tactless. They really wounded me. Herr V. von V. (alias Liesmann) saw it at once, for he laughed and tapped me on the cheek, and said, "You mustn't take offence so easily, little girl. All these things are part of the life, and it's a fine, free one – the life of the Open Road."

I didn't know what to say to that. But when we were going home, those two arm-in-arm and I beside them, I felt very very lonely and desolate.

For when I think of it, it seems to me that there is something quite unique about my fate, which makes it more than usually sad; and I know what it is. It is that there is no "other one" to sympathise with me in my suffering, and for whose sake I suffer. If I could only feel that I had loved a man infinitely and given myself to him, and that I was now making the necessary atonement, it wouldn't all seem so dreadful. But as it is . . . . often it seems to me as if it was all my fancy, and as if I wasn't really going to O God!

Frau Rammigen is a very nice woman, but she's very seldom at home. "Frau" Liesmann is gone to St Pauli's to-day to a dressmaker; I couldn't go with her, I felt too tired; so I got out my book, and here I am writing.

. . . .

She really is Frau Liesmann! We have made great friends, and call each other Thymian and Connie – Constance is her Christian name. She has told me all about her life. She was brought up by her grandmother, a laundress in Hanover, and was married at seventeen to a widower with three brats of children. She stood that for three months, and then ran away. Since then she has had a great many lovers, and was on the stage for a while. Now she is with Herr V. von V. that is Victor von Vohsen a rich factory-owner, who has taken her entirely under his protection. She says she is overjoyed at having a child of his, for it's a certain way of keeping him, and men are not to be trusted without something of that sort. I asked her if she loved him very much. She laughed and said that had nothing to do with it, (he certainly isn't exactly handsome). She says, when you've had as much love as she's had you've got past that stage, and the principal thing is to secure your future. She wouldn't give twopence for good looks, she says; all she cares for is a bit of the devil; that's essential everywhere in the street, in the house, in the bedroom. And he must have "style" everything else is nonsense. That made me think of Osdorff's faultless boots and exquisitely kept hands. And I think Connie Liesmann's right.

No one would notice that there is anything the matter with me as yet. It amuses me to see how the men turn round to look after me in the street. I never noticed them doing that at home. When Connie and I are walking in the afternoon in the "Lovers' Walk" there is always sure to be a pair of them stalking us. We've even been spoken to once or twice. Connie says I'm exquisitely pretty, and that if I only had sense I could do very well for myself even now. . . . We've settled to write to one another often, for Connie says you never know when you may want a friend.

Osdorff wrote to me lately. He is quite near Hamburg, on Count S—'s estate, and means to come and see me shortly, which I'm very glad of.

.   .   .   .

Connie Liesmann had a little boy four days ago. About eleven o'clock at night she began to be in pain, and the sighing and screaming and groaning lasted all night until the child arrived at eight o'clock in the morning. I never closed an eye the whole time, for our bedrooms are next door to one another, and I could hear everything through the thin partition. I never dreamt that it was so terrible, but now the fear of hell has come upon me.

If only I had got through with it too!

I can't stop looking at the little baby. It looks too comical, rather unattractive in spite of its lace-trimmed frocks and embroidered pillows. I shouldn't like to kiss it, but Connie kisses it passionately. Yesterday Herr V. von V. came. He brought Connie a big gold brooch set with diamonds, that she had wanted for a long time. Connie complained that he wasn't nice to the baby, and then I learnt for the first time that Herr V. von V. is married and the father of three children! Extraordinary! If I'd been in Connie's place I wouldn't have gone in for a married man. I hate the way she talks about nothing but money and settlements and presents.

While I am writing this, Connie's door is open, and she is calling out to know what I am scribbling at. I tell her it's my Diary. She shouts with laughter, and insists on reading it. But I haven't the least intention of letting her. She laughs at that too. All her troubles are forgotten. She's well over them now.

"Well, if *I'd* kept a Diary" and she screams with laughter "it would have been interesting, Thymian; there'd have been some things worth reading in that, I can tell you!"

.   .   .   .

Connie went away yesterday, with her baby and a nurse that Frau Rammigen got for her. It's very lonely and dull for me here now. I had grown accustomed to her; she was so amusing and jolly. She has asked me to pay her a visit in Hanover, but that won't be for some time. Herr von Vohsen was here last Sunday, and gave me a gold brooch as a souvenir of "his wife" (as if I didn't know all about it!), because I had so often kept her company and cheered her up. It's a pale gold basket, with forget-me-nots in turquoises very pretty, and I love to have it. . . . The baby had grown quite dainty and sweet, and she had let me dress it and give it its bath once or twice.

Osdorff was here too, last week. I was very glad to see him again. I am really fond of him, though I don't take him seriously, either as a man or as a person. It sounds horrible, but I really think I love him as one loves a dog that one has got used to. And then, except for his silly face, one doesn't mind being seen with him. He looks tremendously smart. Connie shook her head, though, when I introduced him to her as my friend, and afterwards she said that if she were in my place she'd drop him. A man of that sort was a drag on one – one could never get on while one stuck to him. Ah! but Connie doesn't understand. Poor old Osdorff will never prevent me from getting on. . . . He can't bear being where he is; he has to get up early and go out on the estate and work in the office, and Osdorff has never been over-fond of work. He won't stand it much longer, he says. He's sorry now that he didn't go in for diplomacy. Good heavens!

.   .   .   .

Oh! but these are dreary days and weeks and months. Christmas was perfectly awful, though father sent me a heap of presents, and Aunt Freda wrote a long, loving letter. Connie Liesmann sent me a big Marzipan cake and a rose-coloured silk-lined basket, full of baby things, which are quite enchanting. It was really very curious: at first I was delighted, and couldn't let the tiny dainty garments out of my sight they were like doll's clothes, I thought. But all at once I remembered that the little frocks and shirts and caps were intended for a real live child, and that that child was to be mine! It is strange that I can't realise it properly even now. . . . I couldn't help crying, and my tears fell on the sweet wee garments. . . . I am very miserable.

On New Year's Eve I was quite alone in the house. Frau Rammigen was with friends. The servant-maid was grumbling because she had to stay at home on my account, so I told her she might go, that I didn't mind staying by myself and she needed no second telling. Oh, but it was dreadful! that silence and loneliness on the last night of the year. I kept walking up and down in my room, and all the things that I had lived through in the last twelve months seemed to hover round me like specters. I saw Elizabeth again, lying on the grass, with her distorted dead face. And I thought of my dear mother, who found it so hard to die because she was leaving me defenceless – and how well I could understand it now! I think the shadow of what was coming must have haunted her then, and that she saw the future with the wonderful second-sight of the dying. She prayed so fervently for me – she and the dear old pastor. . . . Why didn't God hear those pure prayers? Why did He let it all happen? I don't believe in God any more.

Much the best thing for me would be to die in my confinement. But I don't want to. I'm so afraid of death of sinking into eternal night and nothingness. . . . I want to live and be happy. Can there still be any happiness for me in this world? I think perhaps there may. I am young, and I am beautiful. The world is great, and life is long. One must *will* to be happy. I often wonder what happiness is like to look at. I think it must look like a strong, handsome man, with kind hands and a beautiful kind voice, and clear, wise, gentle eyes. That's the sort of man I want. And he must have some money, so that I can wear pretty clothes and look lovely for him. If ever I meet a man like that, I will give myself to him without reserve, without calculation of any kind. For marriage doesn't attract me at all. To be obliged to live together! That, I imagine, must be horribly tiresome; it must kill all passion and all emotion.

. . . .

Beloved Diary! Dearest friend and consoler in this my evil day, I had such a lot to tell you, but I can't write much; I am too tired. Osdorff has left Count S—; the "disgusting amount of work" was making him ill, he said. He spent six days in Hamburg, because he was too frightened of his guardian to dare to go home. I gave him all the money I had, for the poor fellow had only just three marks in his nurse, and I had forty left. We dined in the Alster Pavilion, and the waiter called me "Madam," and treated us with great respect. Osdorff looks like a Count, despite his stupidity. When the money was all spent, he went off; that is, he telegraphed to them to send him some money for his journey, and then somebody came and took him back to S—; but the Count said he wouldn't have "the lazy hound" back, and so he went to

Berlin. Last week he wrote and told me that his uncle had sent him to study for the Diplomatic Examination with a man in the Wilhelmstrasse; and he has to work in the office, and copy letters, and do all the little things that demand no particular intelligence. But he calls it "strenuous intellectual labour.". . . Well, well!

. . . .

It is all over now. Five weeks ago the baby was born. It was very awful, but now I am all right again, though somewhat pale and thin.

It's a girl, and its name is Erica Susan. Now I understand how Connie Liesmann loved hers, for I love mine just the same, and would like to hold it in my arms all day long, and hug it and kiss it on its rosy mouth and on its blue eyes, and stroke its dear little fat hands.

On the tenth day Aunt Freda and father came and spent a week with me, and during their visit Frau Rammigen propounded what seemed to me a very extraordinary and ridiculous idea.

It appeared that on the very night that Erica was born, a baby was born also – and a girl-baby! – to a very rich family in the town. And the baby died the next day. The people were very unhappy about it, for they had been married twenty years and had no children, and had rejoiced mightily over arrival of this one. Fran Rammigen told them about me and Erica, and they asked if we would be inclined to give or sell the child to them. They would like to adopt it, and they would bring it up and educate it exactly like one of their own.

I laughed at Frau Rammigen, and said that I wouldn't sell my sweet little darling for a whole basketful of money; but father and Aunt Freda thought differently. They said it was a great piece of luck for the child and for every one concerned, that such an opportunity should have offered itself of settling its future. I cried and screamed and pleaded, but nobody would listen to me, and they arranged it all behind my back with Consul Peters – that was the name of the family and five days later my baby was taken away from me.

It was a fearful parting. I don't know how to describe it. . . . Just as if a bit of my heart had been torn out. . . . I threw myself flat on the ground and shrieked in my anguish. Father tried to console me, and Aunt Freda said in her old, stern voice that I ought to thank God on my knees for His mercy, instead of behaving as if I were mad. But old Herr Peters stroked my hair, and promised me that I should have news of Erica now and again. And he needn't have done it at all, for father had, in my name, renounced all right to the child but Herr Peters promised. Finally I fainted, and when I came to myself, they were gone with my baby.

I can't realise it yet. I feel as though I had suddenly grown very poor. At first I cried all day and all night, but now I am a little calmer. . . . Well, at any rate I know that there's one thing in life to fight for. I must get rich, so as to be able to have my child again, for with money one can do everything. If I could marry a rich man it would be all right. I will get rich, and then I'll see whether they can keep my little child from me my little child whom I brought into the world amid such anguish, and for whom I had to bear so much.

For the present, of course, I can't do anything.

They have arranged for me to go *en pension* to a clergyman's family in the country-part of Holstein. Aunt Freda discovered the place. She is almost as unsympathetic to me now as in the old days, with her everlasting admonitions and preachings about repentance. I don't feel in the least like a repentant Magdalen. Goodness me! I've made a mistake and I've suffered for it, and that's the end of the whole thing, in my opinion. . . . I'm glad they're gone.

.   .   .   .

Decidedly, at one time I should never have dream
in Aunt Fohns's confirmation-present would some
only joy and solace, and *that* even that would
forbidden fruit.

Seven months have gone by since my last entry. I have been all
that time in the Penitentiary – call it Reformatory! – of Pastor
Daub and his wife Ulrica, whose maiden name was Von Schmidt,
in G—, near Lübeck. There's no denying they are conscientious
people; they "improve" me for all they're worth all day long, but
whether they are really going to affect the good work is quite
another question. How topsy-turvy everything is! for the
atmosphere of godliness, high moral character, and austerity in
the pastor's house, seems swarming with the bacteria of knavery,
hypocrisy, avarice, cruelty and cunning to such an extent that one
absorbs them involuntarily.

When I was turning over my book just now, I came upon the
place where I so fervently resolved to be good and go to church
every Sunday, and live in the fear of God. Well, if anybody had
the systematic intention of thoroughly disgusting another person
with everything relating to religion, of giving him an utter horror
and loathing of Christianity, the best thing to do would be to send
him here to G—, to live with Pastor Daub and his Ulrica. They'll
do the trick! Their dearest enemy must grant them their piety.

Everybody gets up at six o'clock in the morning, and works –
works hard. Idling and dreaming are unheard of here. And when
at half-past seven the pangs of hunger are gripping your inside,
you are summoned to "worship." We stand straight up, side by
side, all round the table, and listen while the pastor reads a
prayer, which is then made the text of various edifying remarks.
Well, of course nobody really listens; we only bob our heads, and
as soon as "Amen" sounds, up they all go, and everybody looks

at everybody else, as if he were silently saying, "Thank goodness, that's over!"

The Daubs have three good-for-nothing boys, aged from six to twelve, and a niece of one-and-twenty, who is engaged to the curate. She is a stuck-up creature, stupefied with her own virtue; and she and the meagre, half-idiotic curate suit one another like two peas; in fact, the whole lot of them are as like one another as a podful of peas. Then there are two servant-girls and a boy, who are changed every month, for nobody can stand Frau Ulrica and her "Godfearing ways." The servants are frightfully over-worked in the big house, with its big garden, a lot of farm-labour besides, to say nothing of the religious duties. The day begins with morning prayers, at twelve o'clock comes on the second edition, and in the evening, before they go to bed, they have the third which is the chief course, so to speak, of the Spiritual Dinner. For at that we sing three hymns as well, and by way of dessert there's a sort of General Confession of the sins of the day.

Mrs. Pastor says at every second word, "with the help of God." It was with that, I suppose, that she lately hit the kitchen-maid across the mouth, so that her nose bled and her two front teeth were loosened; and no doubt it was also with that that she has escaped paying the innumerable fines which have been imposed upon her for ill-treatment of her servants.

I've never before heard such abominable language as she makes use of when she is in a rage, as she continually is. Pig, beast, carrion, hog, blackguard, image, are the merest politenesses in her intercourse with the farm-people. She keeps everyone's nose to the grindstone, and most of us have felt the weight of her hand. She hasn't hit me yet, but out of the flowering garden of her speech many rosebuds have fallen on me. I am, so to speak, the black sheep of the flock. Everyone, with the exception of the servants, puts on a solemn, stern face in speaking to me, and I get an extra helping of religious admonition every day. The niece, Fräulein Toni, was too delicious at first; she always looked away whenever I asked her anything, or if she was absolutely obliged to speak to me, her young virgin modesty made her tremble violently at having to look at such a person. And the curate – Schaffesky – (I call him Sheep's Head) is quite wonderful in his demeanour with me. I had, and still have, to listen to many allusions to "lost ones," and "rejected ones," and "outcasts." Well, that leaves me cold! I suppose one can't blame them for it, since I've been sent here for a sort of moral drill, and they probably think they are doing their duty in giving me as bad a time as possible.

What I *cannot* stand is the fact that I haven't the smallest personal freedom, but am watched like a criminal every minute of the day. There's something frightfully humiliating and wounding about that. For instance, I never get a letter which isn't opened and read first in the pastor's study. Two letters, one from Osdorff and one from Connie, were actually kept from me. Luckily I found it out, and since then I get them to write to the poste-restante at Lübeck, and the cobbler's wife next door, who does the messages, brings them to me on the sly. And in the same way no letter goes out from me which hasn't first passed the censor in the study. So I scribble a few lines to Osdorff and Connie now and then, and send them off without a stamp, for since I've been here I haven't had a penny of my own. Once I succeeded in smuggling an unstamped letter off to father (by-the-bye, there's been a baby at home), but father didn't answer me directly; he wrote to the pastor saying I had complained; and that caused a fine shindy. And since then I get one mark for pocket-money each Sunday, but on Saturday I have to give an account of every blessed penny of it. It is a hideous life. Father evidently doesn't dare to fetch me away, for fear of Aunt Freda. I can't forgive father for still keeping Meinert, in spite of all that has happened.

I shall never go home again. I hate Meinert like poison. My soul is full of bitterness and rancour. I hate everyone in this house except the servants, who stick by me, but they are always changing.

To-day the Daubs are at a wedding. Fräulein Toni is in bed with toothache, and Sheep's Head is away.

I have been a couple of hours writing at Frau Klock's. Her husband is the cobbler, and she runs messages for the house. She is a very clean, hard-working, kind woman, and very fond of me. What particularly draws me to her is her little eight-months old daughter – a dear little thing, exactly the same age as Erica. I love to hold her on my lap and play with her; she crows and laughs and tries to talk little darling! Oh, if only I could see Errie! I do so long to! It's terribly grievous. . . .

CHAPTER VIII

DOUBTLESS, if one had no active – or rather, indeed, passive – part in it, it might be quite amusing, for a time, to watch with the eyes of an unprejudiced outsider this idyll of family life in a pastoral household. One could make a good many interesting comparisons between words and works, theory and practice, high-sounding moral axioms and their application to the day's work.

There can hardly be anything much funnier than the contrast between the canting and preaching of these sanctimonious gentry, whose eyes are perpetually turned up to heaven, and the actual course of their lives – their relations with one another, their intercourse with their "dear neighbours," and so on.

I noticed long ago that the pastor and his sweet spouse were not a pattern married couple. They quarrel like cat and dog when they think they are safely alone; but hitherto I could never find out what it was all about. Frau Klock, however, told me today that the pastor has a little affair with a handsome peasant-woman in the village, and that Mrs. Pastor somehow got wind of it, and last year went away and took the youngest boy with her, expecting that her husband would come to fetch her back. But he knew when he was well off, and she had to do the fetching back all by herself Well, there's nothing nice about a husband's deceiving his wife, yet I can't be sorry that this old wretch, with her vile tongue and her brutality and her miserliness, should have something to make her justly angry for once.

One thing I know: nothing will ever make me set foot in a church again, when once I get away from here. *Nothing*! Church is done for, as far as I'm concerned.

In former days I was allowed to sleep as late as I liked on Sundays, and I wasn't obliged to go to church unless I chose. So I went often and enjoyed it. Now I have to get up an hour earlier on Sundays, so as to get my work done in time, for I must be ready to start punctually at a quarter past nine. Then I trot along down the village street between Mrs. Pastor and Toni, to sit for an hour and a half in church. That hour and a half appears to me to stretch out till the crack of doom. In winter one's feet get stone cold, and in summer the flies buzz on the walls and one feels drowsy, and might doze off if the pastor's drone wasn't afflicting one's ears and making any escape from present miseries quite inconceivable, even in a dream. I wish I had time to give some idea of the kind of sermons we have here. Perhaps I shall some day. They're all cut out after the same pattern, and they all have the same refrain: "Miserable sinners are ye all!" Hell-cats, brands fit for the burning, ripe for the Infernal Roasting-Oven; and then, as a finale, glib unctuous palaver about the Promise of Divine Grace, and Love, Love, Love. For my part, if this divinely-promised Love is anything in the least like what the firm of Daub & Wife dispense "on tap" – I think I shall beg to be excused from my share.

Mrs. Pastor and Miss Toni sit up straight on each side of me, distended like open umbrellas, with pious self-satisfaction. On leaving, Mrs. Pastor dispense honied greetings full of "love" and gentleness, and it fact does the benevolent Mother of the Congregation all round. But woe to the unfortunate wretch responsible if, on crossing the threshold of home, she draws her finger across a chest of drawers or a mahogany wardrobe, and discovers a speck of dust. Then the band begins to play! "What dirty hog was supposed to have dusted here today?"

Of course I turn out to be the delinquent.

"You? And do you think that your father gives me a beggarly few marks a year which barely pays for your keep, so that you may make my house into a pig-stye?" And so forth.

80

I am so hardened to it now that it is as much as I can do to keep myself from shouting with laughter. She's too funny when she's in a real fury. What I mind much more are the petty taunts and furtive insults. A little time ago there was some talk of our pastor's colleague in a distant village coming to spend a Sunday here with his wife and two daughters, girls of seventeen and nineteen. I was delighted. It's long since I've talked with girls, and I do enjoy being with companions of my own age; and I was actually idiotic enough to give expression to these feelings one day, at dinner, in the presence of the whole household. From the dead silence which instantly ensued, I guessed that something was rotten in the state of Denmark.

"But, Thymian," said Toni, reprovingly, "surely you cannot suppose that aunt will present you to these young girls?"

"Why not?" demanded I, like a fool.

The pastor laid down his knife and fork. "Thomas and Johnny, leave the room!" and as soon as the boys were gone: "My niece is perfectly right. We have no wish to wound you, dear Thymian, but as things are it would be an unpardonable solecism on our part to let you come in contact with the innocent young daughters of my colleague."

"Of course it would never do," said Mrs. Pastor, bluntly. "Thymian must remain in her room the day the Roswars come. Surely it is the best plan, for her as well as for them. She has nothing in common with girls like that."

They scored *that* time! So here I am, sitting in my room, under arrest, as it were, for the afternoon. Well, it gives me a little time with you, my Diary!

The Roswars are downstairs; I have locked myself in. Really it's too silly of me to mind so much. I ought to be above it. But oh, it burns and aches, the pain of it, as if my soul had been scourged with nettles. I have cried and cried about it. Till to-day I had never actually realised the consequences of my misfortune. But now I have been shown that I am an outcast for ever from the ranks of respectable women and girls – of women "fit for society." Though, goodness knows, they have made me feel it here often enough, I had never really "caught on" as they say, so thoroughly before. Now I know it well.

Fool that I was! I imagined that I had paid my debt paid it in the anguish and terror of those past months; in the fearful hour by the black flowing water, when the will-to-die and the will-to-live fought in me like two madmen. I suppose that there was still alive in me a last little scrap of the childish happy faith in the Gospel promise: "*With our God is forgiveness.*"

Now I know better. "Our God" has a Janus head with two faces. One, promising Love and Forgiveness, is for the good people, the people of childlike faith, the people who never make a false step, and so never need to be forgiven at all. And the other face – vengeful, terrible, inexorable – is turned towards the wicked, hardened, impenitent sinners, threatening them with Hell and Damnation and Vengeance and Punishment to the third and fourth generation.

No! I would rather believe in no God at all, than in the God of the Daubs and their like. The master is judged by the servants he has. And what kind of a master can He be, whom those people believe themselves to be serving with their hypocrisy, their pitiless cruelty, and all their odious ways?

I cannot endure the eternal praying and palavering and piety-mongering that goes on here. I feel that I shall grow really evil if I stay, I am getting so bitter, so acrid. "A strict but kindly supervision!" That was what was advertised for, when they wanted to pack me away from home. The strictness is abundant, but the kindness is to seek. I should like to know what the Daub idea of kindness of love is! I am treated as a good-for-nothing, superfluous creature; I hear ten times in an hour that they have five thousand marks worth of trouble with me, and only one thousand marks of pay; and that I can never be grateful enough to a respectable Christian family for taking an outcast like me into its bosom.

I have often thought of running away. But where could I go? for I haven't any money. I have no home now. . . . Old Herr Peters has not kept his word. I haven't had a syllable from them. Or can the letters have been kept from me? I think I must write and ask. Luckily I have the address.

Little Maria Klock had the measles lately, can say "Mamma" now. She's too sweet! I stole away on the sly to see her, which got me a terrific rowing from Mrs. Pastor. She could have torn me in pieces, I think, for fear of the infection which I might have brought back to her boys. Fortunately nobody caught the measles.

. . . .

I had a letter from Lena six weeks ago. She wrote to say that I really ought to be seeing about a situation as "help." It was unpardonable of me to go on costing father so much money, when the whole business had already been so expensive. I wonder if she thinks its luxury for me to live *en pension* with the Daubs! Mrs. Lena has no idea in what a state of mind her suggestion has found me.

I managed to get time that day to write a couple of lines to Connie Liesmann in Hanover, and I intimated to her that I was looking for a situation, and said perhaps she knew of something that might suit me. Some days afterwards she answered, asking me if I wouldn't come to her. She would give me a home, and twenty marks a month for pocket-money, and in return I could help a little in the house-keeping, and she would regard me as a sister.

I was as happy as a grig over it, and wrote home directly. A week after, father wrote that he had been making inquiries about Frau Liesmann in Hanover, and the information he had received was such that he could not possibly entrust me to the lady. That's Aunt Freda's doing, of course. Her reproaches about my bringing-up must have hit father uncommonly hard, for he seems to think now that he must do everything she tells him. She's going to advertise again for a place for me. I suppose I shall be sent to another "Christian household." Heaven have mercy on my soul! If I could only hit upon some way of Escaping from here, I'd manage some how to get to Connie Liesmann in spite of them. I cudgel my brains day and night for a way out.

.   .   .   .

I'm writing at lightning speed to tell about a pretty little episode which I must make haste to chronicle, because it would be a pity if it were lost to posterity. Yesterday, the pastor was at the county surveyor's for a christening, the boys were gone bicycling to Lübeck, and I was supposed to be embroidering monograms on twenty-four handkerchiefs, and mending half a dozen pairs of stockings besides.

After I had been stitching for a couple of hours, I suddenly discovered that I had lost my thimble. I looked for it everywhere, and couldn't find it, and as the work-table is locked tight, like everything else, I thought I'd better apply to Fräulein Toni.

The house was as silent as the grave, for even the servant-maids were out. My shoes have felt-soles (as prescribed by Mrs. Pastor), so they don't make a bit of noise, and I got to the door of Toni's room unbeknownst. I was going to knock, but stopped short, for I heard laughing and whispering going on inside. "Ho-ho!" thought I, and withdrew softly into a corner by the landing, from which one can watch the door.

It kept on and on, until at last I got tired, so I went to the door again and knocked, and then, as I got no answer, I rattled the handle. "Come, this is good fun," I thought; "if they're making love behind locked doors, one knows pretty well what to think" and with that there came over me a nasty malicious joy at having caught these two pious beings "in the act," so to speak. The room has no second exit, so I posted myself beside it, and coughed audibly every second minute, so that they might know I was there. The clock struck seven – the clock struck eight – it was pitch-dark. The maids, came back at half-past eight. The instant I heard them, I rushed to the stairs and yelled to them to come up, saying that I was dreadfully afraid there were burglars in Fräulein Toni's room, and that she might be murdered. Of course the girls began to scream, and then the door was opened, and when I looked round, there stood the curate! He came behind me and shook me and told me to hold my tongue. The wretched creature! His knees were knocking together, and he was blue with fright; but I laughed at him, and then went straight into Toni's room. She was still standing in the dark, and trying to well trying to get things straight!

"I was only going to ask you to lend me a thimble," I said innocently. "Why! haven't you lit your candle yet?"

"Oh! you – you – *creature*" she said, trembling with rage; "you just wait, and I'll get even with you."

"But what? Why? What have I done?"

Then she lit a candle, and she gave me a look! I couldn't help laughing all the same, for the tender experiences of the last hour were plainly written upon her face.

I scored that time!

She began her revenge to-day, the first thing in the morning.

I must stop! The boys are shouting for me.

.   .   .   .

Little Maria Klock died suddenly of dysentery yesterday. Three days ago she was quite well, and now she's dead. I can't get over it, I loved the tiny thing so much. What a little angel she looked in her coffin!

I can't sleep at night. My thoughts are always with Errie. Perhaps she's dead too, and I know nothing about it. Next month she'll be a year old if she's alive. I can't believe she is.

I am quite ill with anxiety and dread and longing; and it's so much worse because I haven't a soul in the world to tell my troubles to. Often when I lie awake in my bed at night, all sorts of crazy fancies wander like black phantoms through my brain.

Isn't it astonishing that things are just as they *are* in this world? Surely the right of a mother to her own little child ought to be absolutely sacred – so sacred that nothing can prevail against it, that scorn and derision must flee before it like owls and bats before the light of day? That Love which the Gospel tells us of, which suffereth long and is kind, which knoweth not strife or impatience, which seeketh not its own, which forgiveth all, which never faileth – surely it is one and the same as the love of a mother for her child? Such love is truly pure and undefiled, and utterly without stain of self-seeking.

I am writing this in bed by the light of a tallow-candle The boys are asleep. . . . If men were truly sincere in their religion, they would not throw mud at an unmarried mother, and make it impossible for her openly and freely to acknowledge her child. They would honour, even in the "fallen woman," the vessel of that holy love which God Himself has said to be the fulfilling of the law, and they would let her go her way in peace.

Where else in the world is to be found a love which more nearly approaches that described in the famous chapter of Corinthians, than the love of a mother? Nowhere, nowhere! And so it must be that which is nearest to perfection; and so a mother's love, must be most like the love of the ideal Christ.

I am not eighteen yet. Youth is called the spring-time of life. But for me there is no more sun, no more joy. All is dark and sad for me. And yet at first one would have imagined that I was intended to be happy and light-hearted, I used to love so to laugh and make fun.

How frightful it is that one wrong step should thrust a human being irrevocably into outer darkness and loneliness and shame! How frightful it is that men and women feeling, thinking beings of flesh and blood, with the same weaknesses and failings as their fellows have should degrade the great, beautiful, sacred Gospel of Love into devilish maxims that are all badness and brutality and horror! When I dream, I dream of a joy which is sweet and pure and clear as sunny air. I dream that I am holding my warm, soft baby in my arms and it wears a little white frock, and laughs and claps its hands. And we two wander on and on in the fair spring morning, through green fields that are full of flowers and butterflies, and my little child runs after them on and on, into another fairer, greater world, where there are no other people at all, but just flowers and stars and clear water. And one can wash away all the stains of the old world in that crystal stream, and stand up pure and good and spotless.

· · · · · · · ·

At the pastor's I had to steal the few moments that I ever got for writing. The last entry was in pencil, and it's hardly legible now. I wrote it by the flickering light of a penny candle.

I have time enough for writing these days, but I've forgotten a good deal and didn't think of my Diary till I rummaged it out to-day. However, as it's a dull Sunday afternoon, I'll write it up now. The last page describes my feelings at that time so exactly! It was a year of experiences at the pastor's; and as my chronicles must be complete, in case they one day fall into the hands of posterity, I will just give the general outlines of what has happened since I wrote last.

When I sum up my impressions of my " Reformatory year" I think I can say truthfully that what disgusted and repelled me so utterly at the Daubs', and made my stay so intolerable to me, was not so much their treatment of myself personally, as the detestable hypocrisy and falseness of the whole lot of them. Something in me is absolutely opposed to that sort of thing. I can't stand it at any price. Piety is beautiful and right, if it has some sort of traceable connection with the first laws of ethics.

But the word "God" in the mouths of a brutal woman and of an iron-hearted zealot is more hateful than the foulest obscenities of the starving wretch in the gutter. I could not do with it; I was all loathing and protest. Otherwise I had nothing much to complain of. The work didn't hurt me, and I always had enough to eat.

If it hadn't been for the sudden overwhelming yearning for my child! After the cobbler's little daughter died, I had not had a moment's ease or rest. It was like a kind of sickness; I grew feverish, worse and worse every day, and thought and hoped and wished and longed for nothing but that just to see my little darling once more, only once.

At that time Aunt Freda paid me a three-days' visit. Mrs. Pastor must have given her a good talking-to about me, for Aunt Freda took me sternly to task, and said that she had found a place for me on a farm in Dithmarsch. There were five children and only one servant, and the house stood quite by itself, and a very rigid, highly-moral Christian life was led there. I let her talk and thought my own thoughts the while, for I had definitely made up my mind that I wouldn't go there. The "rigid Christian life" that I have had for this last year at the Daubs' will satisfy me for the rest of my life.

For I'm like that. I can be ruled only by kindness. And I think most people are the same. Goodness is a weapon that I can't fight against. On the other hand, all my contrariness comes out when I am treated with harshness. Aunt Freda is undoubtedly as good as gold, and she means very well toward me; but as soon as she begins lecturing and preaching, I can't help taking a dislike to her. Dear me! haven't I made atonement enough by this time? I really must have something else to atone for, before I go willingly to another place of repentance! I made three crosses behind her when she was going away.

At that time we had a servant-maid whom the pastor had got out of the Christian Institution in Hamburg, for they couldn't get one any nearer home, as servants knew too much about them. Her name was Rike, and she was rather a firebrand. But I wasn't at all sorry that the Daubs should have some real cause for anger occasionally. There were such never-ending shindies that poor Rike used to say she didn't know whether she was standing on her head or her heels. I got on very well with the girl; I suppose she saw that, in many respects, I was a fellow-sufferer.

One afternoon, when Mrs. Pastor was paying visits in a neighbouring village, and Toni was shopping with her sweetheart in Lübeck, a rich peasant came to bring the pastor some money – I don't know what for, I think it was the rent of a meadow; and when he had gone, the pastor went out. Towards six o'clock, I was coming in from the garden where I had been busy, and in passing the house I looked through the window and saw Rike standing in the study by the writing-table, and taking up some money that was lying there. Of course I rushed in at once and attacked her, and she, in a terrible fright, showed me the money – two twenty-mark pieces – which the pastor had forgotten to lock up, and begged me for God's sake not to ruin her. I thought a moment, for an idea darted into my head all at once.

"Rike," I said, "I have a proposal to make to you. Give me one of those twenty-mark pieces, and keep your mouth shut about it. I'll take all the blame entirely upon myself, and, moreover, the pastor shall be paid back every penny of the money. But I must get away from here. Do you think the old man is hanging about anywhere?"

Rike laughed, and said the old man was with his sweetheart, so he was sure not to come back very soon. She entered into my plans immediately, so I took the twenty-mark piece, got ready as quickly as I could, packed a few things, and hurried off to the nearest railway-station. By great good luck a train was just starting for Lübeck, and from there I made the connection to Hamburg. I got there about ten o'clock. Of course it was too late to go to Consul Peters. On the other hand, I didn't at all wish to spend the night at an hotel, for I had to spin out my money if I wanted to get to Hanover. I stayed till midnight in the station refreshment-room, but the waiter then came and said it was closing-time, and I must leave. Luckily it was May, and a lovely warm night, and the air did me good. I strolled a little along the ramparts, sat down on a seat for a moment, and then turned back and walked through the colonnades to the "Lovers' Walk" and along by the Alster.

The streets were very quiet. A carriage went past every now and then, and isolated foot passengers hurried by. Suddenly I noticed that a gentleman was following me. I was frightened and hurried on, but in the Alster Arcade he caught me up, and spoke to me, asking why I was walking alone so late. I looked at him and noticed that he was very elegantly dressed, and looked nice; he had on a tall hat, and his moustache was long and fair. I told him I was a stranger in Hamburg and had only just arrived by train, and that I had to kill time until the next day, when I was going on to Hanover. He remarked that he was afraid I would find it rather tedious, as it was only just two o'clock, and kept along beside me, and we soon got into conversation. There was something very nice and kind about him, so that when he suddenly came out with the suggestion that I might come to his house with him, and spend a couple of hours, I really didn't see anything against it, and willingly acquiesced. He lived close by, at the corner of the Market Square and Gerlachstrasse, or thereabouts – only a step or two, and his name was Emil Reschke, for I read it on the door-plate.

I've never seen such charming rooms as the three into which he led me. They all opened off one another – a reception-room, a dining-room, and a bedroom, in which a red lamp was burning. Every one of the three rooms was full of fresh, fragrant roses. I took off my things, and Herr Reschke brought a bottle of champagne and glasses, and all sorts of cold things to eat lobsters and cold meat and cakes and sweets, all of which I enjoyed very much, for I was tremendously hungry.

I sat on the long chair, and Herr Reschke sat beside me on a stool; we clinked glasses and I felt better every minute. All my difficulties and troubles seemed to fall away from me, and my soul was free and happy for the hour.

When I had eaten my fill and Herr Reschke had put the things back on the sideboard, he sat down beside me on the long chair, and put his arm round my waist. I permitted it, and I let him kiss me too. But when suddenly he drew me to him, and I saw his eyes glittering close to mine, I tore myself away and all my pleasure fled, for it was Meinert's hateful eyes that seemed to be looking at me, and I knew if I stayed I should lose my head, and that must never happen again. I think I must have turned deadly white, and I know I trembled, and all I could say was that I must go I must go.

"Why! what on earth is the matter? I'm not going to eat you, child," said he, and he persuaded me to sit down again. He talked to me very nicely – very quietly and kindly, so that I gradually got calm and regained my confidence in him, and when he begged me to tell him where I came from and what was the matter with me, I felt as if somebody had turned the key of my inmost heart, and the door of it seemed to open, and I poured forth everything that had been pent-up there for all these years. I told Herr Reschke of my childhood, and the things that had happened in my father's house, and then I told him about my own tragedy, and about everything – everything, even to the purloined twenty-mark piece! When I looked at him again he seemed quite changed; the hot, restless glitter was gone from his eyes, and there was nothing but kindness and sympathy in his fresh, handsome face.

"Poor little girl!" he said compassionately, and stroked my cheek with his hand. "You've been through so much already that you must be cautious in future, and never go again to a strange man's house at night. You may thank God that you've fallen into no worse hands than mine. I'm a bit of a rake, I daresay, but not the common sort that draws no distinctions. To make an unhappy child like you still more unhappy – no, Emil Reschke doesn't do that sort of thing. But you're a great deal too pretty to be alone without anyone to take care of you. Well, don't be frightened; nothing is going to happen to you now. Lie back comfortably in the chair, and rest a little."

So he spoke, and I lay back obediently. And he spread a rug over me, and went out and locked the door. I soon went to sleep, and never stirred until my host waked me at six o'clock. He had made some coffee himself, for his servant didn't come till half-past seven, and I should have to be gone before then. When we had breakfasted he gave me a box of sweets, and a twenty-mark piece to send back to the pastor, so that I mightn't be "a little thief," as he said.

I told my adventure to Connie Liesmann, and she shouted with laughter, and said I mustn't try to take her in with that sort of nonsense. The idea of a man taking home a girl at night and giving her twenty-mark pieces, and getting nothing at all in return! Noble creatures like that were only to be found in novels.

But it's perfectly true, or else I wouldn't write it down here, for I have no secrets from my Book. Emil Reschke was a good man. Thank God, there are some like that.

I wandered about in the streets until the shops were open, and then I bought a little doll and a rattle and a fluffy lamb, and went down the Eimsbüttel to Consul Peters. I asked the maid who opened the door for the Consul, and was shown into a room, and after a short time the old gentleman came in. He knew me at once, and seemed somewhat embarrassed when I said that I would like to see Erica. He said he would speak to his wife, and went out and was away for a long time, and then came back with a very haughty-looking lady in a pale-grey morning gown. She greeted me condescendingly, and said it was quite an unreasonable request, but as the child was too young to understand, she would take me to the nursery, where it had just had its bath. I followed her upstairs, and my heart beat so with excitement that I could scarcely breathe.

There she sat in the nursery in a tiny white chair, like a little angel, all in lace and embroidery!

Oh, God! there's not another thing in the world so sweet and precious and enchanting. She has long black silky curls, and dark-blue eyes. I devoured her with love. I kissed her little face and her little hands and her little neck, and she opened big eyes at me, and tried to slap me, and stretched out her arms to Frau Peters, and called her "Mummie, Mummie."

Frau Peters looked transfigured and not a bit haughty while she was playing with Erica.

Oh, it was a half-hour of heavenly sweetness, but alas! it was too short. Frau Peters said the darling must have her sleep now, so of course I had to go. I was taken back to the Consul's room, and a servant-maid brought me port wine and caviar-sandwiches and pastry. The old gentleman spoke very kindly to me, and quite reasonably. He said I must see that there was no sense in these occasional visits. They only kept the wound open. Erica was entirely and in every respect like their own child. They had adopted her, and in doing so had acquired all parental rights, and she was to be their sole heiress. I must be reasonable, he said, and be satisfied with this one meeting. I was still so young, he added, that I should probably marry some day and have other children. I said "yes" to everything, for my thoughts were still with the little darling angel in the nursery. Pretty soon the audience ended. When I was taking leave, Herr Peters pressed something into my hand, and it wasn't until I got outside that I realised it was a blue hundred-mark note. I went straight to the post office, where I changed the note and sent forty marks to the pastor so that little incident is closed.

I scarcely noticed anything on the journey to Hanover, for I was crying the whole time – my heart was so heavy with longing!

Months have gone by since then, but still I can think of nothing but the child. I can't root out the yearning that overflows my heart, and seems dimly to illumine my soul with the sense of an experience so compact of joy and grief that the light it makes there is like the vacillating, eerie, flicker of a carried candle. The tears which wet my pillow at night are not wept for my unhappiness nor for my desolation, but for the injustice of Fate, and of those human laws which oppress me. I feel that I might be a good woman if I could have my child with me, and watch her growing up. I know that in my soul the light and the darkness are now very close together; they are not separated from one another as they were before, making sharp contrasts; they are closely interwoven – and the shadows threaten to put out the last faint remembrance of any former sunshine. But all would be sweet and good again in me, if I might but be Erica's mother. I *am* her mother! yet she stretched out her arms to a strange woman, and called her by that name. The strange woman has bought the right to it. She has more money than I have, and she has her own place in life. Enough, enough – I must forget; I will forget. Perhaps a time will come when I, too, can stand forth and make my claim.

Connie Liesmann received me most kindly. She has a very pretty flat here, so elegantly furnished, and indeed the whole establishment is on luxurious lines. Little Conrad has his own nurse, and passes as Connie's nephew. That appears to me indescribably foolish, for in the first place it's horrid of her to deny her child: and in the second place everybody she knows must be perfectly well acquainted with the facts of the case. Conrad is a strong, unusually well-developed child – much more robust than Erica. It gives me a sort of mournful pleasure to look after him and play with him. We have another servant besides the nurse. I have nothing to do but keep the accounts, which is certainly very easy work, and everybody who comes is nice to me. When I had been here a week father came, and wanted to take me away. He has altered shockingly in this last year – got so grey and heavy-looking. He told me that he has a lot of worry; he took over the business at a loss, and now the mortgagees, who are almost all mother's relations, are pitiless in exacting their dues. Lena is expecting another baby. Meinert is still there. Father says he's got accustomed to him, and can leave the business to him whenever he chooses. I said nothing to that. I consider it scandalous that father hasn't kicked the scoundrel out long ago.

It's sure to have been Aunt Freda who told father that he must take me away from Connie Liesmann's; she would be certain to dislike the idea of it; but I said definitely that I would not go, and my old influence over father still prevailed. After three days he went away, leaving things just as they were.

CHAPTER IX

The whole show here is run by Herr von Vohsen. He pays the rent and gives Connie three hundred and fifty marks a month, and any amount of presents besides. Moreover, he has put fifteen thousand marks in the bank for Conrad, in case he should die suddenly, for he has a weak heart. I think it's perfectly splendid of him, but Connie never stops abusing his stinginess, and often she makes him frightful scenes, wailing over her "lost happiness," and saying when once he pops off she'll have to go begging with her child, because he has provided so inadequately for them. At first I was inclined to think she was right, but now I'm of a totally different opinion, for the truth is that Connie is not faithful to him. She has a love-affair with an officer, Captain von Kronen, an awfully handsome fellow, whom she is crazy about.

He never comes to the house except when Herr von Vohsen is out of town. They are very cautious, and only meet in the city, where they have hired a room for these occasions.

If I were in her place I should give Vohsen the go-by, as I said to her one day, and stick to the man I loved. (I was still a little naive when I said that.) She declared that a bird in the hand was worth two in the bush.

Kronen *had* money, she said, but he wanted it all for himself; and a good solid settlement was better than love, for one didn't get tired of it and could buy silk frocks with it. One was pleasure and the other was business.

Business and love! I begin to understand. A word to the wise —

Connie doesn't see many people, because Herr von Vohsen doesn't wish it, and the few friends she has are all surrounded by a certain degree of odium. One of them has the same kind of connection with a married man that Connie has, another has already had relations with three, and is now living with the fourth in unlawful matrimony. The third, Frau Anna Kindermann, once an actress (sixth-class, I should think), has had enough adventures to fill three novels, and it is very amusing to listen to her holding forth about this or that chapter of her past. Her last man she's had three too, I believe – was a riding-master in a travelling circus, and he cast her off, and then she ran away, and now supports herself by doing massage. She has learnt it thoroughly, has all her certificates, does very good business, she says, and must earn a lot of money; for she, too, has a beautifully furnished abode, and is always gorgeously dressed. Although she must be about thirty-eight Connie says she can't be less than forty-three, if the truth were known she is still very pretty, tall and sumptuous, with long fair hair, even longer than Elizabeth's was. . . . Ah, God! . . . Poor Elizabeth! The memory of her will never die out of my heart.

Frau Kindermann gives lots of parties, and I used often to be asked to them; but something always happened to prevent my going. To begin with, I didn't particularly want to; and besides, I had no clothes.

On a gloomy rainy afternoon, about a month ago, I was sitting alone by the window in the sitting-room embroidering a little garment for Conrad and looking out at the street between times. Herr von Vohsen was with Connie – he had to take a trip on business to Alsace-Lorraine and was trying to persuade Connie to go with him, for he has lately become rather jealous and suspicious. Connie of course didn't want to go, for she amuses herself here much better without him and it came to a regular quarrel between them. I hate listening to anything like that. I'm on thorns all the time, and longing to get away. Suddenly there came a ring at the door. I went to open it, and in came Frau Kindermann.

"Hullo!" said she. "They're having a little row, aren't they?"

"Oh, no," I said; "they're only disagreeing with each other."

"Evidently," said she, laughing. "Well, that happens in the best families. And what are you doing in the meantime, child?"

I showed her my embroidery, and she sat down beside me at the window and we began to talk. In the course of our conversation she asked me if I was satisfied with my present life? I answered which was the truth that in comparison with the last year at the pastor's it seemed like heaven. She replied that even so, a young girl must long for amusement now and again. I couldn't deny that I had often wished a big change for the better would come into my life some time.

"What do you mean by 'better'?" asked she.

"Just – happiness!" said I.

"And what do you mean by happiness?"

I shrugged my shoulders.

"Oh! you must have a wish of some kind, child," she continued. "Plums don't drop into people's mouths. You'll wait a long time before 'happiness' comes looking for you in your own room. You must go out, you must be seen – then you'll soon find your luck ready waiting for you."

"I have nothing to wear," I said. "And I won't ask father for money. I mean to earn what I want for the future."

"Well, we'll soon remove the first obstacle," she cried, good-naturedly; "and then the other will remove itself. You're not exactly done for yet! But you ought to be with me instead of with Connie, *I'd* make something out of you. Connie, you know, is rather afraid of competition; but I go in for it. I like to have young, pretty faces about me. Do come to me some evening."

And I promised I would. Then Connie came in. Vohsen had departed, but she had been obliged to promise that she would go with him, and was very cross and unhappy about it. I tried to console her and promised to take care of Conrad while she was away, and she said that was nice of me.

"Connie, can't Fräulein Thymian come to me sometimes in the evenings? The poor girl will mope to death here, she'll be so lonely and dull," said Kindermann.

"Of course why, of course," Connie answered, absently.

The other day Connie, gave me a pretty frock and two blouses of hers. The dress had been a present from Herr von Vohsen, and a great failure, for it was pale coral-pink, which Connie hates, because it doesn't go with her hair. It suits me to perfection. Frau Kindermann's dressmaker altered it for me, and now it fits me as if I had been poured into it!

The week after that Connie went off with Herr von Vohsen. A couple of evenings later, Frau Kindermann sent her maid to ask me to come over for a while. They were going to have a party and enjoy themselves hugely. I instantly put on the new coral dress and went.

She seemed delighted to see me. In her bedroom, where I took off my cloak, she said that she wanted to do my hair for me in a new way higher than I did it; and when she had let it down she exclaimed, quite genuinely, with amazement:

"What a beauty! My patience, girl! What have you been doing hiding yourself and your hair like this! It's a sin and a shame!" And she insisted on my leaving it on my shoulders, though I felt uncomfortable, for my hair is so thick and long that it looked very untidy and eccentric. At last she let me "civilize" it a little with a white ribbon.

"Child! child! you're fetching, you're exquisite! she said quite sentimentally. "If you're clever . . . . well, I won't say anything . . . . but you could live like a princess if you liked. What? You don't want to? Well what else can we do for you? What about a pair of diamond earrings in those pretty ears, and some rings on the fingers—"

"I have a whole box full of ornaments," I said; "I don't care a bit about that kind of thing."

"Oho!" said she; and then we went into the dining-room.

About nine o'clock two gentlemen came – friends of hers, both very smart. One of them was slender and clean-shaven, with a single eyeglass, and the other was stout, with a short black beard and a crooked nose. The former was called Albert and the latter Kirschbaum.

We had an excellent supper. There were pies and clear soup, and then lobster mayonnaise and pheasant. In aspic, and finally an ice pudding with brandy-cherries. Massaging must be a profitable business, when Frau Kindermann can do you in that style! We had red wine at supper, and then champagne and port and then more champagne. Frau Kindermann played the piano after supper, and sang some little songs, or, rather, screeched them! Her voice is so funny that nobody could help laughing, and she laughed as heartily as any of us. I got frantically excited, and behaved like a mad woman. Herr Glimm took hold of me and danced round the room with me, and then put me down suddenly with a swing on the sofa beside Herr Kirschbaum, who caught me round the neck and tried to kiss me. But I wasn't going to have that, and, half-fuddled as I was, I took up my glass of champagne and poured it down his shirt-collar, upon which he leaped up and ran about the room as if he was possessed.

Frau Kindermann gently reproved me afterwards, and said I oughtn't to have done that.

"And why not?" I demanded. "Was I to let the disgusting old Jew kiss me? Ugh!"

"Don't be a fool, child!" she said. "The Jews have Moses and the Prophets in other words, if he was a friend of yours, you'd be in clover. He could give you diamonds on your garters if you fancied them."

"I wouldn't be seen dead with his old diamonds!" I rejoined; "and, besides, he's married."

"My dear girl, you have nothing to do with a man's private affairs," said Frau Kindermann.

Well, that's what she is like! She seems to be a queer sort. If she and Connie and the two other are going in for that kind of thing, I'll have to get out I wasn't born yesterday, but there are some things I can't quite swallow.

When I got home that night I couldn't go to sleep for a long time. My nerves were too excited. My heart was fluttering like anything. I wanted to go on laughing and joking long after I was in bed. It's a very good thing to get into that state occasionally, else I should forget that I'm young still. It *is* pleasant to be shaken up a little. And how those two men looked at me!

I could see they admired me. . . .

Oh dear! if I could only have clothes like Connie's and Kindermann's! I don't mean only frocks and hats, I mean everything fine, fine underclothing, cobwebby with lace, and silk stockings, and rustling petticoats in all the colours of the rainbow, and French corsets, and lovely scent that would hang about one like a subtle exquisite emanation. . . .

I do believe one could be happy if one could live like that.

. . . .

One day after the evening at Frau Kindermann's, Herr Glimm sent me a bouquet and an invitation to supper for the next evening. I thought it over a lot, and then Kindermann came and talked to me, and so I accepted.

Herr Glimm came to fetch me. We supped in a private room. It was very nice, and we drank a great deal of champagne. Later on he got a little sentimental, and I allowed him, for I don't object to him at all. But eventually I was rather glad when the door opened and two gentlemen came in, upon which the love-making came to an end.

He introduced the gentlemen to me as his friends, and they were both very nice and polite. Afterwards three more came, amongst them Herr von Kronen, Connie's friend, and then I noticed that they were all officers in mufti. Herr Glimm seemed to be rather annoyed at being disturbed, but of course he couldn't show it. Then the champagne began to flow my goodness! . . . The fun ran fast and furious. All the gentlemen wanted to have philopenas with me, and to be paid that very evening. Oh, it was a high old time! and of course in the end they all lost. So then I had to write down what I wanted from each of them. I was half-seas over, and so I wrote down exactly what I wanted on each of their visiting-cards. "A pair of silk stockings," "a pair of satin corsets," "a silk petticoat," "a bottle of scent," and so on. Only the men roared so when they read the cards that I got shy. I hate being laughed at, so all at once I stood up, flaming with rage. "Please take it all as a joke, gentlemen," I said; "I was only humbugging."

They all assured me that of course they had regarded it as the most utter nonsense, and then I let Glimm take me home.

The next day our door-bell never stopped ringing, and every time it was a servant-man with a bouquet and a parcel. In the parcels were all the things I had wished for: six pairs of stockings, a pair of lilac satin corsets, a silk petticoat, an order for half a dozen pairs of gloves, and a big carton-box filled with scent and soap and powder, all from Roger & Gallet, and the very best of their kind. I didn't know exactly whether to keep them or send them back, but I decided to keep them. It would have looked so silly, so provincial and Philistine, to send them back. After all, it's only right they should pay their philopenas, and what did the few shillings matter to them, who fling money about like water! I'm enchanted with the things.

Yesterday evening, when we came home from supper after the theatre, Herr Glimm was very anxious to come in with me. But I snapped my fingers at him. "There are people and people," says Fran Kindermann; and I'm a lady and insist on being treated as one. If he thinks that I am everybody's game he has made a very great mistake. I have determined never to give myself again except for love. Now I don't love Glimm, although he is a very decent little fellow. I keep on my guard in every possible way, and put a check on my feelings, yet for all that I — no, enough.

. . . .

Monday.

Dear Book! I wish you were a real person. I talk to you as I do to nobody else in the world. You are my only friend; I have no secrets from you, you know me as I am. You are my Father-Confessor. You take in all that I say to you so mutely and so meekly – and what things have I not said to you! Oh, do speak to me, do advise me, do tell me what I ought to do! I am so puzzled I don't know what to think. Shall I? Shall I not? Oh, do speak! If you mean "yes," refuse to lie open at the page I choose; if you mean "no," lie still. Oh, you say "no," do you? Well then, you're a stupid, silly book; you have no soul. Why have I a soul? I wish

I hadn't. Why have people always got to think? Thoughts are so useless and so uncomfortable.

And that's why all morality is so uncomfortable and stupid and tiresome, because it always proceeds from a thought. I never finish Aunt Freda's letters, they irritate me with their moral tone and their hideous dullness. Father scarcely ever writes now. They've another daughter at home these days. I shall soon be quite forgotten. All right! I'll forget too that I ever had a home and a mother and a father. I am like a fallen leaf driven by the wind, trodden down into the mud, yet still wearily fluttering on.

No! for in reality I must confess I don't feel weary at all. A mad joy in life, a hot hunger for happiness and enjoyment, burns in my veins. And for ever the question confronts me – What will my future be?

If I remain "honest" and keep to the "narrow way," that same narrow way of honesty and respectability will end as sure as death in a little poky maiden-solitude *á la tante Freda*. Yes, and if I sit down and look back – what have I had from life? . . .

No, I won't! I won't! I am pleased with myself again as I used to be. I am pretty. It gives me great pleasure to throw off my clothes one after another before the glass, and look at myself as I really am snow-white, and as slender as a cypress, with long soft hair like a black silken cloak. When I plunge both hands into it and spread it out, I look as if I had wings – a white swan with black pinions.

Connie is back again. She brought me a lot of presents, and said she was glad I was enjoying myself, and she had nothing against it so long as I didn't "play in her yard." And of course I won't; that would be unspeakably mean.

The views of Connie and Kindermann upon my present preoccupation are very interestingly dissimilar. Connie sometimes has melancholy fits.

She says that if she could live the past over again, she would do quite differently, and marry a young man, even if he were only a little clerk or an artisan. It would be quite a different sort of life. One would be a real human being then, and could give oneself as that; but as it was, she was neither flesh nor fowl. The men who supplied women like her with money were worse than slave-drivers, for they imagined that their payment gave them the right to tyrannise over one, as if one was a mere chattel. They never talked of loving one. One was nothing more to them than – well, never mind! And unfortunately it was almost impossible to reform when once one had tried the gay life.

Thus Connie. But Frau Kindermann tried to give me quite another point of view. The gentlemen (she said) had complained of my being too coquettish. I was amazed, and couldn't help laughing at such rubbish. But she got really cross.

"So you are coquettish – a great deal too much the fine lady, Fräulein Thymian," she said. "All very well if you were a little white lamb and had had no experiences. I wouldn't say a word then. You would only be showing your sense in playing the game of perfect respectability and good conduct, for then you might marry a post-office clerk, or something of that sort, and have half a dozen children, and cook and darn, and have a beautiful sermon preached over you, and an epitaph — 'Here lies an honest plain, cook and wet nurse' But you! A beautiful creature with a past behind you already, clever and cultivated as you are, with a temperament of your own, and no novice at love-making. . . . No, no; hold your tongue! Anyone can see it. It's all very fine, but you carry it too far, my girl; you overshoot your mark. Gentlemen don't mind for once being drawn on and then given the cold shoulder; they'll even stand it twice, perhaps; but the third time – off they go! There are lots of pretty girls in the world. . . . Good gracious! what does it matter to me? But I'm sorry for you. I was in your place once, and I took what I could get. One isn't young for ever; some day when you're old and can't get it, you'll be sorry you were such a fool."

"Yes," I answered; "that is all quite true, Frau Kindermann. I won't make myself out better than I am; but I have been through too much. I can't think lightly of such things now. When evil thoughts and desires come to me I need only call to mind the hour when I stood by the weir and wished to drown myself – and they all disappear."

"Aha!" she said, and whistled. "So that's it, is it? You're afraid! . . . Well, my lamb, if that's the only trouble, we're all right. Leave it to me. Don't be afraid ; you've only got to trust Kindermann."

"My God! Frau Kindermann, do you suppose that's all I'm thinking of?" I said, sadly.

"No," replied she, "I understand it all. You're a little bit of a Philistine still, and can't quite get into our liberal ways of looking at life. You're not stuck-up, but all the same you have a private conviction that you're a cut above us all. But it's no good, my dear. You have had a child, and respectable society won't have anything more to do with you; you're dead to them all. Then why not do as you like? You'll never be whitewashed really, and even if you did get into society again you'd live in perpetual terror of something coming out – it would be like somebody's sword hanging over your head – Damocles was it ? . . . So you'd better come to us, where no questions are asked and people are free to enjoy life in their own way. With us, you never hear the everlasting refrain: 'Who is she, and where does she come from?' We enjoy our lives; we play fair and fear nobody. So now think it over, and make up your mind to treat poor Glimm better in future. The poor fellow will do himself some harm if you don't take care; he's really in a terrible state."

Thus Frau Kindermann. And I often think of her words; they contain much truth. I was shown plainly enough at the Daubs' that respectable society would have nothing more to do with me. My very presence would corrupt "innocent" young girls. No decent woman would associate with "a creature like me." Well, then! What am I to do? There's absolutely nothing for me but to achieve a resurrection in a new world.

I have no illusions about it. I have long known what type of woman Frau Kindermann is. She was a "masseuse" while it paid her; now she's looking out for some other way of making money. But what does it all matter to me? . . . She thinks of moving to Hamburg and setting up house there. She has a big connection in the town, she says, and she will have an evening party once a fortnight, to which her Hanover pals must come over.

I haven't been outside the doors for nearly a fortnight. Glimm won't take me out any more unless I am "reasonable." Then he will give me a chiffon dress and a diamond ring.

But I don't know. . . . Something in me recoils from it. I shouldn't like to be one of the women whom men treat with disrespect. Glimm is always very respectful to me. He loves me – or says he does; but it's a fixed principle with him not to marry, he declares.

I *should* like to go out in the evening again and drink champagne and be merry, and shake off all these troublesome thoughts that crouch in my breast like dark, hydra-headed monsters, with blazing eyes and grinning lips and claws that reach out to rend my soul.

Dear book, I wish I knew. . . . Oh, I am going mad, I think!

. . . .

Unfortunately, just here, where the mental and moral struggle of the writer is at its height, a great many pages have been cut out of the book. These carefully cut-out pages have given me food for much reflection.

She who in later years could chronicle the most shameful and terrible events of her poor ruined life (despite the degree of sensibility which she retained to the very end) had found too painful for preservation the record of this period, in which with faltering feet she crossed the last crazy bridge between two worlds!

That is the only explanation I can think of. But these missing pages make a deplorable breach in the continuity of the story.

Although at that very time I often saw and talked with the Diarist, I am not able to fill in this gap, for she naturally preserved a great reticence in what she imparted to me of her life and acquaintances. One remarkable psychological fact may be noted here. She was at that time seized by a genuine longing for mental culture. She spent every shilling she could spare upon improving herself in this way. During her two years stay in Hamburg as "companion" (save the mark!) to Frau Kindermann, she perfected herself in French and English, learnt Russian and Italian, and took lessons in various scientific subjects.

Her writing-table was heaped with scientific and philosophical works. I remember that one day when I was visiting her, she drew my attention to a volume of Carlyle, from which she could repeat whole chapters.

I learned later by word of mouth that Frau Liesmann just then made the acquaintance of a Swedish hotel-keeper in Heringsdorf, followed him, with her child, to Upsala, and married him there. In spite of this lady's doubtful past, the marriage (which was abundantly blessed with children) proved a particularly happy one.

Immediately after Frau Liesmann's departure, Thymian went to Frau Kindermann.

The Diarist, in the period between the following entries and the one just read, had completely broken with her own people. I do not know any details of this matter. I imagine that the relatives on the mother's side imperatively demanded that Thymian should leave Frau Kindermann and go again to a "respectable household." But as she was by that time of full age, the family, who doubtless wished to avoid an open scandal, could take no steps to enforce their will upon her.

Thenceforward an estrangement between Thymian and her father made itself felt. — EDITORIAL NOTE.

CHAPTER X

I had yet another row with Kindermann, about a bottle of claret which she tried to smuggle into my bill. That woman is simply awful. I thought she would be satisfied with fifteen marks a day for my keep. I am supposed to have had the bottle of Larose on the evening of the twenty-second of January, and Ludwig is supposed to have been with me. Luckily I am able to prove that it's an impudent lie. On the twenty-second we dined in the Winter Garden of the Hamburg Hotel, and went from there to the Thalia Theatre. In the vestibule Ludwig caught sight of his mother, and as he has a tremendous respect for her, he managed to efface himself, and I had to go alone into the box. I remember the evening particularly, because I made a new acquaintance at the theatre. He was sitting in the stage box and staring at me the whole time. He was exceptionally haughty-looking, so I thought he must be an Indian rajah or something equally gorgeous; afterwards, it turned out that he was a silk merchant from Crefeld, and he wrote himself down as Mayor. However, he left a good lot of money behind him in this house.

That woman! She always tries to make out that I am eternally beholden to her! Harpy that she is! Considering that Ludwig has paid the rent for the last month – which he'd never have done for her sweet sake – I think she might be decently civil. I was in such a rage that I slung a book at her head and told her I'd set up for myself before long if she wasn't careful. At that she sneered and said if I did, I'd better go to the proper street, and I knew what that was, didn't I? *She* wasn't the kind that – et cetera, et cetera.

Saving money takes so infernally long. Ludwig wanted to buy me a brooch for my birthday, and I begged him to give me the money instead. He looked askance at that, and I could see he hated it, the old goose! He'll pay my bills at Meinke's or at the milliner's, or my month's rent, without pulling a long face, but to give me money, naked money. . . . Well, I can understand it when I remember how I felt, the first time I had to take money . . . a year ago, when the knife was at my throat – Bah! what rot! I won't think of it! But it's a beastly sort of feeling to be over-estimated by another person. Ludwig still thinks of me as a lady, and in one way it pleases me, though in another it's a nuisance. . . . But when I asked him that, he opened an account in the North German Bank for me.

If only one's clothes and the thousand and one etceteras didn't run away with such a lot! Often I lose heart altogether. It's a poor sort of life – but what have other women to boast of, after all? Nothing very wonderful! Annie Meier is separated from her husband, and lives now with two little brats in her father's house. And that's no case of "marry in haste, repent at leisure," considering they were engaged at school and had known one another all their lives He is said to have actually beaten her! Strange! I always thought Boy such a good fellow.

Lena Schütt lives here in the Ferdinandstrasse. She married a book-keeper, who then got a year and a half in gaol for perjury, and isn't out yet. Lena lets lodgings and has a wretched time of it. I met her one day and spoke to her, but she was so funny and condescending that at first I wondered what on earth was up. I couldn't help laughing, and yet it annoyed me.

"How are you getting on, Lena?" said I.

"Badly," she answered, with venom. "It's very hard for a decent woman to pull through at all; one doesn't get silk petticoats and hats with ostrich feathers out of letting lodgings, but I'd rather starve than sell my good name!"

I flared up in a minute and would have said a few plain words to her, only I bethought me that it really wasn't worth while to bandy abuse with a fool like that. I told it to Greta afterwards, and she laughed and said, "You can't expect anything but wool from a sheep." And she's right.

. . . .

March 8th.

On Friday Osdorff came.[1] The poor fellow has utterly gone to pieces in these four years. It seems to me that he has positively grown! Involuntarily there came into my head the rhyme about the giant Goliath —

> "He had big, big bones and a look as bold as brass;
> And a big, big mouth, and a face just like an ass";

though indeed "a look as bold as brass" is rather too good, for poor old Casimir hasn't got a morsel of "boldness" about him: swagger enough, on the other hand, for anything – still very much the man with the two "f's." Well, well! America ought to teach him a thing or two. I already see him, in imagination, cleaning boots in the streets. Nevertheless, I'm sorry for him. I like him. He's an old attachment – the only one I have now.

I gave him fifty marks and went to see him off at Bremerhaven. It was as though a bit of my youth was sailing away with him. When the steamer cast off, I found that there were tears in my eyes. I felt a wild desire to start off too for the unknown, but then I remembered that there's no use in it; you may put the whole ocean between you and the past, but you take yourself with you

---

[1] So far as I know, all the efforts of "Osdorffs" family to turn him into a responsible and active member of the community proved totally unsuccessful, by reason of his stupidity and indolence. He was then provided with the means to emigrate to America, according to his own desire. Thymian must have corresponded with him till then. EDITOR.

wherever you go; and you can't eat your cake and have it too, in New York any more than in Hamburg.

When I came back Ludwig made me a scene of jealousy. The dear old donkey! I succeeded in calming him down.

Behrend has been fleeced again. I don't trust Kalkow. The fellow looks like a swell mobsman. I said so lately to Kindermann, and she only laughed at me. Well, then, let her take care of herself; she'll get her fingers burnt one of these days. If there was any sort of a fuss kicked up about this house, it would cost her a pretty penny.

Our aristocrat, von Kosmos, behaved very insolently to me the other day. I gave him a cuff and a kick. I'll stand no nonsense. The next day he came all humility, and apologised. It's queer how mad they all are about me.

. . . .

March 14th.

I don't know why the governess doesn't come any more to the Zoological Gardens with the child. Last Friday I hadn't time to go; but then I went five days running and waited in vain. I'm afraid Erica must be ill. I am terribly anxious, and would go to the house if I wasn't afraid they would chuck me out. Yesterday I went past it, but I saw nobody. Often I have had a wild impulse to kidnap the little thing. But where could I take her? Ah! life is pretty bad, So frightfully uncertain. . . .

. . . .

March 22nd.

Yesterday I couldn't stand it any longer. I went to the Peters', and got the reception I expected.

The maid had scarcely shown me into the drawing-room when the lady of the house, followed by her husband, rushed in and flew at me. She said it was a monstrous piece of insolence on my part to force my way in like that, and if it happened again she would inform the police. But this time I had something to say; and I said it.

"Indeed?" I remarked. "That is charming of you. What have I done to the child that you should need the protection of the police?"

I was shaking like an aspen leaf. I could have boxed the creature's ears. But the old Consul tried to smooth things down. "My wife does not mean it literally. But in fact we have real cause to complain of your continued molestation. You had the effrontery to persuade the child to call you 'mother' – in the presence of the governess! The little girl is no longer so young that such impressions leave no trace – things like that will remain in her memory. You must therefore see that it cannot go on."

"I don't see it at all!" cried I. "I have a right to the child, too. I brought her into the world. I have human rights, mother-rights, which no devilry can take away from me. I will see my child from time to time – I *will*!"

Frau Peters exclaimed that I was an insolent creature, and must leave the house at once. But the old Consul said: "Go, Agnes. Leave me alone with the young lady; she will soon listen to reason."

And when she was gone he took me by the arm and said: "Now look here, my child! If you cause us any more trouble with your extraordinary pretensions, I shall give a hint to the Commissioner of Police to bestow a little of his attention upon you and your way of life. Your father wrote me that he knew nothing of you, and that to his deep sorrow you had entirely rejected all his advice and all his warnings. Your whole appearance, however, is a proof that you have the use of plenty of money. Where you get it from is no affair of mine, nor does it interest me, but you know as well as I do that our police lend no countenance to certain things. I opine, therefore, that a close supervision might prove anything but agreeable to you. . . ."

I longed to answer him and I couldn't. I was so affronted that my cheeks flamed. I was horribly humiliated in the presence of the old man; and the end of it all was that I slunk out like a whipped cur, after having faithfully promised him not to worry about Erica any more (which promise I of course shall break). Once I got outside, I hurried as fast as I could through the streets. I was so wretched! Here was a fresh degradation, and I had such a load of shame already on my shoulders. I don't know exactly what I felt. The rustling of my silk petticoat, which usually I enjoyed hearing, got on my nerves. I ran and ran, as if I were trying to escape from my infamy. Oh! it's an awful life – an awful life! . . .

Yesterday evening we had a great tow-row. Every one of the private rooms was occupied. I drank myself stupid with champagne, and I have a "mouth" this morning.

They had a fine time in the blue saloon. I wasn't there. I couldn't stand that. Besides, there were a few respectable middle-class women there – shopkeepers' wives from St Pauli's. We do have several real "fine ladies," occasionally. When people live as they do, recklessly and extravagantly, eating and drinking their fill, with no anxieties, plenty of money, and nothing whatever to do, it is natural enough that they should come here occasionally to give a fillip to their jaded nerves; but those worthy Philistine women ought to be satisfied with their cooking-pots and their husbands.

I was so befogged that I tore my costly lace dress off my back instead of unhooking it. It's done for now; I gave it to my laundress for her daughter, who wants to go to a music-hall. Kosmos, who was with me, is to give me another in its place.

. . . .

September 10th.

In the early part of the summer I was three weeks it Ilsenburg with Kosmos. But I had my own rooms, and wrote my name as "Frau Gotteball, from Hamburg," in the visitors' book. I did that on Ludwig's account – the good creature is so desperately in love and so wildly jealous. He always came to see me on Sundays, and arranged it so that he arrived on Saturday evening and left late on Sunday for Harzburg, where he was staying with his wife. At the same time Kosmos was in Hanover. Once, at the Brocken Hotel, we came across Ludwig and his wife, whom I had never seen till then. She is a little, slender, delicate-looking thing, narrow-chested and pale, and evidently highly anæmic. They sat opposite me at the table d'hôte, and I couldn't take my eyes off her. She made me feel bad I – don't know why, for she doesn't suffer through me. Ludwig is far too tactful and fine-natured a man to let his little wife see that he doesn't love her. . . . Dear God! yes, I ought rather to have envied than pitied her! And the few thousands which Ludwig spends on me, she, who lives in the lap of luxury and never knows what it is to do without anything she wants, will never miss. She has her parents, too, and she has her home; around her there swarms no hideous brood of snake-like thoughts such as those which writhe and curl about me (except when the drink drugs my brain) and hem me in, and lie across my every way of escape, and circle me around so that my very breath fails me sometimes at the horror of it. . . . I dare not reflect: when I do, it's terrible.

Ludwig devoured me with his eyes. Afterwards I went for a walk alone over the slope. All about me stood and lay and walked little groups of happy, chattering, contented people; the air was clear and warm, and yet with a little freshness in it – it was an ideal Sunday. But my heart was sore. I know many people many men who desire my favours and are ready to pay highly for them and yet, in reality, how utterly forlorn I am! I stand in the centre of my own little world, and life circles madly, intoxicatingly, around me; yet I often feel as if I were alone on a desolate isle in the middle of the sea. . . . As I was standing still and staring up at the sky, Ludwig came quickly towards me. He had plucked a little bunch of "Brocken-myrtle," which is only to be found in certain places, and was bringing it to me. I divided the bunch and gave him back half for his wife. "It will please her when she sees you have picked it for her," I said. "I never knew you had such a pretty little wife, Ludwig."

"She is not a scrap pretty," said he, "and she's ill-tempered and troublesome, and frightfully self willed."

"She is very young, Ludwig," I said.

"No younger than you are, Thymian."

"Yes – much younger," said I. "She is still a child, as far as mind and experience go; anyone can see it. Of a woman like that a man can make what he chooses. If in ten years she is a peevish, embittered, petty-minded, unlovable woman, it will be you who have made her so; but if she is a pretty, lovable, charming, kind one, it will also be your doing, Ludwig. A man should make his wife happy. Certainly it isn't always easy, but with one like yours it is. The sure conviction that they are beloved is to such women —"

"You speak like a book, Thymian," said Ludwig; "but how is one to convince one's wife of a thing which *is* not? I love one woman only you, Thymian!"

"A kindly lie is no sin, Ludwig," I replied. "If you can't love her in any other way, love her as a child entrusted to your care. Be good to her! If you should ever allow her to suspect that you love another woman more than you love her, and I should come to know it, we should be strangers from that moment."

He kissed my hand and said nothing in reply. But the next day he wrote me a wild love-letter and besought me to go with him to Ostend for a few weeks; his wife was going with her parents to Franzensbad. . . . I had no reason for refusing.

We went there in the beginning of August, and came back last week. It was a delightful time. There are few things more extraordinary than the tremendous influence exercised by the individuality of one person upon another, when that other lives in close and continual contact with him. I could have made behind Ludwig's back several interesting and distinguished acquaintances, but I simply couldn't bring myself to deceive him. If he were the average sensual man, or if I believed that it was merely a sensual passion which drew him to me, I shouldn't have had any sort of scruple about playing my cards as suited me best. But he is so good and unselfish that it would be a really despicable thing to deceive him thus – all trusting and confiding as he is. And, thank God! I'm not despicable. What I choose to do – my scheme of life – is my own affair; but nobody can accuse me, up to the present, of any mean action. And indeed I think that life would be more lovely, and nearer to the highest good, if men did not make so many laws for one another, and showed a greater tolerance and comprehension in their mutual dealings, instead of the perpetual narrow-minded suspicion that they so pride themselves upon. Everybody should be allowed to arrange the garden of his own life to his own taste. Let my neighbour have nothing in his plot but useful kitchen-herbs and vegetables, or nothing but roses, or nothing even but poison-plants with which to drug himself – what do I care, *so long as he doesn't come too near me*? If he stays quietly in his own domain, and doesn't steal *my* vegetables, or pick my roses, and the scent of his poison-flowers doesn't injure me, and if he doesn't climb over my fence and trample down my beds surely that is all I need demand of him? In my opinion the only real wrongs are to wound or injure others intentionally (or only to amuse one's self, as some do), and coarsely to betray or misuse the confidence which has been placed in one.

Ludwig's idealising love has a kind of magnetic influence upon me. I don't love him with the true woman's love – I don't suppose I'm capable of feeling it. It seems to me more like a kind of maternal tenderness, although he is ten years older than I am. His kindness and affection seem to flow like a warm sweet stream through my poor weary soul, setting free all that is good and unspoilt within it; but for that very reason I feel that a great danger lies for me in intercourse with Ludwig, which I must not underrate, for if once I were to begin to look at life differently, all would be over with me, and I could do nothing but get out somehow or other. Therefore I am really glad to be back again in Hamburg, breathing the old atmosphere. I make three crosses over the "good spirits," and chase them away.

. . . .

May 7th, 1893.

There's a lot to be written about the last few months. Well, I always told Kindermann that things would take a bad turn some time, but all I thought then was that some fine day our temple would be confiscate, and that there would be a terrific fuss, especially when it was discovered that the business wasn't "kosher." I never dreamed that the saloons and private rooms would be raided too. But I suppose people were going too far. . . . What *cochonneries* may have gone on in that part of the house, heaven only knows! I never had anything to do with that branch of Kindermann's business; but it was evidently a flourishing one, and brought in a lot of money to the old woman. The ladies and gentlemen who patronised it. . . . well, no one would believe who they were!

In short, the police were given a hint. And one evening a couple had forgotten to let down the blinds, and the neighbours at the back saw the whole thing, and next day we had a shindy. Luckily, K. got the tip early in the morning from little L., who always knows just what the police are up to; and so she was able to make arrangements. She could even have got out of the place if she had chosen, but she didn't choose; she had rather, she says, be "put away" for a year, and then be her own mistress again. But she advised me to pack up as quick as I could and be off. She was quite pathetic about it. "I'll swear that you had nothing to do with it, and knew nothing about it," she said. "I've always loved you like a daughter. I wanted to do well for you, and so it would be all the worse if I got you into trouble now. Now remember! if they catch you and make you a witness, you must be sure to swear that you knew nothing about anything."

"But I don't like the idea of perjuring myself," I answered.

"Ah! nonsense!" she said contemptuously; "what are you talking about perjury for? If you believed in God and the dear angels and heaven and all that sort of thing, you might talk about perjury, but heaven is no place for us, and as we can't get into it, what does one thing more or less matter? What's an oath? It's only your word of honour. . . . I can tell you that if I got a groschen for every word of honour that's broken every day in the world, I'd be driving about Hamburg in my carriage and pair." Then she gave me all sorts of good advice for the immediate future. I was to go to Berlin and betake myself to a friend of hers there, a Leipzig woman, who also lets rooms. She gave me the address and a letter, and helped me with my packing. We did it in three skips of a flea. At two o'clock I was driving off with my boxes on a cab, and at three the police had closed the establishment and arrested Kindermann. I drove first to the Berlin station, deposited my heavy baggage, and then went on with a bag or two to Frau Adler in the Langenreihe. I asked her to let me stay a couple of days with her, which she willingly consented to. That day I was so tired and worn out that I couldn't make any plans, but the next day I wrote to Ludwig and asked him to come over. He came at once, very much horrified at the sensational affair, which the evening and morning papers had reported. And he couldn't get over the fact that I had "unsuspectingly" lived in such a hell of iniquity. Then he took me in his arms and set me on his knee and told me that he couldn't any longer contemplate my wandering about homeless and forlorn. He would get divorced from his wife and marry me. He had said something about it to her that morning and there had been a terrible scene, and now she was gone off to her parents, and he was going that very evening to the authorities to take the preliminary steps.

I scarcely said a word. An alluring vision was shaping itself before my imagination of a future filled with calm happiness, a future in which all that now is but delusion would come true for me. I was so very tired of life – and it was sweet to think of living henceforward under the sheltering protection of a true and tender-hearted man who believed in me implicitly. But that emotion passed away, and I knew the truth again knew that the way back was forbidden to me, knew that I had burned my boats; and with the recognition a quite different mood came to me. I resolved to do the right thing, to tell Ludwig all, and send him back to reconciliation with his little wife.

To this day I don't know how I plucked up courage to make my confession. At first it was very slow and faltering, but then the words began to come faster, and at last it was all out, in its dreadful cut-and-dried brutality – the story of my life in plain, unvarnished truth. I told him everything. He got as white as the tablecloth, and then turned livid, and I could see that he was panting for breath.

"It's not true!" he cried. "It's not true! It's your imagination, Thymian. It can't be true!"

"Ah! yes, it is," I said. "I have belonged to many other men – to every man who wanted me, and was able to pay for the luxury of loving me."

Then he leaped up, caught me by the arm, and flung me from him with a vigour which I have never thought he possessed. I fell down; but he was storming like a wild beast about the room, and at last in his paroxysm he dashed open the window and threw down the flower-pots, so that the children playing in the yard yelled out with fright; and then he tore the pictures from the walls and the ornaments from the tables and flung them at me, and pushed me with his foot and spit at me, saying dreadful things all the time, like : "And I've loved a thing like that! . . . I've driven away my wife for that creature, and almost broken with my whole family! . . . And I loved her like a saint. . . . And she's a common —!"

I sat quite still on the sofa and let him rave, for the madder he got, the calmer and easier I got. Quite well I know that I have transgressed against all the recognised rules of morality and social order, and am a pariah, an outcast in the eyes of most people; but I know too that my life has been a great and poignant tragedy, and that if Ludwig had loved me with the infinite, pure, and sacred love of which I had believed him capable, he would have forgiven all and forgotten all in the greatness of his compassion for me. He would have seen in me a tragic figure, and in spite of everything would have taken me into his arms and his heart. And then I should have belonged to him utterly, – body and soul. . . . I should have been faithful to him to my last, last breath. I should have gone to the end of the world with him, starved with him, died for him! . . .

But his abusive fury proved to me that he is just the ordinary average European, whose dull Philistine perceptions never get further than the surface of things, never penetrate to the deep inner meaning of all that goes on around them. Behind my guilt stands the majesty of suffering. . . . But he could only see the sin!

Frau Adler rushed in, and said she would call the police, and he would have to pay damages, and she wouldn't keep me an hour longer, if these were the kind of lunatics I had for visitors.

Ludwig flung three gold coins on the table and took op his hat.

"I have lost all faith in human nature to-day!" he cried.

"But you have gained something in its place," I answered, coldly.
. . .

In the afternoon I went to Eimsbüttel, hoping to catch a glimpse of the child. It was a bitterly cold day. The damp chill of the air penetrated my clothing, and I shivered like a fox-terrier. I hardly hoped, either, for any success, for it wasn't likely that the child would be out in such weather." I was just going to turn back when the door of the Peters' abode opened, and the girl came out with Erica. She looked like a big French doll in her little white coat, with the great white hat on her black hair, and her kittle white gaiters and furry boots. I followed the pair at a little distance, and called the child by name. She looked round, evidently recognised me, and began to cry piteously, stretching up her little arms to her nurse. I must suppose that they have told the poor baby horrible things about me to frighten her, for she was apparently terrified at the sight of me; and the girl, who of course had her orders, took the little thing up in her arms and hurried off like lightning. I let them go, and went my way. I see now that it really is best to cross little Erica's path no more. In the evening I went to Berlin.

CHAPTER XI

MY arrival in Berlin didn't take place under very favourable auspices. I had a heavy cold, a cough, and a good deal of fever. I spent the night at the Hotel Belle Vue, and the next day I made my way to Frau Beidatsch in the Zimmerstrasse. The house looks immensely imposing outside, but the entrance hall is simply awful: pitch-dark stairs covered with shabby linoleum, common doors – in short, utterly vulgar. Frau Beidatsch lives on the second floor, and beside her name-plate there were three visiting cards nailed up. (Mine makes the fourth.)

Heinrich Beidatsch, Solicitor.
The Misses Blunck, Beauty Doctors, Masseuses, Manicurists.
Ella Ronach, Dancer.

I rang. Frau B. opened the door herself. A fat woman in a light-coloured cotton jacket, with a very powerful physique, a sharp-featured, sallow face, an incongruous pair of "nippers" on her nose, and long hands, so thin as to make a striking contrast with her corpulent form.

"What do you want?" she demanded. I introduced myself, and she let me in. "Oh! so you're from Old Anna, are you?" she cried. "Come in, Fräulein. We're a little casual here, but people soon learn to put up with us." And with that she led me into the kitchen, where a great pot of cabbage was boiling, and filling the whole place with its well-known perfume. Along the wall there stood a basket-sofa with a table in front of it, and on that I was obliged to sit down. "Now tell me," she went on, "what Old Anna has been doing."

I told her.

"She must have gone a pretty good pace to get into trouble, for she was always a bit of a dog, was Anna. And oh! she was a downy one! "Then she added: "We were schoolfellows and neighbours in the old days, you know."

I couldn't help comparing her with Kindermann when she said that. Good heavens I she does look a lot older; for Kindermann when she was dressed up really looked quite youthful, and almost like a lady! While we sat opposite one another, enwrapped with cabbage-fumes, I could see how sharply she was taking stock of me, and that gradually her thin face was assuming a more benevolent expression.

We talked of this, that, and the other, and at last I asked her if she happened to have a room vacant.

"For yourself?" she asked.

I said "Yes."

"Well, you've come in a good hour," said she. "Our very best room, the one that looks on the street and has a separate entrance, happens to be vacant. I don't let to everybody, I can tell you. I take only the better kind of ladies not the ones under Government Control. *My* ladies all have their own professions. What do you do? You'll have to specify something. Can you manicure, or massage, or will you go on the stage, or would you rather represent yourself as a nurse?"

I said that I was thinking of giving lessons in foreign languages, that I spoke French and English perfectly, and also Russian and Italian.

"Very good," she replied. "A teacher" of languages is very smart and original. Well, we'll put an advertisement in the directory for you. My son, who is a solicitor, will compose it. I'll call him in a minute."

I said I should like to see the rooms, so she waddled off in front of me and opened the door.

The room which we entered made a very poverty-stricken impression upon me at first sight, although it had a sort of shabby smartness about it. The curtains were dirty, the carpet was threadbare and dusty, the crimson plush furniture was faded. Along the wall stood a sofa with a greyish fur rug on it, and in the corner was the bed, behind a Spanish screen. I must confess that the idea of living in such a place appalled me.

"What is the price of the room?" I asked.

"A hundred and eighty marks inclusive."

I thought my ears had deceived me. A hundred and eighty marks! Then my board at Kindermann's, where I had a charming room, must have cost me literally nothing!

"Monthly?" I inquired.

"Of course. Did you think it was yearly?" she said, and laughed out loud.

"I think it's very dear," said I.

"Dear? Oh, come, Fräulein, you're joking. On the contrary, it's cheap. Think of the risks we run! You won't find anyone to take you for less. Such a stylish lady won't surely make a fuss about a few marks!"

I considered. I couldn't remain for long at the hotel. Perhaps at first it might be a good thing to have a room of this kind – poor enough in all conscience, but one about which no questions would be asked. . . . So I took it, and had my things sent over in the evening.

I was so utterly wretched that I couldn't think at all. The stove smoked in my room, the bedclothes smelt of chloral, and I heard people coming and going all night long. Next morning I wasn't able to get up; I was feverish and had a violent pain in my side. Frau Beidatsch brought me the manuscript copy of my advertisement, with my breakfast. It seemed to me rather strangely written. Like this: —

FRÄULEIN THYMIAN

Gotteball desires to give lessons
in English and French. Also
Russian and Italian.

I asked B. why the first two words were separated so prominently from the rest?

"Why, Fräulein, that's the tip," said she. "Otherwise how are the gentlemen to know? You'd be really taken for a mere teacher if it wasn't put like that. Here in Berlin things are very different – Hamburg's only a provincial town, after all."

I was so sick and weary that I couldn't be bothered saying anything. In the evening I had to send for the doctor, and he said I had inflammation of the lungs. The first day I lay in a sort of lethargy, but later I was frequently unconscious for hours at a time. In the intervals I felt dreadfully ill. My temperature went up to forty, and over. Quite apathetically I watched the figures which moved about my bed, when Frau B. was out of the room. There were two girls, one with red hair and the other with black, both very disheveled, and dressed alike in scarlet blouses and black skirts. The third was a small, very slender, fair-haired creature. All three ummaged among my things in the coolest manner, tried on my hats and coats and cloaks, and behaved as if they were already dividing my inheritance between them! Luckily the two boxes containing my jewelry were locked.

When, after three weeks' illness, I got a little better, I learned that they were my three fellow lodgers. I must confess that the two Blunck sisters, Molly and Dolly, were very kind and sympathetic and nice, often bringing me flowers and fruit, and always ready to do any little thing for me. The dancer she is in the chorus at the Apollo Theatre – I didn't like at all so well. . . . They all have pretty foul mouths: never in my life have I heard such language, although Kindermann, Connie, and all that lot were good at abuse. When they were sitting together in my room, they used to tell one another their adventures, and in this way I got a glimpse into a world and a life that hitherto I had had no conception of. Good God! but it's awful! The gentlemen with whom I had had to do *were* gentlemen, who never showed me any discourtesy nor let me feel that I – But here, where it's a mere question of marks and groschen . . . . ghastly!

My recovery was a slow one. I cried whole nights and days at a time. I had lost all courage. My surroundings humiliated me; I felt as though I had been flung into an abyss of degradation, and I longed to die. But as I gradually got better the desire for death left me. When I got up for the first time, though, I made a dreadful discovery. The box in which I kept my money had been opened with a false key, and the nine hundred marks which I had taken out of the bank at Hamburg had disappeared, as well as a diamond ring (my first one, given me by Glimm) and pin. I of course kicked up a row, but Frau B. got into a terrible state of mind and said I had better not dare to bring the police down upon her; she was no thief, and had no thieves in her house; her "honour" was the only capital she had (my God! then she must be a very poor woman!), and so forth. Of course it had been stolen in the hotel, and I'd never see it again. Hadn't the box been under my nose the whole time I had been with her? . . . The girls, too, implored me not to attract official attention to them, for they had enough to fear as it was. What could I do? I held my tongue; I wasn't anxious to have to do with the police myself. But it was really terrible. Nine hundred marks! Almost all the money I had in the world. When I had paid Frau B.'s bill, and the doctor's and the chemist's, I had exactly four marks twenty left. Frau B. advised me to pawn some of my winter things, as I wouldn't want them again this year. And I did. She herself took my Persian lamb coat and the sable muff that Ludwig gave me, to the pawnbroker's, and actually brought back three hundred and thirty marks! I was glad! I don't know who can have stolen the money and the two ornaments; perhaps it really did happen at the hotel. I have no suspicion of the girls or of Frau B. either, but I shouldn't be surprised if it was her son, the so-called solicitor. He's an ugly, horrid creature, with fawning manners. But so far as I know he was never alone in my room. Well, lost is lost; and, luck is luck. If I get the things again, I'll believe in mine!

The first effect of my advertisement, so to speak, was a quite young lad, an unfledged creature, who wanted to go to extremities at once, and behaved altogether so impossibly that I kicked him out. So he went a doorway further on, and got manicured by Molly and Dolly. They shouted with laughter at me, and said I was a great goose. Later came a few more clients, whom I should have liked to kick in solid earnest, but in the end, I – didn't.

I have put another advertisement in two of the good papers, through which I hope to get some genuine pupils – male or female. Often I positively long for something to do, for some decent employment, and, above all, for some educated human being to talk with. This intercourse with the girls is simply frightful. Molly and Dolly come of poor but respectable parents, and were shopgirls in Wertheim. One day they came to know a woman who did manicuring, and invited them to visit her (*a la* Anna Kindermann). And so it went on, from one little thing to another, exactly as it did with me. In the end, this woman induced them to pick locks and steal things out of the shop, and they were found out and got four months. When they came out, they resolved to stick together and give themselves out as sisters. As they are always dressed exactly alike, they go in their own circle by the name of "The Ponies." They often wanted me to go with them in the evenings, but I *couldn't*. I've never yet gone on the streets, as they do. . . .

I often walk in the Thiergarten. It's so lovely there now. But the fresh green and the spring breezes make me melancholy. The world is so fair – and life is so foul!

. . . .

August 18th, '93.

A heat fit to kill one. The pavements are positively scorching, and the air is like a puff of flame. How I envy the people who can get away to the sea or the country! I can't, for I have no money. I think I'm like a frigate that has been wrecked, and is now being unrigged to make an inglorious end as a collier. But I should be glad if I could *feel* like a collier! That's the tragedy with me. I can't attain to the moral lethargy which is absolutely essential to a life such as the Ponies lead. No one could do it with full consciousness, with awakened mind that's totally unthinkable.

So pretty nearly all my jewelry is at the pawn-broker's. Every week a fresh bit finds its way there, and I don't know what will be the end of it all. I had a few pupils of both sexes, but after the first few lessons they sent me my fees and didn't come again. The *milieu* didn't suit them, I suppose, and I don't wonder!

I'm not really better of my illness, either. The heat pulls me down altogether. I look awful – a perfect skeleton. Once or twice I took a "businesswalk" – a walk for customers. . . . But nothing came of it. I don't know why. The Ponies say that I look too haughty and distinguished and that no one would dare come up to me. Perhaps that may be it.

I am so feeble, so enervated by this heat! Day after day I lie, half-dressed, on the long chair, and dream the time away. I live as economically as possible, so as to eke out my money, but one must eat. And the rent mounts up so. I am terrified of the future. Beidatsch is often very insolent and offensive; probably she is afraid of losing by me – a quite groundless anxiety, since she always demands her money the very second it's due, and I should infallibly be kicked out if I didn't pay on the nail.

The precious "solicitor" sometimes hangs about, trying to induce me to go on the streets. Yesterday evening he was with me, and went on the same tack. "Such a pretty lady as you are, with such fine stylish clothes and such international attractions, would have to choose the best places – the Linden or the Kurfursten Quay," he said. "Those streets are paved with gold for such as you. Most of the girls here are such cattle. . . ."

I have written to K. and R, but had no answers. With them it's out of sight out of mind.

If only it wasn't so infernally hot! Often a frantic longing for the long-ago time of my youth possesses me. I feel so frightfully old. A maddening home-sickness, as it were, for our lovely quiet garden, with the moonlight on the tall white lilies and the red roses – oh! it comes right over me! ... home-sickness for mother's grave, for the wide green country and the silver mists, and the cool, mysterious evenings when the folks sit under the broad-branched lime trees, laughing and talking, while a horse neighs now and then from the meadows, or a sleepy cow lows softly. . . . Gone, gone! Past and gone! lost for ever!

.   .   .   .

Once I've got some money again I mean to send Osdorff his fare home, and tell him to come to me. I've made up my mind to do it. The poor fellow is having a poor time: he actually suffers hunger. His family don't help him at all; I suppose they don't want to have him on their shoulders again. I think it's contemptible and shabby of them. He writes me the most grievous letters. As soon as I have some money, he shall get two hundred marks out of it.

Other people keep a dog or a bird; why shouldn't I keep a poor boy like that, for the sake of his company? Decidedly poor old Casimir would be more agreeable to me than the usual "Louis," who thinks he can play the lord and master over us women – for I've gone on the streets. There was nothing else for me to do.

Old Kindermann got a year and a half. They couldn't substantiate the worst charge against her, so she escaped the House of Correction by the skin of her teeth.

Things are going tolerably with me now. I've been able to take some of my jewelry out of pawn. My old power of fascination seems to work again. I have so many aspirants that I often have to disappoint some of them. In the evenings at Keek's, or at the "National," they swarm like flies round a honey-pot. When once I thoroughly realised that I had sunk beyond retrieval, I threw my last remaining scruples overboard. I often pretend to myself that I am dead, and that the people among whom I now live are corpses. And so they are. They have breathed away their souls – *they have expired*; and they prove by their existence that no one can possibly *live* I write "live" advisedly – without something which can be called by the name of soul.

My knowledge of languages is very useful to me. I often get, by means of it, very rich foreigners who pay well and that's the principal thing for me nowadays. Last night I had a Russian who couldn't speak a word of German; he gave me three hundred marks. "The Ponies" have had luck, too. Molly, in October, made at some bar the acquaintance of an American who offered her a settled engagement for a year. She told him that she would not leave her "sister," and then he engaged the two of them; that is, he has taken rooms for them in the Taubenstrasse and gives them four hundred marks a month; and he is only in Berlin four months out of the year, so they have all the rest of the time to themselves.

Truly I have learnt a deal. At first it appalled me, although I had at Anna Kindermann's a pretty stiff preliminary training. In this world of corpses, the corruption fills the atmosphere, and one has simply to get accustomed to it. The nausea gradually leaves one. These women, and the men they have to do with, are a regularly organised class, and on the whole there is a certain solidarity of interests. There's no perceptible outward difference between the "Government-Control" women and us. *Halbseidenen* – that is the designation for those who are not so "controlled." Of course every *Halbseidene* is frightfully worried and beset by the Public Morality Legislation; not indeed that the "Controls" entirely escape either from the frantic terror of imprisonment. The investigations in themselves are not so bad; it's the hideous difficulty of shaking off the supervision afterwards that scares us. And then, the question of finding a place to live in! That's a ghastly business. It's bad enough for us to find a roof for our heads, but with the "Controls," it's a real terror to have to look for rooms. I really do lodge cheaply. Most of us pay seven or eight marks a day, often much more. The landlady runs a tremendous risk, you see; for if a girl has any trouble with the police, the landlady always lives in the fear of a criminal charge being brought against herself.

I often wonder, when the laws to a certain extent sanction the profession by instituting the "Control," why they don't arrange for the domicile of the women. The outrageous charges for lodging are dreadfully hard to earn; for many, quite impossible. We must dress well, and the life is expensive in lots of other ways besides. For example, I pay income-tax on four thousand marks of income, and am described as a teacher of languages. Do the returning officers really imagine that a teacher of languages in the Zimmerstrasse could possibly earn that? Or have they their own private convictions on the point? Who knows?

People who have no intimate knowledge of these circles think quite erroneously of the relations which prevail between the men and women. I used to think myself that a "Louis" was simply a man who acted as a kind of agent, finding a clientele, protecting the girls against unprofitable or too brutal customers, drawing such men's attention to their obligations of adequate payment, and acting in general as a kind of slave-owner to the women. So he does; but nearly always the relation of the woman to her so-called *souteneur* is simply that of mistress and lover. It is easy enough to see why. Every "girl" has a bit of the woman in her – the woman with her need for dependence, her longing for love, which can find no outlet in the purely professional sexual intercourse of her trade. I myself am like that. What would I not give to have one, just one man in the world who belonged to me, to whom I could cling, of whom I knew that he was there for me and I for him! But then, on the other hand, I could never make up my mind to attach myself to one of these men; most of them ought to be shot at sight.

They would make an interesting study. The creatures are recruited from all classes – *mauvais sujets*, of course, without exception. No decent man would let himself be kept by such means. Scarcely one of them has any occupation, but they have their own clubs, their gymnastic and athletic associations, and they hang about in bars all day long.

Once or twice a fellow of that kind has tried to fasten himself on to me; but I begged to be excused – oh! quite politely, quite in the way of good fellowship! It's bad business to quarrel with these gentry. There is one in particular, " Jew-Frederick" why he's called so I know not; but both men and women have the queerest nicknames in this sphere of life who always comes and sits beside me in the Cafe Keck. He is really an LL.D. – he's shown me his papers; has practised at the Bar, was assessor once, and got kicked out. *He* says it was because a woman ruined him; but I think it was much more likely to have been on account of drink, for he drinks shockingly, and is "blind" every night by twelve o'clock. But before he has got to that stage of intoxication he is quite interesting to talk to; one can see that he's an educated person and a clever man, too. So I rather wonder that his young woman should be, as she is, an utterly common creature; it seems as if he ought to be able to get some one a little better if he chose.

Certainly not me! I wouldn't touch a swine like that with a pair of tongs

In our half-world there are quite as many castes and cliques as in the other. The Upper Four Hundred are those who are entirely kept by a rich friend. I ought really to belong to them, and so I might have, if Ludwig hadn't taken up that crazy idea of separation and marriage, or if I hadn't been such a blazing idiot as to blurt out my confession in his face. One *is* a fool sometimes. . . . Well, between those who have a "friend" and belong to him alone (I am looking out for something of that kind), there is a whole range of gradation down to the very last of the last those who sell themselves for a mark or less. . . Oh! it's not lovely anywhere, but down there it's beyond expression ghastly.

God! the whole thing. . . When I think of it like that, a text seems to jingle in my ear, as if it had been written expressly for us: "*The sorrows of mankind encompass me round about. . . .*"

Finally, to sum up, there hangs over every single denizen of this half-world a lurid, heavy cloud of tragedy and despair. . . Certainly there are girls amongst us who have fallen by their own fault, frivolously and guiltily fallen, but I maintain that *not one* has ever plunged into this mire with full consciousness of what she was doing. I know now many, many women who live only by the barter of their bodies; but I also know, beyond a shadow of doubt, that there are not five in a hundred of them who would not grasp eagerly at an opportunity of getting back to a decent life. There is so much philanthropy and humanity in the world – there are crèches for the children, almshouses for the old, refuges for the criminal, and God knows how many other forms of benevolence – bazaars, theatricals, dances, for the good of the suffering fellow-creature; but into this nether-world of profoundest darkness, uttermost misery, scarcely there falls a ray of loving-kindness, of pity, of real effectual help. How many of us long to be "saved"! But saved, not in reformatories, not in rescue-homes, in Magdalen asylums – no! Not condescendingly will we be lifted up, not with the shibboleth of superior virtue upon our "rescuer's" lips – "Lord, I thank thee that I am not as other men are" – and all the rest of it.

No one would be crazy enough to try the other way! . . . There it is! To change us, to bring us back from this way of life, there would have to be a new system altogether, an entire upsetting of all established ideas and arrangements. Our fellow-creatures would have to put off the old Adam, and cast away their former opinions like worn-out rags. The barriers would have to fall. Did not the ancient Greeks actually celebrate their *hetaïrai*, and the Phoenicians reverence them as priestesses? In those days it was the best and wisest, the fairest and most cultivated of their sex, who were in the service of Venus – and assuredly those people of antiquity were no less civilised than their fellows of a later day. There is no doubt that every woman ought to be free to do what she likes with her own body. Why must the great tribunal of public opinion be set up to crush her who does differently from the rest into an abyss of infamy and contempt? If the profession of yielding the body ceased to be a shameful one, the army of "unfortunates" would diminish by four-fifths – I will go farther, and say by nine-tenths. Myself, for example! How gladly would I take a situation as companion or governess; and I'll be damned – yes, damned! – if I wouldn't put my whole soul into being as good a one as I could, or if I'd ever dream of having anything to do (in that way) with a man again. But apart from the fact that it would be simply a marvel of marvels if one of us women were to get such a situation, there's the further trouble that, if one did, the sword would be for ever suspended over one's head, and as soon as it fell – in other words, as soon as the past became known – one would simply be kicked out with ignominy, and fall deeper in the mire than before. If our condition of *hetaïrai* was no disgrace, and if the return to decent occupations was open to us, the greater number of those who had even for a short time experienced the miseries of this life, would go back gladly. But the doors are locked behind us. "Abandon hope, all ye who enter here."

What enrages me most of all is when these Philistines bring their wives with them to the night-cafe's, and they sit there and whisper and laugh and jeer, and don't know how sufficiently to impress upon us the difference between themselves with their perfect and impregnable respectability, their unimpeachable morality, and us poor devils. I wish I could spit in their silly faces! As if any one of them knew anything of what life is, and suffering is! What do they know of the night-side of existence, where our poor bodies are wearing away? Oh! I should like to cry out and say to them: "Look to yourselves! You have not finished yet – perhaps you have daughters, and death will summon you away from them; and they may sit here one day and be wounded by the cruelty of eyes as scornful as yours. . ." I should like to see the face of one of the many ladies who "do good works" if somebody were to suggest to her to engage a woman from the National Café as help or nurse! Goodness! How she'd toss her head and shiver, and protest against "such ideas"! I wouldn't give *that* for Christian love and benevolence, and the rest of their rubbish. Human beings are all beasts and brutes under one disguise or another.

There's one girl at the National who particularly interests me. They call her Duda. She has very remarkable flaxen hair with red-gold ends, and although she's not bad-looking, she makes a lamentable, downtrodden sort of impression upon one. Her "man" is doing time. She told me lately that he used to regale her with kicks when she didn't take home enough money, and at last gave her such a terrific one that he injured her womb. (I paid for coffee for her once or twice.) She refused to testify against him, but the doctor's depositions got him five months. Now she's waiting for him to come out, and is in terror at the prospect, and yet longs for him, and gets furious if anyone says anything against him.

There are many very *chic* girls here, but few that are really beautiful.

Enough for to-day.

CHAPTER XII

January 8th, 1894.

I ALWAYS come back to my little Book – I don't know why. I often pretend to myself that it's a real living being for me to talk with, a dear, faithful friend, the only one I have in the world. And I delight in writing down my experiences and ideas. I have written to Osdorff to wish him a Happy New Year, and I think I'll be able to send him the money to come home by the spring. Then I mean to find rooms elsewhere and take him with me. . . . All the experiences one has! Fresh ones almost every night but seldom pleasant ones. I am so nervous that I twitch all over sometimes, as if I had St. Vitus' Dance, and often I feel a desperate desire to scold and be abusive, and fling things about and make a row generally. For this is a hideous life but one can't get out, one can't get out! One is walled up in it, and there's never an exit, there's only a window high, high up, and it isn't the sweet sky that one sees in it, but some leaden grey vault that seems to frown over one. . . .

Lately I was sitting in the National with Duda and Keitsche, at a table near the fountain; close by sat two gentlemen, one with a long black beard and a pair of gold "nippers," and the other an old porpoise with a red, pimply nose. The old chap threw a mark-piece into the water, and I stretched my arm down and fished it out. Then he threw in another and another, and Duda came along too, and fished, and then he flung in piece after piece – marks and five groschen and tenpenny-bits, and the whole lot of girls came streaming up, and each tried to get in front of the others, and the old fellow laughed till he shook like a jelly, and got the waiter to bring him a lot of change expressly for this game. In the tumult, "Gold-fish Elsie" lost her tail of false hair, and thought that I'd done it; so in her rage she went behind me and dragged the hairpins out of my head, thinking of course that the same thing would happen to me. But she was jolly well mistaken! Down rolled my streams of hair all over my back, and then got loose, and I shook them out with a will, and stood there, wrapped from neck to hem as in a loose dark garment. How they all gaped! People came from everywhere to look at the miracle; and the tall dark man (who hadn't stirred all the time, but just sat there indifferent and apart, with his hand in his pocket) now got up and gazed at my hair, and said: "Magnificent! Magnificent! You'd do for an advertisement of a hair-wash, my girl." . . . I made a face at him, for the word "girl" wasn't at all to my taste – I don't know why, for I'm not precisely accustomed nowadays to be spoken to with ceremony. All the other girls were envious, and that delighted me, and I let my hair hang loose the whole evening, and everyone who came near me wanted to feel it and pull it about, but I wouldn't have it, and insisted that everyone who wanted to play tricks must first pay five marks; and I soon had as much as sixty, with which I bought myself next day a Paris hat with yellow feathers.

The funny thing was that I couldn't help looking every minute at the dark man, and the more I looked at him the better I liked him. He had such a beautiful profile – an aquiline nose and magnificent brown eyes, and exquisitely beautiful hands, white and firm and smooth. I wanted him to come with me, and wouldn't have anyone else, and after a while he did come and sit at my table, and the old fellow came bleating up too. I found out that the dark one is a doctor; and afterwards he actually said that he would take me home. And I – idiot! instead of taking my chance – got cross and rapped out a "No!" and he laughed and said, carelessly, "Very well, then, I won't, my dear!" and paid and went off. And I was wild with rage; and a horrid boy of some sort hung on to me, and there I was but I thought of the handsome man all night. I am only writing this down because it's really the very first time in my life that I've had any desire for any particular man. I can't stop thinking of him; I want very much to see him again, and I won't let him escape me next time. But I'm like that unaccountable even to myself. All of a sudden, something stands up in me and says: "No, no! Not that! "It's as if somebody else were speaking and I have to do what that somebody says, and not what I want to do myself. That's how it is.

. . . .

February 14th.

It is really too extraordinary. Yesterday I saw the dark doctor again. He was sitting in the window at Kranzler's, Unter den Linden. I went in and sat down at his table. He looked sideways at me over his newspaper and pretended not to recognise me. In a few minutes there arrived a "flapper" with a jam-puff, and sat down beside him, and from their conversation I made out that she was his daughter. So I saw that nothing was to be done there paid, and departed; but waited outside till he appeared with the girl. I meant to follow him and see where he went, and he noticed it and put the flapper into a cab, and then came straight up to me. "Well, my child." he said, "do you want anything?"

I snapped my lips together and said not a word. He walked beside me a long time, as far as Brandenburg Gate.

"Your lovely hair has bewitched me," he said. "I should like to see it again."

"So would plenty of other people," said I.

He laughed. "You're tremendously business-like. The way you made money out of the beauty of your hair was most amusing. And you were perfectly right. If a man wants to see something worth seeing he must be prepared to pay for it. . . . Well, I'm a sober, steady sort of man, and being a doctor I've not much time for nightly adventures. With professional ladies I don't as a rule have anything to do; but your hair interests me. I'm prepared to spend twenty marks on seeing it again. Will you show it to me?"

"You may whistle for it, old Pill-box, old Camomile Tea-pot," said I, as nastily as I could, for again his phrase "professional" had made me wince; it was like a blunt saw on my nerves. "Professional yourself! Aren't you a professional corpse-maker?"

"Oh, come, come! Not so sharp, please," replied he; "I don't want to annoy you, and fair play's a jewel, so you mustn't annoy me. Adieu, my lady." And with that he was gone. And I stood there, swallowing my wrath and my disgust at myself. When I got home I slashed old Beidatsch's table-cover to pieces with rage, and had to pay five thaler for it, though the dirty thing wasn't worth fifty pence. . . .

Certainly one does have amazing experiences "on the road." About a week ago I was in a dancing-saloon one evening, and an old fogey hung round me the whole time, wanting to get in with me, and I couldn't succeed in shaking him off. At first I didn't pay any attention to him, for I saw that there was no business to be done in that quarter. He was quite nicely turned out, with a dash of smartness even, but there was no money in it. His coat was rather shabby at the seams, and his linen and his tie were clean and tidy, but not up to the mark. I took him in at a glance: an old reduced aristocrat, a worn-out rake nothing more and nothing less.

"Leave me alone, you old ass! You're spoiling my market," I said. "An ancient hack like Cimbria is good enough for you. Look! she's sitting up there, watching you. . . ."

But he wouldn't leave my side, and protested over and over again that I was the prettiest woman he had ever seen.

"And you may be proud of that when *I* say it. I've been all over the world, and seen and known and possessed all the loveliest women on God's earth. I've always had the loveliest ones – the exquisites! no matter where – at the *Moulin Rouge*, or Vienna, or Madrid, or Petersburg, and, last not least, Dresden."

"Where lovely girls grow on the trees," said I.

He shook his head sadly and clicked his tongue. "Those were the days of the Brunswick woman Minna's house in the Jüdenhof. I assure you she had the rarest beauties of all Europe in her rooms. Unfortunately she was turned out of Dresden. Afterwards she set up a sort of chapel-of-ease, as one might say, in Riga, but it was never up to the Dresden level."

"'*In those days*,' I suppose you had more cash than you have now?" said I, looking the little fellow up and down. Upon that he pulled a twenty-mark piece out of his pocket.

"Look at that! It's a kind of curiosity. These twenty marks are the last of six hundred thousand of their sisters that have slipped through my fingers. I took forty years to do it, so you perceive that I'm a sensible, level-headed fellow. What do you say? Shall we 'run the fox to covert[2]' in a bottle of Roderer?"

"An idea of Schiller's!" said I, for the old man was beginning to interest me. So we sat in a corner upstairs, and he told me that he had had an un-encumbered estate in Silesia, and a country-seat in Westphalia, and a villa in Steiermark, and every one of them was gone, and the twenty marks were the last of his capital! Now he was to get two hundred marks income from his relatives "too much to die on, too little to live on," as he says. And he showed me the photographs of his former possessions and various papers relating to them, so I saw that he was telling the truth.

---

[2] "Fuchs" is also the German for "gold coin," so there is a play on words here, untranslatable into English.

"And you've chucked them all away!"

He nodded gaily.

"I'm not a bit sorry. If I were to wish for them back, it would only be so that I might give them to you to-night; unfortunately, I haven't for the moment anything at all to present you with. . . ." But as he put the papers back into his pocket-book, he kept one back. "Nevertheless, I'm still a landed proprietor. This here is the purchase-deed of a grave in the Schoneberg cemetery. I bought it ten years ago and have had a railing put up, which cost six hundred marks. There was a stone too, but that I changed my mind about, and got rid of."

"Well, then, you have something to present me with," said I.

"What! the burying-place?"

"Yes. Why not?" I answered. "We, too, would like to know where the worms are to eat us." I lighted a cigarette and ordered some champagne on my own account. "Come, I'll make you a friendly offer," I continued. "I'll give you five free passes for this place, and for that you shall make over to me your landed property in the Schoneberg cemetery."

"What a mad idea!" grinned the old man.

"What's mad about it?" I asked. "I should like to know where they'll plant me some day."

He wouldn't agree at all for some time, but I persisted; at first only for fun, but afterwards in earnest. And before I realised it the bargain was made. I got the Schoneberg ground with the railing complete, and he got ten passes. A crazy bargain!

"Yes," said I. "But who's to certify me that the thing's all square on your side?"

"My word of honour! Hang it, I'm a gentleman!" said he, smiting his breast. A whole crowd of witnesses were present at the striking of the bargain, and at least twenty bocks must have celebrated it. A couple of days later I got the deed, made out in my name. The old man had been princely enough to pay for the alteration out of his own pocket. So now I am the proprietor of a burying-place! I have been out there several times, the first time with him. He says he has a lien also on a burying-place on his own manor. I was glad to hear that, for otherwise I should have been distressed at depriving him of his last possession. The grating is very handsome, and there's a pretty weeping-willow over it. In the spring I'll have a seat put there, and a stone, and I'll plant ivy and flowers. My acquaintances laugh loudly at me, and say I must be mad. But it amuses me. I will lay out a regular little garden and spend hours there in the summer.

.   .   .   .

March 8th, 1894.

These last few weeks I've been doing tremendous business. I had an Englishman, who was staying at the Hotel Bristol, and was clean off his head about me, and threw his money away in handfuls when he took me out. Once he spent four hundred marks on champagne in a dancing-hall, and I got my ten per cent, from the waiter for that. He bought me every single thing we saw! One day we spent twelve hundred marks at Wertheim's on toilet-things alone! Most of them were no good at all to me, and I got rid of them at a profit afterwards. Every evening he gave me two hundred mark notes, and I sent off two of them to Osdorff for his passage home. I should have liked to send him more, but I was afraid that he might spend all the money and not come home at all. What I sent was just enough for the 'tween-decks. Except for that, I don't care a bit for money, it slips through my fingers so! I shall never again be capable of saving.

About a week ago I had a bad time of it. Some infernal spy must have been watching me, for I was summoned to the police court, and the Commissioner, or whatever he was, spoke very roughly to me, and I was called upon to state my means of support.

"Why, I'm a teacher of languages," said I.

"You will have to convince us of that," he shouted at me, and said other things of the same kind. And I was required to furnish corroborative testimony from three persons of unimpeachable character who would affirm that I lived by teaching languages. That wasn't by any means agreeable news to me, for where was I to find the three "unimpeachable persons"? In the evening I told it all to Jew-Frederick, who knows something about the law, and he told it to the others, and they all talked it over as eagerly as if it was their own affair and not mine at all. Well, how shall I put it? In three days I had my three "unimpeachables," taking their oaths that I gave lessons in languages, and that they were my pupils at two marks an hour – and it all passed off beautifully, but of course I'll have to be careful. It's certainly very nice the way people here stick by one when one's in a tight place. In these circles one can arrange for almost any possible situation. There are a lot of women who actually live by what is called "announcing" alone. That means that they "announce" a certain person as being on a visit to them, and get three marks for it, while all the time the person in question is not living there at all. Lately, a woman picked my pocket of my purse with forty marks in it and two subscriptions for hairdressing and manicure, and I was after her, but couldn't find her at first because she had been "announced"; later on I caught her, but never got anything back. Nothing can be done here by force. The lodging-house keepers do the best business of all. In the first place, they get very high rents, and then there are any amount of pickings. For instance, if a woman is in difficulties she usually begins by offering to sell her valuables to the landlady, who buys them for a mere song and passes them on to someone else another "girl," of course generally with a good twenty-five per cent, profit, I needn't say!

Beidatsch has feathered her nest well. She has more diamonds than I have. She means shortly to give up business and take a little place in Pankow. I shall be on the move, too, as soon as Casimir arrives. Later on, I think I should like to go in for letting rooms.

.   .   .   .

May 22nd, 1894.

I have been ill again. I caught a beastly cold in Hamburg, where I went to meet Casimir. The doctor says my heart is weak, and that I must go to Nauheim in the summer. Luckily, I've scraped together enough to be able to do it, and if necessary I can pawn some of my jewelry. Casimir has cost me a lot of money. I had to clothe him from head to foot; he was positively in rags. At first I was a little bit afraid that he might take it badly when I gave him the necessary explanations, but he is really even stupider and more indifferent than I had supposed. His stupidity approaches idiocy. So long as he has the money he doesn't care a bit where it comes from. I had hoped to be able to keep him out of the *souteneur* set, but it was impossible. He's "right in" now; they've even nicknamed him. His designation is Fliebenheinrich, on account of his somewhat prominent underlip. His only anxiety is that his relatives may discover him. In some respects he's extraordinarily cunning. Often I find him inexpressibly repulsive, and I don't know myself what I see in him, for one can't even talk to him sensibly and yet, I shouldn't like to do without him.

I live now in the Markgrafenstrasse, and have a beautiful big room looking on the street, and a bedroom for Osdorff, and I pay three hundred and sixty marks a month, that is, twelve marks a day. The land-lady is a very sensible, nice woman – she's not married – who has had very bad luck and been in trouble twice about her rooms. She has a restaurant-keeper as her friend, who stands by her when she wants him; but she says it's a poor business after all, and she means to marry just for form's sake, so that the police may leave her alone. She has a lodger, a poor silly consumptive creature who may die at any moment, and she's going to marry him. They're by way of being engaged now. In the middle of June the ceremony will come off.

I have put my Schöneberg property in perfect order. There's a comfortable seat under the willows, and there are flower-beds in the four corners, and in the autumn I'll have a stone put up. I often go out there between six and seven o'clock in the evening when it's fine, and sit there a while and lose myself in dreams and fancies, and think how sweet it would be if one could just fall asleep there, on a fair May evening like this, and never wake up again, or else wake up to a new life in which one would be a new person altogether, and could begin again from the beginning.

Close beside my plot is a new-made grave, to which there comes an elderly woman in deep mourning. She never weeps, but one can see that she grieves inexpressibly. One evening we got into conversation, and she told me that she had a piano-manufactory, and was a widow, and that her only surviving son – just seventeen! – had died last March. She sometimes sits beside me on the bench, and has asked me to go and see her, which of course I shan't think of doing. It's better not to; I should be sure to be found out before long.

Sometimes I am so weary that I think I am not going to live much longer. I look wretched so wretched that I have had to take to rouge, which I hate, for rosy cheeks don't suit me.

Molly and Dolly won thirty thousand marks in the lottery, and disappeared one day without a word to anybody. The day before yesterday they wrote to say they had taken a little cottage in Thüringia and were going to start a business. How wise they are! I wish I could get a big bit of luck like that and escape! And then oh! never again, never again ! . . . I am as happy as a child over my landed property. It's too pretty in the evenings, when the birds are singing in the trees, and the whistling and clanging and noise and tumult of the streets seems to fall away from one, as if one had nothing to do with it, as if one were set free from the restless world, like a stone that has been loosed from a ring and were hanging like a dewdrop, pure and still, upon the Tree of Peace in the Kingdom of the Free, the kingdom of those who sleep. When one goes back to the streets, after a time like that, the contrast is overwhelming; it almost turns one sick. . . . It is a source of some satisfaction to me that I have never been spoken to insultingly in the streets. Almost all my "colleagues" bear the stamp of their profession on their faces. One can see what their business is by a peculiar look about the mouth and eyes. I have a horror of this hall-mark of degradation. I study myself daily in the glass, and, thank God! I haven't discovered it yet. I think it's because I keep my spirit apart from the functions of my body. I read many books – good ones, enlightening ones; just at present I'm trying Nietzsche's **Zarathustra**, but I don't understand the greater part of it. . . . Well, so I try to live as if my spirit and my body were two quite separate identities; but the spirit pays its rent to the body by stamping its own impress upon the countenance, so that not yet can the living corpse I am be recognised as a corpse.

Ah, my dears! how happy the dead people are out there!

. . . .

June 18th, 1894.

We had a wedding yesterday. Oh, my goodness gracious me! What a wedding! The registrar shook his head, they say, every time he looked at the bridegroom. The poor fellow could hardly stand. He's eaten up with consumption; he can barely drag himself about; his wrists are as thin as pen-handles, and there isn't an ounce of flesh on his bones. During the official ceremony he got a fit of coughing, and a hæmorrhage came on, and the registrar asked the company if it would not be better to give up the arrangement, for it was a mere mockery. . . . When they came home the young bridegroom had to go straight to bed, and we celebrated the occasion without him – twenty of us – till two o'clock this morning, and made so merry that the servant was able to clean out the room with the champagne that had been spilt – there was no need to use water.

At last I have found my dark man again, and I've really got hold of him this time. I met him in the Bellevuestrasse, and went up to him and apologised for my recent rudeness. He smiled and shook his head. "I wasn't offended with you, dear lady"; and we went into the Thiergarten together, and talked to one another of all sorts of things, like a gentleman and lady, things that girls of my sort as a rule never dream of talking about with men; they are not interested in them. To my great contentment I noticed that his interest in me was increasing every moment. We sat down on a seat in the gardens and went on talking, and I told him all sorts of details and episodes of my present life; and then he told me about himself. He is a doctor and has a very large practice, is happily married and has four healthy, well-grown children, two girls and two boys; but he is suffering from nerves through overwork, and he says he needs an occasional relief from the strain amusement, distraction, whatever you like to call it, and had been long seeking for a passing acquaintanceship. Would I permit him to visit me now and then in the afternoons, between six and eight o'clock? I gave him my card, and he came the next day. I have never before looked forward so eagerly to a visit, or enjoyed one so much as I enjoyed his. While he was with me I realised for the first time that I am genuinely in love with the man. When he wanted to give me money I refused it and all of a sudden I had flung both of my arms round him and kissed him right on the lips from sheer love, and begged him to take me wholly for himself, and I would live only for him. And he drew me down on the divan and pushed my hair off my forehead with such a soft, tender movement, and told me that he could not, without wronging his family, give me more than two hundred and fifty marks a month, and if I agreed to that it would be all right. And he told me, too, that his wife had suffered so shockingly in her confinement last August that they were obliged for the present to live like brother and sister, for a couple of years it might be. . . . So I knew beyond question that I was to be only a make-shift, and that Doctor W— thought no differently from other men about me; and it was so fearfully bitter to me in that moment that I nearly got cross and rude again, but I controlled myself, and he promised to come and see me another time.

When he was going he looked at the books on my writing-table, and he was surprised to find works by Storm and Fontane and Kellar lying there.

"Do you read these, or are they only for show?" he inquired.

"I read them."

"Don't they bore you? Wouldn't you rather have an exciting story?"

"I have stories enough of my own," I answered.

He shook his head and said: "I saw from the first you weren't like the rest of them; but I think you've got even more in you than I guessed."

"Oh, rubbish!" said I. And then he went away.

I thought over the question of the two hundred and fifty marks. . . . Oh! it would be *too lovely*! But it cannot be; I couldn't do with only that much, especially now that I've got Casimir on my hands. For as I've dragged him over here, it's only fair that I should look after him. It's absolutely unthinkable that he should ever be able to keep himself. The most horrible part of it is that he has lately begun to drink too much. Fortunately, he's not quarrelsome in his cups, only just as limp as a wet cloth. The other day I gave him a few good boxes on the ear when he came home like that, and he began to whimper like a little child. It disgusted me, made me feel very nearly sick, but in the end I couldn't help laughing. I keep him tight enough as regards pocket-money, but if I give him a mark or so for supper and beer in the evening, he eats almost nothing and drinks the lot. He is not really healthy; his big body isn't proportionally strong – he has only bones and fat, no flesh, no muscles.

CHAPTER XIII

THE Doctor will come and see me in Nauheim, which I'm very glad of. I go there next week. I love the Doctor; I long for him all the time. It gives me intense pleasure to kiss him – passionately – madly. . . I should like to belong to him wholly. There is nothing I could not do for his sake. I wish that he returned my love, but he doesn't. The only thing that consoles me is that he evidently takes a genuine interest in me. Sometimes I think he pities me: his voice often sounds so tender, and his caresses are so gentle and so dear.

.   .   .   .

It was charming in Nauheim, though the Doctor did not keep his promise, but went with his family to Zoppot. The baths did me a lot of good, and I should like to have stayed there longer, but my money ran out – it goes infernally quick in that sort of place. I enjoyed myself very much, and was glad to find a big bunch of roses from the Doctor awaiting me here on my return. . . . But then came the tug of war! Casimir has regularly gone on the bend during the weeks I have been away, or so my land- lady tells me. He knocked about with women every night of his life, never came in till all hours, and then lay drunk in bed for days together. And that's what's called a *man!* He's nothing but a brute-beast. It seems the creature has taken up with a drab from the Chaussee-strasse. I went to look her up on Monday. If she'll take him on as her "Louis" I shall be glad of it; 'twill rid me of him. Unfortunately, I didn't find her; she had been arrested a couple of days before, and was in the women's prison at X—. With the landlady in the kitchen were sitting two wretched creatures who had come out of prison that morning, and were telling most lamentable tales of all they had suffered there. The wardress never spoke to them without some filthy epithet on her lips; and one of them had had a bed which had been left in an unspeakable condition by the former occupant, and which the newcomer was obliged to take just as it was; and they had nearly starved, too, they said. I must confess that it all sounded a good deal exaggerated to me. I can't believe that in such an institution, where they have every kind of resource at command, things can be quite so swinish as all that. But indeed as regards the starvation, it was plain enough that *that* had been their lot, for how they tucked into the dry crusts she gave them! I felt so sorry for them that I gave them each three marks, though I was quite hard-up for the moment and owed a fortnight's rent. My big room was let while I was away, but when I came back the land-lady at once gave the other people notice, and took me right back. I'm only afraid now that Casimir will do something stupid and be led into some prank that will land him in the punishment-cells for a few weeks. . . . One can have everything in the world for money. I must be wise now and make some more. It is hideous! The Doctor gave me a hundred marks yesterday, but that's not much good.

September 18th, 1894.

Yesterday I was at the Exhibition with the Doctor. We drove out in a droschky, and wandered through the rooms. I love to see beautiful pictures, or indeed anything beautiful. I was particularly delighted with one landscape – a cornfield so entirely overrun by poppies that nothing was to be seen of the golden ears of wheat, only the garish scarlet of the flowers was visible.

"That must be an allegorical picture," I said.

"How do you mean?" asked the Doctor, pushing up his nippers.

"I think the painter meant to show us how it is well that the poppies of oblivion should flame forth above the daily bread of this dreary, dreary life and illumine it with their brilliant scarlet glamour," I said. "The poppies, the poppies! they are what we want most! Here it is all illusion; with them it is all forgetting; 'a closing of the eyes to sleep' ah! that poppy-seed, which is sown by the wind and fostered by no living soul, is often dearer 'to us, more necessary and more helpful, than the good food from the good husbandman's cornfield. ..."

He did not answer. Afterwards, we sat up on the terrace and had supper in the open air. Suddenly he put down his knife and fork, and looked at me.

"Oh, tell me! Thymian. . . . tell me! You have seen better days, you come of a good family? You have had a good education; you have quite unusual accomplishments. How did you come to this life?"

"Nonsense!" I answered. "My father was a porter, and my mother a laundress, and I was to have been a servant, but the life didn't attract me, and as I couldn't be a great lady I chose the middle course and now am, wrongly or rightly, what you see – a lady of the 'half-world.'"

"No!" he said, decisively. "That's not true. I won't force myself into your confidence, for probably you have very good reasons for being silent about your former life; but a child of the people you are *not*, I'll stake my life on that! Your very appearance proves it. Your beauty is a beauty *de race*, which is seldom or never found in the lower spheres of society. You have soul and you have feeling, and intelligence and culture, too, and none of these things can be hidden in you, but each breaks out from time to time as irresistibly and as brilliantly as do the rays from a well-cut jewel. I won't worry you with my curiosity. No! for I'm not "curious' but interested. You interest me in my capacity of doctor as well as of man. I don't understand how a being like you, with all your undoubted mental and spiritual gifts, and with such a keen and profound intelligence, ever got into that blind alley of a life, that awful spiritual hell; and how, having got there, you can stay there. It's all a psychological enigma to me, and I should like to solve it."

So he spoke, but I answered not a word. I gazed at the red wine glowing in the glass, and then out at the people sitting underneath at the little tables in the glare of the electric light, and eating their suppers. It was a warm evening, and the garden was still pretty full; a train clanked by every now and then, so picturesque, like a long chain of glow-worms, with its lit-up windows. The band was playing *Alterseelen* –

> "Lay by my side your bunch of purple heather,
> The last red asters of an autumn day. . . ."

I don't know what came over me my eye's grew dark and sombre. I felt his gaze upon my face and kept staring down into the red glowing wine. . . .

"It was the old story, wasn't it?" he said, softly. "An unhappy love affair? And then one step after another, down – down – down till you were stuck fast in the mire and couldn't get away?"

I shook my head. A shudder ran all over me, and my heart beat slow and heavy as an iron hammer.

"I have never really loved a man before, in all my life," I said. "I love *you* – I love you!" And I could not go on. I leaned my head on my hand and pressed my handkerchief to my eyes, and said that sometime I would tell him all. And he was silent. In the meantime, the waiter had brought champagne, and while I was lifting the glass to my lips there fell into it a tear, and I drank it down with the rest. . . . We did not recapture that moment's mood, and about nine we went away, drove to the Thiergarten, got down there and walked through the shady avenues. Suddenly, the Doctor put his arm around me and said, softly: "Was it true what you said just now, Thymian? Am I personally dear to you? Or was it only a feeling of the moment?"

"I love you," I said, and my eyes filled again. "I loved you from the first. I should like to belong to you – you only. My heart and my senses both desire you. I don't know *what* I would not do for you. . . . I can take money from all the others, but from you I hate to take it. Money is so sordid, and my love for you is so pure."

"But, my child, this is tragic," he said, gently. "If I were twenty years younger and a free man, I would try to return your love, and perhaps we two might still be happy together; but as things are, you must put this out of your head. I want to be a friend to you a friend whom you can trust. Won't you tell me a little about your former life?"

I nodded. And as we walked on arm-in-arm, I told him the whole story; and although he didn't speak at first, I could see that he was deeply moved. Then he pressed my arm still more closely to him, and said suddenly: "Thymian – dear Thymian! Shall we have another try for the straight road? If I give you a helping hand, will you dare the leap back to safe ground to an honourable, self-respecting existence?"

"Ah! will I not!" said I.

"Good! Then we'll see. If you have a genuine desire it will come right. We'll talk of it again. But you must *will* it; you must throw off the deadening, deadly influences that hypnotise you now; you must awake, you must awake, Thymian!"

"How gladly!" I murmured, and I felt quite happy and light-hearted.

As I lay in bed afterwards, I stretched out my limbs with a feeling of well-being that it was long and long since I had experienced. It was like that other time at Ostend, when a warm, purifying stream had seemed to pour through my soul and loosen and carry away all the evil that had clung to it. Quite blissfully I fell asleep.

But the new day brought with it the daily struggle for existence, the hundred things that life, like an insatiate monster, demands from its victims. . . . That very evening there was a dreadful man beside me in the bar a great fat creature who looked as if he weighed hundreds of pounds – but alas! he *had* hundreds of pounds too, it seemed. . . . He gave me two hundred marks. I had to drink at least twenty-five glasses of liqueur-brandy beforehand. . . . I *had* to, so as to let the poppies of oblivion do their work on me. . . . Oh, God! but it is fearful! I feel that the Doctor is right in all that he says to me. I can't bear this life much longer. I am breaking down physically as well as spiritually; some day soon I shall have done with horrors.

.   .   .   .

December 12th, 1894.

I haven't seen the Doctor for weeks. His younger daughter has been very ill, and that made him forget all about me. Last month I had an amusing experience. Six of us had met by chance, Jew-Frederick and another of the same sort, called Red Georgie on account of his hair, and four of us women; and as Red Georgie was in funds (God knows where they came from!) he invited us all to a spree at his expense, and so we supped at Dressel's, and after eleven went to a café in the Friedrichstrasse. And while we were sitting there, in came a woman who looked shyly all round, and squeezed through among the tables, and I looked at her and thought "Surely I know that face!" She looked very quaint; she had on a cheap coat of last season's fashion, and with it a gaudy scarlet hat which wouldn't stay straight for an instant on her smooth neat hair, but waggled about like a lamb's tail; and altogether her effect was remarkable and yet not smart, a regular provincial turnout – gay, cheap, and tasteless. All at once it occurred to me! Why, of course, it's the eldest married daughter of Frau Lütke, an alderman's wife in G—! Yes, her name is Frau Christiansen, and her husband is a cattle commissioner, and is often in Berlin. . . . And when she had at last found a place at a table, the waiter came and told her what I could have told her that after eleven o'clock no unescorted ladies were served. And of course she jumped up and got crimson, and one could see that she'd like to have sunk into the earth beneath the curious, amused looks that were fixed on her. An impulse of compassion came over me. I stood up and went across to her, and invited her to come and sit at our table.

"Don't you know me, Frau Christiansen? A countrywoman of yours – Thymian Gotteball of G—?"

"Ah! Fräulein Gotteball," she said, greatly relieved, and came along with me, and of course I did the introducing in my very best style – "Doctor Fernror; Mr. Schultze" (no nicknames!); "Frau So-and-so. Fräulein So-and-so." . . . And she looked at the elegant gentlemen with their patent-leather boots and tall hats, and the still more elegant ladies, and her eyes got bigger and bigger, and when she took stock of me and saw the diamonds on my neck and arms she seemed more and more perplexed.

"In G— they say that things are not going well with you, but I see that that's not true," she blurted out.

"As you see, I'm getting on brilliantly," I answered, laughing. It amused me to play the patroness with this little highly respectable *bourgeoise* from G—, I soon had her in full swim of course I didn't ask for father, but I heard everything else in the way of gossip from home. Frederick made violent love to her, and weltered in polite phrases: "Gracious lady!" "Dear lady!" and so forth; and she smiled and was flattered, but soon grew uneasy, because her husband, who was to have met her here at eleven after the theatre, hadn't arrived at twelve. No doubt he was "on the spree." When these rustics come to Berlin they lose their heads completely. She got up about half-past twelve, and so did we, of course, and Frederick offered to take the "gracious lady" back to her hotel. Quite proudly she went off on his arm. Well, she had a story to tell when she got home!

.   .   .   .

There's going to be a big change in my life. I can't stand this existence any longer I *can't!* Many and many a night I've lain tossing, sleepless, in my bed, and wondered and wondered what I was going to do, and now at last I've decided. I'm going to do like the rest and marry Casimir, and start a pension for foreigners (a very high-class one), and finish once for all with all the rest. I have talked it over with the Doctor, and he approves, except as regards marrying Casimir. He was sceptical about that at first, but when I pointed out to him that my position as a married woman would be very much more assured, and that in any case I had Osdorff on my shoulders, he acquiesced; and we agreed that I should take a large house at the West End and furnish it really handsomely from Markiewicz – either ready-money or on the hire-system. The Doctor will pay the rent, and I shall sell my diamonds and other valuables and so have a little something to begin with.

With Osdorff I had quite a terrible quarrel at first. When I told him that we were to get married, he said simply, "No; he wouldn't do that on any account." I was absolutely confounded! I thought of course that he had got a sudden fit of morality, and asked him sneeringly where lay the social distinction between a *souteneur* and a prostitute? He, on his side, was totally at a loss to understand that and then I saw the whole thing! The high and mighty Count with the two f's could not marry a mere Gotteball! At first it struck me as so laughable that I treated it as a pure joke, but then I perceived that he was in deadly earnest, and naturally got very irate in my turn, and gave him a hint as to what I thought of him. I said he was a skunk and a swine! I said he was fed and kept by me, and wasted my money, and wasn't as much good to me as a big St. Bernard dog would be – for at least from the dog I should be sure of fidelity and affection. I said he was as stupid and as sluggish as a crocodile; and was a hound and reptile like him, a great parasite of a creature, to talk about his "nobility" forsooth! and think himself too good for the likes of us! I was so furious that I dragged the fork out of his hand – we were at supper – and took him by the collar and kicked him out, and told him to go to his fine relations in the Behrenstrasse and "get them to keep him, for I wouldn't set eyes on him again. And I slammed the door behind him; and he shouted the house down: "No! he wouldn't!" and "he wouldn't!" Afterwards, I told the landlady not on any account to let him into his room again, for I had put him out. She said she thought I had done well, and that every sensible person had been wondering how I could keep such dirt about me for so long. Late at night he came home drunk, and roared like a wild beast when he found his room door locked, but I let him rave. At last he quieted down. About six in the morning I looked out: there lay the creature across the head of the stairs, with nothing on but his shirt, snoring loudly. I poured a jug of water over his head and sent him to bed, but I gave him nothing to eat all day. By evening he was quite humbled, begged pardon, and said he was ready to do anything I liked. I gave him a few pence for supper at the "Strammen Hund" and kept him pretty low in funds for a day or two, so that in the end he was imploring me to marry him. So we went to the registrar, and in January we shall be tied up.

Yesterday the Doctor came again. We arranged everything, and are now on the look out for a house; there's a beautiful flat in the Schellingstrasse with ten rooms, to be had for three thousand marks. Probably we shall take that. The Doctor says he will be very glad when I have a house of my own, so that he can come and have a chat in the evenings occasionally. When we are quite alone I call him Julius. I love him so. . . . I wish I could be his wife. . . . What a notion! One might as well wish for the moon.

.   .   .   .

"Gräfin Thymian Osdorff! How does it sound?" I said this morning to the Doctor, when I was trying on my new, simply-made but well-cut morning-gown before the glass.

"Very well – most imposing," said he, smiling. "It ought to be Princess. Anybody might think you were a Transparency."

"A nice sort of Transparency!" I remarked, and neither of us could help laughing. Of course I don't intend to use the title; I even deny myself the famous double-f, and call myself simply Frau Thymian Osdorf. We advertise in a good many papers, and I've already let four rooms, but of course we'll have to do better than that if the thing is to pay us. For the present the Doctor pays the rent, but I hope very much that later on I shall be able to meet the entire expenses myself. But it does cost a lot, what with the high rate of hire for the furniture, and then the servants – a cook and a housemaid. I had hoped to be able to manage with the cook alone, but it didn't do; the ladies and gentlemen need so much attendance.

I feel as if I were saved delivered from a prison! A great sense of repose and relief has come over me. I'm often genuinely merry, and find myself singing to myself, which I've never done since my childhood. The snowdrops are in flower already on my "grave" out there. I often visit it. The piano-lady still comes there, too, and she really wants me very much to go and see her in her home; she seems to like me. I think I shall go, shortly. It's such a blessed feeling to be a real human being again. My only anxiety is Casimir. I'm afraid he's not quite in the picture. I had a long, serious talk with him and urged him strongly to help me to begin quite a new life with our marriage and our settling down, and I said that all he had to do, all I asked of him, was to behave himself decently, and above everything else to keep away from all our former surroundings. He can go in the afternoons or evenings to some respectable bar for his "bock"; he can go to the theatre can do, in short, whatever he likes, "so long as he doesn't associate again with the *souteneurs*. I appealed to his family pride also, and pointed out to him that he needn't any longer keep out of the way of his relations, for we are respectable people now, and earn our bread decently, and need cringe before no living soul. What a good thing it would be if Casimir had some regular employment! But I don't see what I could do for him in that way. So he lounges about the whole day long, sleeps till eleven, breakfasts in bed, doesn't dress till two, manicures his nails for an hour, goes for a walk, tumbles about on the divan when he comes home – and the only earthly good he is to me is to do my hair! He does that very cleverly and has great taste. I'm always in terror lest he should run across one of his "athletic" friends – the members of the *souteneurs* clubs! – and betray the secret of our thereabouts, and have the whole crew coming to look us up. That would be the end of all things.

CHAPTER XIV

June.

Doctor was reading my Diary yesterday, and thinks I have extraordinary powers of description. It all read so smoothly and nicely, he said. Yes, indeed! I've got so used now to registering all my experiences that it is a delight to me when I have something out of the common run to set down. I only wish I had some real good to chronicle. . . . For the moment all is well with us. The rooms are all let but one, but very shortly they'll all be vacant again, for everyone is leaving town. Of course *I* can't. If one of the rooms, even, remains empty for a month or so it makes a tremendous difference.

I often go to Schlachtenhof to see Frau X—, whom I got to know at the cemetery. She has a little villa out there, and the poor thing is very lonely, and delights in my coming to her. I should like to go oftener, but I always feel a little uncomfortable about it. I don't know why exactly; but it's a peculiar feeling, if one thinks of it, that this respectable townsman's widow would kick one out and disinfect her house after one if she had the least idea of who her guest was. She shows a very marked liking for me and I believe I could easily get a loan from her. She would give me what I wanted for the asking, I know, but I need not say that nothing would ever make me ask. Just now I have a nice Russian couple here, besides a Spaniard and a Frenchman, and a brother and sister from Magdeburg, and a Danish lady quite a cosmopolitan lot! They all lunch and dine at my own table, and I act as interpreter, which is often very amusing. They are happy with me, and respect me highly, and I'm convinced that not one of them would believe it if they were told what I had been in other days. On the other hand, they all shake their heads over Casimir, and one of the gentlemen said straight out to me the other day, that none of them could understand how a clever woman like myself had ever had anything to do with such a man. If they knew—!

I'm so anxious to let the rooms that I'll make terms with the first comer.

. . . .

September 8th, 1895.

A solitary evening, so I'll write a little. Oh dear! but I am worried. I have the furniture-hire to pay on the fifteenth, and I haven't got a penny. The Doctor is at the Lakes with his family; I can't write to him, for I hate to bother him. He already gives me more than he can really afford. I have only four rooms let, and I've taken a schoolmistress for eighty marks a month, which I should make a profit on if there weren't such a lot of people eating their heads off all day long. The daily expenses and the servants' wages, and the gas-bill, and all the rest of it, nearly drive me off my head, and I don't believe I'll be able to go on with this business. Moreover, a married couple who stayed here two months and ran up a pretty stiff bill, suddenly went off, leaving a debt of three hundred and seventeen marks and over behind them. The pension would pay, though, if I only had a sensible, intelligent husband. It seems to me that Casimir gets more of an idiot every day. He was ill lately, and the Doctor said he had serious heart-failure. Perhaps he will die soon. We won't exactly hope that he may – we'll leave it to Providence, that's all. I don't know why such a man should cumber the earth. He often takes a fit of not dressing him-self at all, goes about stark naked, and nothing will induce him to put on a stitch of clothing. On such occasions I have to lock him up, or we should be done for. He is beginning to be disgustingly tiresome in other ways besides; if I don't give him enough pocket-money he borrows in my name, and lately he tried to pawn some spoons on the sly, but of course could get nothing on them, as they're only electroplate.

If I speak to him he gets surly and insolent. Oh, dear! life is full of troubles !

I long so for my Doctor. Once he's back, I shall feel brave and hopeful and confident again. But now I am all sadness and discouragement.

. . . .

October 10th, 1895.

I knew it would come to this with Casimir! The fellow is my evil destiny. I knew he would break out in the end. He had been on the bend for weeks never came home till late at night, drank hard, and would not tell me what he had been doing with himself. On Tuesday week I was asked to Frau X—'s in the Schlachtensee for a birthday party, and had left word that I would not be home till rather late, certainly not before ten o'clock. If only I hadn't gone! I had a sort of feeling that something was going to happen, and was uneasy all the time, and if the old lady hadn't made such a point of my staying to supper, I'd have gone home at seven.

Well, as soon as ever I got home at a quarter-past ten, the housemaid came to me in a dreadful state of mind and said that the master had a visitor – a lady – and they had had coffee made, and then she had had to fetch wine and cold meat, and the lady was still there. . . . I guessed it was nothing pleasant; went in and found nobody in the dining-room, and my bedroom door locked. I knew what that meant, but I pretended not to, and made threats about fetching the police, so at last they opened the door. There lay the woman, half-undressed, in my bed, smoking, and Casimir was half-drunk and could scarcely speak. The woman jeered at me when I told her with calm decision to get up and be off, and said she was a boarder in the Pension Osdorff, for her friend, Herr Osdorff, was paying for her. Well, I knew by experience that a little mild coercion is the only thing that's the slightest use with that sort, and called the housemaid to help me – painful as it was to do so – and we soon chucked her out of the bed, and I then informed her that I would throw her downstairs just as she was, upon which she decided to put on her clothes and vanish, not without some appalling language. Casimir contributed his share to that, and screamed at me in the presence of the servant, saying that I was no better than she was, quite the reverse, in fact, and so forth. . . . Ah! it was terrible! To be exposed like that before the maid! I longed to kill the vile wretch of a man. . . . I didn't remember ever having seen the woman before; and afterwards I heard that she lived in the Elsasserstrasse, and that Casimir had been going with her for a long time, and then I knew at once that our fate was sealed. And so it was. A couple of days later there came a ring at the door. A gentleman wished to speak to me. The maid took him into the drawing-room and called me. I thought he had come about a room, went in and there stood Jew-Frederick. He was already rather drunk, and wanted to embrace me, assuring me that he had been quite ill with fretting after me and had thought I must be dead, and that all the friends, gentlemen and ladies, had been longing to see me again. . . . And I – I don't know what came over me, but I forgot all prudence and caution, and refused to have anything to do with him, and showed him the door. If only I hadn't! It was very silly of me. A soon as he was gone I knew what I had done. And sure enough, three nights later, in comes Casimir with a *souteneur* and two girls. They make themselves at home in the dining-room and order supper. This time I was wiser. I clenched my teeth and gave them what they wanted. In the course of the evening ten more came along, and there was a regular revel. They jumped over chairs and tables and kicked up so much noise that all the boarders proper rushed terrified into one another's rooms, asking what was the matter. The dreadful creatures kept on yelling like lunatics, and I didn't know what on earth to do, so sent in my distraction for the Doctor, who came immediately, but didn't know what to do either, and wanted to send for the police; but that didn't commend itself to me, for I couldn't forget how they had helped me when the police were after me, and besides, I knew that it was bad policy to set these people entirely against one. The Doctor stayed with me, however, till at last, about six in the morning, the beasts departed. My house looked dreadful. The Axminster carpet was swimming in punch and beer, the leather chairs were scratched and soiled by many boots, and a lot of things were broken. I shall have to make it all good to Markiewicz, and I owe him three hundred marks already, I'm in debt to so many people that it frightens me I have never been accustomed to owe money. We have had this house nine months now, and in that short time I have disposed of all my valuables and got head over ears in debt. It's dreadful!

. . . .

December 12th, 1895.

On the 1st January we are moving to a smaller house in the Potsdamerstrasse. Julius has arranged everything for me. The other house couldn't go on, especially after the last trick that Casimir played me. One night, when I was at the theatre with some boarders, he and his friends carried off a lot of furniture – quite enough for a room – down the back stairs, and there's not a sign of it to be found anywhere. Probably he had it taken to his drab's abode. I haven't gone to the police about it – what would be the good? I should never get it back. . . . I couldn't keep on the big house, and indeed I didn't want to, for the servant had blabbed, and the boarders all looked askance at me. After the big row every one of the ladies gave notice, and the landlord, whom I asked to let me off my contract, wrote that the sooner he was rid of us the better pleased he'd be. Julias has arranged everything with Markiewcz. He is to replace all losses and damages, and give the rest of the stuff back. . . . I have bought some new furniture on installment. We have only five rooms here, and I let four of them. Casimir is scarcely ever at home; often he is away for a week at a time, doing goodness knows what! Can't say I care either! I'm only too glad to be quit of him.

. . . .

January 17th, 1896.

I am in luck, and have let all the rooms in the new house at once. It's not precisely a Tom Tiddler's Ground, though, and I shall have to go in for some other paying work as well take pupils for languages, I think. That won't be so easy to achieve, but I shall have a good try. I do so earnestly desire now to earn an honest penny. In the other house the gentlemen tried in these latter days to make overtures to me, but I made short work of them. I can't stand anything like that now. I have all I desire in my Doctor, to whom my whole heart belongs. He is too good – much too good for me. . . . Casimir is ill again. When he's ill he stays at home; otherwise, never.

. . . .

February 10th, 1896.

Another bit of bad luck. Whenever I think that the goal is almost reached, down comes a fresh avalanche and turns me back. Casimir got frightfully ill about a fortnight ago. His whole face swelled so shockingly that he wasn't fit to be seen of men, and we had to call the doctor in. When he came he told us a pretty tale. The creature has got some appalling, unmentionable disease. The specialist who was giving him an injection broke the needle, and he shrieked and groaned the whole night through. . . . My Doctor says that with his heart-failure and his poor constitution he's hardly likely to live long. The world is certainly big enough for everyone, and I grudge nobody his little bit of life, but I can't think it would be a calamity if Casimir were to go under. . . . Now the door is besieged by his precious "pals," who come in hordes to inquire for him. I wonder very much what part he plays among them; he surely can't be much good, considering what a fool he is. I fear they make him do all the dirty work, all the horrors that nobody else will do. What does it matter to me? If I had the money I should put him in a sanatorium, for it's a terrible burden that I've bound on my shoulders in undertaking him.

I am beset with anxieties. My present lodgers have all their meals outside the house, and when they do happen to take one here, they don't pay enough to keep the pot boiling. I don't make more out of them than the installments for the furniture. I hate, too, to take the whole rent from the Doctor. He's done more for me already than he can really afford; but one must live. It is frightfully depressing to get up every morning and go to bed every night with the same anxiety gnawing at one's vitals. Soon I shall have no clothes to put on for I can't bring myself as yet to wear cheap things. I have two pupils, a young volunteer and a student, at one mark an hour. I make nothing by that. Sometimes I say to myself: "Come, Thymian, don't be silly! Nothing matters. The little bits of blue paper are still to be had in the streets, when you're a pretty, well-made, intelligent female. Just you shut your eyes and clench your teeth, and in a minute you'll have earned the notes you want, and have peace for a while." . . . I won't go back to that hideous life, but the temptation to make existence a little easier, to shake off some of these disgusting anxieties about ways and means. . . . it's powerful, powerful!

. . . .

Funny! I didn't want to – but I've done it again. It was after the evening that I met Mimi in the bar. She was swilling champagne and getting a little tipsy. . . . I drank a glass or two to give myself courage, and got hold of a smart man, who took me to his very luxurious bachelor-chambers. His name was D—, and he was so infatuated with me that he offered me a regular arrangement. But I wouldn't agree; for it was to be an exceptional occasion, I had resolved. But the fifty marks were spent by the end of the next day, and so the old troubles were in full swing again. Life is an interminable battle! You kill the days one after the other, and the dead things lie behind you and fester, but there's always a fresh one in front, and you've never won your fight against the hydra-headed monster, Life.

One evening I was with Nix at the Apollo Theatre. We had two stalls. I rather hated being with her, for she was plastered all over with diamonds, and I hadn't a single ornament of any kind – they're all gone. Of course she was kind enough to remark upon it, and turned up her nose when I told her that they'd all gone to keep my pension going.

"I thought you still had Doctor W—," she said.

I explained to her that it wasn't an affair of that sort, and so forth.

"Oh, don't tell me. I know all about the old miser," said she, and told me that a year and a half ago she had consulted him in his capacity of nerve-specialist, which cost twenty marks. And he had "taken her on" for the evening; and it's well known that Nix has her fixed price as well as he, and that no consultation with *her* costs less than fifty marks. When she was leaving he gave her only thirty, and it 'makes her indignant even still when she thinks of it.

Well, the devil had a hand in it that evening, for as we were walking about a little in the *entr'acte*, whom should we meet but the Doctor! Such infernally bad luck, that he should select that very evening to take his wife to the Apollo! He stared at me, and I knew that he knew what to conclude from seeing me with Nix.

I should have thought, though, that he might have asked for an explanation, but no! he simply stayed away, and sent me the money for the rent by post on the 1st. I was terribly annoyed by that, for I care for him so much and would never have let another man come near me if necessity hadn't forced me to it; and in my anger I sent him the money back, so that he may know that the likes of us can have our pride too. But as the rent had to be paid I wrote to D— and asked him for a rendezvous. He came at once, and I told him my troubles, and he said he was quite ready to pay the rent for me, only too glad, in fact, and declared that he had been looking for me everywhere, for he had fallen in love with me the moment he saw me. Well, so D— is my friend now in place of the Doctor, and I am really better off, for he is very generous. But it's the Doctor I want, and my heart beats quicker every time the bell rings, and I feel sad and sorry when it turns out not to be he.

· · · · · · · · ·

New Year's Eve, 1896.

D— is just gone. He had an invitation to a house which he felt he must go to, for politeness' sake. I can't sleep yet, and so I have got out my Book to write something in after all this time. The last entry was in April, and since then there have been many changes. In the beginning of May Casimir stayed out all one night, which made me rather uneasy, for since his illness he had been quite decently behaved. Certainly, I had sometimes wondered at the amount of money he had, for I couldn't imagine where it came from. Once or twice he actually had gold. In his set, though, money quickly burns a hole in the pockets, and it was quite possible that someone or other might have given him ten marks or so out of good-nature, or as a return for some small service; so I didn't bother much about it.

But I did feel uneasy about his staying out all night, and next morning I nearly had a fit, when a constable came to the house and said that Casimir had been arrested the night before. They had caught him at some unspeakable infamy. There was nothing to be done; the thing had to take its course. The *souteneurs* collected two thousand marks to bail him out with, but the Court refused it, and six weeks later the investigation in the Higher Court came on I was summoned as witness, but I refused to give evidence. In the end he was sentenced to three months' imprisonment; and they say that it's an utterly inadequate sentence, and was only given because his solicitor proved that he was of weak intellect.

The day after, all the papers were full of it, under the headlines:–

**STEP BY STEP,
OR
A RUINED LIFE.**

And then, this sort of thing:—

"An investigation, from which the public were excluded, was yesterday held before the Criminal Court of Justice into the conduct of Count Casimir Edmund Maria Osdorff, accused of a breach of public morality. The accused is the fourth son of the late Count Knut Osdorff, one time Member of the Reichstag. The young man was at school abroad, and later, after vain attempts at procuring an appointment suitable to his station in life, had gone to America. By the request of his boyhood's sweetheart a lady well known and much admired in the Berlin 'half-world' by reason of her beauty and charm he returned to Germany, lived for some time in illicit union with her, and finally married her. The lady, who wisely disdained to use her husband's title and simply called herself Frau Osdorf, seems after the marriage to have lost all interest in her husband, for the man, who is morally and intellectually feeble, and had long lost all power of self-restraint, has now become a criminal of the most atrocious type. Yesterday's proceedings ended with the sentencing of the accused to a three months' term of imprisonment, in which the period of detention already undergone will be included."

Well, there was nothing to be done against that, for the solicitor advised us not to appeal. I should have liked to have had Casimir out on bail, so as to try eventually to have him sent to Z—, for I knew quite well that he would never survive a term in a regular orison. But the authorities refused our application for bail, because they were afraid of an escape from justice. Where the poor devil was to escape to is a puzzle to me!

Hitherto I had often secretly wished that Casimir might die, for he was such a trial to me; but I felt immensely sorry for him now, in spite of all that, and when I went to see him in prison and he came towards me looking so haggard and so wretched, all my anger vanished, and I felt nothing but compassion for him. He looked terribly ill and complained of "being hungry, for he couldn't stand the food; it was simply too awful; it made him sick every time." I begged the governor to send him to the infirmary, for he is still quite ill, but it was no good. About eight days after Casimir's sentence, the servant one morning announced an old gentleman. The hair dressing woman was with me, so he had to wait a little, and some instinct made me put on my white morning-gown, which becomes me so extraordinarily well.

When I went in, I saw at once that it was an aristocrat of some kind. I saw, too, that he started when he beheld me. Then he introduced himself – Count Y—, Casimir's one-time guardian. I imagine that he came to tell me his high-and-mighty opinion of me in no measured terms of scorn; but I put on my sweetest expression, and that has never yet failed in its effect. It didn't this time, either. He said that the Osdorff family had had no idea that Casimir was in Germany once more; they had thought him dead and had already instituted inquiries through the German Consulate over there. Now, to their consternation, they had seen the account of the criminal investigation in the papers. Casimir's mother had died six months ago, but his brothers and sisters were still alive, and this would of course be a terrible blow to them. They would take care that when his sentence was over, he was put into some institution for the cure of nervous diseases; and perhaps I would be satisfied with a legal separation?

I answered: "My lord, I beg respectfully to say that I do not care one farthing for the wishes of the Osdorff family. When they had sent Casimir to America, they never afterwards troubled to inquire what had become of him, although they must have perfectly well known that he could no more earn his living there than he could here, and could come to nothing but a bad end. It was I who took pity on him. I sent him money to come home with, and during these last few years I have provided for him entirely, even to the roof over his head, and tried by means of our marriage to make a respectable and respected existence for both of us. I did all this out of pure affection for Casimir, because of our childhood's days together; and I have had nothing in return for it but trouble and ingratitude. But I have gone through with it till now, and I will go through with it and bear it to the end, and I refuse the aid of the family. Casimir is my husband, and I shall look after him. That is all I have to say."

So I spoke! and the Count nodded, and said that indeed the family did recognise all that I had done for Casimir, but that it must be a terrible thing for me to be tied to such a man.

"I have chosen my own lot and will keep to it," said I. "Nothing will make me give up my husband."

The Count stroked his grey beard. He is about fifty, a nice-looking old gentleman with blue eyes; and he took stock of me with a connoisseur-like penetration, just as a sportsman takes stock of a horse. I have keen perceptions, and knew exactly what he was thinking. We talked for about an hour. I told him how I had come to know Casimir, and of my vain strivings to keep my head above water with my pension.

"You're married and yet you stand quite, alone, totally isolated in your struggle for existence," he observed; and then went on to tell me that he, too, had been alone for years – a widower, and his only son was lieutenant in a regiment at Posen. When he left, he promised to come and see after us again, and pressed my hand, and I knew that he had a very kindly feeling for me, and that perhaps my future lay in the hands of this haughty, handsome old gentleman, if I was clever, and knew how to strike the iron while it was hot. . . .

When Casimir came home, he went to bed directly, and got worse and worse every day, couldn't even lift himself in bed, could do absolutely nothing for himself. I had such a desperate time with him that I had finally to consider the family's offer, for it was really more than I could manage alone. His friends of both sexes stood by him splendidly, to their honour, be it said. I doubt very much whether there is anything like the same kindliness and good-nature and sense of comradeship in "respectable" circles. Whatever he wished for, or was ordered, arrived like magic – whole baskets full of wine and champagne, and the most expensive fruit, and every kind of strengthening thing. Hardly one of them ever arrived with empty hands, and at his worst time, from the beginning to the middle of September, when we couldn't leave him alone for nights, they came by turns and sat up with him, and I never heard one coarse or rough word by his sick bed. On the contrary, I learned in those days that amongst the "dead men" there still were living souls, with kind hearts and eager neighbourliness. To some of them I was drawn more closely than ever before; for instance, to "Flaxen-haired Doris," the barmaid at a night-bar in the Friedrichstrasse, of whom I had never hitherto imagined that a decent word could come out of her lips. When we sat together in the evenings, she told me the story of her life, of the unspeakable squalor in which she had grown up. Her mother was put in the House of Correction for a very bad offence, and afterwards sent to a rescue home; her father was a drunkard, and she and her brother were brought up in the workhouse. Afterwards, when she went back to her father and brother, she had to run away from them. . . . Oh, heavens! what horrors that girl has gone through, *I* always managed to find rich, or at any rate tolerably well-off men, who treated me decently; but she, who has no other attractions than her unusual, almost white-gold hair, had to take what she could get, so it's no wonder that she's outwardly coarse and half-brutalised. But I found out for certain in that troublous time that many good qualities of fidelity and unselfishness still dwell unspoiled in her heart.

Casimir dragged on till the end of November; then, one night he got so bad that he couldn't breathe, and we had to rush for the doctor, who gave him a camphor-injection; but it was no good, and at half-past five in the morning it was all over with him.

The Count, who had kept his word and visited us from time to time, gave me as much as seven hundred marks for the funeral, and I bought the coffin and a grave and paid the necessary expenses out of that. It was a big funeral; the whole of the Berlin "half-world," and everyone in any way connected with it, was there. My abode could hardly hold the wealth of flowers, some of which were wreaths of exquisite beauty; and the coffin was literally covered with blossoms. About fifty carriages followed the bier, so that traffic in the Potsdamerstrasse was stopped for some time. The men all wore mourning-bands on their tall hats, and the women were dressed in deep mourning. The church choir sang, "How they so gently rest!" by the grave; and the pastor spoke beautifully, saying things that really went home to one. He must have been rather Broad Church, for he didn't say much about God or heaven, but what he did say got right at one. "When we survivors stand beside an open grave" (he continued), "we realise keenly, as otherwise we seldom can, the nothingness of earthly things, and how the wind of fate drives us across the theatre of this world. And 'character is fate' – for it is our wills, our tendencies, our passions, which decide for us the direction in which we are blown. And, driven thus by our passions, we often forget the one immutable sign-post of human destiny, pointing with inexorable anger to the end of all things the grave. How different many things in this world would be, how different many a destiny, if everyone would but remember steadfastly that this life is nothing but a short pilgrimage, which we take together on the great high-road that leads to the everlasting peace. . . ."

It was a beautiful discourse, and in the black-garbed circle round the grave there was many a pale, earnest countenance to be seen.

It sounds like sentimental affectation, but it is true, that when I got home I felt that in spite of everything Casimir's death had made a great gap in my life. His death could not but bring me a feeling of emancipation, and so it did; yet still – I could sleep at night now, which I had not done for long and long; I was not obliged to look on at suffering and listen to groans of pain all the same, I missed him. It was as if my life had lost its last and only meaning, and I stood more alone than ever in the world of men.

I could not weep, but I mourned for poor Casimir with my whole heart. . . .

Five weeks have gone by since then. In the course of the summer I had a reconciliation with the Doctor. I couldn't help it – it was more than I could stand, and so I begged him to come; but it has not been as it was before between us, especially as I did not feel that I could now throw D— over entirely. The Count comes very often now that I am a widow, and displays a "fatherly interest" in me. I have a sort of feeling that I am standing on the eve of a great alteration in my life; but I won't anticipate, I won't put down in so many words what I think and even expect, for I'm superstitious in that way. If I were religious, I should pray on this New Year's Eve: "Dear God, let it happen as I desire! Give me a few sweet, easy, peaceful years. . . ."

CHAPTER XV

DO you see, darling Booklet, how right I was? Truly I have keen perceptions. I saw it at once in those bright blue eyes with the youthful sparkle in them, that go so well with the grey beard – I saw that any amount of vitality and love of living were still waiting their chance to express themselves. At his very first visit I saw that. *"He's your man!"* . . . And I knew that I had made an impression on him, and that I only needed to please him a little more and the business was done. I am quite happy. And the best of it all is that he is so very sympathetic to me, and that it doesn't cause me the slightest pang of any kind to belong to him. I always like those haughty old men with their perfect manners and their distinguished appearance. Certainly, I should like the Doctor still better, but nothing is perfect in this world of ours.

And he did it all so cleverly, tactfully, diplomatically! Very gradually, the tone of fatherly benevolence became a little warmer and more intimate, so that the definite proposal came not too suddenly for either of us, but seemed to have been led up to by all sorts of delicate transitions. We were at supper one evening in a private room at the Kurfürsten Café, and during dessert he looked at my arm, admiring its beautiful lines, and expressed great astonishment at my wearing no bracelets or rings. I told him my pension had swallowed them all up. He smiled at that and said, "A charming young lady like you is intended for the sunny side of life, and should never know the sordid cares of a daily struggle. You must find a friend who can give you back your life and your joy in it."

I looked into his eyes and said, "Where am I to find that friend?"

And he: "Well, but tell me – Could you think of one much removed in years? I should be too grandfatherly for you, shouldn't I?"

I was silent for a moment, and managed to blush, and I knew that I looked lovely and girlish as I did so.

"No," I answered, gently. I have had quite enough of young men. If I should ever fall in love again, it could only be with an older man."

"Will you entrust yourself to me, Thymian?" he said. "I have admired and loved you ever since I have known you, and you will find a true friend in me, who will show you what happiness is. We both understand the world and life, and need make no pretences to each other. I shall never marry again. But I will put my hands under your feet; and I will give you everything, and do everything for you, that a young and beautiful woman expects, and rightly expects; and I will make only one condition – 'Thou shalt have none other gods but me.' You must belong to me alone. I must be able to trust you."

Instead of answering, I threw myself on his breast and kissed him wildly from pure gratitude and utter gladness. But he took it as the outbreak of a genuine passion, and got quite hot and red, and we were like a young, happy pair of lovers. . . .

On 13th February we go to the Riviera, then to Paris. I have let my house, sold any of the furniture that belonged to me, and am already beginning to pack up. He buys me everything that I express the faintest desire for, and reads my wishes in my eyes. I am very happy, for now at last I have got what I have long striven for: I am the "friend" of a rich, well-born man, a real knight, from whom I need never fear any treatment that could wound me. I need not be anxious and troubled any longer. I have all and more than all I can desire, and I shall soon take steps to have my future assured. I have ordered the most exquisite frocks from Gerson &

Biester. Yes, the old gentleman is head over ears in love with me. I look forward infinitely to the trip in the South and to Paris. Now at last I shall know what real enjoyment means. My friend – I am to call him Otto, but it doesn't come natural to me as yet – need not fear that I shall betray him; I don't feel the least desire to. I am so inimitably grateful to him.

I have already said good-bye to the Doctor. That was a bad hour for me, for I feel more and more deeply how much I love him. He took my revelation very coolly and stiffly, shook his head, and said he had thought I was made of stouter stuff. Oh, dear me! It's so easy and so cheap to give good advice to other people and that's the way I'm made, and I can't change it. I am too weary to wage any longer the struggle for existence and the fight against the thousand worries of life. And this last year I've had scarcely anything of the Doctor, for his family and his profession make such great claims on him. But it was a hard parting. He seemed a little upset by it, after all, and I cried the whole night long. I won't write to D— till I get to Paris. That's a little painful to me also, for he was the first to help me when I was in trouble, and now he's cast off *nolens volens*; but it's the way of the world. Life is such a mob, everyone treading on the other's heels, and he who uses his elbows best is victor.

But I am as happy as a child at the thought of the halcyon days which life is offering me now. I am taking my Book with me. I hope that now I shall often have happy things, sweet things, to put in it.

· · · · · · · · ·

Between this and the page following lies a newspaper cutting with the announcement of a death, in large print, surrounded by a black border:—

"This morning at 7.30 o'clock, after a long and severe illness, died our only and passionately-loved daughter

ERICA,

having just completed her eighth year. We stand by her coffin inconsolable, as we have never before been in all our lives. "We beseech our friends to pay us no visits of condolence. The funeral will take place on Sunday, April 25th, at 10.30 a.m., from the house of mourning.

> CONSUL WILHELM PETERS AND
> FRAU AGNES (BORN SIEDETOPF)."

. . . .

Strangely enough, in the sequel, no remark whatever referring directly to this news is to be found – a peculiar, but psychologically, perhaps, a not inexplicable circumstance. – EDITOR'S NOTE.

CHAPTER XVI

Paris, May 22nd, 1897.

THE "happy days at Aranjuez" are drawing to an end. One can't do anything while one's travelling, and if I didn't chance to have an hour or two to myself this evening between dinner and the opera, and to have suddenly taken it into my head to do some diarising, I should bring my Book back to Berlin precisely the same as I took it away.

The trip was glorious; the months went by like a dream. I had never thought that the world was so beautiful. I had often read descriptions of Southern travel, but the most glowing and highly-coloured pictures of it are nothing but a weak reflection of the fairytale-like truth.

But in the very middle of such wonderful surroundings, there come to one involuntarily very bitter and poignant reflections. Why should such a glorious world have been created unless it was the Creator's will to people it with beings as splendid, as perfect, and as happy? He is no kind God who makes a world so rich in beauty, and puts into it so much human misery and ugliness.

We went to Nice and Monte Carlo and further along the Riviera. And at Nice we took a suite of rooms in a villa by the sea. We often sat on the balcony till quite late in the evening, looking at the sunsets, which are so splendid there, and of such wonderful colouring that when one has seen them one no longer thinks the "Secession" pictures, with their mad colour effects, are at all so exaggerated. The flaming fiery red, and the soft subtle crimson, contrasted with the hard cornflower blue of the water have such an extraordinary and fantastic effect that one must see it to believe in it. The most beautiful moment of all is when the gleams are dispersing, and the round ball of the sun has disappeared, and everything seems to be bathed in a rose-coloured mist, which glows on the horizon, and glimmers on the sea, so wonderfully that one often holds one's breath with ecstasy. And the most beautiful of all is to have a man with one, of whom one knows that he regards the wonders of Nature with the same appreciative eyes as oneself, and to whom one can talk about it, feeling sure that he will understand. The Count is a very clever, intellectual man, who has travelled a great deal, and really seems to know the whole world. He has been round it twice. I learn a great deal from him, and I never get tired of hearing him talk. I'm quite proud of having succeeded in enchaining this man so strongly as I have done. That isn't always easy, for these aristocrats are so highly schooled in self-control that they never fail to keep a certain watch over their feelings, and manage to tone down their desires and passions so admirably that in any given case a separation may not give them too much pain. But I know that my friend couldn't now give me up with a light heart! It is comparatively easy to attract a man like the Count; but to hold him, to enchain him, is difficult. I know quite well that when he first won me for himself, he was firmly determined to be on his guard, and to let me get no influence over him; but however strong and proud and hard such a man's will may be, the subtle, elastic will of a woman is stronger, and brings him under at last. I have an influence over him; he doesn't know it himself, but I can bend him to my will and my desires. I could demand and have from him now whatever I wished. Undoubtedly one has to take great care; one can never let oneself go, nor show one's own feelings, but must always suit oneself to the other's mood; and in this art I had never formerly trained myself, because it hadn't been necessary but I haven't found it in the least difficult.

Certainly the Count is a lovable old man, and I cannot be sufficiently grateful to the fate which has led me to him. But still I don't feel so happy as I might. Often I can't sleep at night now, and then I think of all sorts of things. I believe there are people who can't be absolutely happy, because the capacity for it is wanting in them, and to those I certainly belong. In my heart there is unrest, and an unsatisfied longing for something that I don't know, and that I cannot express in words. And then I long so for Julius! My heart beats quicker when I think of him, and a wild yearning for his love overwhelms me for I think sometimes that it is love that I want. I have been much admired, much desired in my life, but I have never been really loved. . . . It was only my body which men desired whether I had a soul or not, nobody ever asked.

When I lie awake open-eyed at night, like that, and think and think, and the remembrance of all the hideous, disgusting things that I have lived through rushes over me like a murky river, the longing for love rises in me like some heavenly being with quivering, widespread wings. I should like to have a child. I should like to be a mother again. And this time neither gods nor devils should tear my child from me. Oh, how I should love it, and how happy I should be in its love! And if it was a girl, how I should guard and protect her, and take care that her eyes never saw anything except what was beautiful, that her ears never heard anything but what was pure and good Oh, I would keep all the soils of life far away from her! Why should this longing be unfulfilled, after all? I am still young; many women do not marry before my age, and they often bring seven children into the world and I live a regular, well-ordered life now.

My wish is so strong that I told it one night to the Count. He was at first greatly perturbed; but when I told him the reason for my desire, and said that I would take the child entirely upon myself in every way, he only asked me if I really had the courage to bear all the consequences which fulfillment might bring with it – and when I said "yes," he remarked that I had better see a lady-doctor.

And as in the Rue de la Paix in Paris there dwells a renowned midwife, who is said to have made her fortune at this kind of thing, I persuaded my friend to stop here for a week on the way back.

I have already been with her. She advises me to take mud-baths, and gave me all sorts of good advice besides, which I shall carefully follow, in the hope that it may be of some use.

We always stay of course in the same hotel when we are travelling, but we have separate rooms.

Yesterday we dined at the Hotel Ritz. We were at the fish course, when suddenly a tall, gaunt lady, beautifully dressed, and wearing a splendid lace trimmed chinchilla cape, came rustling up to us, and said to the Count: "*Bon soir, mon cher cousin*"; and couldn't make enough of the delightful surprise of meeting him there. The Count was at first evidently a little confused, but he soon got himself in hand, and introduced me – "*Ma niece, la Comtesse Osdorff – Madame la Princesse Tch—*." Upon which the lady fell upon me with a heap of questions about the different branches of the family, and which and what Osdorff I was. Luckily I was tolerably *au fait*, for the family-chronicles and the family-tree were the only things that poor Casimir had in his stupid head. A thousand times he had held forth on it all to me, not that I had listened, but I had picked up enough to be able to give her Highness the necessary information without making a fool of myself. Then two gentlemen came up, Prince Tch— and a nephew, Count L—, and they all three sat down at our table. The young Count paid me great attention, and I saw the old Princess whispering to my Count all sorts of flattering things about me, and insisting that we should go and see her; but the Count refused, and said that we were obliged to go away to-morrow. I couldn't help looking at the old lady, and thinking that the nobility of her birth was certainly not written upon her forehead. If all her laces and diamonds and silks were taken off her, there would be nothing left but a big-boned Northern peasant-woman.

When we were driving home my friend said: "Well, Thymian, it's time for us to go! The sooner the better. Wasn't that bad luck? Good heavens! How small the world is! I haven't seen the woman for thirteen years, and she comes along to-night!"

Berlin, June 13th, 1897.

I find the time very long. The Count is busy, and goes a great deal into society besides, so he can't give himself up to me entirely, though he would like to well enough. I am afraid to go out lest I should come across some one I know, and be spoken to, I do nearly all my shopping by droschky, and never go out alone in the evening.

For the moment I am at the Central Hotel, as it's difficult to rent a house before October. We've taken a five-roomed suite on the Kronprinzenufer from 1st October, and I am to live alone there. I go next week to Elster, and in August to Kreuznach for a few weeks. In the meantime my friend goes to his estate in East Prussia, where his son will join him; and in the late autumn I accompany him to Vienna, where he has official business.

But it is so frightfully slow! And yet my window looks out on the Friedrichstrasse, and it's very amusing to sit there and watch the street. It bores one in the long run, though. I've read such an enormous number of books lately, and I've taken up my Spanish studies again but the day has twelve hours, and I can't sleep at night. To fill up twelve empty daylight hours is no joke. How I'd like to have a talk with Julius now and then, or even with D—; but I dare not. If the Count were to smell a rat, I should come to grief with the very same miraculous rapidity that I have come to the top, and should find myself sitting in the gutter again, one fine day. I often stand at the window in the dark, and look down upon the movement in the streets, and watch the girls walking up and down, offering their bodies to the men – and then something wells up in me that I can't describe a frightful loathing, and at the same time a burning, helpless anger against the abominable injustice and tyranny of fate, which turns human beings into brutes; and, with all that, a profound and almost tender pity for the unfortunate creatures whose comrade I really am, and a raging hatred for the rich, the morally unexceptionable people, who pronounce with such a magnificent, inimitable, haughty, "Don't-touch-me" sort of tone, the word "prostitute." O God! If they knew what goes on sometimes in the soul of one of those "prostitutes," they would be ashamed to despise her. Therefore "Father, forgive them, for they know not what they do.". . . I have read Dumas' **Dame aux Caínélias**, and many other books of the same kind, but they don't satisfy me, for I find nothing true in them. I could write a book on the "Psychology of a Prostitute," for I know my own soul. It's a pity that I have no talent for it. I have such lots of time now.

．　．　．　．　．　．　．　．　．　．

Vienna, October 30th, 1897.

You have had to wait a long time, old comrade, for another talk with me! You always seem to me like a living being only you're much wiser than any one of' them; you let me tell you everything, no matter what, and you keep silence and are patient as is the way of paper, and not of living beings! But because I like to fancy that you have a soul, I should never dare to lie to you, and so you know my innermost thoughts.

The summer was rather *triste*. First I was in Elster, and then for four weeks in Kreuznach. A couple of weeks after that I spent in Berlin. I have conscientiously followed my prescriptions, and live most carefully, but up to the present there are no traces of any result.

I furnished my abode in Berlin very delightfully, and would gladly have set up house there, but as the Count had to go to Vienna in September and wanted me with him, since he had seen so little of me all the summer, I had to acquiesce, and am now looking forward to getting home in December. For I must confess that this life in the long run is not very agreeable to me. It is too "*dov*" as old Kindermann was always saying. The Count is thirty-three years older than I, and he doesn't manage well, and despite his cleverness and his knowledge of the world I find him often dull and tiresome. He's a very strong Conservative, and very proud of his noble birth, though he's too wise and tactful to show that to everyone. But he can't hide anything from me, and I notice it in all sorts of ways – in his opinions and little things of many kinds. When Casimir used to prate of his family-tree and his aristocratic connections, I used merely to laugh; but this irritates me and gets right on to my nerves, and all the contrariety in me longs to break out, and I have to hold myself very tight so as not to say anything, for there's nothing I hate so much as to be cross to my old friend. I can't help it, but it all seems to me so silly! I simply cannot see what right the aristocracy have to regard themselves as a privileged class. Once, indeed, we did have a quarrel about it. We were sitting that day in the Matschakerhof, and happened to get on the subject of a reigning European house which certainly has no reason to pride itself upon its offshoots, and I gave expression to my opinion, which is that a republic is a far healthier form of government than that of a royal house with an unalterable succession. It doesn't matter whether the heir to the throne is stupid or intelligent, evil or good, capable or incapable of reigning he becomes King, Emperor, or Prince, as the case may be, just because an Emperor, King, or Prince has begotten him and a mother descended from another royal house has given him birth; and thus the fate of a whole nation is given into the hands of an incompetent or evil man. I said all that to him, but he merely, smiled ironically and observed, "You are well aware, Thymian, that I hold quite the contrary opinion" and then instantly spoke about a costume which I had bought in the morning at Zwiebeck's, and that made me so boundlessly angry that I couldn't quite control myself, and only wished that I could have thrown my glass of wine in his face. I'll say this! If the Count wanted to marry me tomorrow, and if my whole future maintenance were dependent on whether I did it or not, I should beg to be excused. For to live year after year, day in, day out, with such a wearisome man, would positively drive me crazy. And he's suspicious now, besides; and whenever I've been out alone, it's always "Where were you? How long were you here? How long were you there? What did you do? What happened?". . . . My goodness! it drives me out of my senses.

Luckily there are a great many claims on his time here, and I am left a good deal to myself, and when I stroll down to the Kärtnerstrasse I sometimes have some fun. Directly I enter a café, all heads turn to look at me, and wherever I go I attract attention. Oftentimes I *would* like to go in for a little bit of adventure again, just absolutely *en passant*, to have a little intermezzo to amuse myself; but in the first place I am afraid of Otto, and in the second I do delight in looking scathingly at any man who is insolent enough to come up to me, so that he can't understand how he ever could have made such a blunder! One afternoon lately, I was in the Café Scheidl in the Elizabethstrasse, which the Viennese call "Café Gapeseed," and there a gentleman sat down beside me, and we soon made friends. He was from Munchen-Gladbach and was an author, and was spending a couple of weeks in Vienna studying; and I represented myself as Frau Osdorf from Berlin, and told him that I had come to see Vienna on my own account – which after all wasn't a lie. Afterwards Dr. Martin – that was his name – asked if we couldn't spend the evening together, and as the Count was dining out, I was able to acquiesce.

We went to the theatre and saw the "Mikado," and afterwards supped at Leidinger's, and then my companion wanted to show me "Vienna by night." So we went to a night-cafe, which was very much on the same lines as those in Berlin, only more so! The doctor said: "Do you notice, clear lady, how angrily they're staring at you? They're very much afraid of competition here, and in this Kingdom of the Queens of Night a respectable woman is regarded as an interloper. These sort know their own kind at

once, and never make a mistake as to who belongs to them, and
who doesn't."

I said nothing, but I thought "Dear me! you are clever!"
Afterwards he asked me if it would interest me to see another bit
of the night-side of Vienna, to which I of course said "yes." Then
we went into a cellar near the Cathedral, which apparently is only
known to the initiated, and my companion said: "Now this is the
real modern slave-market – a regular shambles for human flesh."
In a tolerably large room there was music going on, good
Hungarian string-music that set one's blood on fire. The men
really did move about exactly as if it was a market. But what
wares! Our Berlin "half-world" certainly doesn't suffer from a
superfluity of loveliness, but there are a lot of very pretty girls
there, and even the least good-looking, if they're clever, know
how to make something out of themselves. But these women
were absolutely below par, and if that is, as Dr. Martin says, the
élite of the Viennese "half-world," it isn't fit to hold a candle to
Berlin. At any rate that night I didn't see one really pretty
woman. They all looked tawdry and badly-painted, and coarse
and loud and thoroughly bad style. Unattractive as the women
were, the men were just as bad all old fogies, or else raw
bumpkins of twenty and under, who ran about singing comic
songs and making a noise, and there wasn't a single decent-
looking man there. Of course the quite old and quite young men
form the greater part of the *clientèle* in Berlin too, but one does
find men of an interesting age amongst us occasionally. Here
there was not one – at least not that night. . . . A bell rang for a
side-show, and it turned out to be a half-naked woman singing
songs in the Viennese dialect in an impossible voice. I couldn't
understand a word, and the whole entertainment was a penance
from which we got away as quickly as we could. I told the doctor
I was thirsty, and we sat down in the big room against the wall,
and ordered wine. There were a few provincials there, and the
women stared at every individual face as if they'd never seen
anyone before. Certainly it was no pretty picture, this modern
slave-market, and yet . . . . and yet! The hot, luscious Austrian

wine ran through nay blood, and involuntarily I shut my eyes and listened to the heady, fiery music that gets so into one's brain, and it stirred up something in me that I can't call anything but a "home-like" feeling. The felling that this world was my world came over me and caused me, instead of discomfort, rather a sense of well-being. I really think that anyone who has once breathed this atmosphere has drawn the infection of it into her blood, like a disease which is never wholly healed, but always ready to break out again. I thought of my dear love in Berlin, for whom I have longed so madly these ages, and if I had had him there that evening, I shouldn't have cared for anything I should have thrown everything to the winds, the Count and all his money and everything – everything – if I could only just have had my desire of him. Oh! I *will* have him again when I get back to Berlin, no matter what happens! I don't care a hang. Love is the most beautiful thing in the world, and there's nothing to beat it. Yes, I dreamt of my Julius, and as I did so, I grew warm and desirous; and when I opened my eyes, I noticed that my companion was staring at me in astonishment. I smiled at him, for indeed I would have gone with him if he had wished, but the idiot noticed nothing and only paid me the "most respectful attention." Funny! there have been times when I was almost sick with longing for a little respect and homage; and *then* it was a bore to me, and I got cross and ill-tempered. We arranged a rendezvous for the next day at the Pratereingang, but I didn't go – I couldn't in any case, because the Count was there, but I really didn't want to see the man again.

. . . .

As we were supping at Sacher's on Monday evening, there sat opposite to us a gentleman and a lady in white. The lady had her back to us, but I seemed to know her copper-coloured hair and her figure. The Count drew my attention to her strange way of eating fruit. I looked. Well, one knows the ropes! Water boils in kettles all the world over. She ordered the most expensive fruits peaches as big as your fist, strawberries that cost goodness knows what, grapes and what not, each of which cost from two to four gulden, took one bite and then threw them away and took more, and of course her cavalier had to pay for the lot. These are the little side-doors by which one makes a friend of the head-waiter and gets ten per cent, or so commission.

When she turned round at last I recognised her. It was the beautiful Emma, a bosom friend of "The Ponies," who was in great request in Berlin in '94, and then got home-sick for her beloved Dresden, which is her native town, and went back there. She knew me at once, and I think the desire to speak was equally keen in us both, but on account of our cavaliers we couldn't acknowledge one another. So I got up and went into the dressing-room, and she followed me directly, and we embraced and kissed one another, and were greatly delighted at meeting again. She told me that the head cashier at Sacher's is her lover, and she has come with a gentleman to Vienna on purpose to see him. He was formerly head waiter in the Linkschen Bad in Dresden, and next week she is going home again with her gentleman. She asked me if I'd heard of "The Ponies" lately. Of course I hadn't. Then she told me hastily that Molly had poisoned herself six weeks ago with phosphorus, and she had gone to the funeral. As we couldn't stay long away, we arranged to meet next morning at a café near the Votivkirche. There I heard the whole story of the Ponies. They had bought a tapestry business in the little town in Thuringia and were getting on very well, thought a lot of, and all that; but there it was! They began to take to the old ways, and people talked, and nobody would buy anything more from them, and they had to give up the business. After that they didn't care what they did, for it was all up with them. Last August, Dolly married a farmer who had a "bespeak" business as well, and Molly was left alone in the little house that they had bought. There she had the bad luck to fall in love with a young doctor who was attending her for the influenza, absolutely head over ears in love, so that she simply couldn't live without him.

But the doctor was secretly engaged to quite another sort of girl, and her parents persuaded him to give up the treatment of his notorious patient and hand it over to a colleague, and the poor thing took it so much to heart that she poisoned herself six weeks ago with phosphorus.

They found her in convulsions on the ground in the morning, and in a couple of hours she was dead. Well, she's at peace; but it's very sad all the same, and Emmy cried a lot while she was telling me. She went over to the funeral, and she says that I simply wouldn't know Dolly again; she's got so fat and slovenly all in one year. I had to promise Emmy to visit her in Dresden this winter, and she is going to come to me sometimes in Berlin. She's tremendously smart. In her embroidered white cloth dress, with her big white feathered hat, she looked like a Princess.

CHAPTER XVII

Berlin, December 24th, 1897.

CHRISTMAS EVE! And out you come again, my trusty companion, dear old Book! I don't know how I should get through the evening without you. I fear nothing so much as the memories that in such hours creep about the rooms on tiptoe, and grip at one's heart and make it sad and tender. I had so few real Christmas Eves in my far-away childish years! Only those when my dear mother was alive. It was never the same thing with the various housekeepers, and in later years – well, I had rather not recall those Christmas Eves. But even then, I was never alone; somebody was always with me. For instance, at old Beidatsch's in the Zimmerstrasse, we had a tree and all spent the evening together and in the quiet time afterwards I thought to myself, I remember, that not one coarse or obscene word had been spoken the whole night. And last year D— and I kept Christmas together in my own house.

But this year I am totally alone, for my Count has his son on a visit, and they've both gone to a Christmas party at some big swell's in the Wilhelmstrasse. He has given me some gorgeous presents. They're all upstairs in the drawing-room there's a belt-buckle of diamonds and sapphires in the "Secession"-style; and that enchanting tea-service from Raddatz, with rosebuds all over it, that I wanted so much, and a lovely white opera-cloak, besides lots of costly trifles, and an extra thousand-mark note. He wanted me to have a Christmas-tree too, hut I wouldn't. What would have been the good? I've lit all the lights and pushed back the doors, and it is very bright and very warm, and very elegant and luxurious, and it's all my own. If only it wasn't so dreadfully, so oppressively silent and lonely! My Count won't let me have any sociability at all. That's natural enough, for I myself don't want to meet my former acquaintances again, and "proper" ladies would soon find out how I live and move and have my being. But I shan't be able to stand this solitary life much longer.

I am down in the Directory as a lady of property; I pay any amount of taxes, and am treated all round with great respect and attention, and the police naturally do not think of troubling me with their attentions, nowadays. But that's precisely the injustice of the thing. If one has found a rich man to buy one, body and bones, one is left alone; but woe to the poor things who haven't had the "luck" to get hold of a friend of that kind, and so sell themselves, as it were, by fragments in the, streets! . . .

Indeed, sometimes it seems to me that I am really worse and more contemptible than before. When I came to Berlin, I did everything I could to earn my living honestly, for the other sort of life made me sick. But as I could find nothing, and as one must live, I was forced to degrade myself, and I did it with an inward loathing, as an unwilling tribute to the Moloch of self-preservation. But now I sit here in a comfortable home, and allow myself to be "kept," and lead a life of absolute idleness, for which the only equivalent I have to give is to satisfy my old gentleman's not too-exacting passions.

Life leads men over heights and depths. I was wandering in the depths, when the impulse came to climb the heights and get a free outlook, but I was no longer strong enough to retain my place there. The first storm overwhelmed me, and, before I knew, I was slipping downwards again to where I had been before – only with this difference, that now I don't stumble about in the morass, but stand upon dry ground and have no need to soil my shoes. And the atmosphere which I now breathe is not corrupt as the other was; for a delicate nostril it has merely the oppressive perfume of utter indolence, which is like that of dead leaves and withered flowers.

It will not and cannot go on. My blood is too hot, too vehement, to endure the loneliness and quiet of this life. I have too much time for thinking, and that drives me crazy. I often think I should like to do as poor Molly did. Life really isn't worth the amount of trouble that it gives one to live it. But then again I think, "Wait! Nothing lasts for ever. You're not old yet. Take the goods the gods give you. . . ."

For I have such a terrible longing for Julius. It's like a fever. And the Count is so frightfully suspicious and jealous! Often he says that he is going away, and comes back all of a sudden to see if there is anybody with me, and hasn't the least idea that he is thereby cutting his own throat; for if anybody trusts me and depends upon me absolutely, I consider it an infamy to deceive him, and would rather cut off my finger than do it; but suspicion and spying and shuffling, when there's no cause for it, makes me ruthless in going my own way.

Once, immediately after our return from Vienna, I did see Julius, and in the Winter Garden of all places. I was sitting on the terrace, and he was with his wife and another lady, below us. And I heard and saw nothing of what was going on, for I couldn't take my eyes off him. And the next day I went to him in his consulting-hours, but he didn't want to have anything to do with me, and told me quietly and kindly, but quite decidedly, that he didn't poach on other people's preserves, and that as the Count was looking after me on the condition that I was his alone, I must most certainly make up my mind to be content with him. But I wouldn't listen to him, and literally threw myself into his arms; and I think he was sorry for me, but he didn't yield an inch, and I came away sad and utterly depressed. For I can't help it. I simply can't live without him, and I keep on wondering what I can do to have him for my own again. I suffer in this longing for my dear one. I rack my brains for a way out, and find none. When I was sitting alone just now on the sofa, I was picturing to myself how he was keeping Christmas Eve with his family, how the children were crowding round the Christmas tree, all so happy! And I so lonely! . . .

Emmy sent me an embroidered sofa-cushion from Dresden. I was so glad that she had thought of me. She very much wants me to come to her in January at Dresden. I'll see whether I can get leave from the old man. . . . I'm tired! I'll go to bed. Thank goodness, the evening's over. Christmas and New Year's Eve are the most hateful days in the whole year to me.

. . . .

January 29ᵗʰ, 1898.

Yesterday I came back from a week's stay in Dresden. In a fit of generosity, my protector gave me leave to spend the time that he would be on his estate – exactly a week – with my friend.

I didn't know how Emmy stood with regard to money, but as she's always very smart and dresses exquisitely, I thought that she was all right. But it seems she isn't at all. Apparently she carries her whole property on her back in the form of pretty frocks; and at least three-fourths of her diamonds are imitation. She tells me that she has bad luck with her lovers; they always break off with her so quickly. That's a thing I can't complain of; men hang on to me like chains. I can have them all, except the one I want; him I can't; he doesn't want me. Well, Emmy lives with a laundress in a little shabby room whose principal ornament is an oil portrait of Lassalle, bigger than life. That's because the laundress's husband is a great social democrat, who talks very big and calls himself "the Working Man," and makes bombastic speeches at all sorts of meetings and demonstrations, while in reality he's a lazy hound who has allowed his poor wife to keep him entirely for years. I learnt a great deal that was very interesting in connection with them. In Dresden the arrangements are very different from what they are with us. The police operate there in a mediæval sort of way, which seems very strange to anyone who has been brought up in the more civilised Prussian fashion. For example, the authorities consider it a sacred duty to prevent all loose living, and so are on the watch day and night to catch the offenders *in flagrante*.

This laundress is a poor respectable woman who has tried to keep straight all her life long, and who has worked too hard ever to have had time to go astray. Seven years ago she got to know this fellow, and took him up and lived with him, because his "principles" were against marriage, even a registry-office one. But the police soon had their fingers in the pie; they kept up a continual supervision, and caught him several times in her house, and over and over again the poor woman got short terms of imprisonment. Six times she was punished, and if she had been caught a seventh time she would have been banished. Once Emmy came in for a critical episode. In came the police one night – on the very stroke of midnight it was! – and the woman knocked at Emmy's door and begged her for heaven's sake to hide the man in her room, and Emmy felt an impulse of compassion and let him in, and he hid himself between the other door and the wardrobe, and she got into bed again. That very instant the police, three men strong, broke into the house, searched all the rooms, and called upon Emmy to open her door. At first she wouldn't, but "in the name of the law" she had to, in the end, of course. So in they came and poked into every corner, and Emmy says she could scarcely keep from laughing when one of the constables lay down on the ground and peeped into the tiny space under the press where the man, who had hidden there, must have been lying as flat as a pancake (and he was a pretty good size in reality!). The constable's helmet slipped off on to the ground, which certainly must have looked very funny; but the man, who was frightfully squashed, must involuntarily have made some movement, for the door behind him, which wasn't properly latched, flew open with a rattle, and then they had him! The woman would undoubtedly have been banished that time, if they hadn't got married at once. I believe the wedding was a magnificent affair: twelve little girls in scarlet dresses, strewing scarlet carnations all the way to the registry-office! The poor woman didn't gain much by her marriage, for, as I said, she has to keep the "working man" entirely. He lies on the rug the whole live-long day, and makes speeches in the public-houses in the evening about "the sweat of honest labour." I am an ardent democrat, but it's certainly instructive to see, once in a way, what sort of realities are to be found behind the grandiloquent clap-trap of the party. Here is this fellow, who has never had a blister on his hands in his life and allows himself to be kept by a woman, posing as the mouth-piece of "the slaves," of the "oppressed and disinherited." It is the purest irony!

Emmy is to marry her head waiter next August, and then they are going to set up an inn or a café. She is very happy and hopeful about it all, and I really think that she will keep straight. If I had only found a decent man at the right moment, who would have been a help to me, I too would have been contented and would have scoffed at the idea of returning to the old uncertain way of life. I feel great sympathy for all girls who come to this life through a succession of misfortunes. Emmy comes of a respectable family; she is the daughter of a sergeant-major, who lost his health altogether in the campaign of 1870-71, and died in 1879. She was the eldest of six children, and had just been confirmed when her mother died. The younger ones were put into an orphanage, and Emma went to an old grandmother, who kept her very close, so as to save her from the fate of her aunt, her mother's sister, who also belonged to the "lost legion." This aunt had been picked up by a Bavarian Prince in a house of ill-fame. He took her away to Munich, where she lived as his *maitresse en titre*. Well, Emmy had a stiff time with the old woman, but now and again she got a chance to break out. A neighbour's daughter, who was a few years older, and possessed by all the devils, taught her the tricks of the trade and often took her the rounds, and as Emmy was then an extremely pretty girl, she was very much run after. Later she went to a hotel to learn cooking, and there the chef went in for her, and persuaded her to hire a room for herself so that he could go and see her. And thenceforth it was down, down, down the hill. . . . Indeed and indeed, that's just what life is like!

I had a very good time that week. It was a blessing to talk to somebody who had trodden the same road as I had myself. One evening we were with an acquaintance of Emmy's, an hotelkeeper, and there was a gentleman there too, a very "'cute'' American; and the latter, Mr. Stark, made violent love to me, but when he became pressing on the way home I snubbed him thoroughly; not that I had anything against him, but it would have seemed to me a wrong to my friend and protector. He allowed me to go on this little trip because he believed in my promise to keep true to him; and I have never yet broken a promise or betrayed a trust.

. . . .

March 2nd, 1898.

I have been very ill. It began in the first week of February: a cough, a cold, pain in the chest, a high temperature. I sent for Julius, who of course came at once, and said it was inflammation of the lungs. I must have caught cold on an automobile drive to Potsdam which I took with the Count; it was blowiing tremendously hard, and I wasn't dressed warmly enough. I can't stand much nowadays. Julius came to me twice a day, mornings and evening, and always stayed over an hour, and his presence consoled and calmed me. And one night when I awoke, he was sitting by my bed; the maid had fetched him because I had been delirious and had frightened her. But when I came to myself the fever was gone, and I was only very tired, but so happy to find him there. And I implored him to stay and be good to me again as he used to be, for I longed so desperately for his love.

"What have I done to make you so cruel to me?" I said.

He shook his head, and answered, gently: "I have never wished to be cruel to you, Thymian. On the contrary! From the very beginning of our acquaintance I have always felt a great interest in you, and my sympathy for you was very near to being a deeper feeling, and would perhaps have turned into that, if the thought of my duty to my family had not made me keep a tight hand upon myself."

"You despise me, Julius," I said.

"No, indeed I don't despise you though at one time I did hope for better things from you. But there! I know what desperate difficulties you had to struggle with. Only, after your husband's death it certainly seemed as if you might have found another way of life. I make you no reproaches on that score. On the whole, it must be frightfully hard to come back to ordinary existence, and keep to it, after you have sounded those depths. I can't help saying, all the same, that I never could and never shall understand how a woman with your intellectual and moral qualities could bear to stay in such a slough of despond – and how you could *go* back to it! . . . But now, the thing's settled; and I daresay that many and many a steady woman with no past at all would have succumbed to such temptation as the Count offered you. For you, no doubt all is for the best. I don't know what more you could have desired. Your old friend is rich; he's a gentleman; and he lays everything you want at your feet. You have all that thousands of other women long for in vain; you are surrounded with comfort and luxury, and can spend your time exactly as you like. Can't you see yourself that you would be risking a safe, comfortable existence, by having an affair with another man behind the Count's back?"

I flung my arms above my head and looked up with streaming eyes to the ceiling. "You are quite right," I said bitterly. "A creature like me is no better than a doll, only filled with lust and cupidity and paltriness. A soul and a heart – an aching, longing heart – are the privileges of the honourable, the respectable. . . ."

"No, no, no!" he cried, and moved from his chair to my bed, and drew my right arm down and held my hand tightly. "I didn't mean that, Thymian! You *have* a heart, you *have* a soul. If I thought you were the ordinary sort of 'creature,' as you say, I should perhaps have no scruples about stealing my neighbour's cherries—"

"No," I broke in. "That's not a good comparison. To steal cherries from your neighbour's garden, you would have to climb the walls which make it private property. But if a cherry-tree stands by the open road, the fact that somebody fosters it and digs about it gives that somebody no exclusive right to the fruit which the wild tree offers."

"You are clever, very clever, Thymian," said Julius. "But just because you are, you must see that in any compact, each has a right to demand fidelity from the other. The Count protects you; and you owe him fidelity."

I only sighed. And he went on in his soft pleasant voice: "Ah, Thymian dear, life is so uncertain! No man knows how long or how short his span may be. The philosophy of philosophies is to find one's happiness and one's deepest satisfaction in abstract rather than in concrete things. You know what I mean—?"

I nodded. My brain was so tired and felt so empty, and yet I grasped at every word he said and held it fast, and especially that about the shortness of life.

"I shan't live much longer, shall I?" I said. "My lungs are affected, are they not? I'm not surprised, for it's in our family. My mother and her two sisters died that way."

He shook his head. "God forbid! Don't think such things. Your lung is a little affected, and if you were leading your former fast life I would answer for nothing. But living quietly as you do now, you may live to be a hundred."

"God preserve me from that!" I cried. "If I may have nothing better from life than food and drink and clothing, I've done with it, thanks! So be kind and give me a morphine injection, a good strong one that'll keep me sound asleep until the Judgment Day. I can't stand any more – I can't indeed!"

I couldn't go on, for I was too tired to control myself, and I cried bitterly.

But the Doctor bent over me and said tenderly, "Poor little Thymian! poor little woman!" and let me put my arms round him and kiss him, and said he would always be my friend, and I must always depend on him. . . . And since then it has been as it used to be between us.

He comes to me every day, and the Count thinks nothing of it, as he's my doctor. And as soon as I'm stronger, I'm to go to the South of France, which I kick against, because I'm so happy again now. But Julius says I must, because this climate is too severe for me; and the Count, who can't come himself, has engaged an elderly lady to accompany me. He does everything possible for me, and I am heartily grateful to him and wish I could truly love him. But I can't give Julius up! No, I can't do that!

. . . .

Nice, April 17th, 1898.

I should like to write a lot, but I don't know what to write about, for nothing is happening to me. Fräulein Wagner is an old dragon. She appears to have her instructions, and I suppose she is acting on them when she "looks after" me and "nurses" me so energetically that it nearly drives me mad. And then she has such an unbearable manner! Whenever I get into a nice, comfortable rage, she smoothes me down with a soft answer and a gentle smile. Unfortunate wretch! she's spent all her life like that as companion, as finishing-governess, as chaperon, always in the most high-class houses, four years with a Duchess in Marseilles, and three years as governess in the family of a Russian prince. She is very cultured and has the most perfect manners; in her long years of dependence and upper-servitude, she has learnt the difficult art of suiting herself to every kind of mood and temper, of always doing what other people like and never what she likes herself, of making herself agreeable, and never giving herself away. With all her smiling, pliant amiability, she usually succeeds, though, in getting her own way in the end. She can talk very interestingly and amusingly, but she is not the person for me. Her virgin past is so immaculate that mine seems like pitch beside it, and the contrast is too glaring to be effective.

I am quite well and strong again. The Wagner lady watches me like a lynx to see that I don't over-do myself. We drive every day for several hours, and take little walks, too; I should like to get home, and the sooner the better, but I daren't try it yet. The Count writes very lovingly and anxiously, and doesn't let me want for anything. He really is a charming old man; as a fatherly friend, absolutely ideal, but I can't help it if I love somebody else. I hardly ever get any news of Julius. He has so much to do and very little time for writing, and his letters are not really love-letters, but all the same I read them over and over until I know them by heart, and kiss them and try to think that I have kissed him. He keeps on preaching to me to put some meaning into my life, to do some work – it's not yet too late to begin, he says. I wish I could, for I feel that he is right, but what am I to go in for? I don't think he knows that himself! For it certainly *is* too late to train myself for any profession.

The sea is so blue, and the sky is so bright, and the sun is so warm. If I had Julius here, it would be Paradise. But then the angel with the fiery sword would be sure to come and turn me out, for Paradise is not intended for people like me. For us is the desolate and unfruitful land, which must be tilled in the sweat of the brow before it will bear fruit.

CHAPTER XVIII

Autumn, 1898.

HOW the months do go by! I made my last entry in April, and now we're in November. When I turn over my Diary it all seems to me like a dream, particularly when I think of what an enormous amount more I've lived through than I've written down. Many people in their old age can look back upon a long, monotonous life, in which no adventures, no experiences, have come to them. That's because their life has been like a small private business; they have sat, as it were, in a little shop where all the articles are of the same description, and have looked at life-only through its tiny windows. It never occurs to them to chase a butterfly over hedges and ditches; and everything that is strange and incomprehensible they dismiss with a disapproving shrug and a shake of the head, or else with a gesture of contempt. But my life is more like a large international warehouse, full of variety, full of rubbish, full of plunder! And yet I wouldn't like to exchange with them in their little dens. In me there is an ever-burning longing for the intangible, the infinite; my feet cling to the earth, but my soul soars upwards to the blue heaven, to the sunny distances, wishing that it could assume there another form, perhaps that of a lark or a flower, but never of a human body again.

I think often of the life on the other side of the grave. If one only knew that, one would have done with this life for ever! I am not religious; on the contrary, I hate churches and parsons, but all the same I believe in another life. If I ever do reach that world, I should like to be a wild animal; or else a man, for a man never gets into an impasse as we women do. There's always at least one door open to him; his whole existence is not ruined by one false step as ours is. The world belongs to men. We women are only suffered as a means to an end.

I often feel very impatient to know what comes after death. I should like to die, so as to know it. If I came before God, I should accuse Him. For He was a clever architect, but a bad builder, when He made the world; and if He means to be the Father of Humanity, He is a bad and unjust one. Almighty! What Almighty Father could see His children suffer and not console them? What father could see his child go astray and not pick it up and bring it back to the right way which leads to happiness? What father stands by and sees his child fall into the water, and does not stretch out his hand to save it? To believe in an Almighty God is an insult to God, for to be Almighty, and to be a Father, and not to will to help us and save us, is to be! If I were God, I should create a godly world. I should change the gloomy purlieus of humanity into blooming rose-gardens. I should break down the walls which prevent them from seeing me and knowing me in my greatness and goodness; and if I were to perceive that one of my creatures was hopelessly diseased by its own evil propensities, I should gently but relentlessly remove it, and put a new person in its place. That would be a Great, Divine Love, and would make men happy, and would be more worthy an Almighty Being.

．　．　．　．　．　．　．　．　．

I have all sorts of curious, confused ideas in my head, which I can never express to other people because they would think I was mad. I still think I shan't live long, and that I have got consumption, because whenever I catch cold I cough so terribly and spit blood, and that was the way my mother died. But Julius says it's just a fixed idea of mine and that my lungs are perfectly healthy, and I don't think he would deceive me; still I can't get rid of the idea.

When I came back from Nice in the beginning of the summer, I went again to Elster, and the Professor was astonished that the "cure" had had no results. But I don't think I wish any longer to have a child. What would become of it if I were to die? It would go under as I did, when they buried my dear mother.

Of course I'm not always in these melancholy states of mind. It's only sometimes, when I think of how absolutely useless a life like mine is, and how there won't be the tiniest trace of me left when I depart one day. I'm not afraid of death itself, but of the slow suffering and languishing decay. My friend would never forsake me, he is too much of a gentleman and a knight for that; but for myself it would be appalling to be able to inspire nothing but pity.

I have a woman friend now, as I have long wished to have. When my Count fetched me back from Elster we went to the Engadine, and afterwards to the Great Week at Baden, and from there to Berlin; and as the Count then took a trip to Norway, I was alone in September, and often went to the afternoon concerts in the Thiergarten.

One day a young woman was sitting opposite to me, who was also alone, and who attracted me in some indescribable way. She was younger than I – three or four-and-twenty – pretty, with black hair done low over her ears, and she was most exquisitely dressed. She looked at me and I looked at her, and we felt instinctively drawn towards one another. Afterwards, as I was strolling about a little in the gardens, I met her at the bear-pit and we began to talk, and told each other our names. She is Frau Maria von O—, and lives in the Nollendorfplatz; and her husband, who is twenty-five years older than she, travels a lot, and so she has a great deal of time to squander, for she was away from Berlin for years, and therefore has few acquaintances. We enjoyed our talk so much that we decided to dine together that evening at the Garden, and it was very nice. She, too, knows Paris and Vienna, and has often been to Monte Carlo; and we've made great friends and go about together every day now, walk or drive in the gardens in the morning, frequently go to the theatre in the evenings, and visit one another continually. She is just about as well off as I am, but hers is a large house with eight rooms.

I will not maintain that I am a great connoisseur about people, but I have a certain instinct which has never yet misled me, and this infallible instinct which drew me to Maria – we call each other by our Christian names and say "thou" tells me too that her past is not irreproachable, and that there are certain incongruities about her. For instance, I've never been able to find out what her husband really is and does. For the moment he is in Monaco. She is a native of Berlin, the daughter of a post-office official, and is always talking about Privy Councillors, Barons and Consuls, and yet, at the same time, certain words and expressions escape her which are only used in the very lowest circles. When we talk together, we are both on our guard the whole time and we know it, and that cannot go on. I don't mind *her* doing it, but it bores me to wear a mask; if I am to have a real woman-friend, I must be able to be completely at my ease with her otherwise, the thing's tiresome.

Once I was invited to supper at her house, and she had a post-office clerk with his wife and her sister there too. An exquisite supper was sent in from the best caterer in Berlin. It was easy to see that the guests were quite unacquainted with most of the dishes, and were very nervous about helping themselves, because they didn't know how to eat them. I was served first, and they watched me to see what I did and then tried to do the same, which wasn't really astonishing for how should a post-office clerk and his family, in an ordinary sort of way, know anything about the kind of delicacies which Maria set before us that evening? They picked at the dishes, like the stork at the cucumber-salad, and didn't know what on earth to do with the lobster! They poked away at it and couldn't get out the flesh, till at last the post-office man in despair took the carving-fork. Well, their uncouth way of eating didn't surprise me very much, but the fact of their being there at all made me think. The ladies called

Maria "thou," and the girl, an impertinent minx about Maria's age, with detestable fair hair and a somewhat, plebeian manner, behaved most rudely, in my opinion, to her hostess, continually interrupting her and making saucy remarks, sneering at her, and, in a word, making herself thoroughly disagreeable. In the course of their Conversation, I learnt that Maria and she had been schoolfellows, It is very strange, too, that Maria never talks about anybody under the rank of a Privy Councillor, and yet one is merely told that her father was "in the Post Office" a "Privy-Clerk," I suppose! I have my own opinion; I'm not easily taken in. Next week Herr von O— comes home. I'm quite excited about it. Maria says they'll give lots of parties then, for her husband has a large circle of acquaintances from his bachelor-days. It doesn't matter to me, any of it, only I hate mysteries. But I'll take my oath that Maria, before her marriage, was no innocent dove.

. . . .

January, 1899.

Chance plays a great part in life. Twice within the last few months it has given me some fun. A short time ago, I was in the Berlin theatre one evening. As I was coming out of the box in the *entr'acte*, the chain of my lorgnon caught in the key and I couldn't move until a gentleman came up and helped me, and this gentleman was none other than D—, whom I hadn't seen for two years! I got crimson, for I really felt a little awkward with him after the insulting way I had thrown him over, but he was plainly delighted to see me again, and shook my hand and assured me several times that nothing more delightful could have happened to him than this surprising *rencontre*. He took my arm quite blithely, and we walked up and down, and he made me tell him everything that had happened to me in these two years. He had got engaged last year, but now it was broken off.

"We shall have some little suppers together, shan't we, dear lady?" he asked, and I told him that that couldn't be.

"Aren't you really angry with me," I inquired, "after the way I threw you over that time?"

He said that he hadn't been at all. "I couldn't blame you for it," he said. "It's in the nature of things that everybody should cut his coat according to his cloth. But I did regret, enormously regret, that I hadn't been born a millionaire, so that I could cut out your old Maecenas."

I was silent, and the blood rushed to my head. Even still, there are moments in my life when it hurts me frightfully, the way in which everyone estimates me by his money's worth, and tacitly implies that I can have no nobler and finer emotions than are awakened by the striking of a bargain. D— certainly didn't wish to offend me, if a "creature" like me can be offended! Besides, he is not a coarse man, but a sympathetic and cultured one; and yet at that moment I hated him for what he had said, and had to put great restraint upon myself not to show him what I felt I should only have made myself ridiculous.

He implored me to give him my address, and as he would have found it in the Directory anyhow, I gave it, but begged him not to come to see me, and he promised he wouldn't. But as I was alone in the theatre, he insisted upon my supping with him somewhere afterwards. I didn't want to, but for peace' sake I at last consented, so we went together to Hohne's and supped in a private room; and I wasn't sorry in the end, for we had a very pleasant little time. D— declares that I am prettier than ever and have got even more slender, but he thinks I look rather ill.

"Your face seems to me quite altered – I should say it was much more *spirituelle* than it used to be," he said.

"That's not surprising, considering the platonic life I lead now," I answered.

"Well, good luck to platonics!" cried be. "Long live platonics!" He took me home about one o'clock.

Well, now for my friend Maria. Her husband, Herr von O—, came home in the beginning of December. One look at him was enough for me. Poor dear Casimir was certainly nothing to boast of, but he could well bear comparison with the "Baron" von O—, as he calls himself. Von O— will never see seventy again; a dried-up, emaciated old rake, with a head as bald as a billiard-ball, except for a fringe of sparse hair and a white "goatee" to match. Maria was rather uneasy, and thought it necessary to whisper in my ear that her husband was not exactly young or handsome, but had, after all, the one thing needful a good heart.

I take her word for that, and indeed I think she might have given the heart a further certificate. I should say it was not only good, but capacious. As far as I can make out from what I know of this house up to the present, Herr von O— is perhaps not precisely a common swell-mobsman, but he's as near it as possible. And now I know what they want such a big house for. They have an evening for gentlemen every Thursday, and on that night play runs high, and Herr von O— almost always keeps the bank. On the Thursday evenings that I spent there about thirty gentlemen came, and they started a little game of roulette, and some of them played poker and faro, which are quite amusing to look on at. I tried my luck a little at roulette too, and won two hundred marks, which was a great joke. The men are real gentlemen; many are officers; and each of them has a certain pass-word which he gives to any newcomer whom he introduces, and this latter says it unobtrusively, as soon as he enters, to the master of the house, so that Herr von O— may know who has been responsible for each introduction.

It has interested me very much to observe how the passion for play obliterates all others. My fascination has no effect once play has begun – it only works before the business of the evening is taken in hand. So soon as the tables are set, the men have no eyes or ears for anything but the red and white balls or the cards; it is as if their senses were actually paralysed by the lust for gold – the gold that they so untiringly strive for. They are all quite evidently people who never touch a round game. Extraordinary! I don't understand what the attraction of these games of pure chance can be for thinking people. They used to play round games at home in my childhood's days, and they seemed to me to have much more in them. There's some play in those; but in these, chance is the sole arbiter.

When I went to see Maria a few weeks ago, I found her in a very excited state, and she looked quite disfigured. Her face was covered with spots as if she had scarlet fever, and her eyes were red with crying. I thought at first that she must have had a row with her husband (though he's always very affectionate to her), and then by discreet questioning I found out that she had been annoyed with her friend Fräulein Wiegand, the post-office clerk's sister-in-law.

"She's an abominable person," Maria said. "I've done everything I could for her, and instead of being grateful, she's merely impertinent. That's the worst of having anything to do with people of that class."

"Yes, indeed," said I, laughing in my sleeve. "I've always been surprised that you allowed the girl to be so rude to you. What happened, then?"

"Oh, a lot of nonsense. One ought to snap one's fingers at it," Maria went on. "We went to the same school when we were children, and lived in the same house and played together, so I can't treat her *de haut en bas*, when she makes up to me."

"What was her father, then?" I inquired.

"He was in a barber's shop; they were quite poor people."

"Ah! then they lived in the back rooms at your house."

"Of course," said Maria, and got crimson, recognising her blunder.

I had quite forgotten this little episode, but as I was buying a pound of pralines at H—'s in the Leipzigerstrasse yesterday, suddenly one of the shopgirls spoke to me by name, and when I looked up I recognised Maria's old school friend, the impertinent blonde Fräulein Wiegand.

She was quite excited, and said, "Well, dear lady, the 'Baroness' has been abusing me to you because I told her some home truths, hasn't she?" . . . Of course I pretended to know nothing at all, so she began, and her tongue went like the clapper of a bell, and I had the whole of Maria's history slung at my head. Just as I had thought. Her father was a letter-carrier, and they lived in the "two-pair-back" of a house where the Wiegands had the ground floor! Maria was the youngest of five children, and the idol of her parents, on account of her beauty. After her Confirmation she went as apprentice to a dressmaking-business, and two years later ran away with the proprietor to Paris, and her parents are said to have died of grief. Of course that's all gossip, and Fräulein Wiegand's whole story was so compact of envy, hatred, malice, and all uncharitableness, that it almost made me sick to have to swallow so much venom at one sitting. But as it was utterly impossible to cut her short, I heard a lot more. How nothing was real about the Baron except his title; all the rest was a swindle, and not so much as a duster in the big establishment belonged to him – everything was Markiewicz'! And then I heard the story of the quarrel. . . . And how Maria had lived with the Baron for a year before he married her, and so forth, till I had been told everything there was to tell, and at last since I couldn't stop her tongue I simply turned my back on her and departed. I had heard nothing but what I had long suspected; it did not surprise me in the very least! I was only disgusted at the girl's baseness, for I'm perfectly sure that she would have done just as Maria did, if she had got the chance.

The next time Maria and I met, and she began to boast, I took her hand and said, "Maria, we won't have any more of this rot. My father was an apothecary, and yours was a letter-carrier, so there's not very much to choose between us. But we have both sounded the deeps of life; and if, amid all the infamies that surround one there, one keeps one's vision clear, one soon gets a wide outlook which passes far beyond the paltriness of superficial things – one sees much which is hidden from those who live the sheltered life. It is easy to say *I defy temptation*, when one has never known temptation, when family affection and home and friends and all one's environment set up palisades around one, through which no mocking devil can reach to show one the 'kingdom of this world.' But we, who have had no such protecting walls around us, we who have heard the tempest roaring in our very ears when death or destiny had left us defenceless – we know quite well that only he who is without sin should dare to cast a stone at the sinner. And we are all sinners, every one."

Maria began to cry and said she knew that that false cat, Clara Wiegand, would give her away – that pig! that – I interrupted her, and told her that she had lost nothing in my estimation through Clara Wiegand's betrayal, but that, on the contrary, I felt that a wall of division had fallen from between us at last. And to make a beginning, I told her the principal facts about myself; and then she gave way altogether, and confessed that she too had long wished for an opportunity to speak out, and had always intended to tell me everything.

Which I took with a pinch of salt!

CHAPTER XIX

May, 1899.

I DON'T know what is the matter with me. I am ill and yet not ill. An incessant restlessness drives me on and on into the strangest activities. It is some time since this came over me – this mania for spending money, for buying and giving away; and I don't know what will happen if it gets any worse. It is really just like a disease.

I never used to be like this. In that respect I had inherited my mother's solid good-sense. I have always had a great dread of debt. I still think with horror of the time in the Schellingstrasse with the boarding-house, and what I suffered there through my debts, when I didn't know how they'd ever get paid. It had always been my fixed principle to buy nothing that I could not pay for at once.

But for some time now I haven't been able to help buying and buying and buying. And even though I swear to myself a thousand times *I'll spend no money to-day*, as soon as I get into the Leipziger or Friedrichstrasse, something draws me into the shops, and I buy and buy, and it's just as if I were intoxicated with the sheer lust of it, for I buy things en masse that I don't want at all. My cook and kitchen-maid simply don't know what to do with the blouses and petticoats and aprons and hats that I buy and present to them. And I take such wild fancies to ornaments and bronzes and silk hangings, and I buy them, and buy them and pay what I can, and have the rest charged to my account. And so it came about that this month I had spent all but a few shillings of my allowance by the 8th, and I stuffed all the bills into a drawer in my writing-table, and haven't had the heart to look through them, and they get bigger and bigger every day, for I never go out without buying something. Lately I bought twelve Dresden figures for nine hundred and eighty marks the lot; and when they were sent and I saw the bill, I got into a terrible fright lest the Count should see them and ask me about them, and in my despair I smashed them all to pieces, and stuffed the bill into the drawer. I did the same with a little silk hanging from a curio-shop in the Wilhelmstrasse. Its colouring was divinely exquisite, and it cost eight hundred marks. And I didn't know what to do with it either, so in sheer terror I cut it to pieces, and Julius caught me at it and was quite shocked at the vandalism.

"For God's sake, Thymian, what are you doing?" I was half-paralysed with fright, and murmured, "I only want to get rid of it. If the Count were to see it, I'd get a lecture."

He shook his head and said I was terribly neurotic, and ought to go for a short time to a sanatorium for nervous diseases. But at that I got quite wild, and shrieked out that I wasn't mad, and that I wasn't going into a madhouse, and that he ought to go to an idiot-asylum himself; but he kept perfectly cool, and since then he comes every day as he used to, and once I saw him and the Count whispering together and that made me so crazy with rage that I wanted to kill them both, and went out and slammed the door behind me, and locked myself up in my room. D— is my best friend after all, and I have asked him to come to me. I wish myself that I could get rid of this buying-mania, but I won't go into a nerve-sanatorium, for I'm not a bit off my head and know exactly what I'm doing. I should like to help all poor people, to feed the hungry, to clothe the naked, and it makes me so miserable not to be able to that I often cry about it for hours. When I see a poor child in the street I get hold of it, and buy it shoes and linen and clothes, and tell them to send in the bill to me; and the shop-people all give me credit because I live in the big house on the Kronprinzenufer, and because they've seen me with the Count, who is known to be a millionaire.

When it comes into my head at nights that so many poor people in Berlin have no place to lay their heads, I get so miserable that I cannot go to sleep again, and would like to sell all that I possess and give it to the poor, and go on the streets once more myself.

On the 11th of May, I was at one of the "men's evenings" at the O—'s. It was the last for this year; Herr von O— is in Paris again now. They were playing faro, and I was sitting beside a fat Italian banker, who couldn't speak a word of German, but made desperate love to me in his mother-tongue. He was winning tremendously, and as I was sitting beside him I collected all the gold and notes in my lap, and afterwards asked him jokingly what percentage he was going to give me for having brought him luck. Upon that, he said in Italian, "Certainly, dear lady it is all for you; and I count myself truly happy in being able to lay it at your feet."

Well, I didn't see why I should make any fuss about taking his winnings, so I just said *Grazie, O Signore,*" and put the money in my pocket. But then I looked at Maria, who was sitting opposite. I was simply terrified. I had never seen her like that. She looked positively livid, and her eyes were awful. I got up and went out, and she came after me, trembling with rage, and said, "I'm beside myself, Thymian! How can you, a lady, make so little of yourself as to take all that money from an absolute stranger?"

"Rather much, than little!" said I. "And more-over, I have never represented myself as being a lady."

"Well, you might have some regard for us and our name," she said grandiloquently. "You are not in a low gambling house now; you are the guest of Baron and Baroness O—."

At first I took it as a joke, but then her high-and-mighty airs began to incense me.

"As Frau Osdorf, you can do what you like, of course," she went on; "but we know what is due to our name——."

"Oh, come!" said I, "if I cared about that sort of rubbish, I could call myself Countess, and no one would have a word to say, for my husband was a Count, but I wouldn't be bothered doing it. If I were living on my own property, and had horses and carriages, and went to Court, there might be some sense in it; but as things are, I prefer to call myself what I am, a free lance. Besides, as your husband wins all the men's money at play, I may just as well have it as he. We can both get some good out of it if you like, for I am going to make a suggestion to you. Let's divide the spoil – like sisters – half and half! Yes or no?"

"Yes," answered Maria curtly; and we divided it, and each got one thousand and eighty-two marks. I believe that Maria had had designs upon the Italian, and is jealous of me. She has been so for a long time. But lately I don't seem to care a hang about men. All I want is to buy, to buy all day long, and give presents, and see happy faces around me. Yes, buying is my only joy!

. . . .

Yesterday the Italian bank-man took me for a drive in the Grünewald in his automobile. Maria was there too, and I think she wished me further! But how could I help his making love to me? It was in the nature of things that he should rather talk to me, because I can speak Italian, and Maria can only manage a little bad French. Goodness knows I don't care twopence about him! We drove to the Hundekehle, where we had ordered dinner.

As we went in, Maria said to me, "You look positively consumptive again to-day, Thymian – most wretchedly ill. Why on earth don't you paint a little? It makes me feel quite sick to look at you. You look as if you'd been buried and dug up again."

I answered not a syllable, but the word "consumptive" went like a knife into my heart. It was as much as I could do to eat anything. My very soul seemed to shudder. . . .

In the evening I told it to Julius, who often comes unexpectedly to see me now. He consoled me, and said that I ought to give her up, for I could never get any real joy out of intercourse with her.

"You can't make a silk purse out of a sow's ear," he said; "and no amount of paint, inside or outside, can hide the real nature of that sort of woman – the natural coarseness always breaks out. You don't belong to that class, and can never sympathise with them, for, in spite of appearances, you are innately prouder, tenderer, sweeter than they."

I daresay he's right, but one does so want to have at least *one* friend! Julius was so sweet and good that evening, that I took heart, and confided all my troubles to him. He insisted on my showing him the bills, which I did reluctantly. The drawer was crammed full! He added them up and compared them, and his face grew sterner and sterner, and more and more perturbed.

"Good God! Thymian, have you any idea how much it is?"

"No," said I, anxiously.

"Thirteen thousand marks! Child, child! what on earth have you done with all the stuff?"

I didn't know myself. Much of it I had given away, much I had destroyed, and a lot of it was still unpacked in the attics.

"Well, *those* at any rate you must send back," he declared.

"No," said I; "I won't disgrace myself like that for anything."

"Well, really, you've funny ideas of honour and disgrace!" cried he. "What *are* you going to do then? Some arrangement must be made, or they'll come some day and seize your furniture. What on earth made you do it?"

"It was like a disease," I said.

"Yes, you're undeniably ill," returned he. " I saw that long ago. You're thoroughly neurotic. Well, don't worry for the present. I'll think of something to do. By far the best thing would be to tell the Count."

But I wouldn't agree to that, and he had to promise me not to do it. I'm very frightened. I feel very ill too. Julius thought at first it was my nerves, but on examination it didn't seem to be that. I am *so* ill.

. . . .

December, 1898.

A lot to record.

The summer months were ghastly. The Count couldn't go away, for official business kept him in Berlin, and I didn't want to travel either. My house is beautifully cool, and Julius was only away for a couple of weeks, and I always felt ill and weary. The end of August was the fatal day.

It had been raining, and the air was so exquisitely fresh and sweet that I went out about five, down to the Gardens, and stayed there nearly two hours, for I was feeling so happy, and ever so much better that day. I delighted in the children who were playing about there, and the grass was sparkling with rain-drops, and the sun shone splendidly, and I thought again, "How beautiful the world is, after all!" When I came out of the Gardens, I was thinking too hard to notice anything, and as I was crossing the

Siegesallee, I suddenly slipped, and at the same moment a carriage dashed up – and I know nothing more of what happened except that I got a frightful blow on the side, and fainted. They picked me up, and carried me to the ambulance station, thinking I was dead; and thence I was taken, still unconscious, to my own house for I had my card-case with me.

Then I lay for a long, long time in high fever, and knew nothing of what was going on; and in my few conscious moments I always fancied that I was back at home, and that everything which had happened to me since was a dream. I used to call for father, and thought my nurse was Sister Anna, who had brought mother home from Davos that time.

Then I gradually got better, and came back to my senses, and recognised Julius, who often sat beside my bed for hours at a time.

"What on earth has happened to me?" I said at last, for I couldn't remember anything clearly, my brain was so weak.

"Yes, indeed, what has happened to you, my poor child?" said Julius. "You yourself know best. Do try to remember! If we'd only had the least idea! Why on earth didn't you say anything to anybody?"

"Ah! I was run over, wasn't I? I seem to remember that," said I.

"And the rest! All is over now."

I didn't know what he meant; and then he told me that I had been pregnant, and was nearly half-way through with it, and that the frightful blow had brought on a miscarriage. And of all that I knew nothing – nothing!

There had been so few of the usual signs. . . . It didn't affect me very much. I think it's better so, for what could I have done with the child? But I had suffered terribly, and it was late autumn before I could get up again.

They were all very good to me. And the money trouble has been settled, by which I mean that Julius and I have agreed that I am to sell the greater part of my diamonds, and pay off some of the debts. Then, in April, I'll take a smaller house, and sell the superfluous furniture. What do I want with five rooms? Three are quite enough. And then I can dismiss the cook, and save enough out of my monthly allowance from the Count to pay off everything gradually.

The buying mania must have had something to do with my condition, for now it's quite gone, and I'm just as I was before.

I've heard nothing more from Maria. In the middle of June she went off to Ostend, and in July the establishment here was given up, and Markiewicz took back the furniture. There hasn't been a direct communication of any kind from her since then.

But there has been an indirect one. For in November, when I was up again at last, my Count came to me one afternoon and gave me a letter which he had received, and which had been posted in Cologne at the beginning of July. This was what it said, in very bad spelling:

"HONOURED SIR, —

"One who cannot endure to see you betrayed by her who owes you everything, warns you to be on your guard. Thymian is utterly corrupt and evil. She flirts with other men; she has a *liaison* with a doctor, and another with a business man. She goes about with these two behind your back, and deceives you. That is the woman's gratitude for your great goodness to her. She flirts with every man who comes in her way. She can't help it.

Badness is in her blood. Let her be watched by a detective, and he will tell you more than I have told you.

"A WELL WISHER."

I couldn't believe my eyes, and had to read the letter twice. My first overwhelming feeling was absolute consternation, so great that it gave me actual pain, and increased to anger; and with it there was a sort of feeling that I couldn't believe in such atrocious infamy. I had never done the woman the very least bit of harm; we had parted as friends, and I had been so devoted to her that I would have gone through fire and water and shared my last crust with her. And I had confided in her wholly, because it had never entered my head that anyone could be so base as to betray such a trust. When I had recovered from my first stupefaction, it seemed to me almost funny – the unconscious humour of the superscription, "A Well Wisher"! And yet I never realised that this anonymous scrawl was perhaps going to endanger my whole existence. *That* first occurred to me when I felt the stern and piercing look which the Count fixed upon my face.

"As a general rule, I pitch anonymous letters into the wastepaper basket," he said, "and this will go the same way. But I – I thought I'd just ask you. . . . Your hand on your heart, Thymian! I want the truth. Is that pure calumny? Or is there a grain of truth in it?"

Then I knew for the first time the risk I ran. But no matter what was to happen, I could not lie at that moment.

"Yes," I answered very low.

He didn't say a word at first He turned his back to me, and went to the window and looked out silently into the street for fully ten minutes. Then he turned round slowly, and I saw that he was deeply moved.

"I should never have thought it of you, Thymian," he said gently. "No; I trusted you. . . . My God! I was a fool. I might have known—"

I didn't catch his last words, but I bent my head and covered my eyes with my hands, and never in my life have I felt so small and contemptible and evil as in that moment, and never had I known utter shame till then. I was crushed to the very depths of my being, and it would have been a relief to me if he had struck me and ordered me out of the house there and then, and never given me another penny. But nothing, nothing of all that did he do.

"It's really tragic that I cannot be as angry with you as you deserve, Thymian," he said, after a short time. "I won't even reproach you. How could an old man like me expect fidelity from a beautiful young woman like you—"

"From a prostitute, you mean," cried I, and then I couldn't restrain myself any more, but broke into wild sobs and tears. And for the first time in my life I was crying over *myself* – crying because I really and truly was a prostitute, not a bit nobler, not a bit better, than the poorest of the poor creatures on the street who sell their bodies for a few pence. For if I hadn't been, I would have promised him in that moment to break off with everyone else, and henceforth belong to him alone, in gratitude for all that he had done for me, and was doing then.

But I couldn't promise it, I couldn't! For I knew that I should not keep my word, and that would have been worse than bad – that would have been infamous.

Oh! if I only hadn't this wretched love for Julius, or if I were only strong enough to conquer it! But I am not. I am a prostitute.

"Let it pass, Thymian. We won't speak of it again," said the Count "Everything shall be as before."

And everything is as before. That is what tortures me. I seem so horrible to myself. I can't look the old man in the face, I'm so ashamed. His goodness kills me.

When I sat up for the first time in bed, and the Sister combed out my hair, and the long tresses streamed over my shoulders, I drew my fingers through them, and discovered in the black masses one snow-white thread. I was terrified at first, and afterwards it made me melancholy. I'm only just seven-and-twenty years old, and already I have a white hair. . . . Perhaps I shall be quite an old woman when I'm thirty-five. Oh! if I could only die! My heart is filled with such an infinite longing for death.

.   .   .   .

January 1st, 1900.

I had fully intended to write up my Diary again on New Year's Eve, but last night D— was here, and ate his New Year's Eve supper with me. I was delighted that he came, for one's thoughts are not pleasant company on that particular evening; and the Count was out at a supper-party, and Julius never comes on these occasions – he belongs to his family, he says. But D— is just as lonely as I am. We told one another all sorts of things, and exchanged opinions on this, that, and the other. There is something very nice and fresh about him, and we harmonise in many ways. We got a little silent towards midnight and suddenly he gave me a long look, and said, shaking his head, "What a glorious wife you would have made, Thymian! If I could only put my hand on the scoundrel who brought you to this, I'd make his knees knock together. The hound!"

"It was *in* me anyhow," I sighed.

"Ah, don't talk nonsense!" he cried, almost angrily. "A woman like you could only have come to grief by great ill-luck."

The Count might know all about my friendship with D—, for ever since our meeting again we've been only friends, the best of good comrades.

We heard the bells ringing-in the New Year.

"A Happy New Year!" said D—, as we clinked glasses.

"And may I get my wish!" said I.

"What is that?"

"To rest," I answered mournfully. "To die."

"Child, child! Life is sweet, and the sleep under the grass is long. What you want is the salt of life, Thymian – work! Work that will absorb you, body and soul!"

I didn't answer. What could I have said? Everyone who wishes me well gives me that advice. Oh, find me work, then, that will absorb me, body and soul – I am ready for it? But it's all idle talk. Nobody can help me. My life is utterly ruined. I wish I was away out there on my Schöneberg property!

CHAPTER XX

May, 1900.

LAST month I got, early one morning, a letter from Councillor Ellbaum of G—. I instantly felt a presentiment that it contained some very bad news, and opened it with a sinking heart. My instinct had not deceived me. The Councillor wrote to say that father had died on the eleventh of March. He had been ill for a long time.

The business is to be taken over by Meinert, who the Councillor wrote was very shortly to be married, and was getting such a good dowry with his bride that he would be able to pay off some of the mortgages. The first claim was one of forty thousand marks which I had inherited from my mother, and this could be paid on the first of October, or sooner, if I wished. He added the further information that the widow, Frau Helene Gotteball, had been obliged to leave the house which had been her home for all these years, and, with her two as yet uneducated children, had been left in absolute penury. She would have to turn to and find something to do, if they were to live at all, for the sale of the business had brought in only a very few thousand marks more than was needed for the outstanding debts.

I was deeply moved by the news of father's death. And that I should hear it in such a manner, that Lena should not even have taken the trouble to send me a word herself – oh, that filled me with hatred and bitterness against the vulgar woman who had been the sole cause of my father's estrangement from me, who had literally turned me out of my childhood's home! She had no excuse for not knowing my address. The Councillor's letter reached me all right, though it was addressed to "Frau Gräfin Thymian Osdorff."

The first day I spent in utter grief, and my heart was filled with memories and mournful thoughts, and it was only the next day that it occurred to me why the Councillor had written, and that I must answer him. And then I thought it all out. The poor brats couldn't help it; none of it had been their fault, and after all, they were father's children. From what I knew of our relations – the North-country lot on mother's side were the only prosperous ones – they would never move a finger to help the woman, nor care in the least what became of the children, whether they starved or went under altogether. I'm pretty much of a good-for-nothing; no one thinks much of me; but I couldn't find it in my heart to live in luxury and have to think that those poor little creatures wanted the necessaries of life. No! the food I ate would stick in my throat if I had to think of that. They are my half-brother and sister, when all's said and done, and who knows that the little girl mayn't have a drop of the much-dreaded blood in her the legacy of the French *cocotte* who made my great-grandfather lose his head over her! What is, in reality, the greatest danger of all, the rock upon which "virtue" (so-called) and innocence most often split? Is it not Poverty? the impossibility of getting what one wants in a legitimate fashion? I can't protect her, that's very certain; and what will be, will be. . . . But at all events I don't want the money so badly as they do, and therefore I've resolved to take twenty thousand marks myself and pay my debts out of it, keeping what's over against a rainy day, or to help somebody else with – Emmy and her bridegroom, for example, who would like so much to buy an hotel business, and want a thousand dollars before they can do it. She sent me an embroidered cushion that she made herself, last Christmas, to show me that she remembered me. . . . The other twenty thousand marks I'll put in the Savings, Bank in G—, and Lena shall have the interest on it for the children's education until they're of age. And that I mightn't repent of my resolution, I wrote off at once to the Councillor. A few days afterwards, Lena sent me a long letter of thanks, in which she informed me that father had suffered internally for more than a year, and had endured great agony at the last. Of course she managed tactfully to insinuate that his

229

grief for me had broken him down, and concluded with the equally graceful assurance that she would put the money to a good use, and bring her children up to be honest decent people. Well, well, what else could one expect? . . .

I should like to know whether father had any wish to see me at the end. He *did* love me, and it can never have occurred to him, surely, to bear me any grudge for my moral downfall! I can't get it out of my head that they may have prevented him from writing to me and calling me to him. . . .

I live in the Bulowstrasse now – four rooms, a pretty, comfortable abode.

The Count hasn't come nearly so often lately. I don't think he is angry with me, but he seems never to have been able to get over my not having been quite faithful to him. But really that is folly. Fidelity can only be where love is, and he cannot have imagined that I loved him!

. . . .

August 14th, 1900.

The smell of pines – and woods with streams murmuring amid the trees! I *had* to come to the Harz again. . . . In June I was with the Count on his estate for three weeks. I was surprised at his taking me with him. I had my orders, of course – I was to call myself Frau von Osdorff to the servants. Why, I know not! The stay there was very pleasant, only a little irksome on account of the secrecy of it. We were always making *détours*, so as not to run across some of the neighbours. The Count said I wanted country air – I don't mean "paint" this time, but literally![1] For

---

[1] "Landluft geniessen" is slang, in these circles, for "schminken," which means "to paint the face."

I've never got really well since my illness. I would rather have sent in my place that poor sickly creature, the "Black Swallow," as we used to call her, a former acquaintance of the dancing-saloons. I met her in the street this spring, and she looked so wretched and hopeless, slinking along so timidly by the side of the houses, that I spoke to her. Good heavens! to think that any one can come to such utter grief! A few years ago she was one of our smartest girls, and now she looks positively dreadful. She is ill; I don't know what's the matter with her, but she is thoroughly out of health. And poor, into the bargain, for of course nobody wants her when she looks like that. She told me that a little while ago she really had nothing to eat, and had lived for a week on dog's meat. I have let her have dinner in my kitchen every day since then.

The Castle is very fine – a majestic building in the true Romantic Style. I liked being there very much. My old friend and I get on very well together; in those weeks we really drew much nearer to one another in many ways.

I particularly delighted in the library. When it rained, it was always so cosy there; I could have sat all day in one of the deep morocco-leather chairs and read without stopping from morning till night. One afternoon there was a thunderstorm and the air was very sultry, so that I had dozed a little over my after-coffee reading; but the thunder woke me, and as the lightning was wonderful, and the rain was coming down in bucketsful, I got up and went into one of the deep window-embrasures to look out at the tempest. I was wearing my white point-lace dress with the long train (for the Count likes me best in white), and I was stretching up a little, so as to look through the clear panes above the stained-glass, and the pale lightning kept flashing through the window and filling the deep embrasures with a sulphurous half-light.

"If a painter were to see you now, in that position, with the light falling on you like that, he would want to sketch you on the spot, so that there might be some record of the effect," said the Count, reflectively. "The high, pointed frame of the window, the broken, many-hued light, the pale quivering reflection of the lightning-lit sky, and you in the midst of it all, so tall, so slender, so white and queenly to behold – it's all so perfectly harmonious. . . ."

"Yes, it must be. An old castle is exactly the right setting for me, isn't it?" I answered drily.

"Do you know that a couple of years ago I really had for a short time the idea of marrying you?" he said gravely.

"I can scarcely believe it," I answered.

"It is better as it is – for us both," said he.

I was silent, but involuntarily I pictured to myself what it would have been like to be mistress of this castle. I don't care a hang for nobility and that kind of nonsense, but I think that a glorious possession like this, inherited from generation to generation, does give to its inhabitants a certain supremacy, a feeling of independence, of isolation from the common herd, fighting and toiling for mere existence. I have more veneration for these old splendid buildings, whose walls have watched the flight of centuries, than for their proprietors!

We did not say anything more about that. The Count doesn't seem to be jealous or distrustful any longer, and certainly he has no reason to be. I see so very little of Julius, and with D— my intercourse is entirely platonic. At the end of July, the Count went off to Holstein to stay with his brother, whose son was getting married; and after that he was going to Bohemia.

By my desire, he brought me to Ilsenburg. Ever since I was in the Harz some years ago I've always longed to go back, especially in the summer months in Berlin. The time that I was so ill, I was always dreaming of the coolness and quietness of the fragrant pine-woods, and the memory of the murmuring streams seemed to me like that of a sort of Paradise. Secretly I hoped, too, to find some Hamburg acquaintances there. Some of them I should like very much to see again, The Harz country is always crammed full of Hamburgers, but up to the present I haven't met anyone I know. All the faces are strange to me. I sent D— a picture post-card, and one evening, four days later, there he stood in the flesh! He had intended to go to the Ostsee, but as soon as he got my card, he felt a wild fancy to take a trip to the Harz country; and now he is regularly settled down at Ilsenburg, and we wander daily through the woods and over the hills, and are the best of comrades. He sometimes gets sentimental fits. Yesterday we found a delicious little nook in the wood. I sat down on a moss-covered stone, and he stretched himself on the grass, and we spent two solid hours there without saying a word. It was a real forest sanctuary. The brooks rippled and babbled and murmured by, and the grasshoppers chirped, and a little bird was singing, and the sun shone down from the blue sky, glittering golden-green through the trees, and all the place was so solemn and so still! Such rest environed us that it seemed as if one could fill one's soul with great draughts of that divine tranquility, and keep them there always to refresh one in the waste of life. Oh, if one only *could* take to one's self the peace of such hours and carry them in one's soul for ever! It was all so sacred, so wonderful, so glorious! It was only one's own heart that beat like a knell in one's breast, and told one that true peace never comes from the outside, but can spring from the deepest depths of the soul alone.

"Yes, yes, Thymian; I wish I'd known you ten years sooner," said D—, unexpectedly, as we were going home.

"Even then it would have been too late," said I, "for I had barely celebrated my sixteenth birthday when I had a child."

He shook his head, and wanted me to tell him about it I didn't feel inclined to just then, but on another evening, when we were walking in the wood, I told him how it had all happened. And he said that he would never marry, because whenever he met a woman who might do, he couldn't help comparing her with me, and none of them was fit to hold a candle to me. As a general rule I'm not vain, but I did like hearing that. I shouldn't at all like to lose him as a friend, and that I undoubtedly should do if he were to marry.

Emmy and her man are enchanted that I am going to lend them the money. I intend to go myself to G— on the first of October and get it. I have a sort of home-sickness for the graves there. Graves are the only things I have in the world which are mine, really mine.

. . . .

November, 1900.

You and I, my little Book, are both falling into the sere, the yellow leaf. Your leaves are coming to an end, and so is my life; but as I'm afraid we can't make it coincide exactly, I am going to get a refill for you! Well, well! you haven't learnt much that's good about me. I read you right through this afternoon and felt as if I was living it all over again. I should like to have written ever so much more than I have, but I never had simultaneously the time and the inclination to set everything down.

Sorrow constrained my heart when I read my first childish entries:—

"Spread out thy two white wings, O Jesus, King of Kings,
  And take this little birdie in ;
Then through the evil day, she'll hear thine angels say
  'This little child shall do no sin.'"

Good Aunt Freda, ministering angel! Your star was not in the heavens; no kindly saint carried your pious prayer for your poor motherless little birdie to your Saviour. In the evil day she *did* know sin; she has quite gone under, she has been consumed by the lust of the flesh.

Ah! that going home again stirred everything up, and made me feel like a ploughed held. It would have been better if I had not gone.

As soon as I came near Hamburg, and heard the Hamburg accent again, my heart sank like a stone. It sounded so strange to me, as if I'd been away a whole lifetime instead of only eleven years. The sound of the voices there is so totally different, so much harsher, simpler, more honest, somehow; and I felt as if I was separated from my home and my people by an abyss that could not be bridged over.

It was already dark when I arrived, a cold, gloomy autumn evening. Upon the level land which stretches all round the town there lay a sullen, reddish light, amid which the clouds moved like black birds. I left my handbag in the "Deutschen Hof," and took a room there. I had supper in my own room, and afterwards I wandered about the streets for a while in the dark. As I crossed the market-place and stood before our shop, my knees trembled and my heart almost stood still with emotion, and a mad longing to go in came over me; and before I had time to think, I had gone up the steps and was standing in the entrance-hall. I went into the shop and asked for some peppermint-drops. I had put on a thick veil, but the young man who served me would not have known me in any case. The door of the counting-house was half open, and at the desk stood Meinert. I saw him plainly. His hair has grown thinner and his features are sharper, otherwise he looks the same.

The little hall was in disorder. Lena had moved a few days ago. The wardrobe from father's bedroom, and some furniture from the best room, were standing there, and boxes and cases lay about in wild confusion. I stood there quietly for a little time, and I cannot describe my feelings. Like lightning, many visions passed through my mind. I saw myself as a child running through the hall; I thought of the evening when Meinert had carried me upstairs on his shoulders; I saw mother's coffin being carried through the folding-doors, and lived again through the hour when, on that terrible evening of Elizabeth's suicide, I crept up the stairs in the twilight – that evening upon which the die was cast for me. And as I went out of the door, I knew that I had crossed the threshold of my childhood's home for the last time in my life. . . .

After that I wandered about for an hour in all directions through the streets. At Aunt Freda's the green roller-blinds with grey-and-brown Watteau pictures on them were let down, and the lamp was burning behind them, the old lamp with its well-polished brass stand – I knew so exactly how it looked! And on the window-sill stood the pots of flowers and ferns just as they used to. And I knew that she was sitting on the sofa knitting, counting her stitches, and occasionally glancing at the newspaper or a good book – and perhaps, in that very moment, a fleeting thought of the lost one who was standing out in the street in the dusk of the evening passed through her kind little maiden-soul. . . .

I slept very little that night. In the morning I breakfasted in the coffee-room, and the landlady, a comparatively young woman, who was a stranger to me, was very cordial, so I entered into conversation with her and asked about the Gotteball family, saying that I had once as a child been on a visit to them.

"Yes, it's very sad for poor Frau Gotteball that she's so badly off now," said the landlady; "and the children still so young, just coming to the age when they cost money. Her husband suffered frightfully before he died, but no wonder, considering the life he led."

"How do you mean?" I asked.

"My God! He was a regular devil after the women! Hereabouts they all called him – I can't say what. Before he married, he used to have great goings-on with his housekeepers. One of them drowned herself. Well, he was punished for it. He got his deserts in his daughter – her by the first wife, you know—"

"Yes, of course Thymian! I went to school with her for a little while. What has become of her? Has she married?"

"*That* one – not she! I didn't know her. I've only been here seven years, and she was gone when I came. They say she was awfully handsome, but she was the sort that's not to have nor to bind, you know, as they say. Frau Gotteball told me about it herself. Of course it was a trial for her to have such a girl as a step-daughter. When she was only just fifteen, she started her games with Herr Meinert, who has the shop now, and had a child by him. It was born in Hamburg, and she never came home afterwards. They say she went on the streets in Hamburg and Berlin, and no one knows what's become of her, but most likely she's come to a bad end altogether. That sort always dies in the gutter."

"Yes, yes," I answered; "that sort always dies in the gutter. Then she hasn't married?"

"Once there was some talk here that she'd married a Count in Berlin, but of course that's all nonsense. Frau Gotteball doesn't believe it herself. Why! a Count wouldn't touch a thing like that with a pair of tongs, to say nothing of marrying her. I'll bet my hat nobody believes it. Old Gotteball got quite soft at the last, and wanted to have his daughter here, but of course Frau Gotteball wouldn't stand that, and small blame to her – I wouldn't like to have such a creature in any of my beds! And besides, she didn't know where on earth she was."

I nodded and said, "But after all, it was really the man Meinert's fault. And did he stay on in the shop?"

"Yes, he did. He's clever, and the old man was shaky at the last. Besides, men never get the blame."

"Didn't Thymian inherit anything from her mother?" I asked. "She had some property, I know."

The landlady was quite uninformed on that point, so I saw that Lena had sagely held her tongue about it.

"And how is old Fräulein Gotteball?" I continued.

"Oh, she's absolutely gone to pieces," said the woman; "but she manages to rub along. She hadn't seen anything of her brother for years, but she was there when he was dying. The sisters-in-law hated each other. Frau Gotteball is vexed because Freda has nothing to leave her children, for she made a fool of herself over the other girl; but now of course Freda has cast her off too."

"Ah! she has cast her off too?" I said, and asked for Lena's address. She lives now in the Weihgasse. I had arranged to be at the Councillor's at one o'clock.

I used to know the old gentleman long ago. He glanced at me keenly through his spectacles, and I, with my knowledge of men, could see that his face changed agreeably as he took me in. He addressed me as "Frau Gräfin," but I politely corrected him and begged to be called Frau Osdorf. Immediately afterwards Meinert arrived.

If he had met me with courteous indifference, I should not have moved an eyelash. I had had plenty of time to prepare myself for the encounter, and my only feeling for the man is one of abysmal contempt. But he smiled mockingly, made me a low, ironic bow, and addressed me, in an exaggerated tone of jeering respect, as "Frau Grafin."

That was too much!

I felt myself turn deadly pale. I trembled, and it all got dark before my eyes. I had to sit down quickly, for everything was turning round and round, I lost all self-control and spoke only one word.

"Scoundrel!"

"What did Frau Grafin condescend to say?" he said, insolently, drawing out the bundle of bank-notes.

"Will you be kind enough to pay the lady the money?" said the Councillor.

"Oh, yes! I will pay the – 'lady,' "echoed he, with a marked intonation on the word, and laughing derisively.

That was the end of my composure.

"You – you devil!" I said. "You have every reason to bow your head before me, instead of mocking me. Truly, shame ought to crush you in my presence, if there was one spark of conscience or honourable feeling or sense of right in your whole composition. I – I can answer before God and before men for what I have done. For *I* have injured myself alone; have not ravished from any living soul the greatest good of all – honour and fair repute; *I* have no ruined life upon my conscience. And if there is a Divine Judge, and we both stand before Him one day, He will pronounce between us. Yes, you may sneer. You have not finished yet. Never in my life till now have I wished evil to anyone, but I wish for you that you may know in the children of your own body what you have done to me. The sins of the fathers are visited on the children. . . . Perhaps we shall one day speak together again, and perhaps it will be my turn to laugh or would be, if I were so evil as you are, you scoundrel."

"You will not make me angry," he said. "A lady of the street has a privileged tongue—"

The Councillor was sitting at his desk, turning over various documents, but all at once he struck the desk with his hand, sprang up, and thundered out —

"Not a word more, Herr Meinert! I forbid you to speak another offensive word to this lady – yes, lady!" he reiterated, "so long as you are in my office and my presence. You will be good enough to pay the money, and Frau Osdorf will give you a receipt, and let that be the end of this interview."

Meinert sneered, and paid out the forty thousand marks, and I took the pen which the notary handed me and signed the paper, and never looked at Meinert again. As soon as he was gone out, I sat down once more, for I was so agitated that I was afraid of fainting.

The Councillor put his hand on my shoulder and asked me to come into his sitting-room and have a cup of coffee with him; and I acquiesced, for I felt so miserably upset. When I looked at myself in the glass I was horrified, for my face was livid and my lips were blue, and I cannot give any idea of what my feelings were.

The hot strong coffee did me good. . . .

The Councillor's wife had died about a year ago. The old gentleman was very nice to me. I took heart of grace, and asked him if it was true that father had expressed a wish to see me once more before he died.

"Yes," he said. "I know that for certain. He would dearly have liked to see you; he even expressed the wish personally to me. But as things were . . . you were not in good odour with your stepmother, and women in these little holes well, you know what they are. And then the end came very suddenly, much more so than anyone had expected. Otherwise, of course. . . . You were very dear to him, to the very last. It was well for him that the end came soon he suffered terribly."

Towards three o'clock I took leave of the Councillor, and went to the Weihgasse. I wasn't anxious to see Lena again, but the children interested me, and I wanted to get to know them.

Lena evidently didn't know me at first, and when she did recognise me she got quite confused. She wanted to make me some coffee, but I thanked her and refused, saying I would wait till the children came home from school at four o'clock. Our conversation was somewhat halting and monosyllabic, for I was not in the mood for small talk, and I couldn't speak to *her* about anything I really cared for. She has got enormously fat, lost her shape altogether, and looks very old and rather sad, so I couldn't bring myself to reproach her for the past.

At last the children arrived. The boy has a sort of likeness to father, though at present he's very ugly, with rough red hair and a regular clown's face. The girl is Lena all over. Not very tall, but robust; with a thick straw-coloured plait on her shoulders, simply but very neatly dressed; a fresh, oval face, with big but rather nice features, only somewhat spoilt by a fat nose.

I had brought all sorts of things for them – a couple of boxes of sweets, and a gorgeous doll, and some toys for the boy – children's hands are so easy to fill! They were told to shake hands with me and say "Thank you," and I tried to talk to them a little, and was glad when I could get away. The visit set my mind at rest on one point, at any rate. My little step-sister has very certainly not a drop in her veins of the wild "Claire Gotteball" blood! She won't come to grief; she'll stand firm through life on her own sturdy legs. She is no antelope, to be hotly chased by men. Even if she should "fall," it will be as the cattle fall to the butcher's hammer, but I am convinced that she never will. She is Lena the second! Some day she'll be an honest wife and mother, and tell her children as an awful warning the legend of the bad

Thymian, who was not to have nor to bind, as they say, and who died in the gutter. . . .

By the time I got away, it was five o'clock. The sun was shining down into the streets and setting a crimson spark in the bright window-panes, and glowing upon the red-tiled roofs; and the air was as warm as May. But outside the town, where the streets ended, and the gardens and fields began, one noticed the approach of autumn. Gay Virginia creepers curtained the boardings, the leaves of the trees were turning colour and rustling with every breeze; it was as if the wind were playing through funeral-wreaths, I went down the narrow path between the hoardings to the weir. I felt irresistibly drawn to the place which was connected with the saddest memories of my life. In the meadow, on the very spot where Elizabeth's dead body had lain, some boys were playing. They were flying kites, screaming and laughing, and having mock battles – oh! happy childhood! . . . But I stood for a long time at the weir, looking at "the water which rushed, noisily foaming, through the open sluices, and I wondered what would have happened if that black water had closed over me then! Should I have been another person now? For I believe in re-incarnation. I wonder, though, if one carries some little remembrance of the old life with one into the new just a glimmer of consciousness, if it were only for a warning and a help towards better things?

And then I went to the churchyard. By the wall stood the old mountain-ash tree, covered with coral berries, out of which we used to make chains when we were children, and pretend to be queens. I walked ever slowly and more slowly, till I stood by the graves of my parents. My emotions at that moment I cannot describe. I know not how I felt. In these long years I had, so to speak, forgotten that any soul existed in the world with whom I was connected by the ties of blood and affection, but in that moment an ineffable, passionate longing awoke in me, and filled my eyes with tears – a longing to see father just once, once again, and kiss him and say good-bye to him. I had often thought that he was much to blame for my misfortune, but in the moment that I stood by his grave, everything was forgotten except the certainty that he had infinitely loved me – loved me in his own fashion. It was not his fault that that love had expressed itself in a way which was not good for a growing girl. His temperament had been the curse of his own life, and he could not prevent my inheritance of it.

I stood a long, long time beside the two graves: one so fallen in, and the other quite freshly piled. . . . It seemed as if I were speaking to them both – and they didn't turn me away. For them I was not the "prostitute," the despised, lost creature, the homeless wretch; for them I was only the child who after long wandering had come back to its own.

And as the mists of the autumn evening veiled the graves, I fancied that I saw the forms of the two dead ones rising from the damp churchyard-soil, and stretching out their arms to me to take me into their own deep rest, to give the homeless one that surest home from which nobody could drive her away.

Dreams! Dreams! It was only the wind shuddering through the withered leaves, while the dusky twilight fell and hid my graves from me.

It was time for me to go.

The poignant pain of parting constrained my heart. Suddenly I fell to my knees, and bitterly weeping, kissed the earth in which my dear ones lay, murmuring half-unconsciously the two words – "Father! Mother!". . .

I know not how long I lay there. When I stood up at last, my feet were as heavy as lead, and before I could go, I had to lean for a while against the wall, for I was sobbing bitterly and my eyes were blinded with tears. Then I went quickly away. The lamps were still burning at Aunt Freda's as I went by; I hesitated a moment, wondering if I might go in, but resisted the impulse, for what would have been the good? It would have been a grievous meeting. The past is irrevocable, and she "has cast me off like the rest," and would perhaps have shut her door against me.

I hurried back to the inn, so as to get off as quickly as possible. It wasn't to be expected that either Lena or Meinert would hold their tongues, and in a couple of hours the whole little place would know of my presence in it; and then undoubtedly the landlady would have turned me out, body and bones, since "she wouldn't like to have such a creature in her beds."

About half-past eight, I left G——, travelled all night, and was in Berlin early next morning. When I got into my comfortable rooms again I drew a long breath, and it all seemed like a ghastly dream – that mournful journey in the October fog to the home of the dead. But days and weeks went by before Meinert's taunts left my mind, and I couldn't think of my last visit home without my blood running cold at the memory of that frightful quarter of an hour in the Councillor's office. But now I am calmer. A quiet sense of sadness is all that is left. Often I think that I drew nearer to father in those moments by the grave than ever in my life before. From the living man I had been estranged, but the dead one is all my own.

Who knows how long—? I wish I were religious, so that I might hope to see him again.

CHAPTER XXI

April, 1901.

I AM gradually beginning to have some intercourse with the town society, to which I really belong now in outward show. What can't one do with money! I wish I'd realised that sooner. If it goes on, I believe I shall be decorated, some day!

It *is* nice to have lots of money; one can give so much pleasure with it. Not that I ever feel the want of it myself for my Count gives me richly all that I need, and Julius and D— take a pleasure in providing for any little extra fancies that I may have. But other people do want it so dreadfully! I have only to open my eyes, and I must see it. There is so much misery and poverty in the world; and truly there is no greater luxury than to give indiscriminately to the poorest of the poor.

I've had my unfortunate experiences all the same. I offered "White-haired Doris" the position of housekeeper, and she came along, and I hoped that she would feel thoroughly happy and comfortable with me. I gave her a generous wage, and a good room and lots of presents, and in the evenings we used to sit in my sitting-room quite comfortably together, and talk. But she only held out two months! One Sunday evening she went out, and didn't come back again. On Monday she wrote to say that she was sending for her things. She had met an old lover in the dancing-saloon, and had gone off with him; and she said in her letter that she had been very happy with me and would never forget my kindness, but that she would rather take another place as waitress. Twice again I tried the same thing with old acquaintances. One of them stole everything she could lay her hands on; and the other, after behaving quite decently for six weeks, began to bring men into the house at night, and one afternoon I found her lover (the worst description of "Louis") in the kitchen with her, and of course after that I 'couldn't keep her.

I have now got into quite a different circle, through playing the Lady Bountiful. My laundress was confined and had puerperal fever; and I went to see her and found her in the most shocking poverty, did what I could, and took the two little brats, who were helplessly crawling about, away with me to my own house. One day a Deaconess arrived to see if the children were being well cared for; and when I told her that I loved little children, she asked me if I wouldn't help in the newly-organised institute for the care of babies. I said neither yes nor no; but about a fortnight later, a lady came to me with a list and asked me for a subscription, telling me that it was to go towards a new scheme, namely, the support of unmarried mothers and their children. I liked that idea so much that I instantly gave a hundred marks, at which the lady was evidently very much delighted, for she told me her name and got quite cordial. She was a Mrs. S——, the wife of a doctor, an extremely nice woman. Of course she contrived to insinuate some questions, and was informed by me that I was a widow, did not go into society at all, and lived a very quiet life. She asked me if it wouldn't give me pleasure to spend my spare time in the service of such a good cause as this. The field of benevolence was so wide, she said, and many willing helpers were needed for its effective cultivation. I answered evasively, but Mrs. Doctor must have chattered, for soon after that, ladies began to come frequently with lists and prospectuses of all sorts of benevolent institutions, and some of them went in for being quite intimate with me, and asked me to join their branches, and in the end I took the plunge, and actually went to a meeting. And now I'm up to my neck in it! I had nothing to do with it, but the tale must have spread that I was a rich and benevolent lady, because I am received everywhere with open arms, and even somewhat courted; in on branch, I am shortly to be proposed for the Committee, and am very well received at all the general meetings. That's the way, nowadays! One can get on without moving a ringer, if one only has a little superfluous cash, or better still, superfluous "blue paper," in one's purse. Truly it's the purse that makes the man.

My Count, whose opinion I of course asked before I took any steps, had nothing to say against it, only he warned me not to take too prominent a part. I don't want to in the least, but it seems to me that whether I wish it or not, I am going to be brought to the front.

In this way I have made a number of new acquaintances, who, as they are educated, well-bred women, really suit me better than my former friends of the Friedrichstrasse and thereabouts. But whether the fine ladies really tower so high, morally speaking, above the world which they name derisively the "Half-world," seems to me highly questionable. I don't mean in what is generally called "morality"; for in my opinion that word applies to many other things to all the finer human attributes, in fact, and not solely, as some seem to think, to that little bit of existence which has to do with sexual relations. There is a finer morality of the soul, quite unconnected with that grosser and really more superficial sort which men have fabricated for themselves. One may wade deep in mire and dirt, yet keep one's soul clean and pure; and one may be an apparently "honourable" lady, highly respected by all, yet be in reality wholly unworthy of esteem, because one's whole nature is soiled by the paltriness and baseness of one's disposition and point of view.

For example, never have I heard one of our "creatures" so shamefully slander her comrades as Mrs. H—, a doctor's wife, does her enemy, Mrs. Z—, a solicitor's wife. When one of the "creatures" does get into a tantrum, it's something like the trumpeting of the hippopotamus at the Zoo – it doesn't sound nice, but it hurts nobody, for one merely laughs at it; but when these ladies turn spiteful, it's like a snake-bite, quiet and deadly. . . . Oh, my dear! these women of the West End of Berlin, who do so much good, who organise so many charities, certainly haven't tongues to match their good deeds!

I could tell many a tale, but my time and my Book are too precious to waste. And this charity, too! To think, so long as one says nothing, can hurt nobody – and I have my thoughts on the subjects! These charity organisations are a real social scourge. Anyone who buys and pays for thirty tickets becomes a member of the Society; and for a hundred tickets you get an Order! The great guns of the organisations seldom pay out a single copper coin of their own – they foist off their tickets on other people, and do all the talking themselves. . . . It's a rotten system.

In February I was selling raffle-tickets at a bazaar, and got rid of them all like winking. The young girls were every one of them jealous. I enjoyed that. If I take the trouble, I'll back myself to cut them all out – these more or less pretty little donkeys. But I'm always afraid of coming across some former acquaintance. Up to the present it has been all smooth sailing. The Count shares my apprehensions, and is always advising me to keep in the background.

He gave me lately an exquisite petticoat which cost three hundred marks – white silk with incrustations of cream point-lace, a real work of art, good enough for a Queen. I was childishly delighted with it, but after that had gone on for a week, I began to think of all the good one could do with the money that such a thing had cost; and, to make a long story short, I sold it to my dressmaker for a hundred and twenty marks, and she sold it again to a customer with thirty marks' profit; and the hundred and twenty marks I gave to the divorced wife of a constable, who lives in the yard near by. She bought herself a sewing-machine with it, and had her lame boy operated upon he can scarcely walk, his feet turn in so. Of course I had to pay my shot towards that too!

When the Count asked me yesterday if I still had the petticoat, I made him my confession. He was not cross, but said that it was silly of me, for it simply meant that we had thrown away a hundred and fifty marks. That is true. In future I'll try-to make him give me the money instead of the things.

.   .   .   .

September, 1901.

My Count wanted me with him all this summer. We again stayed a while at his castle in Silesia, and then I went with him to Holstein, and stopped at the Grunsmühlen, while he went to a place of his near Plön. There were a lot of Hamburg people in the hotel, but mostly *bourgeoisie* – none of my one-time friends. At the very end of my stay there, I did meet a woman from Borgfelde, whose sister lives on the Uhlenhorst; and this sister, who also stayed a couple of days at the Grunsmühlen, knows Ludwig and his wife, but she could tell me very little about them. They have no children.

I also made the acquaintance there of a nice elderly gentleman from Altona, a one-time Counsellor to the Government; and later of his nephew also, a very smart, and still quite juvenile, soldier. We often made up parties, which was really charming, and went to all the places that are mentioned in Voss's *Luise*. In the beginning of August the gentlemen went to Zoppot, and they implored me to go too, which I was only too glad to do, as Julius is always there in August with his family.

It happened very luckily that the Count had to go to the Rhine in August with a friend who wanted to show him a property that he was thinking of buying there; and so I could go wherever I liked. We took rooms together in the Kurhaus. Julius and his family had a villa in the locality. I hadn't been many days there before I met them on the beach. I had only seen his wife once before, years ago in the Apollo Theatre, and then she looked pale and ill and insignificant. I didn't know her this time – she is such a pretty, smart woman! That sent a pang through my heart, for now I understand why he can give me no warmer feeling than friendship. When I saw him with his charming wife, and their children on each side of them (the eldest is a lovely girl), my heart was filled with envy, hatred and malice, and I had sternly to control myself, that I might not betray my feelings.

So I went away in the middle of August.

Now that I'm back in Berlin I go in for all my Societies again, and last week I was at a garden-party at a Baroness L—'s, for the good of the motherless infants. I was selling roses there.

"You are just like a young girl, dear Frau Osdorff," said the old lady, who is distinguished by the fact that she really does give large sums of money to her charities. "All the gentlemen want to buy your roses."

Well, I'm afraid it wasn't because I'm like a young girl. . . . I got ten, and sometimes twenty, marks per each bloom, and was able to hand in a nice little pile.

My small capital is pretty well melted away. It doesn't matter.

. . . .

December, 1901.

Whether I am happy or whether I am sad *you* are the friend I want, dear Book. I am very ill. I am afraid the road is all downhill for me now. In November I had a hæmorrhage. I am so lonely and desolate. Often I wander for hours from one room to another, and feel like crying all the time. D— hardly ever comes now. I heard by change that he is "courting" a rich widow, who lives on the Kürfurstendamm. Well, well! Everything comes to an end in the end. And yet I have a wild fear of death, of the long night in the narrow grave.

. . . .

March 18th, 1902.

Yes, dear Book, here we both are, back at the old game again! Life is an everlasting circular-tour. Round and round, round and round we go! All my fine-lady acquaintances have their knives in me now. And it happened in this wise.

One evening in February, I was asked to tea with Frau K——, a doctor's wife, whom I had met at the Institution; and when we were all assembled, there arrived a newly-married couple, Frau K——'s brother and his bride, a shy young thing; and the bridegroom, too, was quite young, about five or six-and-twenty. I can't remember ever having seen him before, but I saw at once that he recognised me, for he started back, put up his eyeglass, and stared at me insolently. And when there was some music going on afterwards, he came up to me and whispered, with a look which was meant to be annihilating:

"How did you get here, Thymian?"

I looked at him haughtily. "What do you mean?" I asked.

"Oh, come! don't try to take *me* in," he said, brusquely. "I have seen you often enough in the Café Keck and the National."

I turned my back upon him, but I felt very much perturbed all the same. I knew that he would undo me entirely, if he chattered. After a little while he came up suddenly behind me again, and murmured, "My friend Abraham may be here at any moment. *He* knows you too. I won't have him meet you here, at my sister's. You must arrange it somehow, please."

The insolent young Jewish dog! I could have run him through with a dagger. "You are making some mistake," I said, but he cut me short.

"Don't be a fool, Thymian. If my brother-in-law knew whom he had as a guest in this house, you'd have a pretty bad time of it. And if you don't go of your own accord—"

I understood the threat that was conveyed in his last words, which he hissed out between clenched teeth; and I had no doubt at all that he would make it good. What could I do but clear out, if I didn't wish for an open scandal! But it was like wormwood to me. I didn't close an eye that night.

A few days later I got a communication from the Committee of our Society, in which, without any reasons being given, I was courteously, but very decisively, requested to resign voluntarily my place on the Committee.

That was clear enough. The detestable Jew-boy had not held his tongue, and I am done for in these circles, once and for ever. By calling him a young Jew, I don't mean to say that one must always expect such insolence from a son of Israel. On the contrary, I have always found Jews most chivalrous until now.

.   .   .   .

The affair has done me more harm than it's worth. My excitement and indignation brought on a hæmorrhage, and I had to stay in bed for a fortnight.

Julius and my Count both say the same thing that they foresaw that something like this would happen, and the only wonder is that it didn't come sooner, for I am far too remarkable-looking to pass unnoticed in any assembly.

In reality it doesn't matter much. I haven't lost a deal! I could never have been really friendly with those ladies. And if I want to do good, I know lots of other ways of doing it, apart from these charity-mobs. But it's very detestable all the same. I feel most awkward at the idea of meeting any of the women. People really ought to be more humane.

D— comes often now again. The courtship of the widow came to nothing. He always says he regrets that he can't marry me. I never can help thinking to myself, "Why shouldn't you?" and laughing in my sleeve.

How paltry men are, after all! How narrow are their souls, how limited is their outlook! They are always dashing their heads against the wooden boarding of social considerations and stupid, owlish pre-judices, which they have erected round their own lives; and instead of boldly and blithely leaping over the planking and taking their happiness on the other side of it, they creep along timidly close by, and peer, with sentimental sighs, through the cracks, at the "Unattainable," the "Impossible."

. . . .

June 12th, 1902.

Man proposes, and God disposes!

Julius had to go to Basle at the beginning of May, and as he is very overdone and nervous, he thought he'd make use of the opportunity to take a holiday for a couple of weeks, especially as he now has a very clever assistant to take his place here. He wanted to take me with him, and I was overjoyed at the idea of having him all to myself for a few weeks. I was most blissfully looking forward to it. I told the Count that I was going to a friend in Dresden, which I really *did* mean to fit in, too. By-the-by, it's a great pleasure to me that Emmy and her man are getting on so well; they paid their interest punctually last year, and always write so gratefully and happily.

I was already far on with my packing – it was Thursday, and we were to go on Friday when all of a sudden I was called to the telephone. It was a strange voice which told me I must come at once to the Behrenstrasse, for the Count wished to speak to me. Terror seized me at once, for I knew it must be something particular, else he would never let me come to his house. This was the very first time I'd ever been there. Of course I hurried off at once, and found him ill. He had frightful sciatica, and was altogether very bad, and what he wanted was for me to stay some days with him, to nurse him and keep him company.

What was I to do? I couldn't say no, and indeed in any case I wouldn't have said it – it would have been abominably mean when he has done so much for me. I comforted myself with the hope that he was sure to be better in a few days, and that then I could follow Julius. But he got worse every day.

At first the thought that my trip, which I had been so eagerly looking forward to, was utterly smashed up, seemed to me quite unendurable, and I sobbed like a little child. But gradually I made up my mind to it, and then I was almost glad to be able to make this little sacrifice for my old friend. Another thing that greatly tranquillised me, and made me almost happy, was to find how much he liked to have me with him; indeed, I seemed almost indispensable to him.

"Yours are the real nurse's hands," said the old physician who was attending him, taking mine in his one day and gazing at them. "Soft, tender, womanly hands like these are the doctor's best assistants."

But all the same it was a terrible time. The old gentleman suffered agonies, and had high fever at night. Often I had to sit up with him. It is frightful to see anyone suffer so, and have to sit there unable to do anything. In such moments one realises very clearly one's humiliating impotence. One seems like a marionette; one's wishes and desires are nothing but threads worked by invisible hands. One becomes conscious of the slavery of mankind; of how not one single atom of power is bestowed upon one. Destiny gives us duties only – no rights.

For a few days and nights I was prepared for the worst. After a bad night, when my old friend awoke from a short, troubled sleep, he took my hand and pressed it, and said that he had taken care of me and that if anything happened to him my future was assured, but that I must promise him one thing never again to return to my old disorderly life.

I am no surgeon of the soul, to be able to vivisect and analyse my own sensations, and in that moment truly my feelings were very mixed indeed. His request seemed to me deeply humiliating, but I couldn't blame him for it, for had I not already betrayed his trust? Well, trust—? No. . . .

It was exactly because he never *did* wholly trust me. Ah, never mind! But this I can take my Bible oath of, that in that hour I never once thought of what might happen if my old friend were to die, for in those anxious days I genuinely longed that he should live. I have never loved him as a wife loves her husband, but my deep gratitude had awakened a kind of filial tenderness in me, and I'll swear that I had no base thoughts of any kind at the back of my mind all the time I was nursing him.

When he got better he wouldn't let me out of his sight. To the gentlemen who came to see him now and again he introduced me as his niece, Frau von Osdorff, who was nursing him; and of course they all treated me with the greatest consideration. At the end of a week, exactly on the day that Julius came back, we took our first drive to the Gardens, and next week we are to go to Wiesbaden. It will be a very pleasant stay there in the sun. And I am gladder than I can say that I haven't lost my old friend. His illness and my nursing of him have made him for the first time really dear to me. I have the feeling that we belong to one another, and that's a great deal when one stands so alone in the world as I do. Julius thinks that the stay in Wiesbaden will be good for me too. I haven't got rid of my cough yet; there is really nothing the matter with me, but sometimes I feel so unspeakably tired and run-down. I have been writing this during the many night-watches of the last few weeks.

. . . .

September 1st, 1902.

We got back to Berlin a fortnight ago. The cure in Wiesbaden has done my Count a lot of good. He's quite lively on his legs again; but my cough has not got a bit better. The doctor at Wiesbaden advised me to go to Schlangenbad for a few weeks, and the Count insisted on my doing so. This Schlangenbad is a hideously dull hole. I take a sun-bath every day at twelve o'clock by doctor's orders. I believe I'm thoroughly anæmic; that's what is really the matter with me. In Schlangenbad I met an old acquaintance, namely, the girl we called "the Amma" from Hanover. She lives in Leipzig now, and makes any amount of money, she says; but this spring she had the bad luck to get an eruption of the skin. So off she rushed to the most famous specialists, here and everywhere, and it's pretty well cured now — at least her face is quite smooth again; but she's taking Schlangenbad for the after-cure, as it's supposed to be very good for the complexion. Her landlady was with her there. I heard from Amma that Kindermann now lives in Leipzig-Gohlis, as an independent lady, and has a sort of matrimonial agency. So she's got respectable in her old age, and works in the cause of Hymen! I should very much like to see her again, and seriously think of making an excursion to Leipzig when I'm paying my visit to Emmy this month.

Amma is just the same, if possible perhaps a little thinner. I don't know how she manages to get hold of paying clients. Her face has such a very common expression; one sees at a glance what she is, despite her fine and really quite tasteful clothes. The landlady was a shockingly vulgar person. She was for years in the

"Grünen Affen" at Leipzig, then wandered all over Europe, and finally came back again to Leipzig. Saxon women seem to be very patriotic, for they always do go back to their beloved mother-country, in spite of the rigorous police regulations which prevail there. I find that I don't really get on with my former colleagues now. I am very far from thinking myself above them; but their coarse expressions, and especially their very plain speaking on various delicate topics, absolutely repel and disgust me. I know well that when one's in the middle of it all one gets acclimatised; it's just the same as it is with cocaine-injections – when one has had them too often in one spot, that spot becomes insensible to them. In the same way one quite forgets that sexual relations are a tabooed topic in respectable society. But I have got out of all that, and now I can't endure it; and I had rather hang myself than ever lead that sort of life again.

CHAPTER XXII

September 12th, 1902.

I CARRIED out my plans and made a little circular tour; and it didn't do me any harm, although owing to a terrible draught in the railway-carriage, my cough has got so much worse that it is almost unbearable. The night before last I couldn't sleep for coughing, and it hurt me so much and gave me such a pain in my side that I was really afraid it might be inflammation of the lungs again, but to-day, thank goodness, I feel much better. Well, first I went to Emmy, or, as she is called, Frau Haüsling. There is not the slightest doubt that everything is going very well with her, and it gives me extraordinary pleasure. She had asked me often to pay her a visit, and I was most cordially received by them both. They get on splendidly together, only Emmy is frightfully jealous of her "Schani"! They have a nice little restaurant in the "old town," and supply only good wine and pure beer. Emmy is a capital little landlady. She has changed most amusingly in the one short year. She keeps a very firm hand over her kitchen-folk; dismissed her *chef* on the spot because she found him kissing the kitchen-maid! For she has suddenly become intensely moral, and doesn't allow her servants to carry on in any way with each other. Well, everybody has a right to do as he likes, and I do think that it's absolutely necessary to keep a look-out upon your servants in that way, at any rate while they're in your house. But Emmy was furious with the head waiter because she heard that he had "an affair" outside, and over that, as I said to her, *I* don't think she has any jurisdiction whatever. One thing she did really vexed me. We were sitting in the public room about ten o'clock one evening, drinking a bottle of wine together – Emmy, a friend of her husband's, and I. In comes a lady, sits down at a table, and orders a dozen oysters and half a bottle of wine.

I saw at once that she belonged to the "herd" and not to the Upper Four Hundred, for she was abominably dressed and very commonly painted. Emmy had scarcely set eyes upon the girl before she jumped up, rushed over to her, and hissed a few words in her ear. The poor thing looked round in astonishment, smiled awkwardly, answered something, but was curtly cut short by Emmy. At that moment the waiter came up with a dish of oysters and the wine. Emmy nodded to him, upon which he grinned and took all the things back to the buffet again, and the girl got up and went away. Emmy scolded the waiter a little, and then came back in a terrible state of moral indignation to our table.

"The impudent minx!" she said, panting with rage.

"Why, what was it?" I inquired.

"Didn't you see?" said she. "A regular bit of street dirt comes in as bold as you please to a respectable place like this, trying to pick up customers, I suppose – the beast!"

"But she was sitting there quite quietly, and not bothering anybody," I objected.

"What difference does that make? A thing like that would drive all my respectable customers out of the place. For instance, supposing his Excellency the Councillor had come down with his ladies to have a bock, as often happens in the evenings, and saw that creature there. . . . No! I won't have goings-on like that in my place. Schani is such an old donkey that he winks at it, but I won't have it – not I!"

I couldn't very well say anything, as there was a strange man with us, but I was frightfully disgusted with such detestable intolerance. When we were alone together, I couldn't help going back to it.

"Why, Emmy dear, what do you mean by it?" I said. "Supposing anyone had treated *us* like that in the old days! I must say, I can't understand your being so intolerant."

But she stared at me, and was evidently very much offended at my reminding her of the past.

"What is past is past," she said curtly. "Old clothes fetch no price in the market. I am a respectable married woman now, and I must think of my reputation, especially in business-matters. Besides, I never went trapesing about the streets like that sort."

I saw it would be absolute waste of time to discuss it with her. Curious and interesting, isn't it? What short memories people have for the things they want to forget!

From Dresden, I went to Leipzig to see the Kindermann woman. She lives in the heart of Gohlis, on the ground-floor of a pretty villa, and has everything very nice. She knew me at once, and was visibly pleased to see me again. But she has changed, got so much older-looking, and her features have grown sharp and rigid.

"Well, I can see you've got on, Thymian – there's no necessity for asking *that*. But you look ill, child. You should be thinking of your future now; one can carry on up to thirty, but after that one has to stop, or else one's a wreck for the rest of one's life. Have you saved anything?"

I told her that I had been married, and now had as protector an old rich friend; and she nodded approvingly, with a sly smile.

"Yes, yes, I knew you'd get there, and it was Kindermann who showed you the way," said she. "But I should advise you to marry again; it's always dangerous with old gentlemen. They'll promise you the stars out of the sky, but if they die without putting it down in writing, what then? One simply has to look round again. The best thing is to break off in good time and make a decent bargain, and then marry. For instance, now, if you had thirty thousand marks in ready cash, I could put you in the way of a capital match."

"I haven't as much as that," said I.

"But you could easily get it, if your old friend is so rich and such a swell. All you need to do is to get up a quarrel, and then he'll be so afraid of a scandal that he'll give you whatever you like. If you are clever, you ought to be able to get fifty thousand and more. I have lots of gentlemen who would do for you – an orchestra-conductor with seven thousand marks income, and a bookseller who publishes medical works, and a picture-dealer; or, if you care for academical distinction, I've got a head master; also a doctor, but *he* wants eighty thousand. They're all respectable nice gentlemen between thirty-five and fifty. The doctor is a Jew, but the others are Christians."

I declined her friendly offer with thanks, but K. said she thought I ought to think it over and come back to her.

"If I had your business capacity, I should try to do something independent," said I. "I find life very unsatisfying, through having no regular occupation."

"Yes; unfortunately you've no common sense at all, my dear child," she said somewhat cynically. "I always told you – you were too romantic. It's pure luck and no thanks to you that you've got on so well, in spite of your 'ideals,' and all that sort of stuff, and haven't come to grief long ago. You don't realise how much of a business transaction love is, nor all that's to be made out of it. You should really look at it from the practical side. I did that at first, and then I changed my mind and went in for ideals; 'first love, and then business.' But now I've changed round again, and it's 'first business, and then love.' A full purse on one side, and a nice title, or even only a fine figure of a man, on the other, are quite strong enough magnets to draw two hearts together."

A remarkable woman, Kindermann! but in one respect I admire her. Her elasticity and good-nature are really astonishing.

She made me stay for the day. Her business hours are between three and five, but on that day only one gentleman came. We dined at six, just as we did in Hamburg, and it was the same plentiful and excellent kind of meal, and afterwards we had coffee in her sitting-room; she offered me cigarettes, but I dared not smoke on account of my cough. She herself smoked a cigar, and over it initiated me into the mysteries of her craft. Her services are in much greater request with gentlemen than with ladies. She has a quantity of agents who spend their whole time looking out for rich unmarried women or widows. Kindermann's function is to procure introductions to these ladies, which she is clever enough to manage easily. Her resource is truly astonishing, when one thinks that she has to get hold of absolute strangers and introduce them to each other and get them married. But she has lots of successes, she says. The most interesting thing is the fact that in nearly every case the ladies are quite ignorant of the state of affairs, and never know that instead of "marrying" they have literally "*been married.*" K. gets from four to ten percent of the marriage-portion, and makes a nice little pile out of it.

"I've brought about so much legitimate happiness in the last few years, that my illegitimate crimes must be quite expiated," she said, laughing. "But if you come to me, I'll do the whole thing for nothing, for the sake of old times, and I'll look out for the handsomest man, and the one with the best income, in the whole place."

Time went by quicker than we thought. She took me to the station herself, and I had to promise her to pay a few days' visit at Whitsuntide, when we would take a little trip together to the Saxon Switzerland.

When I got home, I found nobody there. The maid thought I wasn't coming till the last train, and had gone out. The yellow blinds in my sitting-room were drawn down, and the whole place was full of flowers. The Count had sent roses, and Julius a basket of lilies, while D—'s offering was a small wagon-load of roses. They were standing about everywhere, in vases and jardinières, on tables and shelves and window-sills, and even on the ground, and the scent was overpowering, especially of the lilies. As I looked round, a strange oppression fell upon my heart. I couldn't help thinking of a death-chamber, I seemed to notice a slight smell of decay in the midst of the perfume; probably the room hadn't been aired for a day or two, and perhaps the yellow blinds had something to do with the effect – the light they made was so curious, like candles. . . . It was very strange altogether, I pulled up the blinds hastily and opened the windows; and when I heard the noise of the street, the feeling passed away.

. . . .

September 30th.

I still get a great many begging-letters, and really have very little now to give, but I never can bear to refuse anyone.

Yesterday, at the Thiergarten I met the whole clique of my former fellow-workers in the cause of charity. Unspeakable, inexpressible was the disdain on some faces, and the stiff, contemptuous coldness on others. I felt cold all down my back, and I should have liked to hit out right and left into the cackling crowd, and knock a few sparks out of them!

I can bear most things, even serious, honest contempt; but this kind of mocking scorn and derision I cannot bear!

Contempt – yes, when it is justified. For instance, if some poor beautiful girl standing alone in life, sad and embittered and forlorn, with temptations and enticements assailing her on every side, repels them all, rejects them all, and from inward conviction elects to tread the grey, monotonous path of renunciation and tame respectability – in *her* I recognise an individual who has a certain right to look down with contemptuous pity upon a weaker sister But these geese who have fed in the same flat green pastures all their lives, under the vigilant eyes of their keepers, have no right whatever to jeer at those who have not had the same good fortune. The Bible says truly that he who calls his brother "Thou fool!" is in danger of hell-fire.

Mocking contempt is more evil and more wicked than murder and fraud and thieving and arson, or any active wrong-doing, for it kills the divine part of a human being. Mockery and contempt are devilish!

. . . .

Since my visit to G— last year, the past has been coming back into my life so curiously! First my meeting with "Amma," and then seeing Kindermann again – and now comes the third time.

I had been shopping, and was just turning from the Mauerstrasse into the Leipzigstrasse, when somebody called my name.

"Thymian!"

I turned round and recognised the lady standing behind me. It was my old friend Greta. We hadn't seen or heard of each other since the time in Hamburg. How people lose sight of one another!

She certainly hasn't grown any younger in these ten years. She is no longer so slender, so supremely elegant, as she was then. It's *other* people who show one how time is going, how quickly the spring-tide of life flies by. . . .

"I have been walking some time behind you, but didn't feel quite certain of you," she said gaily. "I am so glad to see you! Do you live here in Berlin, or are you only on a visit?"

"I've been living here for years," I said, as we shook hands cordially and walked on together. I didn't feel quite sure if I was glad of this meeting or not. I had always liked her, because she was not so paltry and narrow-minded as the others; but then, on the other hand, things have got more complicated since then, and I don't feel at all inclined to be looked down upon again. But I couldn't get away at once, and had to stand it for a little. We went together as far as Wertheim's and into the tea-room there, and then she told me that eight years ago she had married a man older than herself, who lived in the Rhine country and as they didn't get on together, she had separated from him a few year ago, and had now been living with her only daughter for some time in the Western Berlin suburb of Friedenau. I only half-listened, for I was still debating whether this was to be taken as good or bad luck. She further imparted to me that she had been writing novels for some years, first under a pseudonym and afterwards under her married name. And then I remembered having read some of her books. I said very little at first, and confined myself to the somewhat evasive intelligence that I was a widow. She asked me nothing more; but gradually our conversation became more intimate, and I got warmer, for she really has something very nice and sympathetic about her. Her cordiality delighted me, and the longer I looked at her, the better I liked her. I went with her to the Linkstrasse, and then we took the train to the Bülowstrasse, and when we were taking leave of one another, I promised to go and see her soon.

Afterwards, I was almost sorry that I had. I couldn't sleep for thinking of it, and I pondered deeply what I should do. She attracts me. I have been longing for a woman-friend for years; one gets so sick of being with men only. One can talk so much better to a woman, and be so much more easily understood. Unfortunately, most women are petty and jealous, and suffer from a kind of moral shortness of breath, which totally prevents a comprehension of other people's troubles. Now Greta is not like that; one need never be afraid of her being base in any way. She's not like Maria or Emmy, and neither is she so conventionally short-sighted and intolerant as most women are. She has had her own experiences; and in the by-ways of life people soon cease to cavil and criticise.

Certainly, if she knew all, she might quite probably not want to have anything more to do with me, and that would hurt me dreadfully, much more than the disdain of the society-ladies or anything else. . . . I wondered if I hadn't better give up the whole thing, and then again I thought, "Is it really necessary for her to know? My worst times have gone by; at present I live a quiet, orderly life. I am a widow, and from my husband's relations I receive enough to live on. Is there any lie in that?"

Living out there in the quiet tranquillity of her bourgeois *milieu*, she will never come into contact with anyone who has known me in earlier years. But then again, I can't do it! I can't pretend, particularly to anybody whom I like. And more-over, Greta is clever, very clever, and knows the world, and in the end she would be sure to find out. . . .

I thought and thought, and the next day I wrote a card to say that I would come out on Thursday afternoon. It was extraordinary what an event the paying of this visit seemed to me. I stood for a whole quarter of an hour before the glass, looking at myself from head to foot, to see if there was anything too remarkable about me, and at the last moment it seemed to me as if my perfume – *Bouquet d'Amour* – must betray me; but that was too ridiculous, of course! All the time in the tram I couldn't get rid of an oppressive feeling that was almost like fear. I knew that if she let me feel the slightest thing or hinted that we couldn't see much of one another, I should be rude, poisonously rude, for it's like a sort of gunpowder in me which the slightest spark will explode.

My heart beat quickly when I got down at the Rönnebergstrasse, in which she lives; but Greta had seen me from the balcony and came down to meet me, and greeted me very cordially. I was rather embarrassed.

It was a warm sunny day, like mid-summer. In the small *laggia*, under a huge palm, stood the tea-table. Greta's housekeeper, a nice homely person who has been with her for eight years, brought in the tray; and then came little Kitty, a sweet, small creature, with her mother's fair hair and dark brown eyes. She said "How do you do?" to me, and fetched a chair for herself to the table. Greta talked away so easily that I felt more and more sure that she knew nothing, hadn't a glimmer of a suspicion of my past; but I got increasingly silent. The sight of children always makes me sad, and when the little girl nestled her fair head up to her mother, and Greta, radiantly smiling, pressed several kisses on the sweet rosy mouth, I had to look away, for my heart ached with sorrow and envy. *This* woman is lonely too, and Fate has strewn more thorns than roses in her path, but how rich she is in comparison with me, who am so utterly beggared! If I could have kept my child by my side she would have been a guardian-angel to me, would have saved me from how much! . . .

But that passed, and afterwards I got more at ease, and we talked of this and that and were quite merry.

"And so you write novels?" I said. "I must say it doesn't look to me as if you could have many adventures here."

She laughed lightly, and said it would be splendid if she could herself go through 'everything that she told to her readers, but as a matter of fact it had nothing to do with personal experience.

"But I daresay you'll occasionally be able to give me some copy, Thymian?" said she.

"Rather!" said I. "I'm writing my memoirs in the form of a diary. I have kept one ever since my Confirmation, and I've put everything important into it. When I die, I'll leave it to you in my will; it will give you material for at least five novels."

"I'll take you at your word," said she; "but perhaps you will give it to me sooner?"

"I'll see," I said; "but I won't promise, because I like writing in it so much. As it is at present you could scarcely use it, for it's somewhat condensed, and you could only serve it up to your magazine public with a good deal of extra stuff put in—"

"We'll do everything," said she, "even if we have to thin down our good black ink with water-and-patchouli."

"Yes, indeed; you'd want a good big glass of eau-de-cologne to get rid of a certain strong flavour, which mightn't suit everyone," I returned. "One doesn't live among the thorns and nettles all one's life with-out getting some scratches, and leaving some wool behind one."

Greta nodded. We were silent for a moment. The wind scattered a lot of withered leaves over the table and into the silence there fell the rattling and clanging of the electric-tram, which passes through the Rheinstrasse and stops at the corner. . . . It filled me with uneasiness that Greta should not ask me a single question I did not know whether it was from tact or want of feeling, and that depressed me momentarily, but afterwards we got all right again. I stayed to supper, and helped to put little Kitty into her darling white cot. When she was safely in, she folded her hands, and said her little evening prayer: "Gentle Jesus, meek and mild"; and when she came to the end of the verse, she added out of her own head, "Dear God, keep my dear Mamma well." It touched me so that tears came into my eyes. I thought to myself: "You dear, innocent little pet! what you pray for in your innocence is actually the one thing necessary for your happiness and well-being." . . . Oh! when one thinks of what a child loses in losing its mother! Well, *I* know what it is. . . .

Towards ten o'clock, Greta came with me to the tram-station at the Emperor's Oak.

"When will you bring Kitty to see me?" I asked her.

She hesitated for a moment.

"Or perhaps you don't want to come to me at all?" I said in a hard, suspicious voice.

"Indeed I do, Thymian," she said; "but – you see I live very quietly, and I don't want to make any new acquaintances. I have my work and my child, and they both fill my life, so that I don't want strangers. Whenever you come to me you will be welcome, and I will come and see you; but you will take care, won't you, that when I come, I find you alone?"

I was stupefied for a moment, for I saw at once that she knew all – *all* – just as well as they did in my old home.

At first I didn't quite realise how tactfully and delicately she had opened the way for me to confide in her.

"Yes, I'll take care of that," I said. "Come soon, and bring Kitty. Write to me first or telephone. . . . Adieu!"

The tram rattled up. I got in.

.   .   .   .

November.

I shall never get rid of this dreadful cough. I am utterly worn out, and am often so tired that I can scarcely move my hands to dress or undress myself. . . .

Julius talks of Davos. "Would I like to go there for the winter months?" That frightened me horribly. Am I so nearly at the last stage? I don't believe I am. Doctors always make the worst of things, so that one may be sensible and take care of one's self. This cough is the result of a cold – and it *is* only that kind, but rather harder and more obstinate than usual. I don't want to go away just now. It's too delightful having found Greta again. I often go out to Friedenau. She doesn't come to me very much; she hasn't time, and I don't stand on ceremony with her. It is so home-like and cosy there, when the light falls softly on the table and the clock ticks in the evening-quiet, and the child chatters and laughs – all so peaceful and sweet, so remote from the noise and whirl. . . . I often shut my eyes and dream that I'm really "at home." I think it's very dear of Greta to be so sweet and kind to me, and never to ask any questions. I like her very much, although, in my opinion, some of her views are very peculiar – quite crazy, indeed.

CHAPTER XXIII

January, 1903.

THIS year I passed Christmas and New Year very pleasantly. On Christmas Eve, my Count was with me. He had refused all family invitations, just so as to stay with me. I had a tree this time too, and gave presents to eleven poor children out of the street, and rejoiced over the happy faces. On St. Stephen's Day the Count was with me too, and on St John's Day I was with Greta. On New Year's Eve, D— came as usual, and on New Year's Day I was at Friedenau again.

My cough is pulling me down more and more. I am slipping gradually out of life. If only it isn't any worse than this! Although I know what a mess I've made of my life, and how superfluous my existence is, and that really nothing better could happen to me than to die quickly and painlessly, I yet have an unconquerable horror of death.

For I don't believe in seeing people again, and in the plains of heaven. I *do* believe in a second life but who can assure me that it will be any better than the first, or that I shan't be more miserable even than I have been? And I'm terrified of the dying, the transition-period. My ideas of death are all mixed up with earth and mould, and worms and corruption the gruesome mystery of the Underworld.

. . . .

February, 1903.

Greta is to have my Diary. I have told her to be very nice about Julius in her novel. I insisted on her promising me that. I don't care a hang about any of the rest. . . . Upon my word, I don't feel very cheerful! Yesterday I almost quarrelled with Greta, The day was splendid, and the Count had sent me the sledge at twelve o'clock for a drive. I thought I'd like to take Greta and the little girl, but I didn't find her at home, and the housekeeper wouldn't let me have the child at first, but I begged and prayed until I got hold of the dear little pet. We drove a long way into the Grünewald. It was unimaginably beautiful, with the snow-laden pines and fir trees, glittering like silver filigree-work in the sunlight; and in the midst of them, the busy red-tailed squirrels, and the sledge flying noiselessly along! Enchanting! The child was wild with delight, and so was I. But suddenly the weather changed. A storm came up, and it got bitterly cold, and as the little one was shivering, I wrapped her up in my fur stole.

When we got to Friedenau, it was already dark, and Greta scolded like anything, because I'd kept the child out so long. She had been very anxious, and Fräulein Anna had already come in for some of it, and was weeping tears as big as peas. I took it all quite calmly, and at last she quieted down. But I got another cold from having had my neck bare, and to-day I can't speak, I am so hoarse. I must go to bed at once.

. . . .

March 1st.

I've been in bed for a fortnight. I don't know what's the matter with me; I have no pain, and yet I'm so ill! Greta often comes to see me, and yesterday she and Julius met at my bedside, and they both tried to persuade me to go for a week or two to a hospital. My servant-maid is very stupid and not to be depended upon; and nothing goes right when you have a strange nurse in. I think I will go. One gets better more quickly there, I have had another hæmorrhage.

. . . .

March 15th.

I'm not sorry that I came here. The nursing and attendance are excellent. I was very ill. I am still weak and poorly, but with a pencil I can manage to scribble a little. It gives me pleasure, the time goes so slowly. Greta comes almost every second day. Yesterday Kitty came too, and brought me flowers. The Count visits me too, and D— has been, and Julius often comes twice a day.

They are all good to me. I have a pretty, young nurse. She would like to turn my thoughts heavenwards, and is always wanting to read psalms to me. But I won't have it.

"Do you think I'm going to die soon, Sister?" I asked her, to-day.

She got red and confused. "Nobody can answer that. The Lord alone knows."

"Dying is dreadful," I said. "To be dead is beautiful, but dying is dreadful."

"Oh, no!" she answered; "dying is getting free dying is going home. The Saviour comes, and takes His children to His Heavenly Father's Home."

"Ah! Sister," I said, "for people of my sort there is no Saviour, and no Heavenly Home. The Devil takes *us* when it's all over."

She was frightened.

"It is a great sin to doubt God's mercy," she said uncertainly. "God is love, and he who dwelleth in love, dwelleth in God and God in him."

"Then I have always dwelt in God," said I.

. . . .

March 16th, 1903.

I envy the quiet little Sister her religion. She takes such a lot of trouble about me, and I am so irremediably godless. She has such a young, dear little face. And such a hard calling! Could I ever have gone through with it? I don't think so. With me it was in the blood – in the blood.

. . . .

March 17th, 1903. At night.

I cannot sleep. The Sister is out of the room. If I need her, I am to ring. The night-light is burning. My soul is full of the horror of death. My strength is failing more and more.

Is it Death that is coming for me? Will he fight me for every little inch of life?

A thousand thoughts shudder through my soul, and burn in my brain. I want to write a great deal, but my hand is too weak to hold the pencil long. I have to stop often. Oh, I am so afraid of the long awful night, of the dissolution in the black, infinite Nirvana! Where shall I wake again? To what shore will the dark river of death wash me? Where shall I drift, poor flotsam that I am? . . .

Shall I be a night-bird that dreads the light, and broods heavily in some haunted tower, an evil omen for all who hear the sound of my eerie cry? Or will my soul go into the body of a panther, stealthily stalking my prey, bloodthirsty and cruel?

Shall I return under a good or an evil star?

Anything – anything, so long as I am not a human being, so long as I need not live through this anguish again.

The night will never end.

I am thirsty.

Is not that one of the Words from the Cross? I believe in Him who sacrificed Himself for mankind. Holy God! if Thou art there, assuage this fire in my soul and on my lips.

I am thinking of the roses and lilies at home in our garden.

I have such a longing for the old times, for the old years—

For mother.

For the roses.

For the graves.

I can write no more.

. . . .

March 21st, 1903.

It was very terrible these last few days. They thought it was all over with me. I have given Greta a key for my book, at all events.

I couldn't breathe, and often felt as if I was suffocating. The little Sister always wiped the sweat-drops from my forehead, and whispered to me soft, sweet holy words of comfort.

"'Tis only for a little while we roam,
Then tread the Golden Streets, and are at Home."

It is always sounding in my ears.
The Golden Streets . . . . at Home . . . . at Home.

.   .   .   .

March 23rd.

Julius doesn't wish me to write. It strains me, he says; but I don't think so. I wish I could get up and go out. The air would refresh me. There's really nothing the matter with me but weakness, exhaustion—

.   .   .   .

25th.

I have thought of something. When I'm better, I'll found a Home for children.

.   .   .   .

26th.

Julius will help me. A Home for sick, weak, crippled children, who want a lot of love. It makes me happy to think of it.

The Count was here yesterday, and he will give me the capital for it. I am so happy now at last—

.   .   .   .

March 28th.

I am gradually getting better, only my strength won't come back. I slept well last night, and have no more fever. This morning I wanted to get up, but the Sister wouldn't let me. When she was out of the room I tried, and fainted.

It's only strength I want, nothing else. The Children's Home—

.　.　.　.　.　.　.　.　.　.

30th.

D— was here to-day, and brought me five blood red roses. I must look very ill, for he was visibly moved, and could scarcely speak. But I feel much better. It's only this weakness.

.　.　.　.　.　.　.　.　.　.

April 1st, 1903.

Nurse asked me to-day if I wouldn't like to see the clergyman. I laughed, and asked her if she was trying to make an April fool of me. For I'm ever so much better. But they don't believe me, because I look so wretched, and it isn't much wonder.

.　.　.　.　.　.　.　.　.

April 6th.

My heart is light and free as it hasn't been for years. I should be perfectly well, only lying so long in bed has made me very weak. Thank God, Spring is coming at last! To-morrow I'll get up . . . . to-morrow—

In Poland, Böhme's book was titled **Pamiętnik Kobiety Upadlej**. This striking illustration is from an early Polish edition.

EPILOGUE

THYMIAN made her last short, half-illegible entry in the afternoon, about five o'clock, of the 6th of April. After her death had been hourly expected for a whole week by doctors and nurse, she passed peacefully and without any struggle, at nine o'clock on the morning of the 7th, into the long night of death – into the mysterious region which had always been so filled with horror for her.

In the morning hours of a warm, cloudy day we carried her to her "landed-property," her "summer-parlour," as she used to call the exquisitely cared-for burying-place with the little enclosure round it.

No long parade of mourners, as at the funeral of the luckless Casimir, followed her simple coffin, with its few costly wreaths. It was like the tranquil return to Mother-Earth of an almost forgotten creature. The doctor was the only one of her friends present. What prevented the other gentlemen from showing the last honour to the dead, I have never known. Perhaps the hour for the funeral was not definitely communicated to them.

The rain was falling into the open grave. Softly and noiselessly the grey drops fell upon the black coffin. A maker of metaphors, if he were inclined for them in such an hour, might have thought of tears dropping from Heaven.

The doctor was evidently deeply moved. He waited at the churchyard-gate, and took my hand.

"I have been glad of your interest in that unhappy girl, dear lady," said he. "Poor, poor Thymian! What a sad, ruined life hers was!

It is well with her now. But it is terrible to think of anyone's coming to such utter destruction. So much beauty and intellect so many sweet, womanly traits of character; and all destroyed, all trodden under foot, into what hideous degradation! . . ."

He turned slowly away, with a deep sigh. "Yes, yes. . . . Yes, yes. . . . May God guard our children!"

. . . .

Two years have gone by since then. But in the hour of writing this, the memory of that scene in the churchyard, and of all that had preceded it, is as vivid as if it had happened within the last few days.

From the window I look out on fresh spring foliage and golden sunlight. But there is a shadow amid the rays that gild my writing-table, and my eyes grow dim and dark for I see suddenly before them the black, ominous, raven-haunted wall, which no human power can destroy or penetrate, which stands still and silent and immovable before the life of every single human being, and mocks at all their wisdom, all their courage . . . and a dream-like echo of the doctor's words is in my ears—

"May God guard our children!"

THE END

Louise Brooks as Thymian on the cover of *Illustrierte Film Kurier* (number 1260). This eight-page publication served as a program for the G.W. Pabst film. It was widely distributed throughout Germany, and contained text and illustrations which encapsulate the film's story.

Margarete Böhme's name is prominent on the second page, just below the title. As a famous author, Böhme's name was linked to the film made from her best known work.

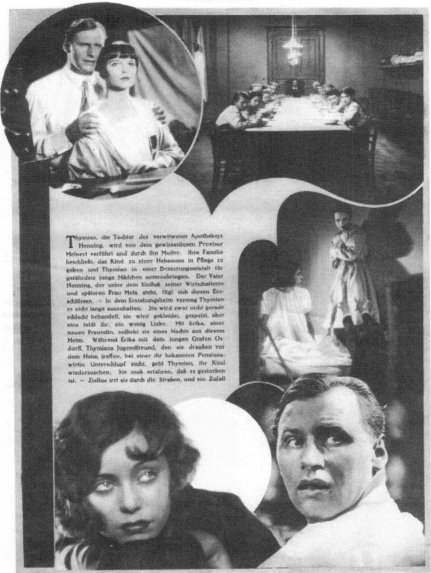

Thymian, die Tochter des verwitweten Apothekers
Henning, wird von dem gewissenlosen Provisor
Meinert verführt und durch ihn Mutter. Ihre Familie
beschließt, das Kind zu einer Hebamme in Pflege zu
geben und Thymian in einer Besserungsanstalt für
gefährdete junge Mädchen unterzubringen. Der Vater
Henning, der unter dem Einfluß seiner Wirtschafterin
und späteren Frau Meta steht, fügt sich diesen Ent-
schlüssen. — In dem Erziehungsheim vermag Thymian
es nicht lange auszuhalten. Sie wird zwar nicht gerade
schlecht behandelt, sie wird gekleidet, gespeist, aber
eins fehlt ihr, ein wenig Liebe. Mit Erika, einer
neuen Freundin, entflieht sie eines Nachts aus diesem
Heim. Während Erika mit dem jungen Grafen Osdorff, Thymians Jugendfreund, den sie draußen vor
dem Heim treffen, bei einer ihr bekannten Pensions-
wirtin Unterschlupf sucht, geht Thymian, ihr Kind
wiederzusehen. Sie muß erfahren, daß es gestorben
ist. — Ziellos irrt sie durch die Straßen, und ein Zufall

Fritz Rasp (upper left and lower right) played Thymian's seducer, the creepy Meinert.
He also appeared in both Fritz Lang's *Metropolis* (1927) and *Frau im Mond* (1929),
and in Pabst's *Three Penny Opera* (1931). Rasp's career as an actor lasted 60 years.

treibt sie schließlich in jenes Haus, wo Erika und Osdorff sich bereits eingelebt haben. Wider ihren Willen wird Thymion in das leichtsinnige Leben und Treiben der Anderen hineingezogen. Sie beschließt zu arbeiten, Gymnastikunterricht zu geben, aber dieser Versuch mißlingt. Ohne Arbeit, ohne Liebe, vergehen die Jahre. Sie ist eine elegante große Dame geworden. Da gibt es eines Abends in einer Bar ein unverhofftes Wiedersehen. Ihr Vater in Begleitung Meinerts und Meias erblickt die „verlorene Tochter" im

The Russian-born Andrews Engelmann played the bald-headed Director of the Reformatory. His best known role, to American audiences, was as a fanatical submarine commander in the Rex Ingram film *Mare Nostrum* (1926).

Mittelpunkt eines Kreises eleganter Männer und Frauen der Lebewelt. Unbemerkt von der Gesellschaft um sie herum, vollzieht sich die endgültige Trennung Thymians von ihrer bürgerlichen Vergangenheit. Jetzt ist sie eine „Verlorene". Doch — nach dem Tode des Vaters gibt eine Erbschaft ihr die Möglichkeit, ein neues Leben zu beginnen. Das ist Anlaß für den jungen Grafen Osdorff, in eine Heirat mit Thymian einzuwilligen. Aber sie verzichtet auf das Geld zugunsten ihrer kleinen Stiefschwester. Sie will das Kind vor einem Schicksal bewahren, wie sie es an sich hat erfahren müssen.

Kurt Gerron played Dr. Vitalis (upper left and lower right). Gerron was a popular character actor, and appeared in many films including Pabst's *White Hell of Pitz Palu* (1929), and in Josef von Sternberg's *The Blue Angel* (1930), with Marlene Dietrich. Gerron was sent to Auschwitz in 1944, where he died. A documentary was made about his tragic life which includes clips from *Diary of a Lost Girl*.

Despite restraint and an emotional intensity Louise Brooks brought to the role of Thymian, some publications gave the actress poor reviews. In 1929, *Variety* described her as "monotonous in the tragedy which she has to present." In 1930, however, the future French director Marcel Carné praised her acting in his review in *Cinèmagazine*, as did the Surrealist poet Philippe Soupault in *L'Europe nouvelle.* Soupault described Brooks as an actress of the first rank. In 1938, an Italian critic wrote, "She suffers and remains unmoved. And precisely this is what counts most: with an almost total 'lack of acting,' she has created around herself a dense atmosphere of intense emotions."

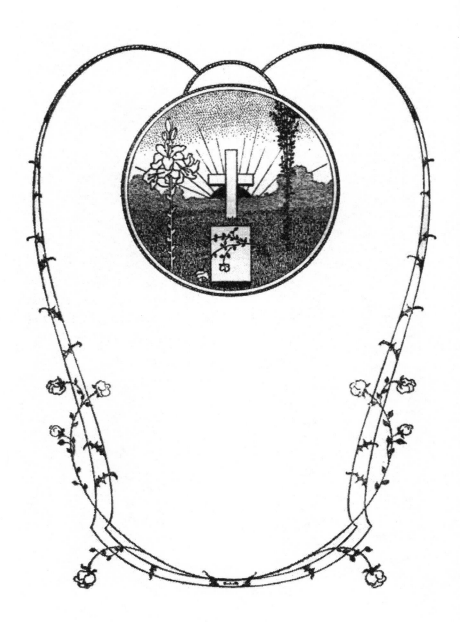

During the early decades of the 20th century, it was common for publishers to include advertisements in the back of books. The vintage ads found at the end of this volume follow in that tradition, and help reveal the widespread fame of Margarete Böhme's story.

This publisher's advertisement from the back of an early German edition of **The Diary of a Lost Girl** lists some of Böhme's earlier books, and promotes her then new release, **Des Gesetzes Erfüllung**. The success of **Tagebuch einer Verlorenen** is noted in the excerpt from the *Leipziger Tageblatt*.

This ad from the back of a 1907 edition of Böhme's **Dida Ibsens Geschichte** notes **Tagebuch einer Verlorenen** had then sold 108,000 copies, and that a special edition ("Luxus-Ausgabe") of the book had been issued. The ad also notes the eight languages into which **Tagebuch** had been translated, and the three into which it would be translated. A Dutch translation was unauthorized.

The Diary of a Lost Girl was issued in Sweden as **Förtappad**, which translates as "reprobate." Here, the book is listed along with titles by Chekhov, Zola, and Oscar Wilde. Böhme's book sold for 95 öre, and was issued in 3 volumes.

The **Diary of a Lost Girl** was issued in Poland under the title **Pamiętnik Kobiety Upadłej**. This 1906 advertisement notes "Every mature man or women should read this book." Also, it warns against an unauthorized edition, and notes that the book is available in all bookshops. The authorized Polish edition was translated by Felicya Nossig, who would later translate Selma Lagerlöf, Josef Conrad, and others of note. Nossig's translation was reissued in Poland in 1929, around the time the Pabst film was released.

Upper left, an early edition of **Tagebuch einer Verlorenen**. Upper right, a look-alike edition of the similarly titled 1906 parody, **Tagebuch einer andern Verlorenen**, by Rudolf Felseck. Bottom, an advertisement for Felseck's take-off of Böhme's book. Felseck claimed a notary vouched for his work's authenticity.

An American advertisement from 1909 lists **The Diary of a Lost One** along with other forthcoming publications from The Stuyvesant Press. This publisher's $1.50 hardback edition was a nearly identical reprint of The Hudson Press edition from the prior year. In both editions, Böhme is named as editor, and no translator is credited.

This magazine advertisement – from a German trade publication, proclaims the film's literary origins and record setting sales of more than 1,200,000 copies. The ad dates from September, 1929 – before the film opened. It also notes the G.W. Pabst directed film would be distributed throughout the nation – in Berlin, Dresden, Hamburg, Münich and Köln.

This 1929 Berlin newspaper advertisement notes the film was made from the "world famous novel by Margarete Böhme." The film received mixed reviews in the many German newspapers of the time. The *Berliner Tageblatt*, however, compared Brooks' performance to that of "a beautiful, tragic Buster Keaton."

This French newspaper advertisement also notes the film's literary origins, though without mentioning the author's name. In all likelihood, Böhme would not have been as familiar to French moviegoers as would her book. The ad dates from 1930 and promotes the film's showing at the L'Empire Theatre in Paris.

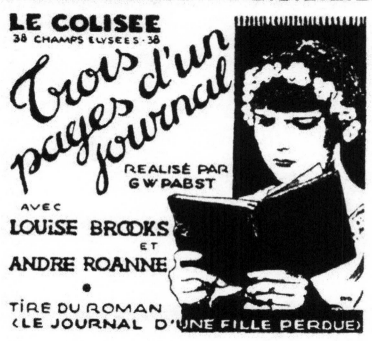

With its phrase, "from the novel," this French newspaper ad likewise associates the film with the book. The ad dates from 1930 and promotes the film's appearance at the Colisee Theatre in Paris. As *Trois pages d'un journal*, the Pabst film was popular and enjoyed a long run in the French capital. It was also widely reviewed in French newspapers and film periodicals.

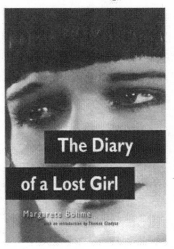